**ALSO BY
ANNA DORN**

Perfume & Pain
Exalted
Vagablonde
Bad Lawyer

American Spirits

A Novel

Anna Dorn

SIMON & SCHUSTER
New York Amsterdam/Antwerp London
Toronto Sydney/Melbourne New Delhi

Simon & Schuster
1230 Avenue of the Americas
New York, NY 10020

For more than 100 years, Simon & Schuster has championed authors and the stories they create. By respecting the copyright of an author's intellectual property, you enable Simon & Schuster and the author to continue publishing exceptional books for years to come. We thank you for supporting the author's copyright by purchasing an authorized edition of this book.

No amount of this book may be reproduced or stored in any format, nor may it be uploaded to any website, database, language-learning model, or other repository, retrieval, or artificial intelligence system without express permission. All rights reserved. Inquiries may be directed to Simon & Schuster, 1230 Avenue of the Americas, New York, NY 10020 or permissions@simonandschuster.com.

This book is a work of fiction. Any references to historical events, real people, or real places are used fictitiously. Other names, characters, places, and events are products of the author's imagination, and any resemblance to actual events or places or persons, living or dead, is entirely coincidental.

Copyright © 2026 by Anna Dorn

All rights reserved, including the right to reproduce this book or portions thereof in any form whatsoever. For information, address Simon & Schuster Subsidiary Rights Department, 1230 Avenue of the Americas, New York, NY 10020.

First Simon & Schuster hardcover edition April 2026

SIMON & SCHUSTER and colophon are registered trademarks of Simon & Schuster, LLC

Simon & Schuster strongly believes in freedom of expression and stands against censorship in all its forms. For more information, visit BooksBelong.com.

For information about special discounts for bulk purchases, please contact Simon & Schuster Special Sales at 1-866-506-1949 or business@simonandschuster.com.

The Simon & Schuster Speakers Bureau can bring authors to your live event. For more information or to book an event, contact the Simon & Schuster Speakers Bureau at 1-866-248-3049 or visit our website at www.simonspeakers.com.

Interior design by Lewelin Polanco

Manufactured in the United States of America

10 9 8 7 6 5 4 3 2 1

Library of Congress Control Number has been applied for.

ISBN 978-1-6680-8553-0
ISBN 978-1-6680-8555-4 (ebook)

For Lizzy Grant

2019

My baby lives in shades of blue.
Blue eyes and jazz and attitude.

—LANA DEL REY

Blue

Blue Velour sat at her vanity and dragged a thin line along her eyelid.

She'd been applying sharp wings since she was sixteen, when she'd shoplifted a liquid eyeliner pen from CVS after seeing Jean-Luc Godard's *Contempt* with her much older boyfriend. She'd been mesmerized by Brigitte Bardot. For an entire year, Blue had worn a thick headband and striped T-shirt with a pencil skirt. She'd stood out among the puka-shell necklaces and Lilly Pulitzer dresses that dominated the school halls in late-'90s Wilmington, North Carolina. They still dressed like that as far as Blue knew. She hadn't been back in nearly a decade.

Blue looked out the window, toward the rippling turquoise water. When she was younger, she'd been terrified of aging, of losing her beauty. But now that she was thirty-eight, nothing really scared her anymore. God had tortured her for many years, and now Blue had finally earned a period of peace and joy. At least that's what she told herself whenever those old fears crept up to say hello, or, more specifically, *This is all too good to be true.*

Nerves danced in Blue's stomach. She braced herself to wing the right eye. Journalists had asked about the eyeliner before. They all assumed she had a makeup artist. But Blue always did her own, even for red carpets. Ever since Sephora had made her look like a freaky pageant clown as a teen, Blue hadn't let anyone touch her face. But now that her hand was shaking slightly as she tried to sharpen the tip of the wing, she fantasized about having someone to help her, if even to just steady her grip. She put the pen down and examined her work. It was not her best, but fine. Sufficient.

The bedroom door cracked open. Max appeared in an oversize cable knit sweater and jeans. Max was Blue's sister, best friend, roommate, stylist, and unofficial assistant. Max had moved to LA to live with Blue as soon as she turned eighteen, less than a year after Blue left home. They were Irish twins, barely a year apart. And in the year 2000, when Max was eighteen and Blue was nineteen—although they'd been Maxine and Beatrice then—they'd shared a studio apartment in Hollywood over a Petco. They'd called it Chateau Velour after the velour couch they'd found on the street. They'd bartended and sugared for money, and on off nights, Blue had sung at open mics under the name Blue Velour, while Max had styled her. Living above the pet store had come in handy when a rich party friend had gifted them two Italian greyhound puppies. They'd named the canine sisters Bijou and Gigi.

When record label money started flowing, they'd moved to Hancock Park, a historic LA neighborhood constructed in the '20s and former home to numerous Old Hollywood legends ranging from Clark Gable to Mae West. They'd adored their cute little bungalow with a small pool and a green lawn for Gigi and Bijou to run free. But then Blue had started gaining fans, which meant rabid paparazzi and unhinged stalkers. So Blue, Max, Gigi, and Bijou had picked up and moved to this house on Sea Level Drive, a gated subdivision in Malibu that was way out of their price range when they bought it. The Art Deco–style home had been built in the '80s and hadn't been renovated since, and Blue had still had to take out a thirty-year mortgage to afford it. She now had the money to renovate it, but Blue sort of liked it as it was, with its terrazzo floors and glass brick, its mirrored walls and sun-bleached teal color scheme.

"She's hereee," Max sang.

Blue's heart thudded in her ears. Again, today was big. She was being interviewed for a feature in the *New York Times*. Her first profile in the American paper of record and one her manager believed was long overdue. Blue picked up her blue snakeskin vaporizer from the vanity and draped a blue kimono over her shoulders. She took a big drag from her vape, then followed Max through a minty cloud.

Blue had of course googled the journalist. Zoe Alexander. She appeared to be from the Midwest, had studied journalism at the University of Chicago. She'd started at *Pitchfork*, then wrote for *Rolling Stone* before moving to the *Times* roughly a year ago. In that year, she'd profiled Rosalía, FKA Twigs, and Phoebe Bridgers. She had nearly black hair cut in a fringe and narrow green eyes.

Sitting at Blue's breakfast nook, Zoe Alexander mostly looked like she did on Blue's iPhone screen—although her hair had grown out a bit, and her eyes were more intense than they were in photos. Blue didn't like journalists. Historically, they made her sound like a dumbass. They'd make her feel comfortable, like they were friends, and then use quotes that alienated people at best, got Blue minorly canceled at worst.

And Blue had been canceled so many times—for telling Azealia Banks that her psych meds weren't working, for telling Dr. Phil she didn't need therapy because she "isn't mental," for telling a journalist he made her want to relapse, for calling Ayn Rand "the original girlboss," for calling St. Vincent a "spooky dyke," for writing Elizabeth Holmes letters in prison, for saying she'd rather talk to pedophiles than critics, for posting a photo of herself with a loaded gun to her head after being snubbed at the Grammys.

Shaking Zoe Alexander's hand, Blue silently vowed not to become friends with this woman. She had to be guarded, deliberate, which was not her nature. It was frustrating, because fans liked that she was raw. But the Interscope execs liked her irreverent attitude to stay in her music and out of her conversations with the press.

"Can I get you something to drink?" Blue asked, wandering over to the wood-paneled fridge. She opened it and peered inside. "We have Diet Coke, Red Bull, Mountain Dew?" Blue was something of a caffeine addict. She was addicted to a lot of other things too—sex, love, older men, sometimes women, nicotine, music, and at one point cocaine, alcohol, and other, more serious downers, but she'd given those up.

"I'm okay," Zoe Alexander said coolly.

Blue grabbed a can of Red Bull for herself. "Let's go outside," she said. "The sun is finally breaking through the fog." Blue headed toward the balcony and Bijou followed. Gigi had become exceedingly lazy in her old age, moving only for the promise of food.

Blue rarely awoke before the marine layer disappeared around noon every day. In this sense, her sleep schedule was tailor-made for Malibu. On the rare occasions Blue did wake up early, either when she had a shoot or a meeting in LA, she enjoyed the moody, foggy vibe. The Pacific coast was infinitely more dramatic than the Atlantic beach city where she'd grown up, where the waves were small and the land was flat, where there were no mountains, no cliffs, no sound of water crashing up violently against rocks.

Outside, the sun shone bright and yellow. It was warm for November. The balcony curved with the building and hung over the water so that it almost felt like they were on a boat. There was a built-in wraparound sofa with faded teal cushions and a white coffee table covered in cigarette butts. Blue sat on the couch.

"Wow," Zoe said, taking in the view for a second, miles of aquamarine sprawling out before them.

"It's something, right?" Blue lit a cigarette. She offered Zoe Alexander one, knowing she'd refuse. No one smoked anymore, it seemed, except for Blue and Max. They used to smoke cigarettes in the house but had recently stopped due to the stench that had lodged in the carpets. Vape inside, smoke outside. That was the new rule, and they mostly followed it.

Zoe shook her head no and took a seat across from Blue on a rickety metal chair with her back to the ocean.

"You don't want the view?" Blue asked. "Come sit beside me, there's plenty of room." Oops, she was already trying to be the girl's friend.

"That's okay," Zoe said. "I won't be able to focus."

Blue should channel Zoe, try to focus on the interview, not the hypnotizing stretch of blue water. Blue had always been a good mimic. She'd learned to sing by mimicking Nancy Sinatra and Julee Cruise. Maybe she could learn to behave appropriately by mimicking Zoe Alexander, who pulled an iPhone from her pocket and started punching on it.

"Cool if I record?" she asked without looking up.

"Of course," Blue said, wishing she could say no.

Zoe put the iPhone on the table between them. Blue could see the flat line from the recording moving slightly as the surf roared beneath them. Bijou barked and the line shot up. Blue picked her up off the ground. The dog didn't bark much, except in the presence of bad vibes. She had a refined vibe detector and had identified several of Blue's exes as toxic far before Blue had. Now she made all her dates meet Bijou first. If she barked, it was game over. Blue was therefore now extra uneasy about Zoe Alexander.

Blue tapped her cigarette on the pink flamingo ashtray in the center of the table. She took a sip of Red Bull and prepared to think before she spoke, for maybe the first time in her entire life.

"So, you've been making music for roughly . . ." Zoe looked up, evidently thinking. Her lashes fluttered.

"My whole life," said Blue.

"Your whole life," Zoe repeated.

Blue wasn't going to say her age if that's what Zoe wanted.

"You must be thrilled with how far you've come," Zoe said.

Blue took a breath. The question, or she supposed it was more of a comment, bothered her. Infuriated her even. The comment implied that Blue had been bad but had improved. That she'd redeemed herself somehow. But Blue had always been good, always been great. The public was just very late to an amazing party she'd been at her entire life. The old Blue would have snapped at Zoe, maybe even threatened her. But that was the old Blue.

"Honestly," Blue said, "I've been at peace since Paz De La Huerta took out her tits at one of my shows."

Zoe laughed, which relieved Blue. This was good. Keep it light. No aggression, no hostility. Be entertaining, elusive. She leaned back in her chair, slightly more at ease.

"Can we do a quick rapid fire?" Zoe asked.

Blue nodded. This sounded fun, but also dangerous. *Just don't get canceled again*, she told herself. *Funny, elusive.*

"Favorite of your albums?"

"*Fluorescent Gloom.*" This was Blue's least popular album.

"Least favorite?"

"*Chateau Velour.*" This was Blue's most popular album.

"Biggest inspiration?"

"My sister."

"Musical inspiration?"

"Kurt Cobain."

"Dream collaboration?"

"Amy Winehouse."

"Dream collaboration with someone who is alive?"

"My gardener." Blue was lying; she didn't have a gardener.

"Dream collaboration with a popular musician who is alive?"

"Dolly Parton."

"Why blue?"

Blue laughed, instructed Zoe to turn around, to look at the layered hues of water and powder blue sky above it.

Zoe turned toward the water for a brief second, then turned back and wrote something down. She looked up at Blue and blinked. All business, this woman.

"Describe your music in three words."

Blue pulled in smoke from her cigarette, exhaled.

"Love." *Drag.* "Death." *Drag.* "Ribbons."
"Describe your fans in three words."
"Sexy." *Drag.* "Gay." *Laugh.* "Rabid."
"What do you want more than anything?"
"Respect."
"How do you prepare for a live performance?"
Blue sighed. "I freak the fuck out."
Zoe laughed. Thank God. Blue looked at the water. This was going okay. She hadn't said anything offensive yet, she didn't think. It seemed like the rapid fire was over. Smooth sailing from here.

"I love *Blue's Beard*," Zoe Alexander said, catching Blue off guard. "I think it's your best record yet."

Blue picked up her cigarette and inhaled deeply to hide her surprise, and, she supposed, joy. The album wasn't out yet; only a few digital copies had gone to journalists. And Blue wasn't used to journalists complimenting her. For the first ten years of her career, she'd routinely been panned by the critics. *Contrived, manufactured,* and *alienating* were the most common insults flung her way, but she'd been called worse. Blue used to take the bad reviews seriously. She thought the critics were correct that she was a fraud. After all, she'd changed her name from Beatrice Clark to Blue Velour as soon as she moved to LA. She'd dyed her hair periwinkle for years until it had started falling out in her early thirties from chemical damage. It had grown out a sort of chestnut, made darker with a quarterly gloss. She was generally more natural now, no longer starving herself or injecting massive amounts of filler into her lips. Back then, she supposed, the critics had been correct that she was fake. But she hadn't realized then that audiences wanted pop stars to be anything but.

"Thank you," Blue said. She pulled hard from her cigarette again to prevent herself from saying something she might regret.

"Can you tell me about the inspiration? How did it come to be?"

Blue hadn't done an interview in a while and suddenly remembered how much she hated answering questions like these, ones in which she was expected to articulate her artistic process. She liked music because it was beyond language. She wrote her lyrics, but that was different. That was poetry. Her lyrics were meant to evoke a feeling, not to make sense.

"I can't totally explain where my music comes from," Blue said. "It's between me and God." Blue laughed and the line on Zoe Alexander's iPhone wiggled. Blue put a hand over her mouth.

"The album title and opening song, 'Blue's Beard'—it's really interesting, an apparent reference to both the French folktale and a shout-out to your LGBTQ+ fan base."

Blue laughed again, a breathy sound that floated off toward the sea. She couldn't take Zoe Alexander seriously. They didn't speak the same language. Blue felt the caffeine and nicotine dancing together in her veins.

"The gays love me," Blue said. She kissed Bijou on the nose.

"A beard," Zoe began, "is a faux romantic partner used to conceal a person's sexual identity."

Blue smirked. "Thank you for that very formal definition."

Zoe Alexander said nothing, just folded her arms. She was wearing a black blazer and must have been very hot. It was probably sixty-seven degrees, but the sun made it feel hotter. Blue was partially in the shade, but Zoe was fully exposed to the ozone.

"Actually," Zoe said, "I'll take a cigarette."

Blue raised an eyebrow. This was a first. She handed Zoe an American Spirit and, for a brief second, wondered if the woman wanted to fuck her. Journalists had tried to get with her before, and on at least one occasion had succeeded. Blue had thought it would make him write about her more favorably. She'd been wrong. He'd called her a clown.

Blue leaned over and lit Zoe's cigarette, then relit her own.

"There are legions of people online convinced that you had, or have, a romantic relationship with your producer Sasha Harlow."

Blue took a drag to appear casual. This question—was it even a question? maybe more of a comment again—tended to irk her. It was hardly the first time an interviewer had mentioned this alleged affair with Sasha, but Blue had thought the American paper of record was classier than this.

"Is that so?" Blue played dumb. The album title was a reference to the subreddit BlueBeards, which was dedicated to piecing together clues that Blue and Sasha were romantically linked. Blue didn't like the internet, but it was hard to avoid. And on a mushroom microdose roughly a year ago, Blue and Sasha had decided it would be hilarious and meta to directly reference the subreddit in the album's title.

Most educated people dismissed the BlueBeards as QAnon-level delusional, but Blue had in fact slept with Sasha on and off since she was twenty-six, when the label had arranged for them to work together. Blue didn't talk about it in the press—not because she was embarrassed or had any doubts about her sexuality, but because fans loved mysteries. Sasha and Blue played into it, leaving little Easter egg hints of their romance for careful listeners, occasionally holding hands on the red carpet. Neither Blue nor Sasha believed in marriage or monogamy, only in all-consuming, passionate, addictive, obsessive, druglike love—what they called an "Aphrodite Bender" in the song they'd written for the *Fifty Shades of Grey* franchise in 2015.

"You tend to be evasive when asked about Sasha," Zoe Alexander said. She dragged and turned toward the water, as if to be polite by blowing her smoke in another direction, as if Blue minded smoke in her face.

"Evasive?" Blue said. "I'm an open book." She inhaled, waited for Zoe to turn back to face her. "Sasha is my soulmate," Blue said when she met Zoe's eyes. "I'll never make another song without her as long as I live."

"Do you mean soulmate in a creative or a romantic sense?" Zoe asked.

Blue exhaled toward Zoe.

"Is there a difference?"

2020

I'm your biggest fan,
I'll follow you until you love me.

—**LADY GAGA**

Rose

Rose Lutz gripped her steering wheel.

Traffic had hit a standstill on the 1. Her phone indicated it would take twenty-five more minutes to get to Blue's house in western Malibu, which was fine, because Rose had left thirty minutes earlier than she needed to. If there was one thing she'd learned after a year of living in LA, it was that getting places always took significantly longer than expected.

The water sparkled on her left, a great expanse of gray. She was roughly twenty-six miles from her apartment in Hancock Park, but she felt further away, spiritually. She opened the windows and tasted the salty air for just a quick moment before resuming her preparation. Rose restarted the audio recording she'd made in her bedroom while her roommate was out eleven days ago when she'd landed this interview. As it played, Rose mumbled along with the stretches she'd memorized, turning portions of her college thesis into a sort of religious mantra.

In eleven years, spanning from 2008 to 2019, Blue Velour has released six studio albums.

In 2008, she released Spirit of Sinatra, *a baroque pop ode to tragic* romance in a bygone era. Her debut established Blue as a cheeky wordsmith, the album chock-full of clever references to soda, makeup, and cigarette brands. It was produced by the then-unknown Sasha Harlow, who said Blue quite literally channeled Nancy Sinatra's ghost during recording sessions, to which an interviewer saltily replied that Nancy Sinatra was still alive, which appeared to come as a shock to both Sasha and Blue. The album was dismissed as frivolous by critics, and after a stiff performance on Conan, Blue was deemed an industry plant and a nepo baby, though she was neither, as she was raised by public school teachers in a North Carolina beach town.

But Blue didn't give up. In 2010, she released Oleander, a softer, more introspective album inspired by Nina Simone, childhood trauma, and film noir. When asked about the title, Blue said, "Oleander is a beautiful flower that can kill you if you aren't careful." After a quick tour, she released fan favorite Chateau Velour in 2011, which paired sweeping orchestral arrangements with trap beats, creating a grandiose sonic quality that caught the attention of several music critics. Sasha Harlow said the album was inspired by Lil Wayne's Tha Carter III and the film scores of Hans Zimmer. Pitchfork gave the album a 7.2/10, calling it "cinematic and desperate." The album featured the single "Death Baby," which topped the UK charts for several weeks, but was unable to outperform the bubblegum EDM bangers by artists like Katy Perry and Lady Gaga in the US. Blue, however, had developed several notable American fans, including Kylie Jenner and John Waters. Her image was also one of the most reblogged on Tumblr that year.

In 2013, Blue again pared down her sound with Fluorescent Gloom, an atmospheric, post-psychedelic rock album inspired by the Doors and the surreal quality of David Lynch films. Blue said the album documented the darkest period of her life, when she felt most misunderstood and rejected, when she'd submitted to the notion that she'd never earn the respect of her peers or find true love. Sadly, Fluorescent Gloom was her most poorly received album at the time, with some critics going so far as to say the album, which featured cover art of a man choking her and a song called "Neon Bruise," glamorized domestic violence and cast Blue as "anti-feminist." However, some fans and critics in retrospect find it to be her best, most poetic and vulnerable album.

Down and out, Blue took several years to make and release her next album. At that point, she'd moved to Malibu and rarely left her gated community. Sasha allegedly built Blue a studio in her new house so she wouldn't have to leave. Rumors began circulating that Blue and Sasha were romantically involved, particularly after 2014's "kissgate"—widely circulated blurry photos of them dancing intimately and potentially kissing at an A$AP Rocky concert on one of the rare nights Blue ventured out that year. A now über-popular subreddit called r/BlueBeards emerged to dissect Blue's music and press for clues about her secret affair with Sasha. Beyond the subreddit, Blue Velour fans who believed Blue was secretly dating Sasha began identifying as BlueBeards. And the subsequent album fueled their fire. Released in 2017, Garbo Gals was thought to reference Greta Garbo's alleged homosexuality (photographer Cecil Beaton famously called Garbo a "furious lesbian") and explored themes of hidden love and secret lives. Moreover, internet sleuths uncovered that Sasha's middle name is Greta, which only amplified their fixation. The hype worked: Garbo Gals was Blue's first record to go platinum and received glowing reviews by several prominent critics.

After the Garbo Gals tour, Blue and Sasha holed up in Marin County north of San Francisco and recorded in the iconic Panoramic House overlooking Stinson Beach. The resulting album sent shock waves through the internet with its name: Blue's Beard. The release was accompanied by Blue's short-lived public romance with suspected closeted actor Jack Willenhall, which Redditors viewed as confirmation that Jack was Blue's beard and Sasha was her one true love. But beyond that, critics were finally listening, retracting former dismissals and rewriting pans. The album eschewed hip-hop beats for stripped-down guitar and piano. With Blue's Beard, New York Times music critic Zoe Alexander hailed Blue Velour as California's poet laureate, a playful genius whose talent rivaled that of Nina Simone, Amy Winehouse, and Stevie Nicks. The album was nominated for five Grammys, including Album of the Year.

Rose's iPhone started speaking, interrupting her monologue and telling her to turn. The sharp, robotic voice of the device made her jump slightly in her seat. She realized she hadn't taken a proper breath in several minutes. Rose inhaled deeply as she approached the turnoff to Broad Beach Road. She cracked the window and again tasted salt. The water glinted silver between massive properties.

Rose had been over here before. As soon as she acquired her fifteen-year-old Saab, she drove straight to Malibu to see where Blue lived. Of course, Rose couldn't get behind the gates, but she'd sat on Lechuza Beach and listened to Blue's entire catalog. And now, Rose was approaching said gates with means to enter, all thanks to connections she'd made on the BlueBeards subreddit.

She'd been a fan of Blue's since *Spirit of Sinatra*, but by the time lesbian rumors began circulating, Rose felt she and Blue had too much in common. For one, they were both raised by teachers. Blue's mom taught biology and her dad taught history at the same public school Blue attended. Rose's parents were math professors at Carnegie Mellon. Rose and Blue both had one younger sister. Rose wasn't as close with her sister as Blue was with Max, but no similarity went unnoticed. Rose and Blue were both Geminis, their birthdays just a few days apart, and they were both type 4 on the Enneagram, "the individualist." They both preferred the Diamond Ice flavor of Mi-Pod vaporizers and they both had been blessed with perfect pitch. And finally and most importantly, they both secretly coveted women.

As soon as she graduated Carnegie Mellon, which she'd attended for its voice program and free tuition given her parents' jobs, Rose had moved to Los Angeles and into an apartment owned by a woman she had met on the subreddit. Ella's ancestors had spearheaded the Georgia gold rush of 1829, and Ella was therefore the richest person Rose knew. (This was also the first Rose had heard of a Georgia gold rush, but she had never really paid attention in history class.) And due to this generational wealth, Ella owned her apartment in the historic El Royale building in Hancock Park, the neighborhood where Blue was living when she made *Oleander* and *Fluorescent Gloom*, the latter being

Rose's favorite of Blue's catalog. Ella preferred *Spirit of Sinatra* and charged Rose only a thousand dollars a month for rent, a major steal in this city, and unheard of in Hancock Park. They lived on the ninth story (out of twelve). At sunset, their entire apartment lit up purple, and on clear days, Rose could see a tiny sliver of the ocean from her bedroom window.

Ella had moved to LA for an internship at Interscope Records, which had released Blue's last four albums. Rose believed it was unpaid, but she didn't ask. When Rose moved in, Ella was about to sell her old Saab, which had been her dad's, and buy an Audi electric SUV ("for the environment, bitch"). When Rose said she needed a car, Ella just gave her the Saab. At first, it all seemed too good to be true.

And it was. Ella was far from perfect. She was self-absorbed beyond comprehension, only interested in subjects that pertained to herself. She often treated Rose like an employee and a maid, which Rose begrudgingly accepted as she was wildly underpaying in rent and Ella had given her a car. Also, Rose was pretty sure Ella had a drinking problem. More than once, Rose had woken up to find Ella passed out in surprising locations—in the bathtub, under the coffee table, in the kitchen sink (it was very big and she was very small). Ella threw parties several nights a week, impervious to the fact that Rose had to wake up at 5 a.m. most days. She worked at a coffee shop in Larchmont Village, and the opening shift was all that was available as no one else wanted to be up that early. Rose didn't want to wake up that early, either, especially given that she was singing at open mics most evenings, coming home to Ella's sloppy soirees, sleeping only a few hours nightly. But that all might end soon.

Rose had been in LA just under a year, furiously trying to network her way to Blue. At first, Rose thought Ella would be her in given her internship at Interscope. But Ella's fellow interns were all people like her—rich girls from irrelevant cities far from LA. Rose talked to every single customer at the coffee shop, forever hoping that one might lead her to Blue, be an old friend from the neighborhood. But nothing.

Until about a month ago.

Rose was on the subreddit late at night while Ella snorted lines with overprivileged idiots in the other room. Rose wasn't looking for anything in particular—she was just expressing herself, rediscovering some lyrics from *Fluorescent Gloom*. She'd posted a few lines—*draped in crimson for the night / common knowledge, I'm chaotic, not quite right*—accompanied by some potential interpretations. As she scrolled through the comments, a familiar username caught her eye: GarboMommy, a reference to a song from *Garbo Gals*. Most users had names referencing Blue's songs or lyrics. Rose's was RoseGhost, after a song from *Oleander*. Ella's was PinkCocaine, after a song on *Spirit of Sinatra* and probably a red flag.

Rose had messaged with GarboMommy, whose real name was Grace, several times before. Grace lived in Wilmington, North Carolina, the same town where Blue and Max had grown up. In her intro post, Grace had mentioned going to summer camp with Max when they were in high school and said they still followed each other on Instagram. Initially, Rose had been excited, thinking Grace might provide an in to get to Blue. But after a few months of talking, Rose realized Grace was probably exaggerating her connection to Max—Grace didn't seem to know any concrete details about Max other than that she loved bubble tape when she was fifteen, as if chewing gum was a unique trait for a teenage girl.

It was not unusual for members of this subreddit to exaggerate tenuous connections to Blue. People bragged about minutiae ranging from living in the same college dorm as Blue's second cousin twice removed to having a friend of a friend who was once in a Sex and Love Addicts Anonymous meeting with Blue to a sister-in-law once selling Max a BB cream at Sephora. And Rose herself had bragged, perhaps excessively, after Blue reposted her video from the VIP section of the *Fluorescent Gloom* tour. Although disappointed that Grace's lead fell flat, Rose couldn't fault her for playing up a link to Max. It was the culture of the subreddit.

But then that one night about a month ago, in between debating whether *draped in crimson* was about sex or vampires or death or all three, Grace had asked Rose where she lived again.

LA, Rose had replied. *Trying to find Blue :)*

Grace had said *omg I thought so* and then revealed that Max had just posted on Instagram that day about looking for someone "reliable, trustworthy, and looking for work in Los Angeles." Grace said she didn't know for sure that the post was about an assistant for Blue, but she "had a feeling." She'd considered recommending herself, but she lived three thousand miles away and her mom was sick. *I trust you given your reputation in this holy subreddit*, Grace had said. *I'll pass on your name.*

Rose had let out a brief and involuntary squeal. But she didn't let herself get too excited because Max might not trust the word of this person she hardly knew. And Rose had nearly forgotten about it when two weeks later, Grace messaged Rose to say, *Blue wants to interview you!!!* Rose had resisted the urge to throw her laptop across the room.

And now she resisted the urge to pinch herself as she approached the gates to Blue's Malibu community—imposing wrought iron flanked by white pillars, frosted glass panels to obscure whatever magic was happening behind them. The interview wasn't for another fifteen minutes, so Rose slid into a parking spot outside of the gates and did a breathing exercise. She was about to pop some magnesium gummies when she realized she didn't really need them. She was oddly calm.

She restarted the audio recording one final time. The familiar words washed over her with the waves crashing in the distance.

In eleven years, spanning from 2008 to 2019, Blue Velour released six studio albums. . . .

r/BlueBeards • posted by u/RoseGhost • November 2019

BLUE'S BEARD?!?!?!?!?

Okay, BlueBeards, are we sitting down?? Are we *breathing*?! Did our resplendent queen really just gift us with a surprise album called *BLUE'S BEARD*!?!? I am in full-blown cardiac arrest—is this real life?!?

    Turns out I am fully lucid, vaping my mango Juul (Blue's fave, let us never forget) and blasting "A Vape Cartridge Named Desire" as loud as it will go. This track is straight-up serotonin wrapped in sapphic yearnings! Blue, you absolute *goddess*.

    Now that my heart rate has somewhat stabilized—well, not really, but whatever—gather round, kiddos, it's time for a classic Rose deep dive:

    So, for anyone who isn't familiar, *A Streetcar Named Desire* is a legendary play by Tennessee Williams—a total icon in queer literature. It stars Blanche DuBois, a haunted woman hiding her truth from a harsh, judgmental world. Blue has referenced Blanche a billion times, starting with "White Moth" on *Oleander*. (In *Streetcar*, Blanche is described as a "delicate beauty" with "something about her uncertain manner, as well as her white clothes, that suggests a moth.") Blanche's fragility and her need to conceal her true self are a proxy for Tennessee Williams himself—a gay man forced to mask his desires in a society that wouldn't accept him. Over and over, Blue suggests that Blanche also reflects her own struggle navigating a double life and projecting a public image while her real self is buried within her art. *Blue's Beard* is literally Blue's *Streetcar*, her diary of longing and defiance hidden in plain sight. It's her way of begging us to *see* her struggle to love openly, and to break free of this beautiful, tortured, closeted life!!

    Okay, and "Lullaby for Jack Willenhall"!?! Blue might as well have tattooed JACK IS MY BEARD across her dang chest! "Tied by a velour thread, but in your gaze, I'm barely there." Are you kidding me? The velour thread is their connection—a fragile, staged performance held together by the demands of the project, the label, the management.

Not real life, not love, not authenticity, but pure *artifice*. And her decision to use "gaze" instead of "eyes"? Very telling! Not only is a "gaze" more soul-deep than just "eyes," but it obvi sounds like *gay*! Jack's *gay* gaze doesn't hold her true self because it can't—it's her way of saying, "I am unseen in this charade." It's like an anthem of pure frustration, her true feelings left as this ghostly outline. Blue is *screaming* this to anyone who will listen!!

And then OMG "A Thousand Oak Trees from You to Me"—HOLY ACTUAL HELL. This is the ultimate love letter to Sasha. Obvi we all remember *Garbo Gals*' "Drive Me to Macy's," Blue's tribute to those 2016 pap shots of her and Sasha GRETA Harlow in Thousand Oaks, hands entwined like they were the only people in the world. Well, this is that times infinity!! "Flashes in our faces, our fingers tracing the legends of a thousand oaks"—she's taking us right back there, like she's guiding us to the holy relic of their love. "Flashes" aren't just the photographers' cameras; they're like tiny, searing memories of that intimate moment, and "fingers tracing the legends"—it's like her hands in Sasha's were touching eternity, reaching into the roots of something unbreakable. The oak trees are towering, timeless, unwavering—just like her devotion. This is her declaration. Her promise to Sasha. Her cathedral of love laid bare.

And everyone who ever called us delusional can sit down!! This album is a *confession* and a *confirmation*—a love letter hidden in plain sight.

THANK YOU, BLUE. WE SEE YOU. WE LOVE YOU.

Blue

*B*lue was still in bed when Max called up from downstairs to say the interview candidate was here. She grabbed a lukewarm, half-empty Red Bull from the bedside table and took a big sip. It tasted like piss but perked her up a bit. In the bathroom, she splashed water on her face, swished Listerine around her mouth. She sucked on the vaporizer on the counter, only to find it was empty. Fuck. She rummaged through the drawers.

"Blue!" Max called again.

"Coming!" Blue yelled back, just as she found a Juul from God knows how long ago with a little juice left. She drew in hard, disappointed to find it was mango flavored. Blue had left her fruity vape days behind her, now favoring only minty varieties. But beggars could not be choosers. She threw on her vintage Gucci kimono and looked for Bijou, her vibe detector, but couldn't find her under the covers. Both greyhounds normally slept with Blue, but last night only Gigi was curled up at the foot of her bed. Blue kissed the dog's nose, then headed downstairs.

"Have you seen Bijou?" Blue asked Max, who was pouring a girl who hardly looked nineteen a glass of Diet Coke, which felt like a good sign—she wasn't too good for diet soda. But why did she need a glass? Blue weaved around Max and grabbed a Red Bull from the fridge, cracked it open, and took a big gulp.

"She isn't upstairs?" Max asked.

Blue shook her head, feeling the timid girl's eyes on her. Blue had interviewed three people already this week, and they were all wrong. The first had seemed like an idiot, Bijou had barked wildly at the second, and the third had seemed capable but deeply unfun. This girl didn't seem fun either, but she'd come via a recommendation from Max's camp friend, which meant Blue already trusted the girl more than the others. The friend said there wasn't a Blue lyric she hadn't memorized, a personality trait that could go either way.

"Blue, this is Rose," Max said, pointing to the girl, who appeared to be shaking.

Rose adjusted her glasses and said, "Nice to meet you."

"Shall we hit the balcony?" Blue said to Rose, who nodded and picked up her Diet Coke.

The fog hadn't broken yet. The air was misty and cool as it typically was in January. Blue grabbed a couple of blankets and settled on the couch, motioning for Rose to join her.

"I don't bite," Blue said, grinning. She needed to loosen the girl up, ensure they could hang. She remembered Bijou and called for her, but Bijou didn't come. Rose sat several feet away from Blue on the couch. Blue threw her a blanket. Rose set down her glass and spread the blanket over her knees.

"Your home is beautiful," Rose said quietly. She had a nice voice, soft but melodic. That was a plus. Blue couldn't stand a grating or nasally speaking voice, like the previous interviewee's. She just wished Bijou would show up.

Blue nodded, lit a cigarette. "So why do you want to work for me?"

Rose inhaled sharply, looked up. Blue could tell she was thinking and that her mind moved quick. She wasn't an idiot like the first girl she'd interviewed. Rose pulled a vaporizer pen—a Mi-Pod, Blue's current favorite—from her jeans pocket and took a hit. This was an excellent sign.

"Sorry," Rose said, exhaling.

Blue instantly recognized the flavor of the pod. "Diamond Ice?"

Rose giggled, nodded. An even better sign.

"Can I have a drag? I ran out this morning." Then, "I'm dying."

Rose handed Blue the vape. Blue inhaled and felt her muscles relax. "Where was I?" Blue asked. "Oh yeah. Why me?"

"I've been waiting to answer this question for so long," Rose said. "It's surreal to be asked it."

"I get it," Blue said, energized by the Diamond Ice plus the Red Bull. "That's how I felt when I first performed on television. I'd been waiting my whole life to be on TV. And then I finally was, and I was so excited, and my voice did all these strange things. I was completely frozen and awkward. I kept doing these weird twirls to overcompensate, which only made things worse." She sighed. "I thought my career was over."

"*Conan*?" said Rose. "That performance is so misunderstood. You were majestic."

Blue laughed. "I really wasn't, but thank you."

"People," Rose said, confidence slipping into her voice, "are so threatened by greatness."

Rose's gaze locked on Blue's, eyes unblinking.

Blue smiled. She was maybe beginning to like the nerd.

"Max says you're a fan," Blue said.

Rose nodded, then laughed. "You could say that, yes," she said. "Does that give me points or take them away?"

"Depends," said Blue. "What's your favorite album?"

"*Fluorescent Gloom*," Rose said without hesitation. This surprised Blue, and did in fact add points.

Rose passed the vape to Blue at the precise moment Blue craved another drag. This was also a good sign. She would need someone who could anticipate her desires.

"What do you like about it?" Blue asked, then sucked on the pen. On the exhale, vapor danced with the mist in the air.

"It's so raw," said Rose. "I love *Spirit of Sinatra* and *Chateau Velour*, don't get me wrong. I love your wordplay, the sense of mischief. But I like you best when the listener gets to hear what's beneath that—the loneliness, the heartbreak, the painful awkwardness of being alive. *Fluorescent Gloom* and *Oleander* do that so beautifully. But, really, I like all your records. And I promise I'm not just saying that. You can ask anyone who knows me. I've defended you from day one and I'm thrilled the rest of the world finally caught up."

This was a good answer. But Rose was not done.

"I wrote my thesis on *Fluorescent Gloom* at Carnegie Mellon," she said, some insecurity returning to her voice, a slight shakiness. "It's not a cool school, I know, but they have a great voice program. And my parents teach there, so I went for free."

"There's no shame in getting an education," Blue said. "I'd love to read your thesis."

"It's completely overwritten, but—"

"Don't do that," Blue interrupted.

"Do what?" Rose asked.

"Downplay your abilities," Blue said. "It comes off as inauthentic. I don't buy it. You're a shark, like me. I see it in your eyes. Own it."

Rose nodded.

"You're a singer," Blue said.

Rose nodded again.

"Sing for me," Blue said.

"Right now?" Rose asked.

"Is now not a good time?" Blue asked.

Rose shrugged, then took a deep breath. A silence fell between them. Water slapped up against the rocks below. Rose adjusted her glasses, then stood up, put her hands on her diaphragm. Blue examined her face. Fair skin, freckles splattered across her nose, wavy auburn hair that fell just below her shoulders. It was thick, though in desperate need of deep conditioning. Blue saw potential. Rose's hair had red undertones, and she had the coloring to pull off being a redhead. Most people didn't. She wondered if Rose would wear contacts or trade her round frames for something a bit more chic, maybe a cat-eye. Behind the glasses, her brown eyes were kind, but intense.

Rose opened her mouth to sing. Blue recognized the first words and notes immediately. Because she'd written them. The song was "Rose Ghost" from *Oleander*. To Blue's surprise, Rose hit the deep notes with ease. Blue's voice was technically classified as contralto, the lowest female singing voice. Most women couldn't go that low, but Rose could. She could go high too, hitting that high C with sharp, almost annoying precision. And like Blue, Rose could move from soft, nearly whispered tones to more powerful, belted notes. When she got to the chorus, her voice seemed to dissolve into the marine layer, syrupy and soft, more intimate than Blue would expect from someone classically trained. Rose's voice lacked Blue's feverish, sultry energy—there was no fire to it—but it was good. Vaguely impressive, but not threatening. Perfect. Blue closed her eyes, zoned into the sounds. Soon, the final note was echoing off toward the water.

Blue clapped and whistled, partially in response to Rose's performance but also as a result of the Red Bull and nicotine swimming in her veins. Rose's fair cheeks reddened. She cleared her throat and did an awkward curtsy.

"What's your sign?" Blue asked.

"Gemini," Rose said.

Blue gasped. "You're hired," she said. Max had wanted her to do background checks before hiring anyone, but Blue tended to act on instinct. And while a lot of bad things had happened to her, she was in a great place right now. Rose was a friend of Max's camp friend. Max said she didn't have many specific memories of this friend, and Blue couldn't remember her name at the moment, but a friend of a friend seemed to circumvent the need for a background check. Rose came across as dedicated. She'd graduated from a top music program, which meant she was disciplined. She was a little uptight, sure, but there was something intriguing lurking underneath—a wild side begging to be unleashed. Blue needed to work with people she could be wild with.

Blue looked at Rose, who appeared to be choking.

Blue stood up and patted her back. "Don't die on me now."

"I'm just so happy," Rose said, catching her breath. "Are you sure?"

"Here's some free advice," Blue said, leaning against the railing. "When someone offers you your dream job, don't give them an opportunity to change their mind."

Rose laughed. "Sorry, right."

"Stop apologizing too," Blue said. "You're a little stiff, but so was I at your age. We're going to loosen you up." She patted Rose's back again. "I can tell there's a little freak inside you."

Rose smiled. "Yeah," she said. "I guess." Mist blew off the ocean. A seagull swooped down and landed on the railing beside Rose. She jumped. Blue laughed. Then she heard barking. Bijou, finally. She was on the patio, barking madly at the seagull. Blue scooped her up and kissed her nose.

"Bijou," Blue said, "meet your new auntie, Rose."

Bijou remained transfixed by the seagull, still barking.

r/BlueBeards • posted by u/GarboMommy • April 2015

Just discovered this sub!

Hey, beautiful ladies!! Massive Blue Velour fan here, completely and utterly obsessed with her angelic tunes and flawless aura. I'm *soooo* excited to have discovered this *glorious* subreddit! For work I'm a graphic designer, and literally everything I make is a subtle nod to Blue's aesthetic—film noir, femme fatales, intertwining freeways, dirty palm trees, velvet drapes, overcast beaches, pink ashtrays, deadly flowers, vape clouds. . . . Blue is basically my entire mood board for life.

    Okay, I don't normally tell people this next part, but I feel like I can trust you all with my entire soul. So here's the tea: when I was a teenager, I went to this summer camp in North Carolina where I'm from, and—brace yourselves—a fellow camper was none other than Max Clark (aka Blue's sister!!!!). Except Blue was Beatrice back then, and Max was Maxine. Maxine and I were like *best friends.* We had this crazy close connection that I swear I'll never forget. We don't talk a lot now, but we still follow each other on Instagram, supporting each other from afar.

    Now for the part that will send you straight to heaven: Beatrice would sometimes pick up Maxine from camp in her baby blue Jetta, and she *always* had this impossibly cool woman beside her, and they'd both be smoking clove cigarettes. I swear, the smell of cloves still gives me actual butterflies. Maxine *worshipped* her sister, always talking about how Beatrice was fearless and did whatever she wanted. Seeing Beatrice with this stunning woman, it all just clicked. The energy was so undeniably sapphic!

    Anyway, I am BEYOND thrilled to join this iconic subreddit and bask in our shared love for our divine queen, Blue Velour!!

    Xoxo, Grace

Rose

Rose and Blue quickly fell into an easy rhythm. It helped that Rose knew everything about Blue—her favorite vape flavors, snacks, scented candles, beauty products—so it was relatively easy to predict her needs. But it was never dull, as Blue's desires were constantly shifting. After all, one of Rose's favorite things about Blue was her dynamism, the way she kept people on their toes. There was always an element of surprise. You thought she was going one way, and she went the other.

Blue's personality was in constant flux. She'd tell Rose she didn't like to drive, then make Rose pull over so Blue could take the wheel, stressing that she had a sudden "need for speed." She'd say she preferred the Stones to the Beatles, then demand Rose put on *Rubber Soul* immediately or she'd "perish." She'd quit cigarettes too many times to count, only to end up chain-smoking on the balcony later that day. Blue was a steady rush of contradictions, which she'd actually referenced on her *Oleander* song "Mercury," about her lack of a fixed personality (and also being a Gemini, as their sign was ruled by Mercury). The song had a lyric Rose loved that she'd only recently realized was attributable to Walt Whitman: *Do I contradict myself? I contain multitudes.*

The biggest shock was how much Blue cared what people thought of her. One reason Rose was drawn to Blue was because of her general air of *fuck it*, an energy so foreign to Rose as to be exotic, as Rose was all effort, discipline, self-consciousness. Blue had always seemed effortless, and she still did, but she also *really* cared. She was also self-conscious. She'd say, "I love my haters, they're my biggest fans one minute," then later that afternoon monologue for an hour about one review from a random blog post in 2013 that "didn't get it," going on to say something like, "If I cared more, I'd kill him." And she'd end up crying. Rose hated to see Blue sad but loved to rub her back while she cried. This was the only time they ever touched, and Blue's skin always seemed to vibrate. Blue was so alive in a way Rose felt she could never be.

One afternoon in mid-January, Blue threw Rose for another loop. Rose was driving Blue back from rehearsal when Blue directed Rose to bypass the turnoff to her house and continue to Route 23. They wound through the canyons as the sky darkened, all the way to Thousand Oaks, site of those famous paparazzi photos Rose had poured thousands of words into analyzing on the subreddit.

"The shopping in Malibu is shit," Blue said as she instructed Rose to pull into a spot outside of Macy's. "Bougie hippie bullshit."

Again, more contradictions. Sometimes, she really seemed to like bougie hippie bullshit. She wore Dôen maxi dresses and loved Crosby, Stills, Nash & Young. Her vintage Mercedes—referenced in the *Chateau Velour* song "Baby Blue Benz"—had an artisanal dream catcher hanging from the mirror and an overpriced palo santo stick in the center console, which she'd burn in between cigarettes. She often wore fringed suede jackets with Ugg boots, and her hair hung below her breasts. But other times, Blue considered herself suburban white trash, exhibiting a near-religious devotion to Diet Coke, Red Bull, and the less luxurious mall department stores. Other times, she was an Old Hollywood darling, with her vintage kimonos and dramatic eyeliner and vintage gold lighter. Still others, she considered herself a redneck, with her Red Bull and old men who rode motorcycles and her vaguely Southern accent that seemed to become more pronounced when the sun went down.

Rose liked all the Blues.

Ella had been weird toward Rose since Rose landed the gig. Ella stopped treating Rose like an employee and started treating her like an ex-girlfriend who had wronged her. Rose and Ella had kissed once, just after Rose moved in nearly a year ago, but they'd both been so drunk. Ella hadn't mentioned it, and Rose wondered if she even remembered. They were by no means exes, but sometimes Ella would climb into Rose's bed and hold on to her in the middle of the night, and by the morning, Ella would be gone.

Ella expected Rose to introduce her to Blue.

"I work for her," Rose had said. "She isn't my friend."

"You're there all the time," Ella had said. "You're there more than you are here."

Rose liked that Ella seemed jealous, although she couldn't pinpoint exactly why. She explained that Blue lived thirty-six miles away, that it made more sense to sleep there most nights rather than spend hours each day commuting. And Blue had needed Rose more as the *Blue's Beard* tour rapidly approached. For the tour, Blue was leaning into her redneck persona. When Blue first mentioned the tour, Rose had been imagining glamorous locations like New York, Paris, Tokyo. But Blue wanted to perform for the "real ones," her "true fans," who she was convinced were located in rural American towns Rose had never heard of. Maybe Blue was right. Rose was a Blue Velour superfan, and she was from the very unglamorous city of Pittsburgh. Ella was also a fan, and she was from a town in Georgia that Rose could never remember the name of. And, accordingly, Pittsburgh and Athens, Georgia, were two stops on the upcoming redneck tour, as Rose was calling it in her head.

And roughly two months before said redneck tour, in Macy's that winter evening, Blue found two sparkly gold dresses by the same designer for her and Rose to try on. "I have nowhere to wear this," Rose said in the dressing room, just as Blue said, "Honey, you look gorgeous."

Rose tried to stop her face from reddening but failed. The problem with her fair, Irish-descended skin, in addition to being allergic to the sun, was that she blushed at the slightest sensation of embarrassment. And Rose was easily embarrassed. Her kindergarten teacher had told Rose's mom that Rose was the shyest child she had ever seen, which Rose's mom liked to repeat at dinner parties. Rose would blush whenever she did.

"What do you mean you have nowhere to wear it?" Blue said. "You're coming with me to the Grammys."

Blue nearly choked. Rose knew Blue had been nominated—five times, in all the major categories, whereas in the past, she'd been snubbed other than maybe a nomination in one of the off-screen categories she never won—but Rose was not expecting to attend the ceremony.

"Sasha can't make it. She's recording with some"—Blue lowered her voice—"Swedish *whore* in Stockholm."

This was only one of a handful of times that Blue had mentioned Sasha. Whenever she did, Rose's heart would go loco.

The saleslady cleared her throat. Blue cleared hers back, mocking the woman. She was wearing her typical disguise—a blue Dodgers cap under a sweatshirt with the hood up, big sunglasses—so she wasn't recognizable, exactly. But the sunglasses inside at night tended to draw attention. The saleslady frowned and turned to help another customer.

"That's too bad," Rose said with a forced casualness. Rose meant this. She was insanely excited to go to the Grammys, but genuinely disappointed that Sasha wasn't going to make it, that she was recording with someone who wasn't Blue, let alone a *Swedish whore*—Lykke Li? Robyn? Tove Lo? The subreddit always got furious whenever Sasha recorded with anyone who wasn't Blue. But as Blue became more famous, Sasha became more famous, which meant Sasha was collaborating with people other than Blue.

Rose was envious of all of them.

And two days later, on Rose's third week of work, she was at the Staples Center in downtown Los Angeles for the 62nd Annual Grammy Awards. Rose and Blue were wearing sparkly gold dresses made by the same designer, the ones Blue had purchased for them at Macy's along with fifteen Jo Malone Wild Bluebell candles, whose scent Rose had come to associate with euphoria. Blue had bought a matching dress for Max too, but Max hadn't wanted to wear it, instead opting for a vintage Prada gown. She also seemed annoyed that Blue was wearing a dress from Macy's, a dress so similar to the one her assistant wore. But she was also Blue's sister and had likely learned a long time ago that Blue was positively untamable.

Rose was seated next to Max, who was next to Blue, who was next to Jack Willenhall. The fact that Blue had brought Jack as her date was sure to get the BlueBeards going. Rose hadn't allowed herself to check the subreddit since she got here, as she was desperately trying to remain present, but Ella had texted her, *Is that Blue with her BEARD on the carpet??* Blue hadn't allowed herself to respond. And right now, Blue was seated beside said beard for all the world to see.

Rose was still sad Sasha wasn't here—even though if Sasha had been, she wouldn't be, since she was in Sasha's seat. But Rose would almost rather see Blue and Sasha interact on a television than be at the Grammys herself. As Rose suspected, Blue and Jack had the chemistry of a cat and a dog. No, that wasn't right—cats and dogs hated each other, and hate was a powerful emotion. There was almost nothing between Blue and Jack. Just air. They were like two very beautiful cats with zero interest in each other.

When it was time to call the nominees for Album of the Year, Rose's heart began thudding in her ears. Max squeezed Rose's hand, which was sweating profusely. The act also surprised Rose, as she'd assumed until this moment that Max didn't particularly like her. Rose knew from interviews, photos, Instagram, that Blue adored her sister, which made Rose uneasy about Max's general disinterest regarding her. Was Max suspicious of her? Had Grace told her that Rose was active on that fanatical subreddit dedicated to shipping a relationship that might not even exist? But now, as Max squeezed Rose's hand, all those worries seemed to dissipate, and Rose directed all of her attention to the words coming out of the presenter's mouth.

LL Cool J, who Rose knew only from the giant words on the screen, was presenting Album of the Year. The other nominees were Billie Eilish, Bon Iver, Ariana Grande, H.E.R., Lil Nas X, Lizzo, and Vampire Weekend. Blue said she liked the Lil Nas X album and thought it might win. Rose thought all the other nominees were shit, that Blue was on a far superior artistic level. When LL Cool J began to open the envelope, Max squeezed her hand harder and Rose squeezed it back. When LL Cool J said, *"Blue's Beard,"* an explosion rippled through Rose's body and then the room at large. Blue screamed, Rose screamed, Max screamed, and Jack whistled. Blue hugged Max, then Jack. Rose wasn't expecting a hug, but Blue not only hugged her but also kissed her cheek before going up to the stage.

Rose had lied to Ella. Blue wasn't just Rose's employer.

Blue was her friend.

r/BlueBeards • posted by u/AutotuneMe • January 2020

OMFG BLUE'S BEARD AT THE GRAMMYS

Ummm . . . who else is losing it!?!? First off Queen Blue looks SO stunning on the red carpet, I want her to run me over with a car?? Jesus, I need conversion therapy!

For those of you all freaking out about Sasha not being there despite being nominated for Producer of the Year, please wake up! Y'all are playing checkers and Blue is playing CHESS!

You know in "Lullaby for Jack Willenhall" when Blue's like "shadows scream in bright lights / it's all a smoke screen now" . . . She's literally telling us Jack is a decoy. It's chaos theory in action, my chicas. I *promise you* Sasha is somewhere secretly watching and laughing at how we've all been *played*!!!

Blue is the QUEEN TROLLLL.

Comment by u/DeathBaby

OMG, YES!! But who is that girl sitting with Max?!? Anyone know?? She looks so familiar, so *normal*, like someone who should be working at the Gap and why is she there and not me?? And is she wearing the same freaking dress as Blue??

Comment by u/GarboMommy

I think that's her new assistant :) And I don't *think* it's the same dress. Blue's is def more sparkly. Maybe same designer? Maybe part of said "chaos theory" to put her assistant in such a similar dress? Didn't she say on the red carpet that her dress was from Macy's? "Drive Me to Macy's" . . .

Comment by u/AutotuneMe

1000% cHaOs tHeOrY !!!

Comment by u/DeathBaby

Ugh so jealous of assistant brb jumping off roof . . .

Blue

"Album of the *fucking* Year!" someone Blue didn't even recognize shouted at her for what felt like the four billionth time that night. She was at the Interscope after-party at some Soho House knockoff in Hollywood. Blue hated industry parties. Hated drunk people. Hated this drunk rando in her face. Blue hadn't had a sip of alcohol since she'd gone to rehab at twenty-six, a year before *Spirit of Sinatra* was released. Before that, Blue always thought she'd end up in the Twenty-Seven Club with her heroes. Amy Winehouse, Kurt Cobain, Jim Morrison, Janis Joplin. But unlike them, at twenty-six, Blue hadn't released a record yet, just a few singles no one cared about. So she needed to stay alive.

While making *Spirit of Sinatra*, Blue and Sasha would often get extraordinarily fucked-up. They'd record with bourbon, cigarettes, coke, and poppers. Sasha could always handle her liquor better than Blue, knowing when to hit the brakes and drink a glass of water. Blue had no limits, recording much of the album in a blackout. One night, an exec came to check in on them and found Blue passed out on the mixing table. She had apparently spilled half a bottle of whiskey on the extremely expensive equipment. The label said they would scrap the album unless Blue got help.

At the time, Blue had been furious, but looking back, she felt extremely blessed that the exec had walked in at that precise moment. And was also very grateful that the label had paid for her treatment at Oro House in Malibu, the best addiction treatment center in California, if not the country. It was also fucking beautiful. Blue fell in love with Malibu. She vowed to move there when she had the money. And thanks to her recovery, she did eventually get the money. After "Death Baby" was featured in a James Bond movie.

But right now, with this random employee's bloodshot eyes in her face, her sweaty palms squeezing her shoulders, Blue wasn't feeling so thankful. She always fantasized about going independent, or to a smaller label with more clout, then remembered the mortgage. Interscope paid the bills. And she paid theirs. Without thinking, Blue lifted her Red Bull over the employee's head, tilted the can, and poured a few droplets onto her head. She couldn't drink anymore, but her destructive spirit was alive and well.

"What the fuck," the woman said, retreating.

Blue poured a little more until the woman ran away like a little baby. What a loser. No one wanted to have fun anymore. Blue looked around for Jack, but she figured he'd left a long time ago for a legitimate romantic prospect, someone more muscular, less supple. Blue scanned the room for Max, who also seemed drunk, flirting with some handsome older guy in the corner. Good for Max. Blue often worried that Max neglected her personal life for Blue's career, so she was glad her sister appeared to be enjoying herself. Max seemed to be taking care of herself a little better since Blue had hired Rose, which was mostly the point of hiring Rose. Also, Blue was sort of starting to like Rose. Sort of.

Blue went to find the little nerd alone in the corner on her phone.

"Come here often?" Blue said, sliding up against Rose and causing her to jump. The girl was so easily spooked. But she'd cleaned up nice tonight in the shimmering Art Deco–inspired gown Blue had bought for her. Blue had encouraged Rose to wear contacts, but she said she couldn't due to a deep-seated fear of touching her eyeballs—such a delicate girl. So Blue had bought Rose new glasses, cat-eye frames that were a bit more elegant. Blue had done Rose's makeup, given her a dark red lip and rosy cheeks. Her hair was a little longer, looked redder under the party lights. She was adorable. Blue felt stage-mom pride at her assistant's light glow-up.

"Wanna get out of here?" Blue asked.

Rose nodded.

Blue drove them home because Rose was overly cautious. She never surpassed the speed limit and followed all traffic laws. She sat erect and very close to the wheel, gripping it hard.

Blue loved to speed in her baby blue Benz late at night. It would have been faster to take the 101 to the canyon, but Blue wanted to take Sunset Boulevard, which went all the way from downtown LA to the ocean. And at this time of night on a Sunday, it was empty. Blue rolled the windows down and sped past the Laugh Factory, then the Chateau Marmont, where Blue used to love doing cocaine with Sasha just before rehab. She shivered at the memory, which elicited powerful opposing feelings—on one hand, of being young and indestructible, at the precipice of fame, excited and eager and not remotely jaded; on the other hand, of being exposed and vulnerable, prey to her demons, powerless, devoid of agency. Blue pressed harder on the gas, not wanting to think about any of it. She was particularly skilled in the art of pressing her feelings down, down, down.

"Put on some music," Blue said to Rose, who hadn't said anything since they'd gotten in the car, which Blue appreciated. She respected a woman who wasn't afraid of silence. Most women were, feeling compelled to fill every little space in the air with the most irritating trivialities.

"Not mine," Blue clarified, knowing Rose was probably about to put on *Blue's Beard*.

Rose froze, looking at the phone with an expression of mild panic, and at that moment, Blue wondered if Rose listened to any music that wasn't hers. The thought was partially flattering but mostly frightening, or maybe just sad. There was so much amazing music to listen to, Blue could hardly find the hours in the day to listen to everything she wanted to hear. But then Rose's fingers moved and then sound came through the speakers and Blue immediately recognized the opening notes of Amy Winehouse's *Back to Black*. Blue laughed at her own hubris. Of course Rose listened to music other than Blue's, and she had good taste.

"I played this constantly before I went to rehab," Blue said. The memory of belting this album at the top of her lungs while Sasha sped to some club flickered in her mind like an old film reel.

Rose seemed unsure what to say. She didn't seem like an addict, not at all—too safe—but then again, Blue wasn't great at assessing these things. It was often the quiet ones who surprised you.

"Before you, Amy was my favorite," Rose said.

"Amy was the best." Blue pulled a cigarette from the pack in the center console and gestured for Rose to light it, which she did dutifully. Rose's quick draw with the lighter was one of her most charming attributes, almost reason alone to hire her.

Amy played and the buildings turned into trees as they glided into Beverly Hills.

"Was that party god-awful, or am I just a miserable old cynic?" Blue asked finally.

Rose inhaled, evidently thinking. Blue liked that Rose didn't just blurt whatever came into her head like most people did. She thought about what she was going to say before she said it. Maybe Blue could learn how to do that. Maybe Rose could teach her.

"I thought it was cool," Rose said.

"So I'm a bitter curmudgeon." Blue laughed.

"I can imagine how they might get tiring after a while, but I felt a bit starstruck," Rose said.

"Ooh, who made you starstruck?" Blue asked. She was charmed by the idea of feeling excited to be in a celebrity's presence, a feeling she'd had all the time when she moved to LA but hadn't experienced in at least a decade. Blue was excited for the tour, to get out of Hollywood and into the real world, to fuck an older man who used bar soap for shampoo and had no idea who she was. When Blue was younger, she hated being from a small Southern town. All she wanted was to move to LA, where everyone was creative and glamorous and no one had a regular job. But now that she'd been in LA for nearly twenty years, it didn't feel glamorous. It felt lame and sad and pathetic, filled with social climbers and sociopaths and pathological liars. Blue was desperate to return to the land of regular people, where no one was pretending to be someone else or name-dropping tenuous connections to D-list actors.

Rose blew a puff of vapor out the window. "Mostly you," Rose said, and Blue smacked her on the knee. Rose jumped, then said, "I wanted to meet Sasha." She said this so quietly, Blue almost couldn't hear her. "That would make me truly starstruck," she said a little louder.

Blue laughed. She couldn't imagine feeling starstruck by Sasha. But the fans loved her, loved the idea of Sasha and Blue together. "Did you know there's a whole group of people on Reddit dedicated to finding clues that Sasha and I are together?"

Rose looked at Blue, adjusted her glasses.

"Well, are you?" she asked. "Together?"

Blue laughed, then Rose did too.

"Sorry, that was forward," Rose said. "My mom always says I have no tact."

"You're cute," Blue said.

A silence hung between them. Blue knew Rose wanted her to answer the question. But secrecy was a large part of the thrill with Sasha. Blue hadn't even told Max about their romance, although Blue suspected Max knew, as they shared a sisterly intuition. But they'd never discussed it. She wasn't about to discuss it with her new assistant.

Blue just laughed and exhaled smoke into the wind.

r/BlueBeards • posted by u/GeminiGod • January 2020

SHAKING CRYING THROWING UP

You guys, ALBUM OF THE FUCKING YEAR?!! After being *snubbed* for her first five albums and enduring critics slamming her for a decade?? And for an album called *BLUE'S BEARD* no less?! This is pure and unadulterated VINDICATION! This album is a straight-up love letter to Sasha, yes, but also to *us*. It's her coming-out album, and Blue is literally *screaming* her queerness to anyone willing to listen.

    I mean . . . that speech!! When Blue said, "Thank you for finally seeing me"—guys, she literally *came out*, right there on national television! After all these years, she's finally revealing her true self to the world!

    Who else is sobbing their eyes out?? This isn't just a win for Blue, it's a win for all of us who've been with her from the start, had her back through every rumor, every hater, every hit piece. For those of us who've had our own tortured years in the closet.

    I'm going to celebrate by blasting *Blue's Beard* on repeat all night and probably the rest of my life. Who's with me?? This is a truly HERstoric (lol) moment, and I'm so blessed to share it with you all, my chosen internet family.

    BLUE TODAY, BLUE TOMORROW, BLUE FOREVER!!!

Rose

Blue's tour preparation was unorthodox.

A classically trained vocalist, Rose would never dream of smoking cigarettes. Blue smoked them all day, every day. When Rose started the job, there was a rule that they could only smoke on the patio, but that rule quickly disintegrated. The house smelled like an ashtray, and Rose was constantly opening the windows to diffuse the stench.

Rose's days fell into a predictable pattern. She'd arrive at Blue's around 11 a.m., meaning she could sleep in later than she could at her old job, although the commute was nearly twenty times as long. On the way, she'd stop and pick up what Blue called "supplies," meaning Red Bull, American Spirit Blues, Cool Ranch Doritos, and vape pods. Blue would still be sleeping when Rose arrived. Rose would tidy up, feed the dogs, and coordinate travel arrangements, meetings, rehearsal times.

Blue would come downstairs at around noon or one, crack open a Red Bull, then join Rose and Max on the patio to go over the ever-evolving set list. Then Rose would follow Blue to the shed out back, which housed a twenty-year-old treadmill covered in dust. Blue would chain-smoke and walk at a slow pace and practice her songs. Rose would give feedback, but mostly compliments Rose learned from hearing Ella talk to her party friends on coke: *Your hair is literally reflective today, it's giving glass. Whatever's happening on your eyelids is straight-up war-crimes levels of slay. Oh my God, was that your voice? I thought it was an actual angel singing? How do you literally have the same body as Botticelli's Venus but also like . . . much thinner?* Blue needed a lot of compliments, and Rose was happy to give them. She'd been preparing her whole life for this precise task.

Four days a week, Blue had rehearsal at Harbor Studios. Rose would drive them, first in the old Saab, but Blue said her Mercedes was more comfortable. It was rickety and hard to drive, objectively less comfortable than the Saab. And driving it made Rose nervous, like someone was going to hit her and the car would crumble into dust.

Harbor Studios had bamboo walls, recessed lavender lighting, and a 180-degree view of the Pacific Ocean. Each rehearsal, Rose would fantasize about one day getting to record here. Blue seemed less in awe of the space. She spent most of rehearsal smoking cigarettes with Trevor, who played drums. Blue and Trevor had apparently gone to high school together, although he looked old enough to be her dad. The rest of the band would often practice without them. Sometimes they'd join, and Blue would giggle and mess around through a few songs. Rose suspected there was something romantic happening between Blue and Trevor, but she didn't like to think about it too much, as Trevor wasn't Sasha.

After rehearsal, Rose and Blue would get burritos. Carne asada for Blue, chicken for Rose, vegan for Max. The three of them would eat on the couch and watch *The Bachelor* or *Real Housewives*. Rose would worry that Max didn't like her again, feel like an intruder, until Blue started doing impressions of all the cast members. She was an incredible mimic. Max and Rose would laugh until they cried, occasionally exchanging glances, and Rose would momentarily feel like she belonged.

After dinner, Blue often went out. She never said where she was going, but Rose suspected it was romantic, or at least sexual. Rose hoped she was seeing Sasha, that one day she'd bring Sasha to the house so Rose could stare at her up close. Max would go into her room, and Rose would feel insecure again. Then she would walk the dogs. Rose preferred Gigi, as Bijou was always yapping at her. Gigi was sweet and lazy. She never wanted to walk, so Rose would often carry her until she wiggled to let Rose know she needed to go to the bathroom. Rose would put her down and look at the few stars she could see—normally just Venus, or whatever that big one was called, and a few others. She'd listen to the ocean and wonder how this had become her life.

Picking up Gigi's tiny shit, Rose would feel like the luckiest girl in the world.

r/BlueBeards • posted by u/CoolRanch • February 2020

Blue and mystery woman again??

Remember the redhead sitting next to Max at the Grammys? Wearing matching dresses with Blue? Did you all see the new pics of them leaving Harbor Studios in Malibu this afternoon? She seems to be Blue's new right-hand woman, like, handing her vapes, driving her around, always so close to her, whispering and shit. Any chance she's more than just an assistant?

> **Comment by u/GeminiGod**
>
> Maybe dating? Idk!
>
> **Comment by u/NeonBruise**
>
> Nooooo, she's just an assistant, please. Nowhere near sexy enough for our sweet Blue.
>
> **Comment by u/RedBullsRunning**
>
> THANK YOU, she's no Sasha!

Blue

At night, Blue would just drive. A younger version of herself would have been driving to meet men—anyone who lacked a smartphone, feigned disinterest, and seemed vaguely dangerous—and sometimes she still did that, but these days, she mostly drove.

Driving was a spiritual ritual akin to attending church. The empty night roads cleared Blue's head and made her soul buzz. She'd listen to her heroes: Nirvana, the Doors, Amy Winehouse, Janis Joplin. Often she'd drive for an hour or two, sometimes four, once twelve—she'd driven all the way to Big Sur, then back, watching the sun rise as she glided through Carpinteria. Another time, she'd driven to Palm Springs just to get out of the car and howl into the desert void, then whipped back to beat rush hour. Blue loved the empty American landscape—just her, a car, music made by someone who'd died at twenty-seven, and miles and miles of anonymous space.

If she craved company, she'd drive to the Rock Store on Mulholland, a biker bar where no one ever knew who she was. These types of places were becoming increasingly rare in and around Los Angeles. She couldn't wait to tour, to hit the road, to go to the type of American city where she could wander into a bar without a disguise and pick up whomever she wanted. Just the thought made Blue's heart skip a beat.

Tonight, she was winding through the canyons, high in the sky but seeing only darkness aside from the headlights of the rare oncoming car. She drove up to her favorite overlook, where she could pull over and see the city lights twinkling below like stars. She got out of the car and the air was cool and damp. She could hear coyotes howling in the distance. She was about to howl back when another car pulled up out of nowhere, throwing up dust. Soon the headlights were in her eyes. The car parked and Blue could suddenly see.

"Bluuuuuue," the driver yelled, hanging out the window of an old Jeep. He had a shaved head and was beside a girl with platinum blond hair. Probably a gay man and his BFF. They looked like most of her fans—twitchy and sad, with artificial hair colors and a smattering of tiny, delicate tattoos.

"We're literally listening to you right now!" the shaved-head boy screeched. He turned up the music and Blue recognized "A Vape Cartridge Named Desire." She loved this song. And since she was in a good mood, she was happy to run into fans. In a decent mood, she loved her fans. They were, after all, why she was here. They were how she was able to afford to live in Malibu and make money doing what she loved, and frankly, they were why she was still alive.

"You're adorable," Blue said. "Thank you."

"We're obsessed with you," the boy said. Men never seemed afraid to talk to her. The woman beside him looked embarrassed, her body language folding on itself the way Rose's often did. "You signed your name on my forearm at Amoeba Records in 2008 and I literally got it tattooed on me the next day." He held out his arm, but it was too dark to see the tattoo.

"Shut *the fuck* up," Blue said, as though this was the first time a fan had said this to her. Fans were constantly showing her tattoos of her own signature, of her face, her breasts, her lyrics, her hair. But fans wanted to feel special and unique just like everyone else, so Blue would perform shock for this cute boy with the shaved head. "You fucking didn't," she continued.

"I fucking did." The cute boy grinned, clearly proud of himself.

"What are you all up to on this gorgeous night?" Blue asked. Perhaps she was lonely.

The boy removed a joint from behind his ear. "Smoking this and listening to you," he said.

"Sounds heavenly," Blue said. She headed back toward her car. "Have a great night," she said before they could offer her a hit of the joint. Blue would break her sobriety for the occasional psychedelic, but weed grossed her out, reminded her of too many bad ex-boyfriends.

The boy called after her, "Hey, Blue, why aren't you playing the Hollywood Bowl on the *Blue's Beard* tour?"

"I gotta get out of LA for a bit," she said. "You know how it is."

Blue got in her car, revved the ignition.

"Wait, do you have any advice before you go?" the boy yelled out the window.

"Fall in love, smoke cigarettes," she called out as she drove slowly toward the road. She leaned out the window. "And open your eyes: poetry is everywhere!" Blue merged onto the road. She heard the boy start screaming "Hell yassss!" behind her, as though this was something revelatory and not what she told everyone.

Soon Blue was winding down the mountain pass, back toward the water, which at this time of night resembled a never-ending black sheet. She put on her high beams as she rounded the corner. Roughly a hundred feet ahead, a bobcat darted into the road. As Blue pressed the brakes to slow down, the bobcat looked directly into Blue's high beams.

Its eyes were neon red.

r/BlueBeards • posted by u/ChateauVelour • March 2020

TOUR IN THREE DAYS

The countdown is on, bitches! It seems like forever ago that I woke up at 6 a.m. to get tickets, but the tour is starting in A-minus three days! I cannot freaking wait to hear "Marlboro Never Dies" IRL—I'll literally off myself if she doesn't play it.

And how COOL is it that Blue's hitting up small towns this time!? I'm seeing her in Franklin, Tennessee, if anyone else is going—let's meet up. Who's going and where?

> **Comment by u/Oleander**
>
> I'm SO excited she's coming to Brandon! I never thought our little town would attract someone like Blue Velour. She really takes care of us!! Such an angel!
>
> **Comment by u/LilacLies**
>
> Are you people serious?? This fucking redneck tour is making me crazy. Why in God's name is she skipping literally all the major cities? Unfair, lame, criminal!!! She could fill stadiums, why waste time in the middle of nowhere, USA??
>
> **Comment by u/PolarVoid**
>
> It's not about filling stadiums. Blue said at the Grammys she wants to make real connections, not just money. It's refreshing to see an artist care about reaching out to fans in smaller towns. She actually sees us as people rather than as a paycheck. That's so rare! An angel indeed!!
>
> **Comment by u/GarboGa**
>
> Hearing about all this novel-coronavirus stuff ramping up—really hoping it doesn't mess with the tour. It would be such

a bummer if they start canceling things. Crossing my fingers. Anyone else keeping an eye on the news?

Comment by u/GlitterGutter

Oh, *please*, Blue won't shut down her tour for a freaking FLU!

Rose

The night before Rose left for the tour, Ella threw her a very bitter going-away party. Rose had no real friends in Los Angeles aside from Ella, unless she counted Blue and Max, whom she did not invite, so the party was entirely comprised of Ella's friends, or at least people Ella interned with and/or had slept with. Ella had even hired a DJ, a pretty blonde who went by Vagablonde. She was often over late at night, blasting trap music and laughing at her own jokes.

"Rose has outgrown us," Ella announced to no one in particular after her third drink. "She's off to bigger and better things. Will she even remember where she came from?" Ella laughed a shrill, cruel laugh. A few people announced that they had to get going. It wasn't even 10 p.m. and the crowd was already dwindling. Ella had a way of alienating people. Rose was glad she was leaving LA.

"And she's leaving me without a replacement, can you believe it?" Ella again asked no one. "I'll be all alone."

Rose sighed, irritated, because Rose and Ella both knew that Rose was going to continue to pay rent while she was gone. Rose was leaving most of her belongings in Ella's guest room. The space would essentially become an overpriced storage unit, but Rose could afford it. Blue was paying for everything from Rose's lodging to her meals on tour. For four entire months, Rose would be making a full salary without a single expense (well, aside from her meager monthly rent payment to Ella). She'd frequently salivate thinking about how much money she'd be saving, money she could spend on music equipment, voice lessons, even studio time.

Rose was still a little disappointed with the tour's stops, but mostly she was incredibly excited. She'd seen Blue play probably ten times in her life—in Philadelphia, DC, New York, and Chicago. But this time, she'd be backstage, by Blue's side, seeing every little detail that went into each show. Rose planned to take copious notes—she hadn't been performing much since she got the gig with Blue, but songs had been swirling around in her head. Historically, Rose had been more a mimic than an artist, excelled at parroting various styles but was unskilled in the art of spontaneous creation. But recently, lyrics and melodies had been popping up on Rose's morning drives to work, during those thirty or so minutes she'd be hardly moving on the 1 while the ocean sparkled beside her. Each day the ocean looked different. Sometimes it was navy blue, sometimes turquoise, others silver. Some days it was rough and choppy, other days smooth like glass. Some days the sun shone bright and white on top. Other days, it was gray with low-hanging clouds. Still others, it was blue and misty. When she told Ella's friends on various nights that she worked in Malibu, they'd all express sympathy for Rose's commute. But Rose loved the commute. In fact, she'd miss it on the tour.

Soon it was 11 p.m. and only Ella and Rose remained. Even Vagablonde, the too-pretty DJ, had left.

"Wow, what a shit party," Ella said. "I guess no one cares that you're leaving." She turned up the music. *Spirit of Sinatra* was playing, as it so often was. Rose and Ella had recently ranked Blue Velour albums on one of the rare nights Rose hadn't been in Malibu, and their choices were almost diametrically opposed. The only album that made both of their top three was *Blue's Beard*. Ella's other top two were *Spirit of Sinatra* and *Chateau Velour*. Rose's favorites were *Fluorescent Gloom* and *Oleander*. Put differently, Ella was drawn to campy, manic Blue; Rose was drawn to depressive, vulnerable Blue. But everyone liked *Blue's Beard*. It had won Album of the Year for a reason. But they weren't listening to that one right now, unfortunately, because Ella mostly thought about Ella.

"My songggg," Ella slurred as "Pink Cocaine" came on, as she always slurred when it came on. She pulled a little white baggie from her purse. Rose said she had to pee but really snuck away to her bedroom, as coked-up Ella was her least favorite Ella, and by this point, none of the Ellas were great.

In her room, Rose shut the door. She opened the window and lit her Jo Malone Wild Bluebell candle to clear the party smells, the vague scents of spilled champagne and sweat. For a moment, she stood looking out the window, watching the city sparkle below, saying goodbye to Los Angeles in her head. Then she put on *Fluorescent Gloom* in her headphones and finished packing. By the time the final song was playing, Ella was barging in. Rose took off her headphones, which she absolutely hated doing mid-song, but Ella's mouth was moving and Rose felt compelled to respond.

"Are you scared?" Ella asked. She hopped onto Rose's bed with her shoes on, which drove Rose absolutely insane.

"About the tour? Not at all. I couldn't be more excited," Rose responded.

Ella laughed. "Not the tour, honey." She gathered her yellow hair into a bun on the top of her head, then kicked off her boots. "The virus." She pulled a stick of gum seemingly out of thin air and started chomping on it. Rose picked up Ella's boots, which had mud caked on the bottoms, and placed them outside the bedroom door.

"God, you're so anal!" Ella squealed, then laughed.

"What virus?" Rose asked.

"Are you kidding?" Ella asked. "Do you consume any information that isn't related to Blue Velour?"

Rose laughed self-consciously. She'd been accused of such things before, of being narrow-minded and obsessive. Before Blue Velour, it had been Amy Winehouse. Before Amy, it had been Britney Spears.

Rose couldn't help that she liked what she liked and didn't care about much else. She pitied other people, really, for not being able to enjoy music as thoroughly and intensely as she did. Sometimes Rose wasn't even sure if Ella liked Blue Velour, or if she just liked having a musical cue to snort cocaine. Sometimes Rose suspected Ella had joined the subreddit because she'd needed friends.

Ella pulled her phone from her jeans pocket and shoved it in Rose's face. A CNN headline read: *CDC reports 60 cases of Covid-19 across the United States.*

"What's Covid-19?" Rose had never heard of it.

"Oh my *Godddd*, Rose," Ella said. "It's like this terrible disease from China that's killing people left and right. It comes from like rabid bats or some shit, I don't know." Ella took her scrunchie out of her hair, put it back on her wrist. Her hair fell down her shoulders like a wave, and for a split second, Rose remembered that Ella was quite pretty: her silky flaxen hair, her sparkly blue eyes, her patrician nose, slightly upturned. She was, after all, a descendant of the Georgia gold rush.

"Oh my God," Ella said. "Do you want to watch *Contagion*?"

"What's *Contagion*?" Rose asked.

Ella rolled her head in a dramatic circle, then hopped off the bed, grabbed Rose's shoulders, started shaking them violently. "It's a Gwyneth Paltrow movie and it's literally what's happening *right now*!"

Since she'd finished packing and was too jazzed up about the tour to sleep, Rose followed Ella into the living room. They curled up on the couch and turned on the movie, which kind of freaked Rose out, as the virus in it seemed terrifying and extremely deadly. Once Ella had finished another half bottle of wine, she rested her head on Rose's shoulder. Rose ran her fingers through Ella's hair. After the movie, Ella asked if she could sleep in Rose's bed. Ella normally didn't ask, just did it, but Rose said yes. Ella curled up beside Rose like a cat and fell asleep almost immediately. Rose couldn't sleep, so she just stroked Ella's hair and looked out the window as the sky gradually changed colors. At around 5 or 6 a.m.—Rose guessed based on the light—Ella stirred awake and tiptoed out of the room. Rose pretended to be asleep.

r/BlueBeards • posted by u/RoseGhost • June 2014

Welcome to BlueBeards!

Hello, my sweet Blue Velour fans! My name is Rose, and I'm *so* excited to start this subreddit! I've been deeply obsessed with Blue since I first saw the "Cool Ranch Kiss" video on my family's desktop computer when I was twelve. Now I'm about to turn nineteen and my rendition of "Rose Ghost" from *Oleander* got me accepted into Carnegie Mellon's music program, where I'll be majoring in voice in the fall. But enough about me! In light of recent events, I felt I HAD to create a space for us to share gossip and geek out together.

 By "recent events," I'm obviously referring to kissgate. Unless you live under a rock or are too busy reading about like, politics, or whatever, you've probably seen the blessed footage of Blue and her producer Sasha Harlow grinding up on each other (and making out?!?) at that A$AP Rocky concert last week. Unless you're still under said rock, Sasha Harlow is Blue's producer who's been in the spotlight separately for her public on-and-off relationship with Zoë Kravitz, but I only care about her because she's produced literally all of Blue's albums. Blue and Sasha arose from obscurity together in 2007, back when Blue was a bar chanteuse and Sasha was a scout at Interscope. Now, Blue is selling out shows worldwide and Sasha is producing for Lorde and St. Vincent (who she also maybe dated?). But it's obvious that Blue is number one in Sasha's heart, and I'm positive the love flows both ways. The way Blue and Sasha gush about each other in interviews has always made me think something else was going on. I've been afraid to articulate this feeling until kissgate, but now I can't keep it in any longer. So I am screaming it into cyberspace: Blue and Sasha are *obviously* dating, right?!

 Re: the name of the subreddit! According to Urban Dictionary, a beard is a "fake boyfriend or girlfriend usually arranged by management to make a closeted celebrity appear straight." Much like the ominous forbidden room in the classic folktale "Bluebeard"—where the truth was hidden behind closed doors until curiosity unveiled its grim secrets—Blue's personal life has its own "forbidden room," or in queer parlance, a closet. And when Blue appeared at the Golden Globes with famously closeted actor Jack Willenhall, she showcased a textbook bearding scenario. First off, Blue and Jack have the romantic chemistry of first cousins. More importantly, Jack has similar features to Sasha—dark hair, lanky body, bedroom eyes—so Blue can sing about Sasha but people think it's Jack! In the original "Bluebeard," the wife eventually frees herself and lives a happy life. I'm hoping that as this subreddit develops, Blue will come closer to living her truth—an out life with Sasha.

Together, I hope we can dissect all the beards, spill the tea, and collect all the evidence—visual, lyrical, or otherwise—revealing the undeniable truth that Blue and Sasha are the queens of each other's hearts.

I can't wait to chat with all of you, put our heads together, and see what juicy shit we uncover!

Welcome to BlueBeards!

Your new leader,

Rose

Comment by u/PinkCocaine

OMG Rose, this is *everything*! You are my QUEEN for starting this sub! Well, my queen second to BLUE, of course! I made an ill-advised (or maybe genius?) decision this year (post–four skinny margs) to get a tattoo of two (small, tasteful) lines of pink cocaine on my inner thigh. I'm telling you, I am *obsessed* with her.

And holy shit, kissgate, I am LOSING MY MIND! No one dances like that unless they're fucking. And Willenhall is 1000% Blue's beard. The name of this subreddit has me gagging!! Your analysis of Blue's sexuality paralleling the "Bluebeard" folktale is absolute fucking genius. Rose, are you single??? Lol, but also I'm dead serious. . . .

And YASS to Blue and Sasha's bonkers chemistry in

interviews. I watch that *Complex* interview from just after *Spirit of Sinatra* dropped almost every freaking night as a bedtime story. Sasha just stares at Blue like she hung the moon and the stars, like her every word is gospel, and I'm pretty sure she's drooling? And at one point (7:32 on the YouTube video, have it memorized, didn't even have to check) Blue touches Sasha's forearm and I swear to GOD I can *feel* the electricity through the dang computer screen. It's SO OBVIOUS there's something psychosexual there. Like, who looks at their "friend" like that? Wake up and smell the homosexuality, people!

AND the way they collab is straight-up *iconique*! They've literally grown and evolved together and stuck by each other in this wack industry. Ride or die since day one and oh God now I'm crying.

Okay, I chugged an iced coffee (it's midnight, why?) and stopped crying and now I'm just so hype about this subreddit! Finally, a place to obsess with people who "get it" instead of annoying my friends who say I'm "delusional" and "need therapy." Squares!

Oh, I'm Ella btw, and Rose, I think I might be in love with you lol

Blue

Blue was unironically thrilled to check into the Hard Rock Hotel & Casino at Fire Mountain. The hotel was just 1.4 miles from the Toyota Amphitheatre in Wheatland, California, which was thirty-four miles north of Sacramento. Blue had been asleep for the first half of the drive up from LA, but the second half had been mostly vast fields, orchards, and farms, with the Sierra Nevadas on the horizon. Blue was thrilled to be out of the smoggy urban sprawl of Southern California.

Blue wore her typical disguise for checking into hotels, particularly because they were so close to the stadium—a blue Dodgers cap under a sweatshirt with the hood up, big sunglasses, baggy jeans. She noticed people hardly looked at her when she covered up her body. She smoked a cigarette outside while Rose got the room keys. Under Blue's direction, Rose had booked the Gold Suite for Blue, the Silver Suite for Max, and Deluxe Kings for Rose and Blue's band members. Max had asked Blue if she really wanted to stay in a hotel with two stars on Yelp, and Blue had said, "Of course, that's what this tour was all about: living it up in two-stars-on-Yelp America!" And Max had sighed. Max had become more spoiled by fame than Blue had, all of a sudden expecting five-star hotels and designer clothes, as if Blue and Max hadn't grown up shopping at Marshalls and vacationing in Myrtle Beach, where they'd be stopping on this very tour. Blue got Max a room with a bathtub to appease her.

A young couple, likely in their early twenties, walked hand in hand past Blue. The woman looked at the man with what Blue recognized as love. An ache bloomed in her chest. Blue longed to be in love, hoped she might meet someone exciting on this tour. In rehab, they'd told her she was a love addict, but Blue didn't consider that a real diagnosis. Everyone was addicted to love, the same way everyone was addicted to music. Those were the free drugs, the guiltless ones. She wasn't going to feel bad about being a romantic.

Blue stomped out her cigarette and went inside. She stood under a chandelier made of guitar picks and eyed the framed gold and platinum records on the walls: The Beatles' *Sgt. Pepper's Lonely Hearts Club Band*; Michael Jackson's *Thriller*; Madonna's *Like a Virgin*. Across the lobby was a bar with a big-screen TV playing the news. The subtitles announced that the World Health Organization had declared Covid-19 a "global pandemic." Blue wasn't entirely sure what this meant. She figured Covid was like SARS or Ebola, diseases that had circulated in the background on the news at various points during her life. She wasn't a hypochondriac; she hadn't been to the doctor since she was a kid. Physically, Blue was tough. She rarely got sick. Emotionally, she was more fragile. She therefore wasn't afraid of Covid, whatever it was, unless it would mess with her tour. Because that would mess with her emotions. And emotionally, Blue wasn't sure she could handle this tour being canceled.

Rose tapped Blue's shoulder and she jumped.

"Here's your key," Rose said, handing Blue a plastic card.

Blue scrolled Tinder in the bathtub. Her friends were all on Raya or some other allegedly exclusive dating app. Those were the worst. Blue didn't want to fuck some idiot who thought they were somebody. She closed out of Tinder and opened Safari, searched *biker bar near me*. She knew she could just go downstairs, but she didn't want to be recognized; the hotel was surely filled with fans. Google located a place called the Silver Dollar Saloon that looked perfect, like real America. It was only eight miles away, an eleven-minute drive. Except her only mode of transportation was the tour bus, and the driver was not on the clock. Did they have Uber here? Probably not, and even if they did, many an Uber driver had fucked her over, squealed to the press that she'd left cigarette ash in their car or some bullshit. Blue just wanted to fuck someone hot, not be fucked over by some rando! She missed when it was easy, when she could just walk into any bar in Hollywood on any given night, drink twelve free gin and tonics, and go home with whomever she wanted. She didn't miss alcohol, but she missed how easy it was to get laid.

Blue got out of the bathtub and put on a robe, then texted Rose, *You up?*

The best thing about Rose was her availability. She always responded to Blue's texts within a matter of thirty seconds, no matter the time of day. This was something Blue had never experienced. Men kept her waiting, played games. So did Sasha. Max could be moody. But Rose's attention was all for Blue, all the time.

Rose knocked on Blue's door less than five minutes later.

"Do you think you can drive a tour bus?" Blue asked.

"Probably not," Rose said. "Why?" She was hanging in the doorway, tugging at the bottom of her T-shirt like a scared teenager.

"Come sit," Blue said, leading Rose over to the seating area. The shades were still open, but the view was only of darkness. Earlier, Blue had smoked a cigarette while watching the sun set over flat farmland, feeling like she was exactly where she needed to be. The nice thing about the Hard Rock Hotel & Casino was that smoking was allowed in the room with a small fee.

Rose sat across from Blue and sucked on her vape.

"I need to get fucked," Blue told Rose, who choked on the smoke. Blue laughed. Rose probably thought Blue was calling Rose in to give her a happy ending, was maybe even thinking about suing her for sexual harassment.

"Not by you," Blue clarified. "No offense."

"None taken," Rose said, although her gaze dropped to the carpet. Blue hoped the poor thing didn't have a crush on her. Well, she probably did. Blue knew that over half her fans were gay, probably more. The gays were tastemakers. Was Rose gay? She was young enough that she might be post-label, which Blue was as well, even though she was older. However she identified or didn't, Rose responded to Blue's texts too quickly for someone who hadn't at least once thought about fucking her.

"I found this bar about eight miles down the road," Blue said. "It looks like a nice place to meet a man."

"You want to meet a man in a bar?" Rose asked, as though Blue had said she wanted to shoot heroin and then jump off the Golden Gate Bridge. Rose was so young, she probably didn't even know that people used to meet romantic prospects in bars, in the world, and not on a dumb app.

"Yes, bitch," Blue said. "I need to let off some steam."

"Shouldn't you stay in and rest up the night before the first show of your tour?"

Sometimes Rose spoke like an algorithm. Blue supposed most twenty-four-year-olds did. They weren't properly socialized. Blue wasn't the picture of politesse, but she did at least know how to talk to people. Or maybe she just knew how to entertain them. Was there a difference?

"I can never sleep the night before," Blue said. "I'd rather go out and get fucked than stay in and stare at the wall. I don't drink, so it's not like I'll have a hangover."

"Well, I don't think I can drive a tour bus," Rose said. This was the first time Rose had said no to Blue, which made Rose slightly more attractive in Blue's eyes. Rose was still the peculiar nerd Blue had interviewed that misty morning a couple of months ago, but she'd changed slightly. She had her new cat-eye glasses, her hair was longer and shinier—maybe she was using that conditioning mask Blue had gifted her—and she was starting to wear mascara and lipstick, dark rosy red, like Blue had applied to her tiny lips for the Grammys. Right now, it appeared as though Rose had just washed her face, but Blue could see the stain of red on her lips and black around her eyes. Blue loved the way a woman's face looked right after the makeup had been washed off, the spectral impression it left behind.

"What if I drive and you come with me?" Blue said.

"I don't think it's a good idea," Rose said.

"If you don't come with me, I'll find a way. I'll hitchhike. And what if I hitchhike and get kidnapped and raped and murdered and it's all your fault?"

Rose's eyes widened, briefly, then she blinked. "What about Trevor?"

Blue laughed. Trevor was her high school sweetheart. He wasn't the world's best drummer, but the drumming on her songs was sparse and uncomplicated. Blue knew bringing Trevor on tour made his life. For the rest of the year, he was a plumber in North Carolina with a wife and two kids. Blue had been the other woman before, but not in years. And if she was going to do it again, it wouldn't be for Trevor. He was like her brother.

"Or just go to one of the bars downstairs?" Rose said. "Seems safer."

"This hotel is filled with fans," Blue whispered. "They're freaks." She paused, realizing Rose was one of them. "No offense, but I want to fuck someone who has no idea who I am."

Again, Rose looked at the carpet. She rested her vape on her thigh. Blue picked it up and took a long pull.

"I'm sure there are people in this hotel who have no idea who you are," Rose said, surprising Blue. "There's a casino here. It's probably half gambling addicts, maybe more."

"But fans will be swarming them," Blue said.

"Wear a disguise," said Rose.

Blue smiled. "Will you help me?"

"That's my job, isn't it?"

The hotel had probably the ugliest carpet Blue had ever seen in her entire life. Primary colors in geometric, kaleidoscopic patterns. It was nearly seizure-inducing.

"Did you drop something?" Blue heard someone ask. She looked up to see a man with a trimmed beard peppered with tiny gray hairs. Blue almost said, *Daddy*.

"Just staring at this fugly carpet," Blue said. She was surprised someone was talking to her. She was wearing a blond wig and big sunglasses indoors, an Adidas tracksuit. The disguise was necessary, but Blue didn't feel her sexiest. She felt silly. She wished she could be herself, in a silky dress with her smooth black hair cascading down her shoulders like a waterfall.

"It's awful, ain't it?" the man said. Blue perked up. He was Southern. But not from North Carolina like Blue. This was a distinctive Texan drawl. They were going to Texas on the tour. But first, Idaho, which looked gorgeous. Blue wanted to meet a cowboy.

"Where are you from?" Blue asked, then sipped her Red Bull.

"Houston," the man said. "Name's Austin, though."

Blue laughed. "Austin from Houston."

Austin nodded. "You know, when *you* say it, it's almost like I haven't heard that a billion times before."

Thank God. Austin was flirting. She didn't even care that he'd just called her unoriginal.

"What brings you to Wheatland, California, Austin?"

"Sales conference in Sacramento," Austin said. "Didn't realize there was going to be some big concert here tomorrow." He leaned in to whisper. "Apparently, some Hollywood pop star is staying right here at the hotel."

Blue shivered, both turned on and afraid, but in a way that made her more turned on. Did Austin know who she was? Was he messing with her? Was he just really dense? Or was her disguise just really good?

"You aren't here for the concert, are you?" Austin asked. Blue still couldn't tell if he was fucking with her, which made the interaction all the more exciting. This was exactly what she needed. Adrenaline.

"Bachelorette party," said Blue.

"You aren't the bride?" Austin asked.

Blue laughed, then shook her head. "My sister."

"Good," Austin said.

Blue couldn't wait to see what Austin's body looked like. She hoped he didn't work out. She wanted a man with muscles from lifting objects, not weights at Equinox. She imagined running her fingers through his gray chest hair and felt dizzy.

The TV above them turned on. More news. More virus. *CDC issues a "no sail order" for all cruise ships.* Blue had always wanted to perform on a cruise. Austin shook his head at the TV.

"Not this bullshit again," he said. "It's just a flu. President said so."

"Yeah," Blue said. She didn't want to talk about some gross virus. It was a turnoff, not exactly foreplay. "Have you ever been on a cruise?" Blue asked.

Austin looked at her. "A billion years ago," he said. Blue liked the sound of that.

Blue had explored her daddy issues somewhat in rehab, but ultimately believed they were best left unexamined. They weren't particularly complicated. She wanted her father's attention, for him to call her beautiful, but he was a nerdy biology teacher with zero interest in beauty. Hence why he'd married her mom, a history teacher who loved God and hated Blue—for her trivial secular interests, in boys and rock music and makeup, and for her disinterest in things that mattered to her mother, like school and the Bible and dressing appropriately for church. Blue never saw a day in North Carolina when her mom wasn't scolding her for something. Her mommy issues ran deeper than her daddy issues, something those only close to her knew.

Blue had waited her entire life to turn eighteen so she could escape.

She had nothing when she arrived in Los Angeles, absolutely nothing, and yet—the day she arrived at the Greyhound bus stop on Skid Row was the happiest of her entire life. The first person she met was a guy twice her age named Chuck. He drove her to his place in West Hollywood on his Harley. Things got dark eventually—he was a drinker with a temper, like her mother—but before that, they were very exciting. Blue was in Los Angeles, three thousand miles from her parents' Bible Belt home, dating a man with a Harley and a grayish beard who called her beautiful every day, said she was a star.

"What's your sign, Austin?" Blue asked.

Rose

Rose had already had an entire day before she went to wake Blue. She couldn't sleep at all given her nerves, owing to both excitement for the first show of the tour and fear that something had happened to Blue. Rose had put Blue in a tracksuit in hopes it would scare men away. She'd told Blue the blond wig could be enough to attract men, but Rose didn't actually believe it. The wig was a bit cartoonish; Rose hoped it would act as a repellent. Then again, Blue had a special power, an otherworldly sensuality that could not be hidden by a tracksuit or a wig or anything else.

And that power had been confirmed this morning at 8 a.m. when Rose had left her room to go on a run and seen a fifty-something man with ruffled gray hair emerge from Blue's suite. Rose exhaled relief. He didn't look like a killer. He looked like a small-business owner from Middle America.

Rose rarely ran—she was sort of allergic to exercise, as well as to the outdoors—but she had adrenaline to burn. Outside the hotel, the sun was hot and white. The landscape stretched out flat and green, making Rose a bit anxious. Also, it was freezing. Not literally, not quite, but close. Her phone read 44 degrees. Rose couldn't run in this. She laughed at herself for even considering it, then went inside to find the gym, which was totally empty. She walked on a treadmill and listened to *Blue's Beard* in its entirety, then got breakfast at the restaurant. Max was also there. Rose considered sitting with her, but Max looked busy on her computer, and then Rose felt bad for not also being busy on her computer, so she returned to her room and answered emails until Blue woke up around noon. Ella kept texting Rose about the virus, accompanied by photos of Gwyneth Paltrow in *Contagion*, which Rose was ignoring. She didn't want to think about any of that. Getting sick or, worse, the tour getting canceled.

Rose greeted Blue with a cold Red Bull as Blue had requested. The tour bus was waiting outside, which would just drive them down the road to the Toyota Amphitheatre. Rose wished they were going somewhere more glamorous, like the Hollywood Bowl or Madison Square Garden, but she was still excited. Blue seemed to be in a good mood.

"Last night was a success?" Rose asked as they rode past flat fields to the venue.

Blue unleashed a breathy giggle but said nothing.

A group was waiting to greet them as the bus pulled up outside the stadium. A stage manager, security, and some kind of coordinator. Rose couldn't keep their names straight. The band members and the tour manager—an old-time friend of Blue from her "partying days" named Jax Jameson—started unloading the bus. Blue, Rose, and Max were escorted to the greenroom, which was actually mostly beige. There was a seating area with brown leather furniture arranged around a low coffee table, on top of which sat a large fruit platter in a clear plastic box. There was a vanity area with large mirrors lined with lightbulbs, beside a clothing rack with Blue's costumes. On the other side of the room were a counter, a sink, a small fridge, and a coffee machine. On the wall was a flat-screen TV and framed photos of various artists who had performed at this very venue—the Backstreet Boys, Blink-182, the Cure, Red Hot Chili Peppers, Tom Petty. Blue walked over to a photo of Gwen Stefani and kissed the air in front of it. Then she picked up the fruit platter from the coffee table and moved it to the counter in the kitchenette. Blue didn't like the sight of food before 6 p.m.

"Sound check at three," said the venue liaison, whose name Rose didn't remember.

Blue saluted the woman, who disappeared; then she peeked around the kitchenette for the items on her rider. Blue irises. Red Bull. Cool Ranch Doritos. Marlboro Reds (her stage cigarette of choice, because Jim Morrison smoked them). White, floral-scented candles. All there.

Rose sat beside Blue and pulled out her phone, read from the schedule over which she and Max had meticulously agonized for weeks.

"Okay, so sound check at three, hair and makeup at five," Rose began, "Then you have a meet-and-greet—"

"You don't need to do this," Blue said. "I've been touring since I was your age. I have the schedule."

This comment stung. First, it made Rose feel bad at her job, but worse than that, it highlighted that Blue had been touring since she was Rose's age, while Rose had never even performed live outside of school and open mics. Amy Winehouse had released her debut album, *Frank*, at twenty. Britney Spears had gone on her ... *Baby One More Time* tour when she was just seventeen. Meanwhile, Rose was twenty-four with no album, no hit single. She hadn't even written a full song yet— just scattered ideas in her notes app and voice memos.

"Sit," Blue said. "Relax."

Rose exhaled. "Okay."

While Blue was at sound check, Rose and Max steamed her outfits, which Max had pretty much chosen all by herself. For the meet-and-greet, Blue would wear a black leotard under vintage Levi's, so fans would feel like they knew her. For the first half of the show, she'd wear a blue velour minidress with matching thigh-high boots, all custom-made. For the second half, she'd wear a blue fur cape over a white baby-doll dress. And for the finale, she'd wear a sequined navy gown while fireworks exploded in the background.

Rose was confident about the outfits, but nervous to be alone with Max. She was harder to read than Blue, who wore her emotions on her sleeve. Max was reserved, chilly, impenetrable.

"How do you know Grace again?" Max asked, while putting the velour minidress on its hanger.

Rose was silent for a second. Grace? Her brain spun. She inhaled her vape, surprised by how fast she was burning through cartridges—one every few days now. At least Blue paid for them.

As soon as the nicotine hit her lungs, Rose's brain sped up and she remembered: Grace was Max's childhood friend whom Rose had met on the subreddit, the one Rose had—yes—founded, who had put Rose in the running for this job. It was Grace to whom she owed everything. How could she forget her name? They'd just spoken a few days ago, but Rose mostly thought of her as her username. GarboMommy had asked how the job was going and if Rose had gotten any insider info. Rose didn't feel comfortable telling Grace anything that wasn't readily googleable, so she'd told her Blue's burrito order (carne asada, extra hot sauce), her favorite sports team (Liverpool FP), and her favorite perfume (Tom Ford's Velvet Orchid).

"We met on a cruise," Rose said. She'd come up with this lie a while ago in case Max or Blue asked. She obviously couldn't tell the truth, that she'd met Grace on the internet, let alone on a rabid fan subreddit that Rose herself had started. A cruise was in person but wouldn't require them to have lived in the same place at the same time or even to have known the same people. She figured she'd message Grace and ask her to verify the story if it came up, so she made a mental note to do that now.

"A cruise?" Max said. "I can't imagine Grace on a cruise."

"It was in college," Rose said. "She said her friends dragged her. My friend from college knew her friend from childhood, who'd actually been my friend's babysitter." Rose forced herself to stop talking. She was giving too many details, breaking the first rule of lying.

Max just looked at Rose, then lit a cigarette. Fuck. Rose's heart thudded in her chest.

"Did you see they canceled all cruise ships?" Max said, plopping down on the couch.

Rose exhaled with relief. "I did," Rose lied. She could extrapolate, probably something to do with the virus. She sat beside Max on the couch, crossed her legs.

"Blue is sort of in denial about these things," Max said. "You know, like . . ." She gestured in the air with both arms. The bangles on her left wrist clinked together. "The state of the world."

"Right," Rose said. Rose was also in denial about the state of the world. "Are you worried about the virus?" Rose asked. "My friend in LA keeps texting me about it."

"Um, yeah," Max said. "It's everywhere. Carla said she's terrified."

Rose nodded. She didn't know who Carla was. Maybe the Toyota Amphitheatre liaison. Rose needed to be better at her job. She was just so on edge today. She couldn't seem to calm down or keep information in her head. She sucked on her vape.

"You really like that thing, don't you?" Max asked. She ran a hand through her dirty blond hair. It was long and thick and enviable, nearly down to her waist.

Rose shrugged. "Being around Blue all the time . . ." She trailed off. Max was being weird toward her. Doom gathered in Rose's belly.

Relieving Rose, Max laughed. "I know, right," Max said. "She's a chimney."

"Be right back," Rose said. She followed a trail of vapor into the bathroom, where she sat on the toilet and pulled up Reddit on her phone. She opened her message thread with Grace and realized there were a few unanswered questions. Rose scrolled up and read the lingering questions, which went back a few weeks: *How is Blue feeling about the tour? Any insight into the setlist? Are you worried about the virus? Is the setlist* Blue's Beard *heavy? Do you think she'll shout out the subreddit at the tour at all? Are you mad at me or just busy? Did Max say anything to you about me? I've changed a lot FYI.*

Rose hadn't been paying much attention to BlueBeards now that she was, well, sort of living it. She put her thumbs in the reply box. *Omg I'm so sorry, just seeing these now.*

Phew! Grace replied quickly. *I was worried you were mad or that Max said something about me being a loser or something.*

She loves you! Rose lied. Grace seemed to be unraveling and it felt important to stay on her good side.

Grace responded with twelve pink heart emojis and one crying emoji.

She just asked about how we met, Rose continued. *I didn't want to out myself as a crazed fangirl, so I said we met on a cruise. In case she asks!*

Rose could see Grace was typing. She kept starting and stopping. Rose's heart thudded.

"I'm going to take a call!" Max shouted outside the bathroom door, and Rose jumped. "Be back in ten."

"No problem," Rose said as Max's footsteps got farther and farther away.

She returned her eyes to the message. Grace had just sent one message, just a bunch of ellipses. She was still typing. Then messages started to come in quick succession.

What do you mean "crazed fangirl"?

You started this subreddit, girl. If we're crazy, you belong in a straitjacket.

The idea of lying to Max makes me SUPER uncomfortable.

Why wouldn't you just tell her the truth?

Are you embarrassed by us now?

You created us!

Rose suddenly felt like she couldn't breathe. She wiped some sweat from her forehead, then shut the phone off.

When Max got back, Rose snuck out to watch Blue's sound check. She recognized "Death Baby" even from the halls. It had dominated Blue's top five songs on Spotify for nearly a decade, but it wasn't Rose's favorite. Blue's voice sounded pretty, though.

Rose entered the empty amphitheater from the side. The stage was set. Lights cut sharp angles in the dimming afternoon. Blue looked tiny up on the stage. The amphitheater was huge. Rows of empty seats seemed to stretch on forever. The air was heavy and cool. Chilly for an outdoor event, but surely the air would warm up once the crowd filled out.

The song ended and Rose tapped her foot waiting for the next one to start. She shivered when she heard the opening notes. She'd advocated for this being included on the set list but hadn't been sure it would really make it.

Blue was playing "Rose Ghost."

r/BlueBeards • posted by u/RoseGhost • September 2016

Rose Ghost Deep Dive

Hi, my lovelies! I'm avoiding my homework tonight (why they make music majors take math is beyond me) and thought, why not deep-dive into my very favorite Blue Velour track? "Rose Ghost," obvi! I love that my name is in the title, but it's so much more than that. . . .

    The echoing guitar notes and Blue's whispery vocals are totally enchanting. It's like a ghost story where the song itself is the spirit, luring you deeper into the afterlife with each note, and haunting you way after it's over.

    And the lyrics are just . . . *ugh*! Blue sings about an enigmatic lover who's both irresistible and dangerous. Most critics say the song is a metaphor for lost youth and fleeting beauty, but, come on. It's obviously about Sasha, right??

    "Under moonlit skies, you haunt my dreams, gripping my throat with your spectral extremes." The lyrics capture the whole forbidden-romance vibe that's all over Blue's music and really resonates with us queers. It's like Sasha only exists in Blue's dreams, hidden from reality, where their love is forbidden. The image of the rose ghost (cough, Sasha) gripping Blue's throat feels almost too intimate to witness! And then of course the rose symbolizes beauty entwined with the pain of thorns, which to me embodies the tension between their visible days and secret, intimate nights. And you can totally hear this in Sasha's production—the way those intense bass lines clash with Blue's lyrical high notes perfectly illustrates the pleasure and pain of reaching for something sublime, no matter the cost.

    Blue told *NME* in 2010 as part of the *Oleander* press cycle:

    "You know how a rose looks all sweet and innocent? And then you reach for it, and it stabs you? And all of a sudden, you're bleeding all over your new favorite silk dress? All because you wanted to hold on to something beautiful?"

Rose

Blue seemed to be fairly calm and in a good mood until about 7:30 p.m., roughly twenty minutes after they'd finished their burritos and exactly an hour before she was scheduled to go on.

They were going over the set list, which was broken up into two acts and an encore, one final time:

ACT I

Death Baby
Rose Ghost
Bauhaus Bathhouse Blues
A Vape Cartridge Named Desire
Auto-Tune Me into Nothing
Running of the Red Bulls
Garbo Is My Mommy
Lullaby for Jack Willenhall

ACT II

God Is a Gemini
Happy Birthday I'm Dead
A Thousand Oak Trees from You to Me
Nicotine in Holy Limousines
Drive Me to Macy's
Tulips on the 405
Cool Ranch Kiss
Neon Bruise

ENCORE

Pink Cocaine
Marlboro Never Dies
Polaroid Is the Void

Blue began to doubt whether "Polaroid Is the Void" made sense as a closer. "Should I end with something more upbeat?" she asked Rose and Max. "Should I switch it with 'Death Baby'?" Blue's uncertainty quickly morphed into anxiety. She was pacing back and forth, smoking furiously, mumbling song titles between drags. And almost as soon as the nerves materialized, they began to transform into rage. Blue was so angry that making decisions was so hard for her, that people wanted so much from her, and that no matter what, someone would be angry.

"And you know who they're going to blame?" Blue yelled, arms slicing the air. She pointed at her sternum. "Me." Then she pointed at Rose. "Not you, who claims to have 'fan insight' and makes all the *goddamn decisions*!" She started shaking Rose's shoulders while she yelled. Max came over and gently pulled Blue away from Rose. Blue shoved Max off and stomped over to the couch. She sat and started hyperventilating, head between her knees. Max went to the fridge and retrieved a Red Bull, walked over and put it on the back of Blue's neck while she breathed. Max rubbed Blue's shoulders, encouraged her to slow her breathing.

"Don't tell me to fucking slow down," Blue screamed at Max, popping up. "If I slowed down, you'd have no fucking money to live on. When's the last time you styled someone other than me, Maxie? Without me, you'd be living in a tract home in suburban North Carolina. You'd be wearing Ross, not the Eckhaus Latta *I* buy you. Without me, you'd be *nothing*."

She stormed off to the bathroom, her four-inch heels clicking hard on the concrete floor. Rose stood frozen, convinced Blue was going to fire her and that the perfect life she'd waited forever for would soon be over. Blue had referenced her anger in songs, in interviews, once telling a *Rolling Stone* interviewer in particular that she "went from 0 to 100 real quick." Rose had seen flashes of it before—more irritation than full-blown rage, like when Rose slowed down before the yellow light instead of rushing to make it, and Blue would shout at her to speed up. Right now, Rose was scared to look at Max, but when she did, Max seemed relatively calm.

"She does this before every show," Max whispered to Rose.

Blue came storming out of the bathroom.

Blue

Blue always knew she loved performing, but somehow she forgot the euphoria until she was onstage. She'd read once that performers often experience amnesia after shows, maybe like women during childbirth. Except the opposite: women forgot the pain of childbirth, while musicians forgot the joy of performing in front of twenty thousand people who know every word to their songs. If women remembered the pain of childbirth, the human race would dwindle. If musicians remembered the euphoria, they might never stop touring, and there would be no new music or something. Blue didn't know if there was any evolutionary explanation for post-performance amnesia. She just knew she was singing "Neon Bruise," her favorite song she'd written off an album for which she'd been ruthlessly mocked, a song for which she'd been deemed hostile to the feminist agenda, and now she saw at least three people in her eyeline crying because they were so moved.

Soon, Blue was crying too.

Afterward, the crowd went wild. Blue ran backstage to change for the encore, high as hell. She had a vague sense that she'd done something bad before she went onstage, that she'd said some rude things, maybe smashed something, but she tended to black out during her rages. She had her mother's temper; Max had their father's patience. Max always forgave Blue, even when she shouldn't.

"You were radiant," Rose said as soon as Blue entered the greenroom, eyes gleaming. Max was already pulling the final costume off the rack, the elegant navy gown. Outside the door, the crowd thundered for an encore. This was always Blue's favorite part of the night. The roar of the crowd in her ears. Rushing to put on her final look. Blue raised her arms and Max pulled the gown over her head. It was heavy on Blue's body in a way that made her feel rich and glamorous. Rose just stared at her.

Blue lit a cigarette and made her way back into the hallway, the crowd getting louder as she approached the stage. Bliss and nicotine surged through Blue's veins. She smiled and returned to the stage for the last three songs, wanting to hold on to the moment as it slipped through her fingertips like sand.

Soon, fireworks were exploding behind her as she sang "Polaroid Is the Void." She wanted to slow down the song, to make it last, but she couldn't. And *boom*, it was over. But then she remembered: she was going to be able to do this for several nights a week for four entire months. Blue wasn't in love, but she was starting to think she didn't need a love interest, at least not in human form. She was in love with her music. Her audience. The celestial voice God had given her. And a different God from the punishing, intolerant God her mom loved so much. Blue's God was benevolent and accepting and merciful and beautiful and probably a woman and definitely a Gemini. Her God was a heart-shaped chemtrail, a silver ripple on the Pacific, cherry Coke on her lover's breath, a fan mouthing her every lyric, Max's laugh, Jim Morrison's torso, Dolly Parton's voice cracking on "Jolene."

Onstage, Blue channeled this God.

And she was—for the only time ever—completely at peace.

Rose

Max pulled out a bottle of nonalcoholic champagne as soon as Blue returned to the greenroom. While Blue had been playing the encore, Carla, who Rose now knew for sure was the venue liaison, said the post-show meet-and-greet would be canceled due to the virus. She seemed frantic. "Apparently the president is going to make some big announcement tomorrow," she'd said. "I just took out a mortgage." Max had patted her back while she cried.

Once she left, Max told Rose not to say anything to Blue. Just let her ride out her high. Let her chill and drink her nonalcoholic champagne and eat her snacks. Take her back to the hotel. Let her think everything is normal until they know for sure it isn't.

Backstage, Blue was glowing. Something otherworldly seemed to radiate off her skin. She was surrounded by a bubble of gold light, a layer of energy Rose felt a mere mortal like herself could not penetrate. This glittering ether seemed to confirm something about which Rose had long been afraid: no matter how good her voice and her work ethic, she lacked Blue's cosmic aura.

Intensifying Rose's insecurity, Blue walked right past Rose and kissed Max on the cheek. The sisters seemed to forget what had gone down before the show. Rose felt like she didn't belong. Grace still hadn't messaged Rose back about the cruise. Maybe she'd told Max the truth, that they'd met on Reddit, that Rose was a creep, and Max was getting ready to tell Blue to fire Rose. Everything was going to shit. The fake champagne cork popped and Rose jumped. Max and Blue laughed. It felt like they were mocking her. Rose was suddenly hot and felt like she couldn't breathe again.

She left the greenroom and saw Carla pacing the hall on the phone. Something was wrong. Rose went outside, where fans pushed by her. A man in a wine-stained shirt told his friend, "No virus could stop Blue." A couple debated whether to stay for the meet-and-greet or heed the warnings and head home. Rose tried to avoid the masses as she made her way toward the parking lot. Everyone was potentially contaminated. She pulled out her vape. As Rose exhaled, vapor mingled with the cold night air, forming fleeting clouds that disappeared into the void of starry black sky above her. Another body shoved past her. She scanned her surroundings, envisioned all these people in the dissipating crowd dropping dead from the virus, imagined each of them frothing at the mouth and seizing like they did in *Contagion*. She pictured bodies piling up in the parking lot and the fields, on the freeways and the beaches.

Back inside the greenroom, Rose went to the bathroom and washed her hands. The fluorescent lights cast a harsh glow over her pale skin. Hearing vague sounds of celebration beyond the bathroom walls, she gripped the sink's edge, steadying herself against a wave of nausea.

And then she threw up.

r/BlueBeards • posted by u/NeonBruise • March 2020

Blue's Beard tour CANCELED (kill me)

Well, it's official. The president just declared a state of emergency, and the *Blue's Beard* tour is freaking canceled. I can't believe this is happening. I was SO looking forward to seeing her in Huntsville. Are you all as gutted as I am?

Comment by u/CoolRanch

Devastated doesn't cover it. Had my outfit all planned and everything. Safety first, I guess, but man, this hurts.

Comment by u/405Tulips

Honestly, it's the responsible thing to do. With everything going on, better safe than sorry. Blue wouldn't want us at risk. Speaking of, is anyone else scared? I'm writing this post through latex gloves lol.

Comment by u/TrashyDemon

Nah, I think it's fine. The tour will probably pick back up once we flatten the curve. Maybe Blue will do something online in the meantime? A virtual concert would be cool.

Comment by u/PinkCocaine

Do we think she's quarantining with Sasha????

Blue

When Blue first heard the tour was canceled, she went a bit loco.

Again, she had her mother's temper. Luckily she'd stopped drinking. If she hadn't, someone might have gotten hurt. But no one got hurt. Well, no living being, at least not physically. Blue had thrown her iPhone against the wall, narrowly missing Max's head, but destroying the phone. She had smashed three vaporizers, which was just dumb, but thankfully she had a fourth. She had pulled out a not insignificant chunk of her own hair, but she and Max had been blessed with very thick hair, and the missing patch was behind her head in a bottom layer, so it wasn't really noticeable.

After destroying the phone, Blue had kicked everyone out of her hotel room and dead-bolted the door. Rage gave way to depression. She stayed in bed vaping and crying and listening to her own music—mostly *Fluorescent Gloom*—for two entire days. Occasionally, her hotel phone would ring, but she unplugged that too. She ignored knocks on the door until she heard a hotel staff member saying they were legally required to open the door for a wellness check.

At that point, Blue happily let them in. Because she had just come up with an amazing idea. The depression had finally started to fade, and the feel-good chemicals were making their way into her noggin. One of Blue's worst qualities was how easily she became upset, how she took it out on herself and others. And one of her best qualities was how quickly and profoundly she moved on from that negativity, how she was able to transform her darkness into blind optimism.

Roughly half an hour before the wellness check, Blue had been watching smoke drift toward the window, outside of which the sky exploded orange over wide green fields, and she had a vision of Northern California. Not where she was, not flat farmland, but somewhere in the redwoods. Surrounded by trees. She couldn't go back to Malibu, where she'd cried herself to sleep for a month and nearly relapsed after the deeply unfair reception of *Fluorescent Gloom*. Blue and Sasha had recorded *Blue's Beard* in a studio in the Bay Area, but Blue wanted somewhere more remote, in the mountains, not at the shore. A cabin in the woods. She wanted to be enveloped by trees.

Blue researched cabins in Occidental in Sonoma County, Guerneville in the Russian River Valley, and Boulder Creek in the Santa Cruz Mountains. She had just found the perfect rental in Guerneville, described as "rustic mid-century luxury in the redwoods," when the hotel staff knocked on her door. The home had the perfect number of bedrooms—four: one for her, one for Max, one for Sasha, and one for Rose. It had a hot tub. It had two decks. And it had a backhouse that Sasha could easily transform into a studio. If there was one thing Blue loved more than performing, it was making music. And what better time to make music than when the entire world shut down?

Blue went to open the door and told the staff that she was doing "absolutely fantastic."

Rose

It was amazing how quickly Blue was able to pivot from utter devastation to sheer exuberance.

Rose had undergone a similar, albeit less extreme, trajectory. She'd thought she was in heaven before, on tour. But she learned she was really in heaven now, at what Blue had christened "Velour Chalet"—a rental home deep in the redwoods just outside of Guerneville, California, a town Rose had never previously heard of. According to the landlord when she handed over the keys, the Russian River Valley was known for its fertile soil, which was ideal for growing a variety of wine grapes, most famously pinot noir and chardonnay. The valley also produced apples, pears, and a range of heirloom vegetables. Sasha had started growing tomatoes and herbs in the garden, which she'd use in pasta sauces and salads she'd make for dinner each night and was stocking the house with local bottles of wine, which seemed to irritate Blue but pleased Rose, who was developing a taste for pinot noir.

Rose still couldn't believe she was sharing the space with *the* Sasha Harlow, the wunderkind who had sculpted the soundtrack of her life. Sasha had arrived at Velour Chalet on their second day with one small leather suitcase of clothes and half a truck worth of music equipment. Sasha drove a black Chevy and cooked all their meals, and when something broke, she fixed it. She was elegant in an unassuming way, wearing tailored black clothes that flattered her figure, delicate silver jewelry, and smudged eyeliner that never seemed to come off, even after a shower. Her hair fell in thick, untamed waves that were mostly black but gray near the temples. She didn't say much but had a calming, easy presence. She looked at Blue like she was the sun.

Guerneville was approximately seventy-five miles north of San Francisco, twenty miles east of the Pacific Ocean, and a hundred and fifty miles west of Wheatland, from which they'd fled after Blue's not-insignificant breakdown upon hearing the tour was canceled. Max had gone back to Malibu after Blue threw an iPhone at her head, narrowly missing her temple but with enough velocity that the phone smashed. At first Blue had been pissed that Max had left—calling her names Rose didn't feel comfortable repeating—but then she'd cooled off and decided it would be good for her and Max to have some time apart, something they hadn't done since Sasha and Blue had recorded *Blue's Beard* in 2019.

"Max needs to fall in love," Blue had said.

Rose was at first skeptical of Blue's plan to head into the woods, as Rose wasn't a huge fan of nature and was generally allergic to the outdoors. When Blue said "cabin," Rose worried the experience would be akin to camping, something Rose hadn't done since she'd been forced to go on a school trip to Laurel Highlands in seventh grade and had gotten her period all over her sleeping bag. But Velour Chalet was far from camping. It was recently renovated and frankly much cushier than the Malibu home, which was low-key falling apart. Located deep in a canopy of tall trees, a far cry from the large cloudless skies that had dominated most of Rose's experience of California until this point, the home was a multitiered modern structure made of dark wood broken up with expansive windows. Several decks wrapped around the home like a ribbon. The lower deck had a hot tub where Blue, Rose, and Sasha spent many a late night.

Inside was an open-plan living room anchored by a live-edge wooden table, its surface polished to a sheen and reflecting the warm glow of spherical pendant lights that hung throughout the space. A leather sectional couch hugged the corners of an earth-toned Persian rug. A towering wall of windows framed the redwoods, which Rose had grown to love as soon as she acquired the requisite Zyrtec supply.

Blue's room was the largest, with the best views and its own private deck, onto which Rose had been invited only once or twice, when Blue was in the midst of one of what Sasha called Blue's "manic moments," when the world was sunny and bright and filled with possibility. Sasha's room was the second largest. It was next to Blue's room, but Sasha didn't seem to sleep there, as the bed was always made. Sasha was frequently emerging from Blue's room, a fact that never ceased to electrify Rose, although she'd forced herself to stay off the subreddit for fear of saying anything to compromise this perfect situation—also, the Wi-Fi at Velour Chalet was spotty at best. The third-largest room was originally meant to be Max's, but when Blue learned Max wasn't coming, she had Rose convert it into a luxurious dog room for Bijou and Gigi, equipped with plush dog beds and toys and treats and their water and food bowls. Even so, Bijou mostly slept with Blue—the dog still seemed to dislike Rose—and Gigi often slept with Rose, in the smallest bedroom. Rose slept in the attic. The bedroom was tiny but cute, with an A-frame ceiling and exposed beams and 180-degree forest views. At night, after taking her Benadryl, Rose would open the windows and smell bark and moist soil, the musky scent of forest undergrowth, and listen to the crickets and occasional hoot of an owl, the scurrying of nocturnal creatures, the faint flow of the river in the distance.

During their first week, Blue said they needed to focus primarily on "vibing," which entailed the three of them renting inner tubes and floating down the Russian River while vaping heavily and drinking beer—Tecates for Sasha and Rose, NA beer for Blue. Rose couldn't remember a time she'd been happier than floating on the ice-cold river, sunlight filtering through the crowns of towering redwoods and oaks, laughing hard at inside jokes between Sasha and Blue that Rose pretended to understand, freezing and shivering and laughing and drunk.

At one point, they passed a gravelly beach where partiers were blasting "Death Baby." Blue paddled her tube over to them, got out, and chatted. She shared cigarettes with several strangers, which had caused Sasha to snap at her, but Blue seemed unafraid of the virus. After Sasha repeated CDC statistics during the first two nights over dinner, Blue had officially banished all news from the house.

"This will be a news-free household," Blue announced on night three after Sasha said they should start wiping down the dogs' paws with Clorox before bed. "News organizations profit from keeping people in a state of hysteria and their project is antithetical to our own, which is to bring sublime beauty into the world." Then she'd slammed her hands on the table so hard that it shook.

The week of vibing also included listening to every record Blue wanted to inspire her next project. Part of Rose's job had been acquiring "supplies," which included two record players—a Cambridge Audio for the living room, and a wireless Audio-Technica for Blue's private deck, both models recommended by Sasha. Rose had searched for and found all the records Blue and Sasha had asked for, some of which Rose had Max ship from Blue's collection in Malibu, some she'd had to find on Discogs or eBay. Once the records arrived, they had to be organized into "morning Red Bull records" and "nighttime mushroom records."

The morning Red Bull records included the following: Nina Simone's *Little Girl Blue*, Love's *Forever Changes*, Cat Power's *You Are Free*, Morrissey's *Viva Hate*, and Patsy Cline's *Sentimentally Yours*.

Nighttime mushroom records included Portishead's *Dummy*, Hole's *Celebrity Skin*, Janis Joplin's *I Got Dem Ol' Kozmic Blues Again Mama!*, Stevie Nicks's *Bella Donna*, and Julee Cruise's *Floating into the Night*.

While listening to the morning Red Bull records, Blue and Sasha would dictate notes to Rose, which she'd scrawl down in a Moleskine notebook because Blue said the sound of Rose's typing was "very annoying." Notes would include everything from themes to lyrics to instrumentation to dinner ideas.

During the nighttime mushroom record sessions, Rose was also the scribe, meaning she could not partake in the mushrooms because she learned the hard way that doing so made it impossible to write coherently. So she'd sip a Tecate or a small glass of wine while Sasha closed her eyes and listened and Blue thrashed around on the splintered wood. Most of Blue's utterances during these times were incomprehensible strings of words, but Rose diligently wrote them down, nonetheless. In the mornings, before Blue awoke, Rose would type up what she'd handwritten the previous night.

By day ten, she'd organized the following notes for Blue's next record:

Instrumentality:

Fingerpicked acoustic guitar, felt-dampened piano, minimal percussion, orchestral layering, soft analog synths.

Genre:

Ethereal psychedelic folk with cinematic textures.

Themes:

Isolation, moon phases, the void.

Vibe:

Spectral, haunting, raw.

Reference points:

Sparse piano chords and smoky vocals of Nina Simone's "Don't Smoke in Bed," remixed in a song called "Always Smoke in Bed."

Flamenco-ish guitar and bittersweet chord progression on Love's "Alone Again Or."

Nostalgic yearning and warm guitar tone in Stevie Nicks's "After the Glitter Fades."

Spacious, dreamlike reverb from Julee Cruise's "The World Spins."

Gritty breakbeat drums and ominous guitar lines of Portishead's "Sour Times."

Aching vocal twang of Patsy Cline's "Strange" and the line "strange you're still in all my dreams."

Blue wanted to shed the cultural satire, the impishness, and hip-hop influences that had defined her most popular records and return to the vulnerable, stripped-down psychedelic quality of *Fluorescent Gloom*. She wanted the new record to heavily reference her unfairly rejected album. Blue talked about opening or closing the album with a remix of *Fluorescent Gloom*'s single "Neon Bruise," the song that had briefly gotten her canceled. She said they should make fun of that, the bullshit, the hypocrisy, because Blue was about the only person in this industry who actually cared about women, she'd said, without citing any evidence.

She talked about calling the record *Fluorescent Girl Blue* or *Neon Indigo*, references to the Nina Simone album they listened to most mornings. Sasha wanted to incorporate the redwoods into the title, something like *Fluorescent Forest* or *Neon Canopy*—ideas that Blue had dismissed with a cruel, mocking laugh while spinning around in a nightgown to Julee Cruise.

Rose felt like she was living in a dream. She had deleted her Reddit account, which—according to Ella—was causing quite the stir in the subreddit but Rose didn't give a shit. She was embarrassed she'd ever been on there to begin with, mortified that she'd founded it. These days, she was too busy living and learning and even connecting with nature—Rose helped Sasha garden many mornings before Blue awoke—to busy herself with fake online fantasies. She would have blocked Ella's number, a vestige of that cringe time in Rose's life, but most of Rose's belongings were still in Ella's spare bedroom, and Ella seemed vindictive. Rose worried that a kinder person would be concerned about Ella's ability to survive the lockdown alone, without drinking or drugging herself sick or worse. Rose was too happy to be concerned about Ella or anything else, like all the people dying and the civil unrest and people out of work and whatever else was happening in the news Rose wasn't allowed to read.

For the very first time, her life was exactly what she wanted it to be.

r/BlueBeards • posted by u/GlitterGutter • March 2020

Where is Blue quarantining??

With the tour canceled and everyone locking down, where do you think Blue has holed up? Is she back in Malibu, recording in some elite studio, or maybe hiding out somewhere scenic? And who's she with? Did she bring her mousy little assistant? Let the speculations commence!

> **Comment by u/NeonBruise**
>
> I hope she's in New York! We NEED her on the East Coast!!!
>
> **Comment by u/DepravedButterly**
>
> I doubt it, doesn't she hate New York? I bet she's somewhere completely off the grid. Hopefully without that redheaded little mouse.
>
> **Comment by u/PinkCocaine**
>
> A little birdy told me she's in NorCal, somewhere in the woods. I have a hunch Sasha just might be there too. . . . I'm BEYOND hype for the album that comes out of this!!
>
> **Comment by u/405Tulips**
>
> Omg I hope Sasha proposes in the redwoods. How ROMANTIC. Side note—has anyone heard from Rose? I can't find her account? Did she delete it? I hope she's okay!!!
>
> **Comment by u/GarboMommy**
>
> Dude, I think she deleted her account and I really need to reach her—anyone have her number?

Blue

Rose was getting on Blue's nerves. She was always just *there*. And she rarely said anything other than to give Blue compliments, which was nice at first but now was grating on her. Did the girl have a personality aside from being a Blue Velour fan? How dreadful.

Worse, Sasha was starting to give Rose that look. That leery one she got around any woman under twenty-six, any woman whose breasts hadn't yet been impacted by the pull of gravity. Sasha was so predictable. Blue knew she was always number one in Sasha's life, the one woman she wanted the most and could never fully have, but Sasha was also incredibly simple. When it came to music production, she was an unparalleled genius, manifesting an extraordinary ability to elevate the artist's vision into something magical. When it came to love, she was like a teenage boy—forty-three going on eighteen. Blue had a better singing voice, prettier eyes, longer hair, suppler lips, better style, larger breasts, and an infinitely sexier aura, but Rose had one thing Blue didn't: fewer years on planet Earth.

And Sasha was starting to look at Rose like fresh meat.

Sasha was an early riser, as was Rose, meaning they would have an entire day together, just the two of them, before Blue rolled out of bed around noon or one. This morning, Blue walked in on Sasha playing guitar and Rose singing in the living room. Worse, it was Blue's song. "Rose Ghost." Did the bitch know any other songs? Blue wished she'd never made the damn ditty.

"Rose," Blue hissed, interrupting the song. "Breakfast."

Rose mumbled," Sorry," under her breath and dutifully darted into the kitchen like an obedient little mouse. Sometimes Blue wished Rose would stand up to her. Tell her to *fuck off*. Do something other than mumble and obey and sniffle. That was another thing getting on Blue's nerves—the girl was *always* sniffling. Blue would have hired someone else if she'd known a global pandemic would force them to relocate to the redwoods when the woman was clearly allergic to trees.

"Fun morning?" Blue said with a tinge of aggression as she sat on the leather couch and put her bare feet on the coffee table. She scanned her surroundings to extinguish her annoyance at Rose, to replace it with gratitude. Outside the floor-to-ceiling windows, lush greens swayed softly in the breeze. The room was filled with green too, large plants soaking up the sun. Rose appeared to be allergic to all of it.

"Is there a problem?" Sasha asked. Sasha always did this, played dumb. She had a smug look on her dumb face, which unfortunately was getting more attractive with age. Lesbians were like men in that way. Hotter the more worn they got. Although Sasha didn't look entirely weathered. Her olive skin was smooth and taut, but not frozen—not Botox, but probably expensive laser treatments. After the success of *Chateau Velour*, Sasha had had a steady stream of work from artists ranging from up-and-coming musicians to household names to ex-girlfriends to future lovers. Sasha had collaborated with her on-and-off girlfriend Zoë Kravitz, which didn't bother Blue and in fact sort of impressed her—not because Zoë was a good musician, she wasn't, but because Sasha had seduced Zoë. She wasn't as pretty as her mom, no one was, but she was as close as a person could get, and that was very fucking beautiful. Blue was also certain Sasha had hooked up with Annie Clark, aka St. Vincent, with whom Sasha had also worked, which annoyed Blue only insofar as Annie had always been very icy to Blue, but Sasha said that was just her face.

"No problem," Blue said. "Just asking about your morning."

Before Sasha could answer, Rose returned with a tray holding two cans of ice-cold Red Bull and Blue's morning vape. Blue snatched the Flum Gio Coffee Pump and inhaled vigorously, hoping it would make her less annoyed. But Rose was sniffling again and Blue wanted to bang her head through the glass. Rose sat on the couch across from Blue, beside Sasha. Blue sipped her Red Bull and stared at them. There was a nearly twenty-year age difference between them. Sasha could be Rose's mother.

Blue squinted at Rose, with her tight, fair skin, the smattering of rouge freckles that Blue knew would turn to sunspots. Rose was now parting her hair on the side in a messy and exaggerated way that read as unequivocally dykey. But she seemed so asexual. Blue wouldn't be surprised if the girl were a virgin. Rose adjusted the cat-eye glasses that Blue had purchased for her. *Virgin asexual*, Blue concluded.

Blue watched Sasha watch Rose, who was now typing on her phone, her eyelashes casting tiny shadows on her face. Sasha ran her fingers through her wavy, nearly black hair, which now had streaks of gray near the part and around the ears. She was wearing all black as she always did. An oversize black button-down shirt cuffed above the elbows tucked into high-waisted black trousers cinched with a slender black belt. The silver padlock necklace she always wore caught the sun's glow. Sasha's cheeks were slightly flushed, which further irritated Blue.

"Rose," Blue snapped. "Can you go to the store? Get supplies?"

Rose perked up. "Of course, what do you need?" she asked.

Blue knew well that Rose had just gone to the store and they didn't really need anything. She tried to think of something that would be hard to find, something that would keep Rose out of the house for a while. "Blue nail polish," Blue said. She pulled up a screenshot she'd taken before she went to bed, an Instagram ad for a dark blue Chanel nail polish that Blue really did want and that really would be hard to find in rural Northern California during a global pandemic. "It's called Fugueuse," Blue said. "It's Chanel."

"You're making her buy Chanel nail polish," Sasha said. "Right now?"

Blue nodded.

"You aren't even seeing anyone," Sasha said. "Why do you need nail polish?"

"It's important to feel beautiful when I create," Blue said. "I like how navy blue nails look with the mic." Blue held her unpainted nails up in the light from the window, glanced at them, sighed.

Sasha rolled her eyes.

"Please," Blue said. "It's not like you're wearing sweats. Those trousers are the Row, are they not?"

Sasha shrugged. "They're really comfortable."

"I'll find the nail polish," Rose said, as Blue had known she would. "Don't worry."

Blue went over to the record player and put on Nina Simone's *Baby Girl Blue*. The frenetic opening notes of "Mood Indigo" seemed to dance with the dust motes, and Blue felt slightly more relaxed, as she knew Rose was on her way out.

r/BlueBeards • posted by u/RoseGhost • January 2016

Sasha 101

Hello, my sweet BlueBeards! We spend a lot of time on here analyzing Blue and how her lyrics pertain to Sasha, but I wanted to dedicate a post solely to Sasha! So here's a deep dive into the elusive genius behind our queen's spellbinding dreamscapes.

    Alexandra Greta Hardy was born in Long Beach, California, in 1977 to a mechanic father from Los Angeles and a nurse mother from Belarus. (Sasha is a Russian nickname for Alexandra, and Harlow is a nom de plume.) Both of her parents were musical, and Sasha shared in her parents' passion from an early age, taking up piano and guitar in elementary school. In high school, she started a band called Witch Fuzz (if anyone can track down digital versions of these tracks, please message me ASAP!), which disbanded in 1995 when Sasha landed a scholarship at USC, where she studied music production.

    In college, she worked part-time at the Roxy in West Hollywood and had summer internships at Capitol Records and eventually Interscope, which hired her after she graduated. Sasha knew she wanted to produce but worked as a scout for years. Then, one fateful night in 2007, Sasha saw Blue sing a cover of Nirvana's "Love Buzz" at Hollywood's Hotel Café and instantly knew she had to work with her. Sasha—who is famously shy—has said in interviews that she was extremely nervous to approach Blue, but once she gathered the courage, the two quickly hit it off and soon started working together. Roughly a year later, *Spirit of Sinatra* was born. Over the next eight years, they'd go on to make four studio albums together, each more interesting than the last. (While *Fluorescent Gloom* was panned by critics, it happens to be my favorite, and I know a lot of people share that *correct* opinion.)

Sonically, Sasha came to be known for her shimmering synths and shattering bass lines, which paired perfectly with Blue's ethereal melodies. After she established her signature downtempo electropop with Blue, a growing list of artists were itching to work with Sasha. She's since produced albums for Lorde, St. Vincent, and Suki Waterhouse, among others, but none of these records touch the alchemy Sasha has with Blue.

Beyond her undeniable musical genius, there's just something so inexplicably captivating about Sasha, am I right? She just has this quiet confidence I imagine it would be *so alluring* to be in the presence of.

And while her romantic timeline of It Girls like Zoë Kravitz and Annie Clark is long and titillating, let's be real—we know Sasha only has eyes for Blue. What's your hottest take or secret tea on Sasha? What details and moments have you picked up on that make you CONVINCED that she and Blue are not only a couple but the loves of each other's lives?! Share your most stalkerish observations and delirious ravings below!

Comment by u/NeonBruise

Um I have no special tea but just want to echo that Sasha is pure sexxxx. Those bedroom eyes? She drives a fucking pickup truck? The way she walks and moves? Her husky voice? I want her to tie me up and leave me somewhere, bible.

Comment by u/RoseGhost

Lol yes to all that ^^^

Comment by u/PinkCocaine

She's kind of corny, no? I feel like she's just, like, a walking fedora?

Comment by u/NeonBruise

Bitch if I didn't love you I'd ask that you'd be kicked out for that one ^. Straight-up delusional. Sasha hasn't worn a fedora in like a decade. You're just jealous because Rose loves her. Transparent AF :)

Comment by u/PinkCocaine

:p

Rose

According to her iPhone, Rose could buy Chanel nail polish at Bloomingdale's, Ulta Beauty, and Neiman Marcus. The closest Neiman Marcus was an hour and a half away in San Francisco, and Rose wanted to avoid a dense urban area right now. She kept forgetting about the global pandemic until she left Velour Chalet. Now, driving through downtown Guerneville, Rose saw signs that said TAKEOUT ONLY or CLOSED INDEFINITELY. There were only a few people on the streets, all wearing blue surgical masks. The town's somber energy stood in stark contrast to the colorful buildings and playful signage from another era.

Rose pulled over in front of Main Street Bistro, a place Blue often cursed for not being open, as it had a piano bar she'd once sung at in her twenties. (Rose knew both from Blue's stories and her own research that Blue had begun her career primarily as a "bar chanteuse.") The neon signs in the window were all turned off. The sun was bright but nowhere near as harsh and yellow as it was in Southern California. Rose pulled out her phone and searched for the nearest Bloomingdale's, which was also in San Francisco. Another swing, another miss.

But thankfully, according to the internet, there was not one but two Ulta Beautys in Santa Rosa, which was only twenty-six minutes away. Rose exhaled relief.

She had driven to Santa Rosa several times to buy supplies. Guerneville had a Safeway and a general store, but the general store was overpriced and the Safeway lacked certain supplies Blue needed, like her Flum Gios and the Mi-Pods and Elf Bars, which Rose bought in bulk at a place called Digital Ciggz. Rose had also driven to Macy's to buy candles—Blue had moved on from Wild Bluebell to Pomegranate Noir, a scent that gave Rose an immediate headache, but Blue loved it. She also now loved the Cire Trudon Ernesto candle, which Rose had to order online and which smelled like leather and tobacco, as if Velour Chalet needed to smell any more like tobacco than it already did.

Now Rose was driving the baby blue Benz through winding vineyards, rows of grapevines sprawling over gentle hills. The drive was so much more tranquil than her previous commute from Hancock Park to Malibu, which she hadn't minded but which had mostly involved moving a few inches every three minutes, staring at other people's license plates, and getting honked at excessively. Now, there weren't many other cars on the road as she sped along the lush Russian River toward suburbia.

Oleander played on the speakers, and when "Rose Ghost" came on, Rose's belly started to flutter. She was thinking about this morning, about singing while Sasha accompanied her on the guitar, an occasion Rose had dreamed of her entire life. This morning in the garden, Rose had confessed to Sasha that she'd been working on some of her own lyrics, was thinking about putting together some of her own music. Sasha had lit up, said she wanted to hear it. Rose felt too shy. Sasha demanded that Rose at least sing for her so she could hear what they were working with. Those words currently ricocheted through Rose's mind: *Let's hear what we're working with.* She'd said *we*. Like they were already working together.

Rose had had a crush on Sasha since she'd first conceived of the concept of having a crush. Growing up, Rose had never understood the way her peers fussed over boys, whom she found disgusting and annoying. When Rose was thirteen and her younger sister, Lucy, was eleven, Lucy came home from a sleepover and called Rose a dyke. Their mom scolded Lucy, but Rose didn't even know what the word meant. She'd looked it up that night on the family desktop computer while everyone was in bed. Urban Dictionary said it was a derogatory term used to refer to lesbians with masculine characteristics. Rose didn't feel masculine. In fact, she had zero interest in masculinity, in sports or building things or whatever else boys were into. She'd looked up *lesbian*. Merriam-Webster said *lesbian* meant *relating to or characterized by sexual attraction to other women or between women*. Rose didn't feel sexually or romantically attracted to anything. Was she attracted to Amy Winehouse? She wasn't sure. She turned off the computer, embarrassed by what she'd seen.

Later that year, Rose was up late at night watching videos of Amy Winehouse performing live on YouTube on the same family computer. At some point, she went to the bathroom, and when she came back, a non-Amy video recommended by the YouTube algorithm was playing. The woman in the video had long, light blue hair and was wearing a baby blue minidress. She was standing in dramatic gold lighting by a pool, looking right at the camera with fearless aquamarine eyes. She wore winged eyeliner like Amy, but drawn in thinner, more precise lines. In between shots of her singing was footage of '70s surfers, '80s Doritos ads, and Britney Spears shaving her head. It was the music video for "Cool Ranch Kiss," Blue's first single. Rose stood staring at the screen, completely transfixed, heart racing.

When *Spirit of Sinatra* leaked on LimeWire, Rose downloaded it immediately and listened nonstop, so many times that she memorized every word and the songs came alive in her dreams. Rose was singing so much in the house that her mom upped her singing lessons to twice a week. At night when her parents were asleep, Rose would search Blue on YouTube the way she used to with Amy. She'd watch live performances and music videos and interviews. And it was in a Zane Lowe interview that Rose first saw Sasha, Blue's producer.

Sasha made Rose feel things she'd never felt before. Rose wanted to be Blue, but she wanted something else from Sasha. She wanted to be held by her, to sit on her lap, to nuzzle her head in the crook of her arm, to put her silver padlock necklace on her tongue. And now, twelve years later, Rose was closer than she'd ever been to fulfilling this long-held fantasy. This morning in the garden, Sasha had put her hand on Rose's to show her where to plant the dill seeds, an act that had made Rose's entire body tremble. And afterward, Sasha had played on the guitar while Rose sang. *Nice voice control*, Sasha had said. It wasn't Rose's dream compliment. She wished Sasha had commented on the texture of her voice, its richness or emotional pull, but at this point, any compliment would do. Blue had been twenty-seven when she put out *Spirit of Sinatra*. Rose was only twenty-four. She had plenty of time to improve.

Rose merged onto the 101. The landscape was becoming flatter, more concrete, suburban. Shopping malls and fast-food chains. Soon she was nearly missing her exit. Once she was off the freeway, Rose quickly spotted the Ulta Beauty. Two clouds above it parted and made way for light that hit the building and made it look holy, like a church.

Blue

"Eat a strawberry," Sasha said. She pushed a berry from a cardboard box toward Blue's mouth.

Blue nearly hurled. Sasha knew she couldn't think about food before dark. Blue pulled her legs off Sasha's thighs.

"I don't like red foods," Blue said. "Red things." Rose's little red hairs that were now all over Blue's furniture. Or her rented furniture. Luckily Rose hadn't spent much time in here, the back house that Sasha had just finished converting into a studio. If production ever dried up for Sasha, she could have a career converting spaces into aesthetically pleasing studios, which she'd now done for Blue several times in various locations. Here, Sasha had set up a mixing console, a sound system, a keyboard, and a makeshift recording booth. A workstation with monitors sat under huge, angular windows that revealed the forest outside, a living painting that changed with the light. Majesty palms were positioned in the corners and pothos trickled down from the shelves. Sasha had kept the Persian rugs and large black leather couch they were sitting on.

"I worry about your diet," Sasha said. "You can't subsist on Red Bull and burritos. Also, Red Bull is red, no?"

"It's actually gold, and the can is blue, and why not?" Blue asked. "Don't I look good?" She stood and did a twirl. Blue's weight had fluctuated over the years, from dangerously thin to ten pounds overweight. But right now, she felt perfect. She didn't weigh herself, but all her clothes fit. And the last time she was in a biker bar, men's heads turned in the precise way she needed them to. Blue wasn't as afraid of aging as most women. She knew her sensuality was of the innate, timeless variety. Gravity could not and would not bring her down.

"I'm not talking about looks," Sasha said. "I'm talking about your health. You're almost forty."

Blue gasped with faux outrage. "I'm thirty-eight," she said. "How dare you."

"I was never a star math student," Sasha said. "But I believe thirty-eight is very close to forty."

"Is this why you've redirected your focus toward my little assistant?" Blue asked.

"*Pardon?*"

"Never mind," Blue said. She didn't want to seem jealous. She wasn't jealous. She was bored. "Should we record a music video?"

"When's the last time you had your blood pressure checked? Your cholesterol?"

"Probably rehab," Blue said. "My blood pressure was a little elevated, but they said that was a natural side effect of the detox."

"You haven't been to a doctor since rehab? Blue, wasn't that over ten years ago?"

"So?" Blue said. "I'm healthy. Anyway, the music video."

"Anyway, fruits and vegetables," Sasha said.

"Listen, Mom," Blue said. "I eat the gross, healthy crap you make every night for dinner."

Now it was Sasha's turn to gasp with faux outrage. "You know I almost went to culinary school—"

"—before you got into USC, I know Sasha." Blue got up and tapped Sasha's nose. "I know everything about you, my little fox." Blue sat on Sasha's lap and delighted in feeling Sasha's racing pulse beneath her. "What about your blood pressure, dear?" She put her fingers on Sasha's wrist. "Pulse feels elevated."

Sasha pushed off Blue's arm and leaned in to kiss her. Blue put a finger over Sasha's mouth.

"What if the girl comes back?" Blue said.

"The girl? Rose? I thought you liked her."

"She's fine," Blue said.

"You turn on everyone eventually, don't you?" Sasha said.

"What's that supposed to mean?"

"Exactly what the words say," Sasha said.

Blue got off Sasha's lap. "Can we film the music video?"

"For what?" Sasha said. "We don't even have a song. I thought you wanted to make a record."

"I do!" Blue shouted, irritated. "And we will. But everyone is bored at home right now. Shouldn't we give them a beautiful woman in the woods to look at? To fantasize about?"

"I don't want to be in a music video," said Sasha playfully.

"Oh, shut up," Blue said. "We didn't make a video for 'A Vape Cartridge Named Desire.' I mean, wouldn't this be the perfect time? Just sexy footage of me vaping and singing in the woods as the light gets all dreamy?"

"I'm not much of a videographer," Sasha said.

"The girl could film it!" Blue said. She was getting excited imagining imminent virality. "And I know you were joking about being in it, but—"

"No," Sasha said.

"Just like, whispers of you. In the background. Your leg. Your hair. Just to create buzz. Get that demented subreddit going."

Bijou ran in through the doggy door Sasha had created and jumped on Blue's lap. Blue held up Bijou, hoping the cute dog would convince Sasha.

Sasha shook her head, but Blue could tell from the tiny smile cracking on the left side of her mouth that she was in.

r/BlueBeards • posted by u/Oleander • December 2019

"Why wouldn't she just come out?"

You, my dear friend, say:
> "I don't think it's appropriate to speculate about Blue Velour's life. If she and Sasha are a thing, why wouldn't she just come out?"

I say:
> "Well, that's the point of queer subtext. It's a way to test the waters—to see if it's safe."

You say:
> "Safe? Please. It's 2019."

I say:
> "Yes . . . it's 2019, and it's still dangerous. Hate crimes happen every day. Globally, it's illegal to be gay in sixty-four countries. Even in the US, being out means risking your career if the industry decides you're 'too niche.'"

You say:
> "But she's so rich. What does she have to be scared of?"

I say:
> "Plenty. People tore her apart over *Fluorescent Gloom*. She knows how quickly fans and critics can turn on her. Being out would make her even more of a target."

You say:
> "Okay, but what's the worst that could happen?"

I say:
> "It's not just about her. The moment Blue comes out, every man she's dated gets accused of being her beard. Every woman she's ever hugged becomes a closeted lesbian. Sasha hates attention, and it would drag her into the spotlight too. Blue's truth affects more than just Blue."

You say:
> "She could just say she's straight."

I say:
> "She's *never* said that. She clarifies everything else—her tour outfits, her diet, her nail polish—but not this. Her silence on her sexuality speaks volumes."

You say:
> "Your theories are so complicated. Why wouldn't she just come out if it's true?"

I say:
> "Maybe she's scared. Maybe she's still unlearning the shame she grew up with in a deeply religious family in the Bible Belt. Maybe she doesn't trust herself. Or maybe she sees how angry people get at even the idea that she's queer and thinks, 'Not worth it.'"

And then you, my sweet but clueless friend, say:
> "She just doesn't seem gay to me."

And I think, "I guess that's why I haven't come out to you."

Comment by u/ChateauVelour

> SO beautifully written, and that ending hit me hard. People forget that growing up in the Bible Belt leaves scars, even for someone like Blue. It's not just about coming out—it's about unlearning years of shame and fear.

Comment by u/BauhausBathhouse

> No! Notes! I've had this argument with my roommate! Blue knows people would dissect her relationships and lyrics if she came out. They're already doing it, and she hasn't even said a word.

Comment by u/PinkCocaine

> Lol I don't think Blue is ashamed I think she just likes being mysterious <3

Rose

Rose couldn't find Blue or Sasha when she came home with the nail polish, which had also been difficult to find. At the first Ulta Beauty, there was no Chanel. The woman working there said to try the other Ulta Beauty, which ended up having Chanel nail polish, but not the navy blue color Blue had requested. The saleslady said to try Macy's, which was massive and chaotic and hard to navigate. Multiple salespeople gave Rose incorrect directions to the beauty counter. Rose ended up in home furnishings, where she sat on a bed and drank some water, then got scolded for sitting on the furniture and for briefly taking off her mask. By the time she finally found the nail polish, Rose wanted to kiss the saleslady. She charged it to Blue's credit card and drove home while the fields shone golden under the afternoon sun.

And now Rose was back at Velour Chalet, and Blue and Sasha weren't in the living room. They weren't in Blue's bedroom, or Sasha's. They weren't on the decks or in the hot tub. They weren't in the studio. Eventually, Rose heard Bijou barking. She followed the barking until she found Blue barefoot in a kimono, singing in the middle of the trees, yellow light creating dots on her face, Sasha filming her with an iPhone. But as soon as Rose got close, Bijou jumped out of Blue's arms, began charging at Rose.

"Fuck!" Blue screamed.

"Maybe we should try a take without Bijou," Sasha said.

"She was fine," Blue said. "Until she got here." Blue narrowed her eyes at Rose, whom she suddenly seemed to hate in the precise way she'd hated her before her show at the Toyota Amphitheatre.

"I got the nail polish," Rose said.

Sasha turned, clearly seeing Rose for the first time and smiled from the side of her mouth. Rose's abdomen fluttered.

"What nail polish?" Blue asked. She adjusted her kimono. She looked gorgeous under the flickering light from the canopy. But she had a mean, wild look in her eyes.

Rose held up the nail polish that had taken her nearly three hours to procure.

"Oh," Blue said. "Thanks." She took the nail polish, examined it in the light, then handed it back to Rose, who put it in her jeans pocket.

"I'm glad you're here," Blue said.

Rose exhaled. "You are?"

"We need you," Blue said. "To film." Blue turned to Sasha. "Give her the phone."

Sasha handed the phone to Rose.

"Don't stop filming," Blue said. "We're making a music video. For 'A Vape Cartridge Named Desire.'"

Rose nodded. This was Ella's second favorite song after "Pink Cocaine." Rose liked it too. Everyone did. And Rose liked the idea of Blue making a music video right now. The lo-fi quality of Blue barefoot in the woods reminded Rose of the video for "Cool Ranch Kiss," which had first endeared Rose to Blue. It had also been filmed on an iPhone, featured footage of Blue singing under a tree, and had been edited by Blue herself.

"Why are you just standing there?" Blue said. "We're losing the light." Blue reassumed her position with Bijou in one hand, her vape in the other. Rose dutifully held up the phone camera, trying to keep her hands still.

"Okay," Blue directed. "Rose, keep the camera pointed on me. I'll sing and"—she turned to Sasha—"on the line 'sweet nicotine kiss,' Sash, I want you to reach for Bijou." Blue turned back to Rose. "Don't get Sasha's face, just her arm taking Bijou."

"We can edit me out too," Sasha said.

"Let's just try it," Blue said. "Now turn on the song," she said. Sasha pressed a button on a small Bluetooth speaker and the song started playing. Blue started singing, her voice louder and more vibrant than the speaker's tinny output.

Bijou started barking again.

"What the hell?" Blue scolded the dog. She glanced at Rose. "Take her inside, grab Gigi. Hurry back. Bijou's not a fan of yours." Blue unleashed a little laugh.

Rose reached for Bijou, who growled at her.

"Easy, buddy," Sasha said, stroking the dog.

"Don't call her *buddy*," Blue said to Sasha. "She's a feminine lady."

"I'll handle the lady," Sasha said, easing Bijou from Blue. Sasha trotted off through the forest. Rose felt suddenly nervous to be alone with Blue, who seemed manic and on the verge of aggression. Rose watched Sasha's boots disappear.

"What are you looking at?"

Rose turned her eyes toward Blue's, which lit up electric aqua in the light.

"Nothing," Rose said.

"You were staring at Sasha," Blue said. She smiled. Bit her lip.

Rose remembered she'd stopped at Digital Ciggz. She pulled out a Geek Bar from her canvas tote. "For you," Rose said. "Stone Freeze, like you wanted."

Blue stared at the electronic smoking device as though she'd never seen one before.

She said nothing.

Rose saw a little flash of yellow by her feet. She looked down and saw a slimy, bright yellow creature.

"What the hell is that?" Rose asked.

Blue laughed. "It's a banana slug," Blue said. She took the Geek Bar from Rose's hand. She inhaled deeply. Exhaled up toward the canopy.

Rose watched as the vapor spread and disappeared. The mint mingled with the forest scents of dirt and pine. Rose sniffled, then sneezed.

Blue

*T*hey were getting some good shit. The light was positively celestial. Softer and more effervescent than in Southern California. The thin mist from the vape danced with the sun's rays and made the smoke seem almost alive, a spectral presence in the forest. Gigi was still and behaved. Sasha was also behaving for once. Right now, Sasha was standing behind Blue with her back turned while Blue sang and they followed the fading light. Blue was singing in a last patch of gold, gradually disappearing. And when it did, finally giving way to the cool shadows of the forest dusk, Blue's phone rang. The device was sitting up against a tree. Blue told Rose to stop filming and went to answer it. She was delighted to see the name on the phone.

"Maxine!" Blue cooed. She was in a fantastic mood. Filming music videos always did this to her: creating art made her feel alive and positive and indestructible. Various exes and friends and family members and colleagues and psychiatrists had referred to such states as "mania," but Blue thought everyone was too online and overly eager to diagnose. Blue didn't believe in the *DSM*. She believed in God. And magic.

She'd been mad at Max when she left, but now she felt delighted at the prospect of speaking to her. And Blue knew before Max said anything that she would finish the video tonight, by the light of candles and the moon. She'd edit it tomorrow, upload it, and then start making the album. She should probably tell her record company before uploading the music video, as well as her manager, but Blue always had trouble following rules. And it had turned out just fine for her. The *New York Times* had called her California's poet laureate. She could do no wrong.

"Blue," Max said, her voice soft and soothing. Blue trotted off farther into the forest for some privacy.

"Be careful, Blue," Sasha called after her. "Critters will be coming out soon."

"I could take a bear!" Blue shouted back as she ran away from Sasha and Rose, the damp soil cold beneath her bare feet.

"Are you safe, Blue?" Max was her younger sister but had always felt older. She was the more practical, protective one, always keeping Blue out of danger.

"I've never been safer," said Blue. "The redwoods are absolutely fantastic," she continued. "I'm like a forest nymph right now, you should see me. I'm just barefoot in a kimono running around the trees. We were just filming a video for 'A Vape Cartridge Named Desire.'"

"Which kimono?" Max asked. Sometimes Max was Blue's stylist before she was her sister. Max had gotten Blue her first vintage kimono—cobalt blue silk, Christian Dior—and Blue had been a kimono addict since.

"The teal Halston," Blue said. "The sort of gauzy one."

"I bet that looks nice against the color palette of the forest," Max said.

"It does!" Blue squealed. She was so excited it was starting to become uncomfortable.

"So," said Max. "I have something to tell you."

"Pray tell," Blue said. She walked even farther into the woods.

"I'm seeing someone," said Max.

Conflicting feelings swirled inside Blue's gut. Delight, confusion, jealousy. "How? It's a global pandemic. Please tell me your secrets; I'm dying for dick."

Max laughed. "You actually know him," she said. "Grayson."

More conflicting feelings. Pride, envy, sadness. Grayson had been one of their first friends in Los Angeles. They'd met him at their go-to Hollywood bar, the Frolic Room, in their early twenties. Those years were hazy, but she vaguely remembered Grayson as being kind, albeit a bit bland. He was a few years older than them, but he was from North Carolina too, so he felt safe. He had a regular job as far as Blue could remember. Tech? Real estate? Finance? Blue could hardly name any regular jobs.

"That's fantastic, Max," Blue said. "How is he? How did you reconnect?"

"We started talking on Instagram," Max said. "He's good, divorced. He lives in Malibu, so that's how he opened the convo. I'd posted a photo of the sunset on the beach and he slid right in asking if it was Lechuza, which it obviously was. He has his own company—contracting. He wants to renovate the house." Max laughed.

Blue didn't. This was so much information. Blue felt dizzy. She was happy for Max. She couldn't remember the last time Max had a boyfriend. So much of her time had been dedicated to supporting Blue. She deserved to take care of herself, her needs, Blue knew that. Blue wanted Max to fall in love, she'd said that when Max went back to Malibu. But she nonetheless felt jealous, like this Grayson dude was stealing her sister, like they had this whole new life together without her, that they were going to renovate the house Blue bought and start a family there and Blue would be alone with nowhere to go.

"And it's serious?" Blue asked.

"I really like him, Blue," Max said. Blue couldn't remember the last time she'd heard Max say anything like this.

"That's wonderful, Max," Blue said. Luckily she was in a good mood.

"You sound happy too," Max said.

Blue nodded, then realized Max couldn't see her. Max kept talking.

"Maybe we needed some time apart, you and I. When's the last time we've gone this long without seeing each other? When we were teenagers and you moved to California?"

"I think it was rehab," Blue said. She tried to remember the last time she'd spoken to Max. They'd been texting every few days, but hadn't spoken on the phone in weeks, not since Blue had moved to Velour Chalet. But why hadn't Max told her about the boyfriend earlier? How long had they been seeing each other? Part of Blue didn't really want to know. She wondered if she would ever meet a nice, normal guy from North Carolina who worked in construction. She hoped.

"The girl is annoying me," Blue whispered. She was far enough in the forest that Rose likely couldn't hear, but then again, Rose always seemed to be lurking around every corner.

"What girl?" asked Max.

"Rose," Blue whispered.

"Oh," Max said. She was quiet for a second. Crickets began to hum. The light was sort of purple now, approaching dark. Blue knew she should head back to the house, but she didn't want to. It was so peaceful out here. She stopped walking and leaned against a tree that was probably hundreds of years old.

"She's just *always around*," Blue continued. "Just, like, sniffling. She's allergic to the outdoors or something. She has real indoor-kid energy."

"I thought you liked her," Max said.

"I sort of did in the beginning," Blue said. "She was shy, but I thought there was something underneath it. A freakiness I could pry out. But now that I've lived with her for . . ." Blue tried to think about how long it had been but couldn't figure it out. Was it April yet? "Who knows what time is anymore, but anyway, I think there's just . . . nothing there. She's just like, empty. And she's a good assistant, don't get me wrong. I have everything I need. She even found me Chanel nail polish today." A cool breeze rustled the leaves above her, carrying with it the distant hoot of an owl. Blue had just realized Rose could film

Sasha painting Blue's nails tonight for the video. Maybe they could find the owl and film it too. "But there's something vacant about her." Blue paused. "And Bijou doesn't like her."

Max was silent for a second. "You know, I was surprised you hired her," she said.

"Why didn't you say anything?"

"I did," Max said. "I told you to get a background check, that I hardly remember the girl who recommended her. And you said you trusted her because she had a good voice and was a Gemini."

Blue laughed at herself. Why didn't she ever listen to Max?

"And I didn't mind her, really," Max said. "Although I did notice the Bijou thing. And Bijou notices things we don't, as you know. And then . . ." Max trailed off. Blue heard a male voice in the background. Again, feelings swirled inside of her. Anger, resentment, rage. Blue tried to will her brain back to the excitement she'd felt a few minutes ago.

"Sorry," Max said. "Grayson was looking for the wine opener." She giggled, as though it was funny. As if Blue wouldn't love to share a bottle of wine with a nice man who built things. But she never could, because she was an alcoholic, and a sex and love addict on top of that, and she confused intensity for intimacy, and danger for love, and she'd likely die alone, or in Sasha's pathetic arms.

"What were you saying?" Blue asked. "About the girl." Blue was having trouble saying her name, like the word couldn't find her tongue, or vice versa.

"Oh!" Max said. "So at the Toyota Amphitheatre, I asked Rose how she knew Grace, the girl who recommended her. I'd had to double-check her name beforehand because I couldn't remember it for the life of me. I believe we went to camp together but God, it was like, twenty years ago?"

"I can hardly remember what I did this morning," Blue said.

"Same," said Max. "Anyway, Rose said they'd met on a cruise."

"A cruise?" Blue said. She couldn't imagine Rose on a cruise. Her skin was so pale it was nearly translucent. She looked like someone who could burst into flames in strong sunlight. She always wore long sleeves and a hat in Malibu.

"Right?" Max said. "Totally random. It felt like a lie. I said I couldn't imagine Grace on a cruise, which I guess was true in the sense that I couldn't imagine Grace doing anything because I don't remember a goddamn thing about the girl. Rose said Grace was dragged along by her college friends. I'd meant to message Grace about it but then the tour got canceled and we don't have to go back there, but I was distracted."

"I'm so sorry about throwing that phone at your head," Blue said,

"The bruise is almost gone." Max laughed. She really was a good sport.

"But a few weeks ago," Max continued, "Grace responded to one of my Instagram stories. And I remembered that conversation with Rose, so I asked her about the cruise thing." Max swallowed. "And Grace said she'd literally never been on a cruise."

"What?" Blue asked. More weird feelings. Dread, distrust, disarray. "So how did they meet?"

"I don't know," Max said. "She stopped responding. I'll try to ask her again. Maybe she just left the phone and forgot about that. I do that all the time."

Something wasn't adding up. She knew there was something off with Rose.

"Send me her Instagram handle," Blue said. "Grace's." She was going to get to the bottom of this.

"Okay," Max said. "I have to go. I'm glad you're happy, Blue. I love you."

"I love you too," Blue said. Max hung up.

It was dark now. Blue put on her phone flashlight to make her way back to the house. When she pointed it ahead of her, the beam connected with two neon eyes. It was a fox. Its fur was silver in the light—resplendent. Blue quickly opened the camera app, started filming the creature. It ran away, darting into the darkness. She'd use the footage in the music video. Maybe she'd write a song about the silver fox, and for once, it wouldn't be about a man.

r/BlueBeards • posted by u/GlitterGutter • April 2020

Vape Cartridge Named Desire video and OMG SASHA!!!

Y'ALL. Did everyone see the new video?? It's legit hypnotic—Blue singing in the woods, vapor swirling in the moonlight, cute AF little forest creatures! BUT I'm totally burying the lead here: *Sasha's hands*. That's 1000% Miss Harlow painting Blue's nails and braiding her hair, right?! They're just being romantic as hell in this off-the-grid cabin, two sapphic icons hiding out from the world, and it's giving me actual LIFE. They literally just confirmed *everything* without saying a single word.

And can we talk about how Rose totally called this? Remember her brilliant analysis on how this song channels *A Streetcar Named Desire*? This music video is like Rose's post straight-up brought to life! The whole hidden-cabin vibe feels like Blanche's need to create her own world, a secret space to be vulnerable and escape all the judgment. It's got that vibe of desire and intimacy away from society's BS, like Tennessee hiding in his plays!

Are you all as shook as I am??

Comment by u/405Tulips

I think Rose deactivated her account! I'm worried about her ;(

Comment by u/GarboMommy

Don't worry, she's more than fine.

Comment by u/Oleander

Do you know her? What's going on??

Comment by u/GarboMommy

You know the redhead who's been by Blue's side the past few months. . . .

Comment by u/NeonBruise

STOP

Comment by u/405Tulips

WHAT is going on??

Rose

Over the next few weeks, Rose didn't see much of Blue.

Roughly thirteen days ago, Rose had finished shooting the "A Vape Cartridge Named Desire" video, a day after they'd started. Blue had spent a day in the studio editing the footage—of herself singing in the forest with the dogs, of vapor curling up toward the trees, of Sasha's disembodied hand painting Blue's nails on her bed, of Sasha's fingers braiding Blue's hair, of Blue spinning in circles in a kimono on the deck under the moonlight, of various forest creatures, such as a silver fox and the wings of an owl—spliced with older clips of Blue vaping with fans at various concerts.

After what seemed like thirty-two hours at the computer—Rose appeared periodically only to bring Red Bull and nicotine and grilled cheese sandwiches made by Sasha, who made an absolutely killer grilled cheese—Blue uploaded the video to her YouTube channel. She was promptly scolded by her manager, who had been scolded by the record company, who promptly apologized when the video amassed ten million views within two days. It had officially gone viral. The BlueBeards in particular were going crazy for it. Rose was still off Reddit, but Ella had texted her the day it was released.

HOLY FUCKING SHIT, she'd said. *DID YOU SEE THIS?*

Honey, Rose had replied, *I filmed it.*

I'M DYING, she'd replied. *THAT'S SASHA RIGHT? PAINTING HER NAILS??*

Rose had responded with the zipper-mouth emoji. She hadn't told anyone where she was, or that Sasha was here. There wasn't really anyone to tell. Rose's parents hardly ever reached out to her since she'd left home for college. Rose had no real relationship with her sister. Ella was the only one who ever texted her, and Rose had only told Ella she was in Northern California with Blue.

Blue had read headlines about the video at the dinner table that night. *Blue Velour's iPhone Music Video Is a Queer Pandemic Fairy Tale. TikTok Teens Call Blue Velour's Latest Drop a "Gay Baptism." Blue Velour's Vape-Fueled Woodland Romp Has the Internet in a Chokehold. Blue Velour's New Video Breaks the Internet and Probably at Least One NDA. BlueBeards Spiral Over Softcore Sapphic Forest Video.*

"That subreddit," Blue had said, "is so gay." She'd looked at Rose right when she said it, in a way that gave Rose chills. Did she know?

"You can't say that," Sasha had said.

"Say what?" Blue had said. She was so good at playing dumb.

After dinner that night, Blue and Sasha had gone straight to the studio. Blue was clearly energized by the video's success, even though she frequently claimed to not care what fans or critics thought. Blue was filled with contradictions; she *contained multitudes.*

Blue certainly contained a multitude of personalities. There was Morning Blue (pre–Red Bull), who was hardly verbal and wore the look of someone who'd just smelled something foul. There was Afternoon Blue (post–Red Bull), who was chatty and exuberant and full of ideas. There was Whimsical Blue, who often appeared in the evening, the one who would want to drive to Kohl's at 9:45 p.m. or go skinny-dipping or have a spontaneous "twerk-off." There was Horny Blue, who often appeared at rehearsal back in Malibu, who really only appeared around men, who had absolutely zero interest in speaking to Rose or any other woman. There was Enraged Blue, who'd appeared before the show at the Toyota Amphitheatre. There was Rude Blue, a cousin of Enraged Blue and of Morning Blue, who was curt and sassy and had been appearing more and more recently. And, finally, there was Manic Blue, who was a cousin of Whimsical Blue, but with a dose of Enraged Blue. Manic Blue wanted to run through the forest at midnight without a flashlight, wanted to take a night swim in the river, would pick up Rose and spin her in circles until Rose wanted to throw up, wouldn't sleep for days, was grandiose, cocky, and had, at least twice in the past week, compared herself to God.

In the past eleven days, Blue had been alternating between Manic Blue and Enraged Blue. She wasn't sleeping much and when she did, it was on the couch in the studio and she'd wake up at around 4 or 5 p.m. Rose would only appear to bring Blue her supplies on a tray, but this morning, Enraged Blue had screamed at Rose that she didn't want to see her anymore, that Rose was interfering with Blue's creative process, and that, effective immediately, Sasha would bring Blue her breakfast and dinner and Rose was to remain in the main house, where she would wait to hear from Sasha whether Blue had any tasks for her.

So now, Rose was sitting in the living room, trying to figure out how to kill the hours until Blue asked her to do something or Sasha returned. Rose and Sasha still had their mornings together. They would still garden, still sing. Sasha was encouraging Rose to listen to music other than Blue's, to expand her palate. She'd ordered some records for them to listen to together, which Rose found incredibly erotic. She was now familiar with most of Sasha's favorite records—Janis Joplin's *Pearl*, Dolly Parton's *Jolene*, Mazzy Star's *Among My Swan*, Mariah Carey's *Butterfly*, Britney Spears's *Blackout*. Sasha was happy to learn that Rose was also a Britney fan but seemed offended that Rose preferred *Circus*.

Rose got up and put *Jolene* on the record player. It was her favorite album that Sasha had played for her, and it made Rose feel so many things. Right now, Rose felt sad, lonely, nostalgic for the early days at Velour Chalet, when she'd been floating down the river with Blue and Sasha, when Blue had been including Rose in listening sessions, in brainstorming sessions, when Rose had been taking notes that would eventually inspire the next album. At this point, Rose didn't even know what Sasha and Blue were doing in the back house.

Rose must have drifted off at some point, because in the middle of "Lonely Comin' Down," her phone dinged and jerked her up. It was a text from Sasha, which always caused Rose's stomach to flutter, even though Sasha was typically just asking Rose to do something on behalf of Blue. This time, Blue had a craving for Warheads. *You know, that super sour candy that was big in the '90s.* Rose wasn't familiar. She'd been born in 1995. But according to the internet, the "go-to candy for sour seekers" was currently sold at Walmart and Walgreens, both of which they only had in Santa Rosa, which was fine—she needed something to do. She grabbed a surgical mask, Blue's card, and the Benz keys, and headed out to the driveway.

Blue

*T*he light outside the window behind the monitors was turning orange. Sasha was at the mixing station with headphones. Blue was on the couch, sucking on Warheads. She couldn't remember the last time she'd slept, but she didn't feel tired at all. The sour candies were doing a good job of keeping her alert. Blue probably could sleep. They'd written and recorded twelve songs in seventeen days, although Blue wanted to record more, wanted to go faster. Kurt Cobain had famously recorded Nirvana's debut album, *Bleach*, in thirty hours of studio time. It had eleven tracks, which felt like the perfect number for this record, which Blue was currently thinking of calling either *Always Smoke in Bed* or *Love in the Time of Lithium*, but she knew she'd change her mind a thousand more times. She knew she wanted to record a few more tracks to give them options to pare down. Maybe Blue needed a little break. She was starting to feel that mounting pressure inside her stomach, a flush rising on her neck and cheeks, a jittery sensation throughout her limbs.

"I need to get fucked," Blue told Sasha. She had to scream it so

American Spirits

Sasha could hear. Sasha turned and slid her right headphone away from her ear.

"Huh?" Sasha said. Her eyes were bloodshot, her hair disheveled. She wore a pained expression on her face. Sasha was a baby. She was sleeping much more than Blue, disappearing back to the main house at around 1 or 2 a.m. while Blue stayed up writing lyrics until sunrise.

"I need to get fucked!" Blue shouted again, this time louder, even though yelling was no longer necessary because Sasha had taken her headphones off.

Sasha rubbed her hair. "Give me a second," she said.

Blue laughed. "Not by you." Sasha and Blue had had sex a few times during the recording, and the prerecording. It was part of their process, infused the music with the libido fans adored. But Sasha could only do so much.

"I need a dick," Blue said. "Inside me." She grinned. "A big one."

"Jesus," said Sasha. "I don't need to hear that."

Blue laughed again. Sasha knew Blue loved men. Sasha loved and hated that about Blue. She loved it because Sasha loved straight women, had once confessed to Blue that she got off on the idea of her with a man. She hated this fact because it meant that Blue would never be fully hers. Beyond her sexual preferences, Blue was incapable of commitment, and Sasha was too, and Sasha hated looking in the mirror—most people did.

"Please," Blue said. "Like you don't like the idea of me getting thrown up against the wall by a man with a grisly beard and smelling of automotive grease?"

"Not really," Sasha said, but her face flushed slightly, giving her away.

"What time is it?" Blue asked. She'd turned off her phone and buried it in a box in the yard weeks ago.

Sasha squinted at the screen. "Five fifteen," she said.

"A.m. or p.m.?"

Sasha smiled. "P.m."

"Perfect!" Blue shouted. "Happy hour! There has to be a biker bar around here! Drive me!"

"Hate to break it to you," Sasha said, "but we're still in a global pandemic. Bars aren't open."

"*Still?*" Blue never read the news. She'd typically get snippets of whatever was important from scrolling social media, but she hadn't looked at her phone for seventeen days. "I thought it was just going to be two weeks of things being closed."

"They said that at first," Sasha said. "Now they're saying years."

"*Years?*" Blue said. She felt panicked. She needed to be fucked more than ever. Maybe she could go into the forest and find solace in the comfort of some large woodland creature. Although that was probably illegal. Maybe she could find a hunter! But what if she got shot?

"Humans are social creatures," Blue said. "They need to gather. Even if the government or whatever says it's illegal, I'm sure it's happening. People are organizing speakeasies and house parties. We have to know someone who knows someone who lives here and knows where the secret parties are."

"I thought you wanted to work on the album," Sasha said. "To fully immerse yourself in its world with no outside influences until it was done?"

"Dick is hardly an outside influence," Blue said. "I'm most myself with one inside of me."

Sasha made a face.

"You just want me to yourself, don't you?"

"I support a woman's autonomy," Sasha said. "I just want this record to be perfect."

"It will be," Blue said.

Sasha was silent, which made Blue nervous. Blue always thought whatever she was making was perfect at the time she was making it. Otherwise, she wouldn't have the energy required to complete it. And as time passed, she tended to find it less perfect, more cringe, cartoonish, sad, pathetic. And sometimes that feeling would go away if critics and audiences loved it, like with the last couple of records, which were universally acclaimed. But before that, that wasn't always the case. In fact, it was never the case. And the disappointment Blue had experienced after *Fluorescent Gloom*'s reception still haunted her to this day. She didn't think she could handle something like that again. It might kill her. Literally.

"The record is good, right?" Blue asked.

Sasha made an unreadable expression. "It's great," Sasha said. "But after *Blue's Beard*, people are going to expect more than great from you. People are going to expect perfection."

"Perfection is impossible?" Blue said.

"We have to get as close as we can." Sasha scratched her wrist and adjusted her headphones, suddenly focused on something Blue couldn't see.

Rose

Rose was typically asleep when Sasha returned to the main house at night, or she'd hear the front door open from her little bed in the attic. But tonight, Rose willed herself to stay up. She took her daytime allergy medicine, the one that gave her energy, and opened a bottle of wine. She lit Blue's expensive candles and listened to upbeat music to stay awake. When Sasha finally returned at a little after 1 a.m., Rose was halfway through Britney's *Blackout*.

"Wow," Sasha said. There were dark circles under her eyes. On day three of recording, she'd traded in her button-downs and trousers for black T-shirts and slouchy Levi's. "I wasn't expecting to come home to 'Freakshow.'"

Rose smiled. She was a little drunk, and high, on the combo of wine and allergy medicine and now, Sasha's presence.

"I wanted to wait up for you," Rose surprised herself by admitting.

Sasha raised an eyebrow. "Oh yeah?"

"Wine?" Rose asked. She'd already poured Sasha a glass as soon as she heard the door to the studio open.

"I really should go to bed," Sasha said. She flipped her hair from one side to the other. Rose held her breath. "But that looks too good." She took the glass and sat down next to Rose, whose body began thrumming with pleasure.

"How's the recording?" Rose asked. She wasn't just asking to be polite; she was legitimately curious, envious that Sasha was a part of it and she wasn't.

Sasha exhaled. She stood up. Rose was worried she'd upset her, that she was leaving. Sasha walked over to the record player. "You know I love this album," Sasha said. "But it's a little aggressive right now." She turned it down, then stopped it.

"I get it," Rose said. "I was trying to stay up." She paused. "For you." She really was drunk, high, whatever.

Sasha smiled out of the side of her mouth. "That's sweet," she said. A silence hung between them. "I have an idea," Sasha said. "Stay here." She ran upstairs and Rose worried she wouldn't come back. While she was gone, Rose pulled out her phone and looked into her selfie camera, examined her appearance. She'd put on red lipstick earlier, but it was slightly faded. She reapplied the lipstick and finished just as Sasha was returning down the stairs.

"Who are you getting all dolled up for?" Sasha said, her boots creaking on the floorboards.

Rose smiled shyly and took a sip of wine. "It's just us here," she said.

Sasha gave an inscrutable smile. She was holding a record behind her back. "Okay," she said. "I'm going to play something for you, but only on the condition that you *never* tell Blue. Ever."

"Okay," Rose said. She didn't know why she'd have to hide this information from Blue, but she loved the idea of her and Sasha having a secret.

"Say you promise," Sasha said.

"I promise," said Rose.

Sasha removed a record from behind her back. The cover was adorned with pink and purple clouds and said the word *Lover* in pink script. On the album cover was a blond woman who Rose believed was

Taylor Swift. Blue wasn't sure. Ella liked her. Blue had never listened to her, other than songs she couldn't avoid in public spaces.

"Is that Taylor Swift?"

"Shh," Sasha said, and playfully ran over to put a finger over Rose's mouth. Rose laughed.

"You're a Swiftie?" Rose said. She knew Blue hated Taylor Swift. Everyone knew this. Blue had famously said in an early interview that she would have "shoved Taylor up against a locker" if they'd gone to high school together.

"I think she's a talented songwriter," Sasha said. She went over to the record player. "This isn't a perfect album," she said while changing the record. "But it has some songs I love. The title track is gorgeous." Sasha pressed play, then turned to Rose. "There's this track on *1989* that's almost exactly a Blue Velour song. Blue was pissed, but I think it's a compliment. Taylor would have sued if Blue had copied one of her songs, but Blue doesn't believe in that kind of thing. She always says great artists steal."

Sasha sat down on the couch next to Rose and picked up her wineglass. "You know, it's funny," Sasha said. "When Blue and I first made *Spirit of Sinatra* in 2008, Blue's sound could not have been more unfashionable. It was all bubblegum pop like Katy Perry's 'I Kissed a Girl' and bouncy synth pop like Lady Gaga's 'Just Dance.' And then we come out with these baroque, cinematic songs, all downtempo, and everyone is like *huh*? And then cut to 2019 and—"

"—everyone is ripping Blue," Rose interrupted. She was excited. This was a topic she knew about. "Billie Eilish, Sky Ferreira, Mitski, Lorde..."

"Well, I made Lorde sound like Blue." Sasha laughed. Rose had forgotten Sasha had produced Lorde's latest album. The second song on the record was playing, and Sasha pointed to the record to redirect Rose's focus. Rose closed her eyes.

"This is nice," Rose said.

"It's a banger," Sasha confirmed.

They listened for a few moments. Rose watched the flame of the expensive candle dance with the song. It had a fun chorus that reminded Rose of Britney's "Circus." The candle flame seemed to be having fun. Blue rarely had a fun chorus. She never wrote anything up-tempo.

When the chorus ended, Sasha sighed, then put her head in her hands. Feeling emboldened by the wine, Rose put her hand on Sasha's back, rubbed her palm in a circle.

"You okay?" Rose said.

Sasha sat up. "I'm okay," Sasha said. She looked at Rose. "Just stressed."

Rose had already asked about the album once and didn't want to pry, but Sasha had opened the door. "What do you mean?"

"I don't know," Sasha said. She took off her boots and put her feet up on the coffee table. She was wearing thick gray socks that looked comfortable. Rose fantasized, briefly, about sliding her foot under Sasha's, about how warm and safe that would feel.

"I never know," Sasha continued. "It's so hard to know. Blue gets so excited when she's making a record. She's been open about this, so I don't think I'm breaking any confidences here, but she's bipolar. And she refuses to take medication for it. I mean, you've seen the way her mood shifts throughout the day."

Rose nodded.

"When we're making a record, she's mostly manic. Which can be a lot of fun. She's all possibilities. No idea is too outlandish or ambitious. And the rest of the world disappears. It's just us, and she truly believes we're capable of anything."

"That sounds fun," Rose said. She was jealous of Sasha, jealous of her access to Blue at these moments from which Rose had been ousted.

"It is," Sasha said. "But it's also dangerous. We've had so many upsets. And it's my job to reel her in. And it's hard to know what's a legitimately brilliant idea and what's, well . . ." Sasha took another sip of wine, swallowed. "Mania?"

"That sounds really tough," Rose said. She was enjoying comforting

Sasha, telling her what she wanted to hear. This was something Rose could do that Blue couldn't. Rose wasn't bipolar. She wasn't fun or exciting or whimsical or moody, but she was obedient. She was predictable. She was safe.

"The notes we took," Rose said. "During preproduction—"

"Oh, Blue abandoned those on day one, threw them out the window," Sasha said. "Literally tossed them right out of the window—even tried to set them on fire first." Rose felt disappointed. She had worked so hard to capture and organize those notes in a coherent fashion.

"She always does that," Sasha said. "Her imagination moves at the speed of light. She's the queen of a pivot, of pulling a one-eighty. She says it's a Gemini thing."

"I'm a Gemini," Rose said.

"I think astrology is bullshit," Sasha said. "You seem nothing like Blue."

Rose frowned.

"I don't mean that in a bad way," Sasha said. "Like, you're polite." Sasha turned toward Rose. "And sweet."

Rose smiled.

"And Blue is on Planet Blue," Sasha said. "Like, when we're not working, she's blasting Travis Scott. She wants to go back to making hip-hop–inspired tracks. She wants trap bass lines. And we're in this tiny studio in the forest. I can't be making trap beats. It's completely at odds with the atmosphere. We're in this little cabin in this quaint forest and Blue is blasting trap music twenty-four seven."

Rose knew Blue loved hip-hop, had used hip-hop influences on her first few albums, but Rose had never been much of a hip-hop fan.

"What do *you* want to make?" Rose asked because she figured Sasha wanted to be asked it.

Sasha looked at Rose. Her eyes weren't brown as Rose had initially thought. They were a sort of hazel in the soft glow of the room, chocolate with specks of yellow and green. "I heard via her producer," Sasha said, pointing to the record player, "that our friend Ms. Swift is making a quiet, stripped-down pandemic album. All acoustic folk songs."

Rose nodded, then whispered, "She's not my friend," for unclear reasons, maybe out of reverence for Blue. But Sasha didn't seem to register it.

"I think Blue should do something like that. Everyone is trapped inside for the foreseeable future. Everyone is alone. No one is partying. People need songs they can listen to in their bedrooms. With candles lit." Sasha looked around the living room, candles glowing on most surfaces. "Like this," she said, and laughed.

"Did you tell her this?" Rose said.

"She never listens," Sasha said. "But yes. I said, *Blue, let's make something quieter. Just you singing and me on the guitar. Laurel Canyon–inspired folk songs.*"

"What did she say?"

"She laughed at me," Sasha said. "She wants to make a deep, dark party album. She wants to make music to play at a club at four a.m. I'm trying to tell her that no one is at the club right now, and won't be anytime soon. But Blue is on Planet Blue. She doesn't understand the practical realities of the world."

Rose nodded. She too had been accused of living in her own world, of being oblivious to everything outside it. Mostly by her mother, who said she should have other interests besides Blue Velour. Rose's mother was a math teacher, always encouraging her to wonder about the way things worked. But music was the only thing that captured her interest. Unlike most children, Rose never asked why the sky was blue. She wanted instead to *be* Blue. And that meant having Sasha.

"Maybe you should trust her," Rose said. While Blue hadn't been the nicest to Rose lately, she really did trust her creative impulses. "You all have never made a bad record."

Sasha laughed. "*Fluorescent Gloom?*"

"*Fluorescent Gloom* is my favorite!" Rose said. "I mean, I know that's a controversial opinion, but I think it's sooo beautiful."

"Really?" Sasha said. "I guess I'm probably too influenced by public opinion." She sipped some more wine. "Blue too."

"She doesn't care what people think," Rose said with a wry smile. They both knew that wasn't true.

Sasha laughed. She drained her wineglass. "God, this is good." She poured herself a little more. "I should probably go to bed soon, but . . ."

"You need to unwind," Rose said. She put her hand on Sasha's shoulder, which was tense. Rose gave it a little squeeze.

"That feels good," Sasha said.

Rose positioned herself so that she could get a better grip, and massaged Sasha's shoulders a bit more deeply. The song playing was slower and softer.

"This is nice," Rose said.

"When did you get into Blue?" Sasha asked.

Rose told Sasha the story, about the YouTube algorithm leading her from Amy to Blue.

"That's so millennial," Sasha said. "Wait, please don't tell me you're Gen Z."

"I'm on the cusp," Rose said. "We can say millennial." She wanted to be a millennial because Blue was a millennial.

"Jesus," said Sasha, and Rose didn't entirely know what she meant by that.

She dug her fingers deeper into Sasha's shoulders. She couldn't remember the last time she'd touched someone so intimately. Rose didn't have much in the way of romantic experience. Sloppily making out with Ella one drunken night was the closest she'd come to sexual contact since she'd moved to LA.

"I made my parents let me stay up late to watch Blue on *Conan*," Rose continued.

"God," Sasha said. "*That* performance."

"I loved it," Rose said.

"You did?"

Rose nodded, then realized Sasha couldn't see her. Rose was behind Sasha, kneading her shoulders. "Mhmm," Rose said.

"Are you close with your parents?" Sasha asked.

Sasha's curiosity about her upbringing caused Rose's cheeks to heat. She was glad Sasha couldn't see her.

"No," Rose said. It was an easy answer. She hoped it wasn't the wrong one.

"Homophobes?" Sasha asked. "Mine are."

"Oh, I'm sorry," Rose said. "Mine aren't. They're professors. Liberal. They're just kind of distant." It was true. There was really nothing to complain about when it came to Rose's parents. They had fulfilled all of Rose's basic needs, had given her singing lessons and organic food and allowed her to stay up late to watch her favorite singer on *Conan*. They just weren't the warmest people. They'd never cared much about her interests (music) or her emotional landscape. And once she'd moved out, they hadn't seemed to care about her at all. They acted as though their job was done. And it was, wasn't it?

Sasha sighed, then said, "The apple doesn't fall far."

Rose removed her hands for a second, hurt. She sensed Sasha tensing, silently begging for Rose to continue.

"I'm not distant," Rose said, slowly placing her hands back on Sasha's shoulders, digging her knuckles into tight muscles. "I'm giving you a massage."

"True, this is incredible," Sasha said. "I didn't realize how much I needed this."

"You've been spending all your energy serving Blue," Rose said.

Sasha laughed. "You could say that."

Six months ago, Rose would have died at this statement. She would have absolutely lost it, collapsed onto the floor. The idea of Blue and Sasha together sexually was her most cherished image in the entire world, holy, like paintings of the Madonna and child during the Renaissance. But right now? Right now, it produced in her stomach a strange and unfamiliar sensation she believed the music she loved would identify as jealousy.

Blue

"I think it's ready," Blue said to Sasha, who was testing her patience. She was being a downer. Always trying to rein her in. But Blue was antsy, high on lack of sleep and sour candy and Red Bull and nicotine and not sleeping and did she already say she wasn't sleeping? The album wasn't ready, but the single was. It was the perfect single. Brooding and electric and unlike anything on the last two albums.

Blue had been listening to Travis Scott's *ASTROWORLD* and Future's *DS2* while she wrote late at night, was feeling inspired by the distorted vocals and menacing synths. She wanted to make something in conversation with these records—a dark, twisted, hyper-produced album for turning up at 4 a.m. The lyrics she was writing felt like poetry, as they always did, but these felt deeper, darker, punchier, more to the point. Her lyrics were an open wound put through a synthesizer and projected into cyberspace. She wrote that down next to an Amy Winehouse quote she'd transcribed after watching the documentary for the five billionth time this morning while the sun rose: *I write songs because I'm fucked-up in my head.*

Blue was feeling extremely confident.

"I'm not sure," Sasha said.

"It's ready, bitch," Blue said. She picked Bijou up off the floor. Bijou had been staying with Blue in the studio because she didn't like the girl, because Bijou had impeccable taste. "Let's just send it to Interscope, see what they think."

"Okay," Sasha said. She swiveled around in her editing chair.

The song Blue wanted to release was called "Insomniac." She'd written it while Sasha was asleep, while the world was asleep. Stevie Nicks had reportedly recorded "Gold Dust Woman" at 4 a.m. with a black scarf around her head to veil her senses, which Blue had also done but with a silk chemise. Sasha had done a pretty good job at making the bass line sound like Future's "The Percocet & Stripper Joint." Blue had given up drugs, but she wanted to make the type of music that was a close approximation of the feeling. Being sleep-deprived was also a near match. Being bipolar meant your mind naturally created sensations nearly identical to those of being on both uppers and downers. Blue imagined winning another Grammy, thanking her chemical imbalance. She started laughing.

"What's funny?" Sasha asked. She was becoming so unfun, even more than normal. She'd been going to bed earlier and earlier, while Blue wasn't sleeping at all, so why was she so fucking cranky all the time? Sasha got up from her chair and hobbled over to the couch, where she collapsed.

"I had an amusing thought," Blue said. "You should try it sometime."

"Okay, we can send it to them," Sasha said. "But if they have notes, we need to listen."

"Yeah, yeah," Blue said. She grazed a finger along Bijou's spine. "Send it to them tomorrow morning. Promise?" Blue put her head in Sasha's lap.

"Sure," Sasha said. "I think it's strong."

Blue smiled. "Finally, some positivity from the local grump."

"I'm tired," Sasha said.

"Well, you're sleeping more than I am," Blue said.

"I don't know," Sasha said. "You're waking up at like four or five p.m. I wake up at seven a.m."

"Well, maybe you should try sleeping in," Blue said. "And what are you doing all that time when I'm sleeping? You should be working."

"But you're asleep in the studio," Sasha said. "All my editing tools are in here." She was being so difficult.

"You could have thought of that before you made the studio," Blue said. "You know I can't leave."

"I don't totally understand why," Sasha said.

Blue sat up on the couch, squinted out the window. It was dark. She heard an owl in the distance.

"What are you doing all those hours I'm asleep and you're awake?" Blue asked.

Sasha was silent for a second. "Gardening," she said.

"With the girl?"

"With Rose? Sometimes," Sasha said. "When she isn't out buying things for you."

"Okay, you're boring me," Blue said. "You'll send them 'Insomniac' in the morning?"

Sasha nodded, rubbed her eyes. Blue walked over to the mini fridge and cracked open another Red Bull. She offered Sasha the first sip.

"It's almost midnight," Sasha said. "I won't be able to sleep."

"You should really try to get on my schedule," Blue said.

"Wait until you're in your forties," Sasha said. "Not too long for you." She grinned.

"You're boring me to tears," Blue said. "Can we talk about the album title?"

Sasha nodded. "But not for too much longer," she said. "I'm out of here by one."

"I know," Blue said. "Baby needs her bedtime."

Using her foot, Blue slid her Moleskine notebook out from under the couch. She flipped through it to find the album title pages. She had pages and pages of ideas. She began reading the ones she'd underlined earlier in the morning.

"*Silver Foxes, Nocturne, Always Smoke in Bed, Mania, Love in the Time of Lithium, Lavender Mist, Silk Dreams, Velour Noose, Blue Lace, Moonlit Vapor, Screaming at the Moon* . . ." Blue looked up at Sasha, whose eyes were closed. Blue slapped her shoulder. "Are you even listening?"

Sasha opened her eyes and nodded. "I like *Nocturne*," she said. "And *Love in the Time of Lithium*."

Blue nodded. "I like those too."

"We have time," Sasha said.

"What time is it?" Blue asked. She gulped some more of her drink. Sasha looked at her watch. "Twelve seventeen," she said.

"No, I mean the date," Blue said. "Like what day, what month?"

Sasha laughed. "It's May sixteenth."

"Is the world still shut down?" Blue asked. Sasha opened her mouth, and Blue jumped in. "Actually, never mind. I don't want to know."

"Okay," Sasha said.

"When should we aim to be done with the album?" Blue asked. "You know Kurt Cobain recorded *Bleach*—"

"—in thirty hours," Sasha finished. "You've told me like seven billion times."

Blue grinned. "Go to bed," she said. "You're killing my vibe."

"If you insist," Sasha said, and sat up.

Once Sasha was gone, Blue went over to the computer and looked at porn. Her search terms were always the same: *hairy, motorcycle, daddy*. She came quickly, then again. This was part of her process. After masturbating, Blue let Bijou up on her lap, who heard a sound outside that caused her to start barking. The barking triggered a memory. She opened her Instagram on the computer, which she hadn't done since she'd taken up residence in the studio. She had thousands of notifications, as she always did. Blue didn't care about any of them. She was looking for something very specific. When Bijou barked, Blue thought of the girl, then remembered her call with Max, how Max said her camp friend said Rose had lied about how they'd met. Blue had messaged her after that to get to the bottom of it. What was her name? Blue searched her messages, but finding a message among thousands from a girl whose name she didn't remember was a near-impossible task, a needle in a haystack. Blue opened her email and sent a message to Max.

Hi sissy,

I miss you dearly. Sorry if you've tried to reach me, I buried my phone in a shoebox in the yard. How is your man? I'm so jealous you're getting dicked down. I'm stuck here on estrogen island. It's a nightmare. But I think I'm making a fucking brilliant record. You're going to die when you hear it. I can't wait to tour again. For things to be normal. To fuck and be fucked. ANYWAY. What's your camp friend's name? The one who Rose allegedly met on a cruise ship but it was a lie? And then she ghosted? Curiosity killed the cat, but here I am. Curious! I have a bad feeling about the girl. As we know, Bijou agrees.

Kisses!
Blue

Rose

Rose ached all day waiting for Sasha to return. She still cherished their mornings, their gardening and jazz, but their nights were holy. Rose had never been confident in her powers of seduction, but she felt she was getting very close to something. She'd just taken another allergy pill and was a quarter of the way through a bottle of wine and was throwing a tennis ball for Gigi, who didn't seem particularly interested in the ball, but it was something to do. Rose nearly hit Sasha with the ball when she walked in.

"Sorry," Rose laughed. "I was playing fetch with Gigi."

"I haven't seen Gigi run in like a decade," Sasha said.

Rose picked up the dog and put her in her lap.

"How's it going?" Rose said.

Sasha sighed as she typically did when Rose asked about her day. She couldn't believe it had been over a month since Blue had left the studio. Although in the middle of a recent night, Rose had heard what she thought was an animal and looked out the window to see Blue in a nightgown, howling at the moon. Then Blue had started running into the forest. Rose was worried for her but also glad she seemed to be getting some exercise and fresh air.

"I don't know," Sasha said. "I'm worried."

Rose handed her a glass of wine.

"Blue made me promise to send a single to the label tomorrow," Sasha said.

"Is it good?"

"I think so?" Sasha said. "I don't know. I'm so tired."

"You should get some sleep," Rose said, even though that was the last thing she wanted, that is unless Sasha wanted her to accompany her. During the day, Rose would go into Sasha's room while Sasha was with Blue and sniff her pillows. They smelled like leather, pine needles, and heaven.

"Is that my sweater?" Sasha asked.

Rose looked down and jumped, embarrassed. Doing the laundry was one of her tasks. Maybe she could say she'd gotten mixed up, instead of the truth, which was that she'd put it on earlier while snooping in Sasha's room and had forgotten to take it off. It was gray and cashmere and felt like a cloud. It was dry-clean only, though, so Rose had no reason to be touching it. She certainly had no excuse to be wearing it.

"It looks good on you," Sasha said, and Rose exhaled relief. "Anyway, I'm just a nervous wreck. Per usual." Sasha took off her shoes and put her legs on Rose's lap. Rose instinctively rubbed her feet. Sasha moaned.

"Can you sing for me?" Sasha said.

Rose's cheeks felt hot. She hadn't sung for Sasha in weeks. But she'd been thinking about it, hoping Sasha would ask.

"Not Blue Velour," Sasha said. "Anything but Blue Velour."

Rose had been prepared for this. She knew Sasha liked Britney Spears and Dolly Parton, so she'd been practicing songs by each while she folded laundry and walked Gigi. Rose reached into her gut and decided on Britney. She'd been practicing one of her slower songs from *Circus*, "Out from Under," which Rose had sung to try out for middle school choir. She still thought it worked well a cappella.

She stood up and started singing for Sasha, who closed her eyes. Rose worried she was putting her to sleep. But then Sasha made a noise of approval, a soft moan. Rose smiled. Singing felt good. Rose felt confident and relaxed. Her voice reverberated in the space. The song was moving and sad, like most songs Rose felt connected to. It was about becoming free from a suffocating relationship, something Rose knew nothing about. She'd never been in a relationship. When Rose hit the final note, Sasha stood up and started clapping.

"That was incredible," said Sasha. "Girl, you got pipes." She was still clapping. "I'm sleep-deprived, yes, but I swear I almost cried."

Rose felt like she could die right there.

Blue

It was 5:45 a.m. and Blue was still staring at the computer.
Interscope liked the single and had given the okay to release it. Sasha had uploaded it at midnight. The two of them had sat at the computer and watched the initial replies roll in on social media. Mostly good, fire emojis and the like, but the type of people who waited up for Blue's releases were primed to like them. Sasha had disappeared at one, her annoying bedtime. Blue had been sitting here refreshing Twitter since. She was searching *Insomniac* and *Blue Velour* in the Google search bar every five minutes. She popped another Warhead. She wanted to sit here until at least 6 a.m., meaning 9 a.m. East Coast time, when the publications would upload their reviews.

In between Google searches, Blue checked her email. She had a new one from Max.

My sweet Blue,

I miss you too. Malibu is not the same without you. I've quit cigs AND vaping—can you believe it? Love changes you!

So my camp friend's name is Grace. She finally responded to my message. And told me she met Rose not on a cruise, but—wait for it—in the BlueBeards freaking subreddit! She was embarrassed to admit she was in there, but she said she "occasionally enjoyed perusing the delusion of others," which felt like a lie but as I said, I don't really remember the girl! I probably played capture the flag with her one time and followed her back on Instagram to be polite, and she's exaggerating our connection to give herself clout among your little weirdo fans? But the bigger point is: your assistant is a BlueBeard!!! Is this amazing or horrible or both? I guess it all depends on your mood at the time this news hits you.

Call me as soon as you finish the album and dig up your phone! I miss your voice so much I've been listening to your music to fall asleep. Oleander. *You know it's my fave!*

Infinite x's and o's,
Maxie

Before Blue could react, she heard what she at first thought were gunshots, but it turned out to be Sasha knocking on the door. Pounding. She charged in with a bottle of Martinelli's apple cider.

"Best New Music, baby!" Sasha shouted. Blue pinched herself to make sure she wasn't dreaming.

"I'm awake, right?" Blue said.

"You're awake," Sasha said, shaking Blue's shoulders. She leaned over Blue to reach the mouse, to open *Pitchfork*. There it was. The two red triangles sandwiching a red arrow that indicated music the editorial team had decided was the very best. Sasha started reading.

> There's a confrontational stillness to "Insomniac," Blue Velour's unsettling new single and spectral elegy to mid-2010s trap. Her signature contralto drifts through glitching melodies and fractured

synths, flickering like a distant signal. Longtime collaborator Sasha Harlow laces the production with an eerie precision. Percussion cuts like a warning. Bass lines lurch and recede. Velour floats just beyond reach, hypnotic in her detachment. The track moves with the logic of a hallucination—heavy-lidded yet hyperaware, caught between lucidity and delirium. "Insomniac" lingers in the suspended hours of lockdown, channeling the restless inertia of a world untethered from time, where night never ends and sleep never comes.

Blue slapped herself across the face. "It's sooooo pretentious and sooooo correct!" she said.

"They got exactly what we were doing," Sasha said, squeezing Blue's shoulders.

"We have to celebrate!" Blue said. "Do we have any more mushrooms?"

Sasha nodded. "I'll go get them."

"No, wait," Blue said. "Fuck it. I'll break my self-imposed exile," she said. "For today."

"Hell yes," Sasha said.

"I need to take a bath," Blue said. "And sleep in my bed." Blue also needed to gather more underwear.

"Yes, you do."

"But first," Blue said, "mushrooms."

Exiting the studio, Blue remembered the email she'd read just before Sasha started banging on the door, the one from Max, about Rose being a member of that creepo subreddit that spent all day dissecting dorky little comic book clues about her sexuality. At this moment, Blue found it hard to care. She and Sasha mocked *Pitchfork* all the time, with their self-serious Midwestern posture, but at the end of the day, all the other music publications followed *Pitchfork*'s lead. A *Pitchfork* review would influence everyone else's perception. And a Best New Music review on her first single from the record was a good sign. It was an excellent sign. And Blue already knew Rose was a creepy fan. She hardly seemed to know any music that wasn't Blue's. But being obsessed with Blue Velour was not a crime.

r/BlueBeards • posted by u/PinkCocaine • May 2020

INSOMNIAC!!!!!!

Holy shit it's 4 a.m. and "Insomniac" just slapped me the fuck awake! Okay, fine, I was already wide awake thanks to some pink you-know-what . . . but if I wasn't already high as a kite, this track would have gotten me there au naturel. Blue's spooky vocals + Sasha's 808s = my brain on absolute fire. I have to go smoke an entire vape cartridge (named desire) to calm down.

    Okay, on my fifth listen and it's like they made this track just for me?? It's a song for the twisted head cases whose minds will never shut the fuck up and let us catch a break. It's for that moment when your exhaustion flips into euphoria and you're just like FUCK IT, who needs sleep?!?! Some of us have brains that are simply too powerful for REM, baby!

    Planning to blast this hypnotic perfection until my speakers blow out, no joke.

    SLEEP, WHO IS SHE???

Rose

Rose was folding the laundry in the living room and wondering where Sasha had gone when Blue burst through the front door for the first time in nearly a month and a half. Her hair was wild and she had a crazed look in her eyes. Rose braced herself. She'd listened to the single at midnight along with all the other fans, then again with Sasha when she returned from the studio. Rose loved the song, more than she'd been expecting, given the influences Sasha had cited. This morning, she'd seen it had gotten Best New Music, but the look in Blue's eyes scared Rose. She braced herself to be screamed at. Instead, Blue ran over to Rose, picked her up, and spun her in a circle.

"Best New Music—did you hear?"

"I did!" Rose said. "Congratulations—I love the song!"

"You do!" Blue said, finally putting Rose down. "What do you love about it?" She grabbed Rose's forearms with intensity. Rose bruised easily and imagined Blue's nails leaving marks.

"It really enacts its thesis," Rose said, repeating something she'd read this morning. "It feels like buzzing with energy while everyone else is asleep." Rose grinned. "In a fun way." Really, she was thinking of her late nights with Sasha. They'd been staying up later and later, until 3 or 4 a.m., talking and singing and playing records. A few times, they'd fallen asleep together on the couch, woken up entwined.

"So you read *The Guardian*?" Blue said, and winked. Rose braced herself to be scolded for plagiarism, but Blue didn't seem angry at all. She was euphoric. This was Nice Blue. "We're doing mushrooms."

Sasha walked in, and Rose's stomach fluttered. She was on the phone. "Blue." She handed the phone to Blue, who cooed an ecstatic greeting. Sasha rubbed Blue's shoulders while she talked to someone who seemed to be wishing her congratulations, maybe someone from the label. Rose hadn't seen Blue and Sasha interact in nearly two months, and the sight of it was difficult to bear. Their bodies had an easy familiarity with each other, an undeniable chemistry that had once excited Rose and now horrified her. Rose suddenly felt invisible. She went back to folding the laundry while Blue giggled on the phone and Sasha hung on her like a little puppy. Rose remembered she needed to feed Gigi, which she went and did.

Blue and Sasha were on the phone for hours while Rose did more chores—cleaning surfaces, watering plants, taking Gigi out to go to the bathroom. They kept touching and spoke in a way that made Rose want to jump off the roof. She wished she could go somewhere. Maybe she'd take the Benz for a drive. But she'd still be alone. She wanted attention. Rose supposed she could text Ella, but Ella typically seemed to dislike Rose unless she was on cocaine, and it was only 11 a.m. Maybe Ella was doing cocaine at 11 a.m. now. Rose opened her phone and fired off a text.

Did you hear the new Blue? she wrote.

OBVI, Ella wrote back, followed by twelve fire emojis.

How are you? Rose asked.

#Sliving! Ella replied. *I was literally born to work from home. I got a dog. Her name is Blue. I gave her your room. No offense, but she's a much better roommate than you. More fun!*

Rose frowned. She wished Ella missed her, wished Ella would ask

Rose how she was doing. But she knew Ella wouldn't. In the other room, she heard Blue squeal something about Travis Scott wanting to drop a verse on "Insomniac." Rose went up to her tiny bedroom in the attic. She wondered if they'd even notice she was gone. Up there, she took one of her allergy pills that caused drowsiness. She put on "Insomniac." And, perhaps ironically, she fell into a very deep sleep.

When she woke up, it was dark. She heard Blue and Sasha giggling downstairs. She took another pill and went back to sleep.

Blue

Sasha was being a downer again. She kept talking about these protests. Black Lives Matter. These victims of police brutality. A bunch of names Blue couldn't remember. She said they should change the direction of the record, that now was not the time to release an album ripping musical styles invented by Black people. Blue said it was an homage. They weren't ripping. They were elevating. Sasha said that rhetoric was problematic. Everything Blue said and did was suddenly problematic.

"I think it's ready," Blue said this afternoon for the fourteenth time.

"I promise you," Sasha said for the fourteenth time. "Not now."

"You were nervous to release 'Insomniac' and look how well that did," Blue said.

"That was a different time," said Sasha.

"It was like a week ago!" Blue said. Her voice surprised Bijou, who jerked awake.

"A lot has happened since then."

"I told you to stop reading the news," Blue said.

"We're living in unprecedented times," Sasha said. "It would be irresponsible to not keep up."

"Travis is on the track," Blue said. "A young Black American man. Doesn't that mean anything?"

"We still haven't gotten confirmation from Travis," Sasha said. "I'm not sure he's still interested given everything that's going on."

"Travis doesn't read the news!" Blue screamed. "He's probably just busy." She picked up her pack of American Spirit Blues. Vaping wouldn't cut it right now; she needed the real deal. "I can't with you," she said, and left the studio.

Outside, the air was warm and fragrant. Purple irises had bloomed all around the house. She wasn't sure if they'd grown organically or if Sasha had planted them. Blue was over Sasha. She was too fucking nervous, too cautious. Blue had gotten this far by being bold, brave, fearless. She inhaled and felt her skin tingle. She had an idea. The last time she'd spoken to a rep from Interscope, they'd said that with the success of *Blue's Beard*, the "A Vape Cartridge Named Desire" video, and "Insomniac," they'd support whatever she wanted to put out next. Blue didn't need Sasha to okay the album's release. Sasha had done what she needed to do; she'd made the tracks prettier than Blue could on her own using fancy computers.

Blue had her title: *Mood Onyx*. She'd been working on the cover art while Sasha was asleep. Blue designed all her album covers. For this one, she'd used a still from the "A Vape Cartridge Named Desire" video, an image of herself spinning on the deck under the moonlight, her figure a light blue blur. She had her track list, which she mentally finalized one last time.

1. Screaming at the Moon
2. Raven
3. Insomniac
4. Love in the Time of Lithium
5. Always Smoke in Bed

6. Manic Everyday
7. Lavender Noose
8. Mood Onyx
9. Silver Foxes
10. Silk Mist
11. Nocturne

Blue put out her cigarette in the damp soil.
It was time.
Besides, it was Gemini season.

r/BlueBeards • posted by u/PinkCocaine • June 2020

SURPRISE BLUE DROP OMG

HOLY SHIT MOOD ONYX. I was literally blasting "Insomniac" as I've been doing when I can't sleep (i.e., every night) and refreshed Twitter and saw Blue Velour was trending and omg I am now listening to Mood Onyx for the second time and losing every bit of chill I never had!! It's like Blue ripped these tracks straight from my DARK TWISTED FANTASIES?!?!?

OK "LAVENDER NOOSE." I know idiots are going to say she's glamorizing suicide but it obviously has nothing to do with that and everything to do with autoerotic asphyxiation. "Tightening grips, I'll be the gasper." When I first heard it I literally had to slap myself across the face to stop hyperventilating. And then I had to SMOKE IN BED. I hadn't smoked a cigarette in YEARS but I found a half-crushed Camel Blue in the bottom of a Marc Jacobs bag I didn't even know I had and just smoked it while staring at the moon that I'm PRETTY SURE is FULL because BLUE is genius enough to release this album on a FULL MOON. And now my room smells like cigs and I don't give a SHIT because I'm too high off this surprise drop. I will most definitely be calling in sick to work tomorrow because becoming an expert in this album is now my job.

OH AND "SILVER FOXES." Morons will say it's about Blue's performative taste for older men. Or literal silver foxes in the forest. But it's obviously about Blue and Sasha growing old together in the woods. "Brows furrowed, sweet woods pining." Remember that *Rolling Stone* interview from 2013 when Blue said Sasha smells like "a sweet forest"??? That lyric is 1000% about Sasha.

I know it's only existed for 1.5 hours, but Mood Onyx is my absolute favorite Blue Velour album. It has it all—lovesickness, madness, ecstasy. It's the album for when you're TOO WIRED FOR SLEEP but TOO IN LOVE WITH THE DARKNESS to do a damn thing about it.

YOU CRAZY FOR THIS ONE, BLUE!

Rose

Rose awoke to the sound of Sasha yelling for the second day in a row.

Yesterday, Rose had grabbed her phone to see a series of texts from Ella, starting with: *OH SHIT SURPRISE BLUE DROP.* Then, *you probably knew!!!* Actually, Rose hadn't known. The previous night, Sasha had been extra stressed. She said she knew when Blue was about to do something reckless and stupid, and she had that feeling, she just didn't know what it would be yet. She'd made them sleep with the car keys under the couch pillow. But as it turned out, Blue was not going to drive anywhere. She had simply released an entire album in the middle of the night without telling anyone.

And Rose had been able to tell from the sound of Sasha yelling downstairs the next morning that she was not happy about it. By the time Rose splashed water on her face and walked down to the first floor, Sasha was gone, likely in the studio from which Rose was strictly forbidden. So Rose had taken to her phone, trying to figure out what the hell was going on. Ella was actually the most helpful, as she spent most of her waking hours scrolling social media and was able to sum up the zeitgeist's opinions on any pop culture topic fairly quickly (albeit chaotically). Rose had pretended that she'd known about the drop to save face and asked Ella about the general temperature.

OK SO: the people who get it, LOVE IT
It's freaking sick yo!!!
But the idiots be whining as they always are
Spitting nonsense about how it's "tone-deaf" or some shit
I literally don't get why
No real reviews yet as you prob know
A few blog posts—mixed
I REALLY think it's one of her BEST
But no one is thinking straight right now
Well, I'm never thinking straight ;)
But I know good music when I hear it, ya dig?!
And this. is. BRILLIANT!!!!!

Weirdly, Rose couldn't bring herself to actually listen to the album. It was the first Blue Velour drop of her entire life about which she lacked excitement or curiosity. Maybe she was scared to listen, anxious that it was bad and that Blue had embarrassed herself. But really, deeper down, Rose knew she was not listening because she was jealous—of this special thing Blue and Sasha had created from which Rose had been barred access, that they'd made during the same time that Sasha and Rose had been spending their precious late nights and mornings together, during which Rose knew but had not yet admitted to herself that she'd been falling very deeply in love. Listening to *Mood Onyx* would be like watching a sex tape of your partner fucking someone else. The idea of it made Rose sick to her stomach.

Sasha and Blue had been in the studio most of the day yesterday—Sasha didn't even come back for lunch. Rose had seen her pacing on the phone outside the studio a few times, presumably reassuring executives and managers that everything was going to be okay, even though the strained look on her face told a different story. A profound loneliness had settled over Rose, reminding her once again that she was on the outs with regard to the very important work Sasha and Blue made together. That she was quite literally the help.

When she'd finished the laundry and cleaning, Rose had played Dolly Parton and sprawled on the couch messaging Ella. *HOLY SHIT BLUE'S IG*, Ella had texted in the afternoon. Rose had opened Instagram to see a still from the "Vape Cartridge Named Desire" video that Rose had filmed . . . a month ago? Weeks? What was time? However long it had been, so much had changed so quickly. Back then, Rose had been thrilled to be included, to film the titillating imagery of Blue and Sasha that had fueled the last decade of her life. But now, seeing this image on Blue's Instagram of what Rose knew to be Sasha's hand grazing the nape of Blue Velour's neck, she'd felt vomit rise up into her throat. Rose had shut off her phone and taken another one of her drowsy allergy pills, tried to sleep the day away.

And this morning, Rose felt déjà vu—hearing Sasha yell, then the back door slam. Sasha was gone again, to the special world she'd created with Blue, the one from which Rose would forever be excluded. Rose hadn't seen Sasha in nearly thirty-six hours, and she was starting to feel like she'd imagined her, that she was just in this cabin in the woods alone and there was no back house where her former favorite musician and the newfound love of her life were making music and probably doing other things that Rose couldn't bring herself to think about.

Rose hadn't checked any Blue Velour news since yesterday afternoon, when there had been no major reviews. But Sasha's aggressive exit from the house made Rose think things online were not looking good. She grabbed her phone. Ella had sent a bunch of texts since Rose had last checked. Kylie Jenner had apparently posted the album cover on her Instagram story accompanied by several fire emojis. Julia Fox had played "Love in the Time of Lithium" on her TikTok. Ryan Murphy tweeted that he wanted to make a TV show about "Silver Foxes." The BlueBeards were apparently "not getting it." The last text was a link to a *Pitchfork* review, followed by the word: *jackasses*.

MOOD ONYX

3.8

<u>Blue Velour</u> • 2020

Blue Velour has never been interested in playing nice. Her debut album *Spirit of Sinatra* introduced her as a lounge singer with a nihilist streak, a woman unafraid to air her ugliest thoughts. Tracks like "Pink Cocaine" and "Happy Birthday I'm Dead" felt engineered for shock value. And in calling the album's inspiration "Nancy Sinatra lost in the hood," she came out as either a master provocateur or an unrepentant troll.

For over a decade, she's straddled that line, feeding her own mythology while generating both adoration and disdain. Her breakout came not from an organic rise but through relentless reinvention. *Oleander* positioned her as a poetic chronicler of self-destruction, *Chateau Velour* made her a Tumblr icon, and *Fluorescent Gloom* was so bleak it nearly ended her career. After featuring a man choking her on the album cover and a single called "Neon Bruise," Velour dismissed feminist critique, telling *Jezebel* that she was more interested in aliens. Then she wore a burka to the Teen Choice Awards, where she encouraged the youth to smoke cigarettes. She's been romantically linked to both a megachurch pastor and a parole officer, she called Roman Polanski "misunderstood," and she told a class of UCLA students, "Real bitches get DUIs." For those who find these actions unforgivable, wishing Blue would fade into the obscurity from which she emerged, there is perhaps no better argument for Velour's cancellation than *Mood Onyx*—an epic misfire amid the tumultuous backdrop of mounting racial unrest and a global health crisis.

Released without warning in the dead of night, her seventh studio album arrives with no clear marketing strategy, the work of an artist fully off the rails. The album's title—a clumsy nod to Nina Simone's "Mood Indigo"—is the first red flag. In a year defined by racial reckoning, Velour's adoption of a "black mood" is glaringly obtuse. "Always Smoke in Bed," a reimagining of "Don't

Smoke in Bed" from *Little Girl Blue*, is yet another ill-conceived invocation of Simone's legacy. Given Covid-19's severe impact on respiratory function, Velour's choice to glamorize smoking feels particularly callous. The artist has always flirted with mortality, famously telling a journalist in 2013 that he made her want to "pull a Sylvia Plath." But this obsession with her own extinction now reads as an affront to the countless lives lost amid a global pandemic and escalating police brutality. Maybe Blue wishes she were dead, but most of us are fighting to stay alive.

Mood Onyx unfolds like a myopic attempt to flatten a century of Black music into a single cheap aesthetic. Sasha Harlow's production is swamped in blown-out 808s and gothic synths. A smog of reverb hangs over everything, blurring the impact of even its sharpest moments. "Insomniac," recently praised by this very publication for its spectral nod to mid-2010s rap, now feels embarrassingly out of place—particularly with the conspicuous absence of Travis Scott, whose rumored involvement might have imbued the track with a shred of authenticity.

The lone bright spot is "Lavender Noose," a stark acoustic ballad that strips away the album's suffocating excess. It is a rare moment of clarity, one that recalls the raw vulnerability of *Blue's Beard* and the gut-punch lyricism that made *Garbo Gals* a cult favorite. It suggests that she is still capable of making music that matters, though *Mood Onyx* provides little evidence that she is interested in doing so.

Overall, the album feels like a regression, a retreat into the reckless stunts that defined Velour's early career. She has always been an artist in tension—with her audience, with herself—but here, that tension collapses into hollow ignorance. While once hailed as a worthy heir to Dolly Parton, Amy Winehouse, and Stevie Nicks, on *Mood Onyx*, she only sounds lost.

Rose

Rose realized she'd been holding her breath. She exhaled, then took a deep breath in. She heard noise across the yard. The studio. Yelling, banging. She wondered what she should do, if she should try to hide or escape with the Benz. Rose had seen Blue rage before, but this would likely be far worse. She decided to go up to her little attic bedroom. She crept up the two flights of stairs. There, she took a drowsy allergy pill and tried to fall asleep. It worked until she woke up to Blue over her bed, pulling off her covers.

"Everything has gone to SHIT since you've been here," Blue was screaming. Mascara ran down her face in near-cartoonish streaks. "I should have listened to Bijou, who HATES YOU. Because you're BAD NEWS! You're a creepy FAN who LIED to Max about how you know WHATEVER THAT GIRL'S NAME IS!!"

Rose's heart was racing. Was this a nightmare?

"You didn't meet her on a CRUISE!" Blue shouted. "You met her ONLINE. In the SPOOKY SUBREDDIT that is obsessed with my SEXUALITY! You FREAK!"

At this point, Blue started to lunge at Rose, who covered her face with her hands and prayed it was a dream. Rose heard footsteps charging up the stairs. Before Blue could get to Rose, Sasha was holding Blue back. Blue was trying to break free. Rose just huddled in the bed with her hands over her head.

"PUSSY!" Blue shouted. "Won't even fight me!"

Once Blue registered who was holding her back, she redirected her focus to Sasha. "Stop me, whatever, I don't even care about this loser girl!" Blue screamed. "It's YOU I'm really mad at. Fucking HAS-BEEN. Working with LOSERS. Sellout dyke FREAK. Also, I spied on you FLIRTING with HER!" Blue eyed Rose and nearly spat. "LISTENING TO TAYLOR FUCKING SWIFT!"

Blue started laughing uncontrollably, like a hyena. She folded over and heaved. Sasha looked at Rose with fear in her eyes.

"You know what?" Blue said when she stopped laughing and caught her breath. "Fuck both of you. You're both fired. And I'm out of here. I'll be gone by this afternoon. You two can clean up the mess."

Blue disappeared down the stairs. Sasha stood rigid, seemingly waiting for Blue to change her mind and return. From downstairs, Nirvana came on.

"She just needs to cool down," Sasha said.

"Do you think I'm safe?" Rose asked.

Sasha nodded. "Just stay up here for a little bit."

"No problem," Rose said. Sasha laughed. Rose wanted Sasha to stay, to comfort her, but she disappeared down the stairs as quickly as she'd appeared.

Rose was left alone with the sounds of *Nevermind* coming up through the floorboards. She took another allergy pill and willed herself to sleep.

Blue

Blue smoked an American Spirit out the window while driving toward town.

She'd put all her belongings in trash bags and thrown them into the Benz. She'd also taken Bijou, but not Gigi, who probably wouldn't be able to handle Blue's life on the road. She'd dug up her phone and was waiting for it to get enough juice to turn on and direct her to a proper biker bar. A semi-violent fuck was the only potential antidote to Blue's rage. After that, she would come up with a plan.

As soon as her phone lit up, Blue pulled over and googled *biker bar near me*. All the bars that came up in Guerneville looked bougie and/or hipster, i.e., likely to contain people who recognized her and thought she was evil and/or problematic like *Pitchfork* did. A seedy-looking dive bar in Santa Rosa called Wagon Wheel came up. It had a pool table and the patrons in the photos looked old and unlikely to know who she was.

Blue put on big sunglasses and a baseball hat and drove ninety miles per hour toward Santa Rosa. The sun illuminated sprawling vineyards. Blue smoked cig after cig and blasted Nirvana. She arrived at the bar in under twenty minutes, even though her GPS said it would take thirty.

After parking, she approached the business and saw a sign that said CLOSED INDEFINITELY. This fucking pandemic.

Blue looked around to see if there was anything else nearby. The area was kind of desolate. Office parks and dilapidated homes. She searched her phone for somewhere else. There was another dingy-looking bar roughly fifteen minutes away called the Zoo. She called the number listed, which sent her to a voicemail that said they were also closed indefinitely. Blue slammed her phone on the wheel. Everything was fucking closed.

"Hey, Siri," Blue said. "Where do I party during a global pandemic?" She'd never spoken to Siri before but she'd seen Sasha do it, and currently she was desperate.

Siri spoke. "Partying during a global pandemic requires a careful approach to ensure safety and compliance with health protocols. Some tips include: following local guidelines, sticking to small outdoor gatherings, maintaining a safe distance from others, wearing a mask to cover your mouth and nose, washing your hands frequently, and considering virtual gatherings—"

"Shut the fuck up!" Blue shouted. She didn't want to know how to party safely. She certainly didn't want to party on a computer. She wanted to go somewhere where there were no safety guidelines. She needed to be around other people, to feel the energy of their bodies. Maybe she should phrase the question differently.

"Where in America are they not following the safety guidelines?" she asked. "So I can know where to avoid."

"Parts of Florida, Texas, and Georgia have begun lifting restrictions and opening bars in limited capacity as of June 2020."

Fuck. None of those states were anywhere near her.

"Are there any states near California that have begun lifting restrictions?"

"Nevada is in the process of lifting restrictions and is moving through its phased reopening plan."

"How far is Nevada from Santa Rosa, California, by car?"

"The distance between Santa Rosa, California, and Reno, Nevada,

American Spirits

is approximately two hundred miles, taking approximately three point five to four hours by car via I-80 east, depending on traffic and starting points," Siri said.

Blue smiled. Three and a half hours was nothing. And with her driving, it would be more like two and a half, maybe even two. She could be there by night. The world might hate her and find her stupid, but the America that read *Pitchfork* was a tiny bubble. There was a whole country outside of that. An America that had no fucking idea who Blue Velour even was.

Blue listened to four albums and smoked six cigarettes on the drive to Reno. With the first cigarette, she wound through rows of vineyards stretching across lush hills lit up gold. She listened to PJ Harvey's *Dry*.

On cigarette two, she merged onto I-80 east, transitioning from pastoral scenery to flat concrete. The freeway moved through expansive fields and the occasional cluster of oak trees as the sun lowered in the sky. She listened to Nirvana's *Bleach*. Just before Sacramento, Blue stopped at an In-N-Out and got a cheeseburger. She ate it while traffic slowed and the sky exploded with pink and purple. Advancing toward the Sierra Nevadas, she smoked cigarette three as the flat landscape gave way to towering peaks and dense forests. The light began to fade, casting the mountains in silhouettes against a navy sky. When Blue put her hand out the window, the air was ice-cold. She put on *Daydream Nation* by Sonic Youth as dusk deepened.

Blue lit cigarette four and ascended through mountain passes. Patches of snow still lingered on distant peaks, remnants of winter. As she lit cigarette five, the forests around her became denser, with tall pines and firs lining the freeway. Soon the road was empty and everything was dark. She put on her high beams and the Doors' *Strange Days*. When "You're Lost Little Girl" came on, Blue started to cry.

On cigarette six, she stopped crying as Reno's lights emerged like a constellation against the night. Soon she was among the casinos and neon signs. Finally. Blue was out of liberal hipster California and here in real America. She saw several hookers on the side of the road. Bars everywhere. People drinking on the street. No one in a mask. There was no pandemic here. She saw a neon sign that said SHOOTERS: FREE BEER, TOPLESS BARTENDERS & FALSE ADVERTISING. She parked and went inside.

Rose

Sasha was convinced that Blue was coming back, but Rose hoped she was wrong, and on day three, Rose was becoming confident that Sasha was wrong, that Blue was gone for good, and it would just be her and Sasha, indefinitely, forever.

"Has she fired you before?" Rose asked while Sasha was making dinner and Rose was drinking a glass of wine.

Sasha nodded. She turned to Rose. She was wearing a black cashmere sweater over faded black Levi's and gray cashmere socks. Rose wanted so desperately to curl up beside her on a couch, her whole body ached.

"How many albums have we made together?" Sasha flipped her black hair from one side to the other.

"Six," Rose said. "Seven if you count—"

"Don't even say the words," Sasha said. For the first day Blue was gone, Sasha was in a state of deep, near-catatonic depression. She curled up in bed and hardly moved. When Rose tried to come in and bring her food, Sasha snapped at her to leave. Her career was over, she kept saying. Her life was over.

On day two, Sasha left the bed but was mopey. She was still saying her career was over, but Rose assured her it wasn't. Sasha had worked with some of the biggest names in the business. And Blue had released this album without Sasha's consent. And also, fans were actually loving the album whose name she was not allowed to say. Ella thought it was one of Blue's best and that once all the "coastal elite libtards get their heads out of their asses, they'll say that too." Rose repeated this exact phrasing to Sasha, who laughed for the first time in days, which elicited in Rose a greater feeling of accomplishment than when she'd gotten into Carnegie Mellon's über-competitive music program.

On day three, this day, Sasha was seeming a little more herself.

"So she's fired you before," Rose said. "She'll hire you again."

Sasha shook her head. "It feels different this time," she said. She put whole wheat pasta in the water and joined Rose in the breakfast nook. Rose had lit one of Blue's expensive candles, which illuminated the curves of Sasha's face as she poured herself some wine. "I don't think she's coming back."

Rose's belly swirled with delight. She didn't want Blue to come back. She wanted to stay here, with Sasha, singing and listening to music and falling asleep together on the couch and never seeing another person for the rest of their lives.

"She left Gigi," Rose said. The dog was currently sleeping on the floor beside Rose.

"She doesn't care about Gigi," Sasha said. "I'm telling you: she's not coming back." Sasha paused. "I guess we should start packing up after dinner."

Rose's heart dropped into her tailbone. "Packing up?"

"If Blue isn't coming back," Sasha said, "I should get back to my life. Besides, we made the album." Sasha let out a sound somewhere between a sigh and a groan.

"It's a six-month lease," Rose said. "We may as well stay here. The world is closed. It's so pleasant here."

"Aren't you, like, deathly allergic to nature?" Sasha asked.

"Not deathly," Rose said. "Just mildly. And I'm really starting to enjoy the side effects of my allergy pills." She grinned.

Sasha laughed, then stopped. "So, what, you just want to stay here and do nothing for another three months?"

"Not nothing," Rose said. She wanted to say a lot of other things but she suddenly felt afraid. She refilled her wineglass and took a big sip for courage.

"Then what?"

Rose stood up, wineglass in hand. She'd been practicing this speech in her head since Blue left. A slight curl formed at the corner of Sasha's mouth as Rose took a deep breath, preparing to speak.

"Remember how you said you wanted Blue to make a quiet, acoustic folk album?"

Sasha nodded.

"Full of songs like 'Lavender Noose,'" Rose said. She still hadn't listened to the record, but she'd read the *Pitchfork* review.

"Please stop mentioning that record that shall not be named," Sasha said.

"Sorry," Rose said. She took another big sip of wine. "Okay, so, you like my voice, right?" Sasha tilted her head in a very slight sign of affirmation and Rose's heart thudded in her chest. "Yes, okay, so." Rose swallowed. "Let's make that album, the one you wanted to make with Blue."

Sasha laughed. When she stopped laughing, she said, "You're crazy."

Rose's heart sank. Then something strange happened. A foreign sensation. Excess moisture formed in the corners of her eyes. Her throat burned. Her glasses fogged up.

"Oh, honey," Sasha said.

Sasha reached up and rubbed Rose's forearm. "You're serious?"

Rose nodded.

"Babe," Sasha said. "I love your voice, but I really have to get back to my life. I have other albums to make. You know, like, for money."

Rose nodded. She was such an idiot. Of course Sasha couldn't just stay here and make an album for some nobody for free.

"Sorry," Rose said. She took off her glasses and rubbed the foggy lenses on her shirt. "I was being stupid."

Sasha pulled Rose onto her lap and squeezed her in a way that made all of her sadness evaporate. But it almost instantly returned upon the thought that this was probably the last time she'd feel Sasha's body near hers. Rose realized for the very first time that she'd been fired by her literal hero. She started crying again, harder.

"Oh, honey," Sasha said, and rotated Rose to face her. "I can't stay here for too much longer."

The tears increased in intensity.

"But," Sasha said, "how about I give you one day in the studio? Tomorrow. You and me. Let's do it."

Rose momentarily closed her eyes as her pulse flickered under her skin. One day was not what she wanted. But it was better than nothing. She'd take it, for now.

Sasha got up to strain the pasta, and they ate a candlelit dinner that was both perfect and devastating, because it might be their last.

After Sasha went to bed, Rose crept into the studio and practiced singing the songs she'd been writing since she started working for Blue. Not long enough to strain her vocals but enough that she would be prepared tomorrow. Her plan was to blow Sasha out of the water. To sound so good that Sasha would have no choice but to stay.

r/BlueBeards • posted by u/CoolRanch • June 2020

Spotted: Blue drinking whiskey in Nevada?!

Guys, my friend just texted me from Reno saying they saw Blue at this dive bar, downing whiskey . . . like, straight from the bottle! Can anyone confirm? Is she off the wagon?

Comment by u/405Tulips

No way! I bet it's nonalcoholic, or just a prop for a photo? Blue's SUPER serious about her sobriety. She's been clean like nine years, right? She wouldn't just throw that away. In Nevada of all places.

Comment by u/Mercury

Even if it's nonalcoholic, isn't it a bit irresponsible to be out partying like that during Covid? Like, stay home maybe? That plus *Mood Onyx* being kind of tone-deaf and low-key racist? Has Blue lost her way?

Comment by u/PinkCocaine

Omg, y'all are SO embarrassing. Cornball behavior, for real. Blue is not your mom, she is not your nurse, or your babysitter, or your ethics professor. She's an ARTIST. You think that dangerous, horny brilliance comes from drinking matcha and following government protocol? As if! This woman cracks herself open so WE can enjoy the most gloriously depraved music. So she can 100% get blitzed if she wants. The chaos is the process. Let the bitch RAGE, creeps!

Comment by u/PinkCocaine

Okay, sorry I was on a lot of pink C last night and I don't know why I got so aggressive lol I hope Blue is okay!!

Blue

Blue hadn't been intending to relapse. No one ever intended to relapse. But when the man with the graying beard and dirt under his fingernails offered her a shot of Johnny Walker at the first bar in Reno, saying no didn't feel like an option. The whiskey burned her throat in a way that made her remember why she sang about God. Alcohol was a sin, and sins were so holy they had to be prohibited.

Or something.

Things had been a bit of a blur since then. She'd fucked the guy with the dirt under his fingernails in the bathroom, come so hard she'd almost said *I love you*. Fucked two other men that night, men she could hardly tell you a thing about. The problem with Blue's desire was that it was a bottomless pit. With most people, the craving for sex and liquor were like an itch you could scratch, and then the itch would be gone. But for Blue, the itch just kept getting more and more intense until she'd dug a hole into her skin and left an open gash, bleeding everywhere, exposing her bones.

And now, Blue was hemorrhaging, driving on I-80 east with no real destination in mind, smoking in between sips of a McDonald's

Coca-Cola half-filled with whiskey. Last night, she'd slept in her car under the stars, somewhere in the middle of Nevada—she'd just driven from Reno and stopped once she'd escaped the urban sprawl and saw no more lights. She'd woken up to a wide-open beige landscape littered with tiny sage shrubs and peaks so far away, they hardly looked real. Now, Bijou was on her lap and she'd been driving for hours but the landscape hadn't changed. The road seemed to stretch on forever. Luckily, she didn't have service here. It was nice out here on the open desert road with no one able to reach her. Blue made eyes at a series of men driving large trucks while handing Bijou French fries.

When her service returned around some billboards and a big RV park, Blue was assaulted by a series of missed calls. From Sasha, from Max, from her manager, from the label. Blue swiped away the notifications and said, "Hey, Siri, are there any good biker bars off I-80 in Nevada?"

"If you're looking for a good biker bar off I-80 in Nevada, one notable spot is Miss Kathy's Short Branch Saloon in Pahrump," Siri chirped. "It's a friendly bar with a lively atmosphere, especially during events like the Fourth of July. For a different experience, along the Cowboy Corridor of I-80, you might consider exploring places like the Old Pioneer Garden Country Inn in Unionville."

Cowboy Corridor? Blue began salivating. "What is Cowboy Corridor?"

"The Cowboy Corridor is a renowned road-trip route that spans roughly four hundred miles along Interstate Eighty in Nevada, from Reno to West Wendover. The journey offers a deep dive into Nevada's rich cowboy culture and history, providing an eclectic mix of experiences that range from historical sites to natural wonders."

Blue smiled. She was on that very route right now. She passed a sign that said MILL CITY.

"What's the very best cowboy bar on Cowboy Corridor?" Blue giggled at the question. Several times she'd thought of throwing her phone out the window, but she needed Siri, who routed her to a place called the Stray Dog Pub & Cafe in a town called Elko, Nevada. It was an hour and forty-nine minutes away. Perfect. She'd arrive by happy hour.

Rose

Rose's plan worked. She'd sung well enough for Sasha that Sasha had agreed to give her a trial run. A week in the studio. Rose was hoping to turn a week into months. She wanted to finish out the lease here with Sasha, then extend it. She wanted Sasha to buy the house, for them to start a family and get more dogs. Maybe some cats too. And just make albums and never leave except maybe to tour. But Sasha would stay home while Rose toured, to tend to the home, the plants, the animals. And she'd throw Rose a welcome-home party every time she came back, even if it was just for three days.

Now Rose and Sasha were sitting in the studio brainstorming, the way Sasha and Blue once had. But this time, it was just Sasha and Rose in the studio. No one knew where Blue had gone. Max had called Sasha this morning, worried. Sasha told Max she'd been fired and Blue had left. Earlier today a fan had uploaded a photo of Blue taking shots at a casino. This distressed Sasha but not Rose. Blue would be fine. Rose had more important things to think about. And Max was flying out to Reno to find her.

"What's your point of view?" Sasha asked Rose. She was sitting backward on a swivel chair with a yellow legal pad in her hands. She'd gotten a good night's sleep and had some more color in her face, seemed more alert, alive.

Rose was sitting on the couch sipping an espresso Sasha had made her. The day after Blue left, Rose had impulsively thrown away all the Red Bull in the house. Sasha didn't touch the stuff—only expensive coffee. Rose hated the chemical smell of Blue's canned caffeinated drinks and was glad they were gone.

"What do you mean?" Rose asked shyly.

"I know you have the vocal chops, and you've written some nice melodies," Sasha said. Rose smiled. "But what are you trying to say?"

Rose's heart thudded. She'd been so focused on perfecting her craft, on getting close to Blue, no one had ever asked her about her point of view before. Did she even have one?

But it felt like an important question, like a test Rose had to pass. She sucked her vape and thought.

"I don't know," she said finally. "Maybe I'm empty." This felt like something Blue would say. Rose bit her lip. "Empty . . . except for my little obsessions."

Sasha grinned. "This is good, okay, 'Empty,' that's a single." She was scribbling on the legal pad. "'My Little Obsessions,' that's another single. Maybe an album title."

Rose lit up. "So you're doing an album with me?" She got up and wrapped her arms around Sasha. Sasha laughed and squeezed the side of her waist.

"Listen," she said, "I haven't agreed to anything yet."

"Right," Rose said, trying to conceal her smile. She sat back down on the couch.

"So you're empty and obsessive," Sasha was saying. "But not the way Blue is empty and obsessive."

Rose frowned. She was so sick of hearing about Blue.

"Blue is obsessive about men," Sasha said. "You're obsessed with . . . ?"

"Music," Rose said. Then, feeling bold: "Women."

Sasha smiled. "Great," she said. "And you aren't empty in that dead-eyed nihilistic way, like Blue. Or like a bottomless pit of desire that no one or no thing could ever possibly satiate." She paused, sipped some of her espresso. "You're empty in a way, like, you're open. You can be whoever the audience needs you to be." Sasha put her cup down on the desk with a clank. "You're empty in a way, like, *Fill me up*."

Rose grinned, nodded. She felt electric.

"Sorry, did that sound pervy?" Sasha asked.

"No," Rose said. "Well . . ." She paused. "A little pervy. But in a good way." Blood rushed to her cheeks. She hoped it wasn't noticeable.

Sasha laughed from her belly but stopped when her phone rang. She quickly turned her attention away from Rose and toward the device.

"Max," she said.

Rose couldn't hear what Max was saying, but Sasha looked concerned. Rose was so sick of Blue's never-ending revolving door of drama. She saw an old pack of American Spirits Blue had discarded on the coffee table. She slid one out and took it outside. Rose had never smoked a real cigarette before, but she needed to take the edge off, to take her mind off Sasha's obsession with Blue Velour.

There was a slight breeze, so it took a few tries to get the thing lit. When she first inhaled, she was shocked at how harsh it was. Like she was lighting her throat on fire. She coughed and hoped Sasha didn't hear, didn't think she was an idiot or a child or both. She was still thinking about the way Sasha had said *Fill me up*. Rose knew that if they made the album, it was only a matter of time until Sasha did, in fact, fill her up. Last night in bed, Rose had embarrassingly googled *how do lesbians have sex?* She wasn't even really sure how straight people had sex either. She hadn't had any of it, and her parents had sent her to a private school that wasn't required to teach sex ed and therefore didn't. The Google search had answered some questions, although it mostly made her horny.

Rose's phone dinged with a text from Ella. She was happy to have *someone* interested in capturing her attention, even if it was just her weird former roommate.

BLUE IS MISSING!!!

Rose wrote back, *She's in Reno, I think.*

Wait I meant my dog and OH never mind she was under a blanket!!! LOL!

Rose had forgotten Ella had named her dog Blue. Rose really did not want to go back to that apartment.

You mean Blue Velour!! I heard she's partying it up in red states!!! Our iconoclast QUEEN!

"What are you doing?" Sasha said, appearing through the studio door.

Rose shrugged. "Is Blue dead?" Once it came out, Rose realized the question was strange and macabre. But the thought had crossed her mind. Blue had fallen off the wagon in Reno. These were the types of circumstances that preceded an untimely death. And after Amy had died when Rose was fifteen, she felt like she was always waiting for her heroes to die. Rose had moved on to Blue at that point, but Amy's death had still hit her harder than anything had since. Rose had worn all black for a month, created a memorial in her room. Her mom took her to a therapist, who diagnosed her with OCD. She stopped going when her mom got sick of driving her there. Maybe she could write a song called "Obsessive Compulsive Disaster." Maybe that would be too Blue, or like a cheap parody of Blue, which so many musicians were these days.

"Dead?" Sasha said. "God, no." She looked disturbed by the thought. Rose was relieved. She was over Blue but didn't want her to die. She wanted her to be alive and well, just somewhere far away from her and Sasha. Maybe in Europe, or outer space. Blue was always talking about wanting to go to Mars.

"But maybe worse," Sasha said.

"What's worse than dead?"

"Max finally got a hold of her," Sasha said. "She sounded completely fucked-up. She was at some random bar in the middle of nowhere in Nevada. She said she was driving east, all the way to New York."

"Well," Rose said, loving the idea of Blue in New York, three thousand miles away. "That doesn't sound so bad. Maybe some time away from California would be good for her."

"She shouldn't be driving drunk," Sasha said. "Blue is a scary enough driver as it is. And Blue on a bender isn't like anyone else on a bender. Blue has zero limits and a strong desire to self-annihilate. The public already hates her, and now people are taking pictures of her partying during a global pandemic with Republicans."

Rose nodded. She remembered Ella's text. "Some people think it's iconic," she said.

"Really?" Sasha said. "Why?"

"I don't know," Rose said. She really didn't know anything about politics. "People seem to like when Blue does the opposite of what she's supposed to."

Sasha paused, looked up, then back at Rose. "Well, it gets worse," Sasha said. "At least from my perspective."

Rose was scared of what was going to come next. She felt so intensely that she needed to stay in the redwoods with Sasha indefinitely, any information that could threaten to change that possibility was terrifying to her.

Sasha sighed, then sat down on the stoop. Rose sat next to her. She took another drag and tried not to cough.

"She's going to New York to, at least according to Max, work with—*ugh*, it's so hard to say this out loud, but . . . Liam Sterling."

Rose blinked at her. "Liam Sterling?"

"Oh God, Rose," Sasha said, and Rose just loved how her name sounded in Sasha's mouth. "I'm so jealous you don't know who he is."

Rose took another drag. "Well?"

Sasha looked down and trailed a circle in the dirt with her index finger, picked up a twig, examined it, put it back. Rose smelled dirt, and also Sasha.

"I don't even know where to start," Sasha said. "He's, like, my mortal enemy. He's this dumb alcoholic Brit and probably my biggest competition, even though I'm objectively a better producer than him. Women just want to work with him because they find him sexy for reasons I cannot wrap my head around and because he worked with Radiohead and Pulp in the nineties, so I guess they think he has clout. But really, he's just connected. A 'nepo baby,' if you will. And he still acts like a baby even though he's in his mid-fifties. Blue always threatens to work with him whenever she's mad at me. And I know he's been dying to work with her." Sasha ran her fingers through her hair. Rose fantasized about running her own fingers through Sasha's hair. "Blue is also sort of in love with him," Sasha continued. "Or at least with the idea of him."

This was getting better by the second. Sasha put her head in her hands and Rose rubbed her back. "Maybe she's bluffing," Rose said, although she hoped she wasn't. The idea of Blue moving on to another producer with whom she was maybe in love was positively thrilling. Oh, how desperately Rose wanted Sasha all to herself. Rose's desires could be so intense. Did other people want things this badly, so badly they felt they might literally die if they didn't get them?

Sasha sat up. "She's not bluffing." She looked at Rose, whose belly fluttered. "She tweeted that she's officially ended her professional relationship with me. She's never done that before."

Rose took another pull of her cigarette, for the first time enjoying the burn.

"Hey," Sasha said, "you shouldn't be smoking that if you want to make a record."

Rose's breath hitched. Gauzy light streaked through the canopy, lighting up Sasha's features in a soft, heavenly manner. Glee rushed through Rose's limbs. Sasha wanted to make a record with her.

She put out the cigarette in the dirt, vowing to never smoke one again.

r/BlueBeards • posted by u/AutotuneMe • June 2020

Blue and Liam Sterling? Seriously?!?

I'm sure you all have seen Blue's positively UNHINGED tweet about driving to New York to work with Liam Sterling? If that doesn't scream relapse, I simply do not know what does! Honestly, I don't blame her for falling off the wagon after the brutal (and utterly clueless) critical reception of *Mood Onyx*, which is literally a masterpiece. But fleeing to New York? Leaving behind the genius of Sasha? That ain't right!

    Now don't get it twisted—I don't despise Liam. I obviously didn't love Radiohead's lawsuit against Blue for "Polaroid Is the Void," but Liam likely had nothing to do with that. I love his work on the Black Keys' *Brothers*, which Blue cites as one of her favorite albums as well. The man's obviously talented. But let's be real—Sasha is the sorceress of sound behind the magic we worship. Liam's gritty vibe is a universe away from Blue's dreamy sound. And isn't Liam like fifty-something? Blue claims to love older men, but we all know that's just a performance piece. The last thing we need is Blue leaving the love of her life with some has-been with a dad bod. Sasha is the muse, the mind-melder who has been with Blue through every high and low. Why ditch a winning formula to work with a dude who probably still thinks prog rock is all the rage? It feels like we're witnessing the prelude to a tragic fall from grace. And also, doesn't Blue hate New York? This whole thing just reeks of midlife crisis.

    Am I spiraling here, or are we staring down the barrel of a gun?

Blue

A cigarette dangled from Blue's fingertips as she thundered through Utah, adrenaline rushing through her veins. She loved the open American landscape, had been longing for it, but she longed for Liam Sterling more. Liam Sterling. She kept saying the name over and over in a British accent until Bijou looked at her, confused.

"It's just Liam fucking Sterling, Bijou!" Blue said, looking at her dog. "Liam fucking Sterling, who's won like fifty billion Grammys wants to work with *me*! *Me! MEEE!*"

Blue had first met Liam at the Grammys nearly ten years ago. Sasha had been nominated for the very minor category of Best Engineered Album for *Chateau Velour*, but they were excited, because the Grammys had never recognized their work before. Max had found Blue this amazing vintage Dior gown. Liam had been nominated for Producer of the Year for his work with Arcade Fire, Radiohead, and the Black Keys. He'd been in another world at the time.

When Liam had approached Blue at the after-party and offered her a glass of champagne, Blue had been so nervous she hadn't even told him she was sober, just brought the glass to her lips and didn't actually sip. He'd told her he liked *Chateau Velour*—actually, he'd said it was "cracking"—then was pulled away to talk to someone else. Later that night, Blue had googled *cracking British slang* to confirm he was complimenting her (he was) and then masturbated to a photo of him with his arm around Karen O from the Yeah Yeah Yeahs. Liam towered over Karen O in the photo. He was six foot three, with broad shoulders and a bit of a beer gut, which Blue preferred to the coastal American obsession with vanity muscle definition. He had all his hair, which was rare for someone of his age, and it was thick and nearly black, peppered with gray. He had piercing blue eyes and a strong jawline with a hint of stubble. He wore a uniform of black Fred Perry polos buttoned to the top over dark jeans with Converse sneakers. Blue liked to imagine removing his polo shirt, picturing the tufts of grayish chest hair that would emerge from underneath. She envisioned him wearing a thin silver chain that she could put in her mouth.

They'd had a few, very brief encounters over the years at various industry parties. During the last two, Liam had alluded to wanting to work with her, although he didn't exactly say that, as everyone knew Blue was committed to working with Sasha. And she was. Blue had always wanted to work with Liam, but she had loyalty. Sasha had worked with Blue when she was a nobody, had helped Blue hone some of her most arresting and personal work. But Sasha had also disappointed Blue. And she'd really fucked her over this time. Letting her put out a bad record, not doing enough to stop her from embarrassing herself, and throwing herself at Blue's nearly underage assistant. Blue felt no loyalty anymore, to anyone, only to herself, her music.

Liam was a heavy drinker, something that in the past would have given Blue pause. Sasha partied too but was generally respectful enough to not do it around Blue. Liam, Blue knew, would not give her the same grace. He was a man who was used to getting his way, to people catering to him. But now it obviously didn't matter whether Liam drank around her or not. Blue was drinking whiskey from a Wendy's cup right this very moment. And Liam had called her up just thirty minutes after she'd tweeted that she had ended her professional relationship with Sasha Harlow. She'd immediately left the bar—it was called Carmen's, in a town on the border of Utah whose name she forgot—and gotten back on I-80 east, which she could take all the way to Manhattan.

Now she was driving along the edge of the Great Salt Lake. She only had thirty-two hours to go. Just over a day. She'd copped a bottle of Dexedrine from a guy with one eye at Carmen's, which would make the drive whiz by. Liam told her to take her time, but she was eager to get back in the studio. She was also itching to see what kind of expensive drugs he had. Nevada was fun, but the coke was shit.

Liam surely had the good stuff.

Rose

When Sasha had suggested that Rose move from the tiny attic into Blue's old room, Rose hadn't hesitated to grab her things. Not only was Blue's room next to Sasha's, but it was huge, with a private deck and a vanity and a mirrored closet that made the space feel twice as big.

Currently, Rose was trying on some of the new dresses she'd impulsively bought in town one day while Blue and Sasha were recording. There was a vintage store next to the market where Rose occasionally bought produce typically requested by Sasha, and Rose had started going in to kill time. She had never really worn dresses before, only jeans and T-shirts. And she'd never really thought much about her personal style. She'd loved looking at pictures of Britney and Amy and Blue, and had always admired their taste, but had never felt like she could be one of them. Rose had always felt frumpy, basic, invisible. Her voice was the only beautiful thing about her. But then at the Grammys, Rose felt physically attractive for the very first time. She had a flash of guilt at taking over Blue's room that Blue was paying for, then remembered how nasty Blue had been, that Blue had fired her. She refocused her gaze on the closet mirror.

The first dress she'd bought was delicate and cream colored with a white lace bib around the neckline and sleeves. It was slightly sheer and made of thin, loose fabric. It turned out a dress was much more comfortable than jeans, and Rose now felt stylish for the second time in her life. The dress paired well with the off-white Converse high-tops she wore every day. The fabric flickered gold in the light from the windows, which Rose had cracked open. Birds chirped madly outside.

The second dress she liked even better. It was short and flowy with a floral pattern—tiny roses stamped all over nearly sheer fabric. It had a scooped neckline and long, sheer sleeves that flared out into bell shapes from the elbow. Rose decided to wear this one for recording today. Her stomach danced at the thought.

Sitting at the vanity, she applied the bright red lipstick Blue had encouraged her to wear. Blue had also taught Rose to put some of the lipstick on her cheeks. "Don't pay for blush," Blue had said. Rose felt another flash of guilt, which she quelled upon remembering how Blue had called her a freak, lunged at her, and might have actually hurt her if Sasha hadn't intervened. Rose thought about applying eyeliner but then remembered that Blue had said something about her glasses being her "eye accessory—no need for liner." Rose smiled like Blue had taught her and rubbed the lipstick on the apples of her cheeks. Then she combed some of the serum Blue had given her through her hair, which was now nearly down to her breasts. Blue had also been encouraging Rose to use a shampoo for redheads, which intensified Rose's natural color.

"Who are you getting all dolled up for?" Sasha asked.

Rose smiled. "You," she said with a confidence that surprised her.

"You look good, Rose," Sasha said.

Rose trembled with desire.

"Hey, do you have an Instagram?" Sasha asked.

Rose shook her head. She'd always been too embarrassed by the idea of posting photos of herself online. Besides, she had no friends. She had a lurker account to look at photos of others, formerly Blue and now mostly Sasha, or the artists Sasha had gotten her into, or other artists Sasha had worked with and Rose was now jealous of, but she had no account attached to her name.

"Really? Aren't you a millennial? Isn't that like your whole thing?" Sasha said.

Rose didn't want to tell Sasha that she was on the cusp of Gen Z, a generation that found Instagram geriatric and corny. Instead she just shrugged and said she had "nothing to post."

"You're adorable," Sasha said, and heat moved through Rose's limbs. "But you should have an online presence if we want this to work."

Rose nodded. She'd do pretty much anything Sasha told her to do. If Sasha told her to climb up on the roof and dive off headfirst into the dirt, Rose would do it with glee. Sasha came over and sat on the edge of Rose's new bed. Rose's mind immediately went to the two of them in the bed together, naked, the same bed where Sasha had once been naked with Blue. Rose felt dizzy.

"Hey, Rose," Sasha said. Whenever Sasha said Rose's name, Rose wanted to record it, to listen to it over and over as she fell asleep. *Hey Rose, hey Rose, hey Rose.* "I just realized I don't know your last name."

Rose frowned. She hated her last name. She had been thinking of a stage name. She was prepared here. She knew Rose Lutz was not going to work. "Okay, so it's Lutz," she said. "But I was thinking of going by Rose Lux."

Sasha nodded. "I like that, but . . ." She paused. "Lux. It's not really you."

Rose felt embarrassed.

"I mean, not in a bad way," she said. "Like, you aren't extravagant. You're sweet. You're innocent."

Rose tucked some hair behind her ear.

"What about Rose Lush?" Sasha offered. "It's softer." She smiled. "And we know you love your wine."

Rose laughed, embarrassed. Was she a lush? Maybe.

"I like it," Rose said.

"Great," Sasha said. She came over and sat beside Rose on the vanity bench. Rose's body trembled. "See if the handle is available on Instagram. Then we'll take your first photo. And then . . . we'll make a record!"

Sasha turned and squeezed Rose's shoulders.

Rose nearly fell over.

Blue

Blue listened to twenty-four albums, smoked forty American Spirits, took sixty milligrams of Dexedrine (doled out in twelve five-milligram pills), and drank a handle of whiskey on the drive from Salt Lake City to New York.

For the first Dexedrine pill, Blue traversed the flatlands of northern Utah. She listened to Radiohead's *The Bends* while passing sagebrush and staring at the distant mountain range. She had decided to listen exclusively to albums Liam had worked on or was inspired by on the drive, to get in the proper headspace.

For the second Dexedrine pill, Blue moved into Wyoming, a wide and open landscape. She listened to *Kid A*, *The Bends*, *A Moon Shaped Pool*. Blue had avoided Radiohead for most of her adult life because this pimply boy in her high school photography class would hog the darkroom record player with *OK Computer* when she just wanted to play Nirvana. And then of course Radiohead had tried to sue her, but the judge had quickly dismissed the case. Blue was over it, really. And thinking back, she supposed it was cool that her high school had a darkroom and a record player, things today's youth probably could not define at gunpoint. Thom Yorke's whiny voice still bothered her—she'd skipped *OK Computer* for PTSD purposes—but she could admit the instrumentation was innovative.

Blue was expecting mountains in Wyoming—wasn't Yellowstone supposed to be around here?—but saw only flat grasslands. She watched antelope run while "True Love Waits" concluded the third album, a devastatingly beautiful song. She wiped a tear from her cheek. Her finger was black, mascara-soaked. She let Bijou out to pee and saw not another living being in her sight line. The barren landscape exhilarated her. She felt like she was on another planet.

As she moved on to Pulp—first *Different Class* and then *His 'n' Hers*, both Mercury Prize nominees—the afternoon sun began to turn the grass golden. To the sound of melodramatic Britpop, the sky exploded into fiery oranges around Cheyenne, which Blue believed was the capital of Wyoming if she remembered correctly. Either way, watching the sky turn Technicolor over a McDonald's billboard inspired her to get a Big Mac. She got a cup of water and an extra patty for Bijou. She fed Bijou first, then chomped on her burger as she moved to Pete Doherty's project, the Libertines. First she listened to *Up the Bracket* and then their self-titled album from 2004, gritty garage pop that made her vaguely horny in a pleasant way. "Time for Heroes" made her want to be thrown up against the grimy wall of a filthy bathroom in a Camden pub. The fantasy kept her going as she shot through the empty terrain. The sky turned navy on the final track of *The Libertines*.

Eventually, the landscape disappeared and Blue was driving through the flat darkness. The road was empty except for big trucks. She popped Dexedrine number three and put on the Kings of Leon's *Aha Shake Heartbreak*, which made her think of her first LA boyfriend, her first love, who'd put out a cigarette on her wrist after she accused him of cheating, which he had been, but so had she. Blue still had a scar. She traced her fingers along it, then took Dexedrine four. She played *Only by the Night* as she traversed dark, empty roads. It was almost too on the nose.

Blue remembered people saying Kings of Leon had sold out with this album, and listening now to its vacant arena rock, Blue could confirm that this was absolutely true. Blue was ready to sell out too. With Liam. *Only by the Night* had been nominated for four Grammys and sold over 6.2 million copies worldwide. High on amphetamines and watered-down whiskey and nicotine and stadium rock made for boys, Blue briefly fantasized about being a billionaire. Would it be unethical for her to have a private plane? Tour buses were so depressing, and flying commercial was so unglamorous. Maybe she could offset the environmental damage somehow, like by planting a forest for every flight. But also Blue didn't really care about the environment as much as she felt she should. The planet would be fine—it would get rid of humans if it needed to, and Blue was going to die anyway. She wasn't precious about the human race. Who cared if it disappeared?

The sun began to rise in Nebraska. Blue popped Dexedrine five and put on the Black Keys' *Brothers*. She'd listened to this album hundreds of times, often with hot men in hot trucks with the windows down. The lead singer, Dan Auerbach, was also a producer who had won several Grammys and who threatened Sasha almost as much as Liam did. Dan had expressed an interest in working with Blue many times and an interest in sleeping with her at least once, an interest to which Blue had given in during a manic episode probably around the time this album came out.

Soon the sky was bright and cloudless. Blue popped Dexedrines six and seven and played the White Stripes—*Elephant*, then *Get Behind Me Satan*, albums that had been important to the men she dated in her formative years. She still found Jack White sexy and had also slept with him—just before rehab. She wished she could remember how he was in bed. For the sake of her ego, she liked to think she had enjoyed herself and performed very well. Bijou licked her hand as if to say, *Of course you did, my dear.*

Blue crossed into Iowa during golden hour, the scenery a patchwork of farms and fields. The landscape was suddenly greener, softer, less expansive and somehow safer looking. It made her think of home, which Blue typically didn't like to think about. She popped Dexedrine eight and played Yeah Yeah Yeahs' *Fever to Tell*. Karen O had always intimidated Blue. She wondered if she'd slept with Liam. She glanced down at Bijou, who was whining softly in the passenger seat, a much prettier whine than Thom Yorke's. Speaking of bitches, Bijou had to pee. Blue let her out and basked in the Midwestern sun while leaning against her car.

As Blue crossed into Illinois, she took Dexedrine nine and played *It's Blitz!*, a fucking perfect album. The sky was a pale blue, then vibrant—oranges, pinks, and reds—the palette of Blue's envy. At dusk, the Chicago skyline took her breath away. Or maybe that was just the amphetamines. And she hadn't seen a skyline since . . . Reno? It had been a while. Blue put on *Cool It Down*. The first song was a banger and then it fell off. Blue started to feel better about Karen O. This album was fine. Just fine!

The light disappeared as Blue moved out of Chicago's urban sprawl and back into rural America. It was just Blue and the trucks again, the way she liked it. She popped Dexedrine ten and played Arcade Fire's *The Suburbs*, which bored her so much she had to take Dexedrine eleven to stay awake, then *Reflektor*, which she had to turn off. Even Bijou seemed to hate it, barking as if to protest. Did people really like this shit? She switched to Sky Ferreira's *Night Time, My Time*, which she'd never listened to mostly because Sky was so fucking pretty. She was talented too, unfortunately.

The sun rose in Ohio, or was it Pennsylvania? Blue was delirious. She saw a sign for Pittsburgh. Wasn't Rose from Pittsburgh? What a shit place to be from. Blue had her hometown demons, but at least North Carolina was green and bucolic with pristine beaches. Pittsburgh was a dump—all factory smoke and dirty steel bridges—fugly even as the sky broke out into intense colors.

Blue put on Warpaint's third album, *Heads Up*. She'd never listened to them before, but Liam had produced their two most recent albums. These bitches could really shred, damn. She googled a photo of them and—fuck—they were all gorgeous? In a really understated and effortless grunge cool-girl way? And Shannyn Sossamon, that stunning actress from the early 2000s, was in the band? She'd left, good. But her sister was the bassist? What the hell? Had Liam fucked all of them in some massive cool-girl orgy? A truck honked and Blue realized she was veering into the lane beside her. She honked back and straightened out. Blue was good at driving intoxicated, bad at driving jealous. As she focused on the road ahead, determination filled her veins, like she was winning a race. Blue wasn't jealous anymore. That was the old Blue. The new Blue knew her worth. None of these bitches could touch her, her raw sexuality, her knack for melody, her je ne sais quoi! The Dexedrine was great.

As Blue entered the lush Appalachian Mountains, she moved on to albums that had inspired Liam. The Smiths' *The Queen Is Dead*, Joy Division's *Unknown Pleasures*, the Cure's *Seventeen Seconds*. She supposed he was a loyalist; Blue was a patriot. She was sick of the British. She deviated from Liam's sonic world as the landscape became less rural, more urban. She put on Blondie, a real New York band. *Parallel Lines*. She took Dexedrine twelve as she passed through a corner of New Jersey. She saw signs for Manhattan and became excited, then hungry. She pulled off and got a Quarter Pounder with cheese and an extra patty for Bijou. They both wolfed down their burgers as she filled up her gas tank for a final time. Lighting her final cigarette, she got back on I-80. Traffic was heavy; the car moved slowly.

When the New York skyline appeared, euphoria washed over Blue.

Towering skyscrapers glittered in the distance. She rolled down the windows, letting the East Coast air hit her face. The smell of exhaust and possibility filled her lungs.

Rose

*I*n just thirty-six hours, Rose had amassed nearly fifty thousand Instagram followers. All it took was uploading a photo she'd taken of her reflection in the mirrored closet, which Sasha then reposted accompanied by the caption *Let's make an album bitches.* Sasha had over three hundred thousand followers, tens of thousands of whom quickly started following @RoseLush.

Ella had texted Rose almost immediately upon her uploading it. *HOLY FUCKING SHIT ROSIE!!!!* Ella had never called her Rosie before, nor had anyone else. Ella sent a selfie of herself and a French bulldog, accompanied by the text: *ME AND BLUE THINK YOU LOOK HOT AS HELL.* Then six fire emojis.

Rose hearted the texts, but Ella was still typing.

I hardly recognized you at first! Your hair is long AF! And REDDER! And your MAKEUP is on FLEEK!! SLAY ALL DAY, QUEEN!!!

Rose knew Ella was likely on stimulants, but her compliments felt good nonetheless. They continued to text back and forth as Rose vaped and paced the yard, as had become her routine before entering the studio each morning. She and Sasha had saged the space and rearranged the furniture to infuse it with "new energy." Now the mixing equipment was against the wall and the couch was under the window, meaning Rose could lie in the sun on breaks. Often, Gigi would lie on her lap.

Currently, Ella was yapping feverishly about *Mood Onyx*, which she probably loved because it sounded like being on drugs. Rose pretended that she'd listened to the album, said that she didn't think it was Blue's best but she thought it was a "successful project," just words that came to her on the fly.

Hey, shouldn't you be coming home soon? Ella said. *With Blue on the run?*

Sasha and I are staying out the lease, Rose told her.

BOLD! HOT! Etc!! Ella said. *Is it true that Blue is working with Liam Sterling?*

That's the rumor, Rose said.

Btw the BlueBeards girlies are SO MAD AT YOU LOL, Ella wrote. *They literally like want to kill you. It's so funny. I am kind of over them and their moralism. Maybe I should dip like you did.*

Rose looked away from the phone, watched a neon yellow banana slug crawl somewhere at a glacial pace. She didn't find the fact that the BlueBeards wanted to kill her very funny. And did they know that the woman Sasha had posted was the woman who'd founded their holy subreddit? Her phone lit up with another text from Ella.

I defended you obvi <3

Sasha appeared from the main house and Rose no longer cared about what was happening on her phone. Sasha's hair was wet, leaving damp patches on her T-shirt. She'd been running in the mornings and would shower before they met in the studio. She already looked so much healthier since Blue left. Her face had color; her posture was more erect. Sasha looked down at her phone as she approached Rose, who put the vape behind her back. Sasha didn't want Rose to be smoking anything. Sasha smiled at the phone, then let out a small laugh.

"What's funny?" Rose asked.

"Nothing," Sasha said. She looked up and squeezed Rose's forearm, creating an electric shock that ran through Rose's entire body.

r/BlueBeards • posted by u/GarboMommy • June 2020

The Truth

BlueBeards, this is the hardest post I've ever had to write. I need to tell you all something really fucking difficult. Something you all aren't going to like. Something about the person who started this subreddit, who she really is, and what she's done. And I have to admit my own part in it all.

    As you all know, I went to camp with Blue's sister, Max. Max and I shared a special bond, and while we've mostly lost touch, we still follow each other on Instagram. Several months ago, Max posted about looking for a reliable person seeking work in Los Angeles, and my intuition told me Blue was hiring a new assistant. Given that I live across the country and my mom is sick, I did not recommend myself. However, one night I was on this subreddit messaging with Rose and realized she lived in Los Angeles. You all can likely see where I'm going with this. I passed Rose's info to Max, who organized an interview with Blue, who ended up hiring her. Yes, that's right, our Rose is Blue's new right-hand woman about whom we've been speculating on this sub. And Rose is also the woman in Sasha's latest Instagram post, the post about which many of you have expressed rightful outrage.

    Back in January, I was excited that Rose got the job, as I assumed she'd use her new position for good—supporting Blue, fostering her relationship with Sasha, and supplying our precious subreddit with valuable information. I could not have been more wrong. Instead of supporting Blue and Sasha and our community, Rose ghosted me (literal Rose Ghost), lied, and has now fucked over all of us in the worst possible way.

    When I saw Sasha's Instagram post, I felt sick to my stomach. Rose didn't just abandon us; she's inserted herself between Sasha and Blue, disrupting the supernatural bond that made us all fall in love with their music. Rose appearing in Sasha's Instagram post with the caption *Let's make an album bitches* feels like a slap in the face to Blue and to all of us, especially now, when Blue is off in New York working with Liam Sterling—a move none of us are happy about.

Here's the real kicker: Rose had the audacity to ask me to lie about how we knew each other to Max. She said she didn't want to come off as—get this—*a crazed fangirl*. Like she was embarrassed by us and this subreddit, the very one *she* started? When pressed, I obviously told Max the truth. Rose had shown her true colors as a traitor who thinks she's above us all, so I didn't feel any need to protect her.

I'm sorry to bring this news to our community, a place built on trust and shared love for Blue and Sasha's music. But you all deserve to know the truth about the person who created our space only to trash it and bail.

With a heavy heart,
Grace

Comment by u/CoolRanch

ARE YOU KIDDING ME?!?! This has to be a joke right? If not, I'm seething! This is WAY worse than my dad cheating on my mom when I was 12, no joke. What are we going to do about it!!?

Comment by u/NeonBruise

This is insanity. I'm not a violent person but I literally want to kill rose.

Comment by u/GarboMommy

Same.

Comment by u/PinkCocaine

Kill Rose?? You all need to chill the fuck out and get your heads checked. How can we even be sure this is OUR ROSE? This seems very farfetched. Even in the off chance it IS our Rose, can you all blame her? Isn't everyone on this subreddit dying to get close to Sasha? Don't we all want to be Blue? Y'all need to get off your high horses and admit that in Rose's position, y'all would do the exact same thing.

Comment by u/GarboMommy

It's def her and I would NEVER get between Blue and Sasha. I would literally rather die.

Blue

Liam Sterling lived in a prewar co-op on Broome Street. Blue somehow found parking, which felt like confirmation that the universe was back on her side. She had clearly been on the wrong coast. New York smelled like asphalt and chestnuts and sewage and suddenly felt like home. The streets were relatively empty. The few pedestrians wore masks and scowled at their feet, which Blue suddenly found preferable to the vaguely friendly but aggressively distant demeanor of Californians. She tried to remember the last time she'd been in New York. Probably her last tour, in 2018. She'd played at Terminal 5, which she thought was maybe near here? Blue didn't know New York well. She never stayed for long.

Blue grabbed a few things from her car—a vape, a toothbrush, a clean pair of underwear, Bijou—and approached the building. It had a redbrick facade and fire escapes zigzagging down the front. The buildings on both sides were boarded up, perhaps due to the virus or to protests. Blue wasn't sure. She didn't even know what month it was. She'd left Velour Chalet on May 29? Or was it June 1? It must be June by now. Was it almost her birthday?

Liam's lobby had marble floors and white walls. A small brass chandelier hung from the ceiling. The doorman asked Blue if he could help her. With a swell of pride, she said she was here to see Liam Sterling. The doorman nodded, then made a call. Blue had told Liam she was coming to New York, but she hadn't said when. She prayed he was home; she hadn't come all this way to wait. The doorman hung up the phone and escorted Blue to a wrought iron elevator. Again, the universe was obviously on her side. The man turned a key on the outside and pressed PH. Blue's stomach surged with adrenaline as she rode up to the penthouse.

The elevator opened into a vast room with exposed brick and tin ceilings. The hardwood floors creaked beneath her. Liam appeared from a doorway on the other side of the open-plan living room. He was holding a glass of what appeared to be whiskey. His mostly gray hair was ruffled and he was wearing his typical Fred Perry shirt, fitted black jeans, just socks. Excess saliva formed in Blue's mouth. She put Bijou on the floor. The dog barked at a bronze statue of a lion.

"If it isn't Blue Velour," he said. "Just in time for a nightcap."

Blue smiled. She approached him, trying to appear as confident as possible. As she traversed the sprawling space, she tried to remember the last time she'd showered. Probably not since Reno? Maybe before that. She'd been spritzing herself semi-regularly with Tom Ford's Velvet Orchid and using dry shampoo, wet wipes under her pits, but she hadn't taken a proper shower in probably a week, maybe more.

"Can I freshen up?" Blue asked.

Liam performatively wrinkled his nose. "Please," he said. "Bathroom's over there." He pointed to the other side of the loft. Embarrassed, Blue followed his finger. She brought Bijou with her into the bathroom, not wanting to leave her to be frightened by another bronze animal statue.

The bathroom had a black bathtub and a separate glass shower. Blue was tempted to take a bath but was anxious to get back to Liam. The shower had one of those fancy rain heads and extremely strong water pressure, so powerful it made Blue horny. The products were all expensive—Molton Brown body wash and Flamingo Estate shampoo.

She lathered up her body, and brown water circled the drain. She supposed she was covered in dirt. She gave her hair a good wash, then toweled off. There was a black robe hanging on the door. Blue put it on. She liked the idea of Liam having worn it before her, of the fabric having been against his naked body, now hers.

"You smell *much* better," Liam said when she reentered the living room. "And you've helped yourself to my bathrobe, I see."

"Sorry, my clothes are kind of dirty," Blue said. She put Bijou on the floor. The dog ran over to the lion statue and began barking again.

"I saw that," Liam said. "Are you okay? And this dog belongs to you, correct?"

"I'm great," Blue said. "And this is Bijou."

Bijou barked and Liam said nothing, just went over to the bar and poured her a glass of whiskey. A record was playing. Blue recognized it. She'd listened to it on her drive. War paint. The hot girls who could play the guitar.

"Are you playing your own music?" she asked when he handed her the glass.

Liam smiled out of the corner of his mouth, similar to how Sasha did. Blue hated Sasha so much, just thinking about her propelled Blue to take a giant swig.

"Good ear," Liam said. He sat down on a brown leather couch. Blue sat on a velvet chair across from him, not wanting to appear too easy, too available. She leaned over to put her glass on the coffee table, hoping to attract his eyes to her décolletage.

"I listened to pretty much your entire catalog on the drive," Blue said, sitting back up.

"Yeah?" Liam said. "Find anything you like?"

Blue nodded. "I like this record. I'd never heard it before."

"These girls are brilliant," Liam said, and Blue felt that surge of jealousy again. She brushed it off. Where were these girls? Blue was here, in Liam's penthouse, in Liam's bathrobe, drinking Liam's whiskey with Liam himself.

"I'm obviously familiar with most of your oeuvre," Blue said. "*Get Behind Me Satan* was very formative to my sexual awakening."

Liam smiled. "You might want to discuss that in therapy."

Blue laughed. Bijou barked.

"I listened to the Black Keys' *Brothers* while watching the sun rise over cornfields in Nebraska."

"So you drove here from California?" Liam asked.

Blue nodded. "Took me only a few days."

"That explains the smell," Liam said.

Blue winked. She enjoyed the way he negged her—his sharp British snark was an electrifying contrast to the languid Californian passivity.

"You haven't mentioned Radiohead," Liam said.

"Well, you know they tried to sue me," Blue said.

Liam laughed.

"But honestly, *A Moon Shaped Pool* was quite gorgeous."

"I had nothing to do with that one," said Liam.

"Oops," said Blue. Now she laughed. She could tell him she liked *Kid A* and *The Bends*, but his ego didn't need any more inflating.

"Anything you didn't like?" Liam asked.

"Arcade Fire," Blue said. "Bored me to tears." She took a big swig of whiskey. She wasn't from California; she could be a bitch to people's faces. "I hope they paid you well."

Liam frowned. "*The Suburbs* won the Grammy for Album of the Year."

"The Grammys are shite," Blue continued, attempting to mimic his accent. "I had to pop an extra Dexedrine to stay awake," she said. She couldn't remember the last time she'd slept. She blinked at the walls, which were filled with framed covers of albums Liam had produced. Blue made eye contact with a naked Sky Ferreira in a shower and looked back at Liam. She leaned over and allowed the tops of her breasts to fall slightly from the robe.

"How are your energy levels now?" Liam asked, his eyes floating to right where she wanted them to be. He put his glass on the dark wood table, then opened an antique box beside it. It was filled with white powder.

"I could always have more energy," Blue said.

He cut a line for himself first, then her. She snorted it quickly, instantly recognized its high quality. Just as the euphoria was hitting her, her phone dinged in her purse, which Liam had put on the chair beside her. She checked it and saw a message from Max. It was a link to an Instagram post, a photo of Rose. All dolled up. In Blue's former bedroom at Velour Chalet. Looking kind of pretty. And it was posted . . . from Sasha's account? What the actual fuck. Blue knew Sasha well enough to know she was trying to get under Blue's skin. The last time Blue had tried to fire Sasha, she'd started working with Zoë Kravitz as payback. Blue had been so distraught that she'd given herself bangs, a decision that had only hurt Blue. She wasn't going to let Sasha get to her this time. She double tapped the photo to show how cool and chill she was. Unbothered. Also she was high as hell.

"Everything okay?" Liam said.

Blue snorted another line. "Peachy," she said, wiping her nose. Blue remembered that Rose was on that delusional subreddit. Did her Instagram followers know this? Maybe Blue didn't need to be so cool and chill. She wrote out in the comment box: *so cute that you're doing community outreach with our online weirdos.* Then she deleted it. She didn't want to alienate the BlueBeards, her most devoted fans. But she wanted to expose Rose. She wrote out: *our best BlueBeard*, followed by a blue heart emoji. Cryptic. Would get people talking, researching. The online sleuths were good. They'd get there quick. Blue clicked send on the comment.

"So," Blue said, and put her phone away. "The album."

"I have some ideas," Liam said.

Blue leaned over, put her elbows on her knees. "Let's hear 'em, boss."

"Well," Liam said, crossing his legs and staring at her tits. "I like *Mood Onyx*. It's a good record."

"Can you not use those words?"

"What words?"

"The words that make up my last record title," Blue said. "Consider them canceled."

"It's a good record. I think there are some concepts on there worth revisiting," Liam said.

"Next idea," Blue said. She snorted another line. Liam raised an eyebrow at her. This coke was good.

"I'm still on this one," said Liam. Blue had heard Liam was stubborn. Maybe this wouldn't work, as Blue was also stubborn. Or maybe it would infuse their collaboration with a nervy and captivating tension of the British and East Coast variety. Liam kept talking. "I like the through line, the liminal space between night and day, insomnia, being awake and buzzing when the world is asleep."

"Are you trying to kill me?" Blue said. She finished the whiskey in her glass and went to pour herself another. Bijou trotted along with her. Liam kept talking at her back.

"The sound is good, it's just not what the world wants right now," Liam said. "For frankly bollocks reasons. I love New York, but no offense, Americans can be so incredibly daft."

"Offense taken." Blue took a shot, then another. "This is a wonderful country." She turned toward Liam, inserted a breathy insouciance into her voice, the kind of affected, ephebophilic quality that had endeared her to essentially every man at Interscope. "We invented blue jeans and rock 'n' roll and airplanes and jazz. Hollywood and skyscrapers and Coca-Cola." This coke was *really* good.

"And nuclear weapons," Liam said. "Mass shootings and mass incarceration, and high-fructose corn syrup and—worst of all—musical theater."

Liam laughed. Blue didn't. She didn't like musical theater either, but this coke had killed her sense of humor.

"I forgot to say cars," Blue said. "And hip-hop."

"Great, back to hip-hop, back to *Mood Onyx*," Liam said.

Blue shook her head, a firm no, but Liam didn't seem to notice or care.

"As you know, I'm no hip-hop producer," Liam said. He smiled. "And I'm not sure Sasha is either."

He'd finally made Blue laugh. Liam was insulting Sasha's production skills. He was right. Sasha wasn't shit. Blue was moving up in the world. Sasha was falling, plummeting even, working with Blue's creepy former assistant with zero sex appeal? She filled her glass to the top, then returned to the couch.

"I think we should remake the record," Liam said.

Blue stared at him like he was insane. Was he insane? "The record everyone hated?" she asked.

"They only hated it because one woke asshole at *Pitchfork* got up on his high horse," Liam said. "Look, all we have to do is take out the hip-hop and soul references."

"That's a lot of the record," Blue said. A siren sped past on the street below them. The sound excited Blue. She hadn't been in a city in so long.

"There's a lot aside from that," Liam said. "Look, keep the themes, the melodies. Just make it more psych rock, less hip-hop. If you take out the bass lines, Travis Scott is basically making psychedelic rock."

Blue nodded. Liam was smart. Maybe he was onto something, or maybe it was just his British accent. Blue's eyes flickered around the space, and she realized there was a balcony. She ran over to it, stepped outside, looked at all the sparkly buildings and listened to the street noise. She picked up Bijou and held her up into the city sky. The pooch had never been to New York before, and she seemed excited. Or maybe nervous, frightened, or cold. A homeless man on the street yelled and Blue howled back, both of them incomprehensible.

"I love this apartment," Blue said, returning inside. "Is it cool if I crash here for a few days while I find a more permanent situation?"

"Definitely not," said Liam. "I can get you a room at the Mercer." He eyed Bijou. "Someplace dog-friendly."

"I fancy the Bowery," Blue said, again with a British accent.

"Fine," Liam said. He picked up his phone and disappeared. Blue went back onto the balcony and smoked a cigarette. The air was balmy and smelled of concrete. She tightened her robe. Bijou peed in the corner. Shortly after, Liam opened the door and joined her. He pulled out a pack of Lucky Strikes. He handed one to Blue, who accepted. He lit hers first, then his own. A gentleman. He exhaled, and said, "The Bowery is ready for you."

"Already?" Blue said.

Liam nodded.

"But we'll finish the coke first, right?"

Liam shook his head. "Early morning," he said.

Blue's heart sank. She wasn't ready for the night to be over. She was awake. She was with the man and producer of her dreams. She'd just driven across nearly the entire country without sleeping. She couldn't just go to bed.

Liam took Blue's hand and kissed it. "We'll have plenty of time for fun," he said, and Blue shivered. "There's a car waiting for you downstairs."

Blue briefly wanted to jump off the building, then remembered she was in New York, the city that never slept. There were a thousand places she could go. A thousand parties. Millions of men. She dropped the robe and sauntered down the hall, hoping Liam would watch, then put back on her dress, which she now realized did smell really terrible—like McDonald's and gasoline.

"We'll start recording Friday, yeah?" Liam said as he led her into the elevator.

Blue smiled, then said, "I'll check my schedule."

r/BlueBeards • u/GarboMommy is the new moderator of r/BlueBeards

Hello, you are the new administrator of **r/BlueBeards**. As the moderator, you now have full control over moderation tools, settings, and overall management of the community. It is crucial to ensure that the subreddit remains a safe and peaceful space. Please be vigilant to prevent hate speech, violent speech, or any content that could harm others.

Welcome aboard and thank you for contributing to the Reddit community!

Rose

The next few months were the best of Rose's entire life—the best they'd ever been, and the best they'd ever be for a good while afterward, as she'd later learn.

Her days transpired as follows: She would wake up at around 10 a.m. Sasha would be awake already, would have already gone on a run, would be reading the news on her phone in the living room while drinking coffee and listening to jazz, or she might already be in the studio. Gigi would be in bed with Rose. They'd snuggle for a bit while Rose scrolled on her phone, admired the steady increase in her Instagram followers. Rose would shower, put on a dress—she'd bought a few more online with the money she'd saved from working for Blue—apply makeup, then go downstairs, where Sasha would hand her a fresh cup of coffee if she wasn't already in the studio. If she was, Rose would head over there with Gigi, who would typically relieve herself on the way.

Sasha would be huddled at the mixing table with headphones on. Rose would tap her shoulder and Sasha would jump, turn, and laugh. She'd spin her chair around and Rose would lie on the couch. Dots of sunlight would push through the trees and the window and warm

Rose's skin in circular patches. Sasha would make them coffee, and Rose would share the ideas she'd come up with in her sleep.

Then Sasha would play scales on her guitar while Rose did vocal warm-ups. Sasha would move into riffing on the guitar to find the right tone for the day. They'd lay down a few rough tracks, Rose singing and Sasha accompanying her on the guitar, recording several takes, improvising, laughing.

At around 2 p.m., Sasha would go back to the main house and make sandwiches while Rose composed more lyrics. Sasha would return roughly fifteen minutes later with cheese and tomato on whole wheat, and they'd eat in the sun and look at their phones. Rose might post a photo of herself, her lunch, or Sasha. Several websites had written articles speculating about Sasha's new mystery artist, wondering who she was, where she'd come from, and why on earth someone of Sasha's caliber would be working with this rando nobody. And of course Blue had commented on the photo, *our best BlueBeard*, which had overly excited Sasha—Blue was being petty, which meant she cared. The comment briefly worried Rose. She knew from Ella that Grace had outed her in the subreddit, but she was afraid that it might hit mainstream news—that Blue's collaborator was working with Blue's most obsessive fan. But that fear quickly evaporated into the high of being in such close proximity to Sasha with no one else around. Ella had texted Rose that the BlueBeards were up in arms about Grace's reveal and Rose's sudden closeness to Sasha, furious about being backstabbed by one of their own, but Rose couldn't bring herself to feel anything but bliss.

After lunch, they'd review the morning recordings, selecting the best takes and noting areas for improvement. Rose would write or refine lyrics while Sasha would experiment with various guitar arrangements to complement the vocal melodies. They'd record a few more takes to fine-tune the sound. Sometimes Rose would play guitar on the recordings. She had been forced to study an instrument at Carnegie Mellon, and she'd chosen guitar because Blue played guitar. But Sasha had recently confided in Rose that Blue did not actually play guitar, that it was merely a prop for her stage performances. Sasha was impressed that Rose could actually play. Rose wasn't exactly Jimi Hendrix, but she knew the basic chords and notes. Sasha had three guitars in the studio. She liked to play the Martin 00-17, and Rose preferred the Gibson J-45, because it was bright red. Sasha said Rose looked good with the cherry-colored guitar and that she should play it onstage. The idea of being onstage with Sasha cheering her on made Rose delirious.

At around five or six, Rose would go into the main house and bring back a bottle of wine. She and Sasha would drink and discuss "big ideas" for the record—themes, subgenres, influences. The big ideas mostly came from Sasha. Rose would write them down in the same notebook in which, months ago, she'd carefully noted Blue's ideas that she'd subsequently lit on fire. For her own record, she'd written down the following:

Ingenue-core. Open, vulnerable, naïve. Raw, unplugged soundscapes. Subtle orchestral elements. Sparse use of synths to add atmospheric textures, mists of sound. Delicate, raindrop piano notes. The sound of lens flare, golden hour, afternoon light filled with possibility. The gentle intimacy of Taylor Swift's vocals. Enya's angelic, crystalline voice. Hope Sandoval's dreamy, ethereal quality. Laurel Canyon folk. Whispers of vinyl crackle. Female James Taylor. Naïve Joni Mitchell. Britney Spears with a guitar.

Inspired by this last "big idea," Rose had written a song called "Britney's Guitar."

Sasha also talked a lot about Rose's image juxtaposed against Blue's, things Rose didn't write down, things along the lines of: Blue is jaded; Rose is green. Blue is world-weary; Rose is fresh. Blue is night; Rose is bright. Blue is depression; Rose is bliss. Blue is cold; Rose is warm. Blue is the moon; Rose is a sunbeam. Blue is contralto, languid, smoky; Rose is mezzo-soprano, gentle, airy.

Rose didn't like being defined against Blue. Rose was suddenly into the idea of being her own person, of having a "point of view," even though it was really Sasha's vision of who she should be. Rose was happy to adopt Sasha's perspective as her own, as long as it didn't involve Blue.

At around seven, Rose and Sasha would take themselves and the wine back to the main house, take the stairs up to Rose's bedroom deck—formerly Blue's bedroom deck—and finish the bottle, watch the sun disappear behind the trees. Then Sasha would cook dinner and Rose would listen to her "homework albums": Enya's *Shepherd Moons* and Mazzy Star's *Among My Swan* and Joni Mitchell's *Blue*, which Rose loved the best except for its color imagery. Rose was over anything blue. She was into red. Taylor Swift had an album called *Red*, which was a little energetic for Rose's taste, but Rose liked the ballads. Both Rose and Sasha were excited about the record that Taylor Swift was working on in the woods on the other side of the country. In particularly delusional moments, Rose felt like she and Taylor were contemporaries, momentarily forgetting that Taylor Swift had seven studio albums, ten Grammys, and hundreds of millions of dollars. Rose had roughly $15,000 to her name, only because Blue's bimonthly checks were continuing to come. Sasha said that Blue was terrible with money sober, and egregious with it when she wasn't sober, and that she was probably too fucked-up to remember to cancel the automatic payments.

After sunset, Rose and Sasha would eat—typically whole wheat pasta with a salad, or a grain bowl—at the breakfast nook with candles lit. Then they'd hang out on the couch and listen to more records with Gigi curled up between them, keeping their feet warm. They'd maybe share a bar of artisanal dark chocolate or a glass of expensive scotch.

After five days of this routine, Rose had consumed enough wine to gather the courage to do what she'd wanted to do for a long time: kiss Sasha. They'd been sitting with their legs tangled on the couch listening to Joni Mitchell when Rose couldn't hold back anymore. When Sasha was mid-sentence—something about some artist who was overrated or bad in bed—Rose lunged. She put her lips on Sasha's, which felt like clouds. At first, Sasha pulled away. Protested. Said things Rose couldn't exactly remember, things that soon became irrelevant, along the lines of *you're too young* and *it's not a good idea*. Rose pushed back. Sasha gave in. Then she became passionate, aggressive. She picked up

Rose and carried her all the way up the stairs, laid her on Blue's former bed, undressed her slowly and kissed her everywhere.

Then she filled her up.

Sleeping with Sasha improved Rose's music, improved their chemistry. They started writing better songs twice as quickly.

Was this why Sasha's music was so good? And why Sasha only worked with women?

Rose didn't let these thoughts consume her for too long.

She was simply too happy.

For Rose's twenty-fifth birthday, on June 17, Sasha greeted her in bed with a coffee cake that she'd baked from scratch. They took the day off and went to the river. Rose thought of that first time, with Blue, when the water had been freezing but Rose hadn't minded because she was so happy to be with Blue and Sasha. This time was even better. The water was warmer and the jokes that Rose had once been on the outside of, she was now right inside. And Sasha literally slipped inside her under a waterfall they stopped at.

Later that night in bed, Sasha told Rose the sun had lit her hair up neon red as she came.

r/BlueBeards • posted by u/Mercury • June 2020

Has Blue fallen?

Ugh, I've always defended Blue but it's getting hard with these new paparazzi shots every day of her emerging from some illegal party while the world is on fire. If she was going to break the social distancing rules, I thought it would at least be for a BLM protest or something. I knew Blue was an iconoclast, but this recent behavior feels straight-up sociopathic. She's out there partying like there's no tomorrow while the rest of us are struggling for today. So much for being our hero. I'm so depressed by all this.

> **Comment by u/GarboMommy**
>
> I'm with you, girl. This behavior is not our Blue. I fully blame Rose. Something shady obviously went down in the redwoods. My prediction is that Rose threw herself at Sasha, maybe even drugged her or something, and Blue saw and lost it. What are we going to do? We need to get Rose away from Sasha. We need our Blue back.

> **Comment by u/PinkCocaine**
>
> PLEASE, people, Blue's recent behavior is 100% consistent with her personality. She's an addict. She's anti-authoritarian. She performed on the rubble of a demolished cathedral and also in a morgue. She wore a dress made of human hair to the Grammys as an homage to *Eraserhead*. After her DUI, she burned her driver's license on YouTube while singing "I'm free" over and over. If three years ago someone asked me what Blue would be doing during a global pandemic, I would say exactly this—breaking rules, not giving a fuck, making dope music, and probably relapsing. Rose has nothing to do with it. My money's on Blue abandoning Rose and Sasha after the bad *Mood Onyx* press, and Rose and Sasha are just trying to make the best of it.

Comment by u/GeminiGod

Are you fucking Rose or something? Why do you keep defending her? She's an obvious monster. Seek treatment, girl, for real.

Comment by u/PinkCocaine

Honestly? I wish! (That I was fucking post-glowup Rose *and* that I was in a glamorous treatment facility!) Does anyone else feel like Blue hasn't fallen, but this subreddit has? What's up with the new self-righteous energy and spooky threatening vibes? Since when is this r/GaylorSwift???

Blue

       *B*lue felt like she was twenty-six again, in the sense that she felt that she was about to die.

    Her time in New York had been a blur. She'd been getting recognized and bullied—even with a mask and disguise—at the Bowery. It was too public. Hotels were no longer safe for her. With the help of Liam's assistant, Blue relocated to a furnished condo so high in the sky she often forgot there was a city beneath her, breaking out in protests and becoming infected with a virus no one seemed to understand. Blue was literally above it all on the sixty-eighth floor of a building in Hudson Yards. It looked out over the river, a view she'd been having trouble enjoying.

    She was also spending less time there. Liam was a tougher producer than Sasha, who'd let Blue call the shots. Liam liked things his way. *Liam's way or the highway*, Blue would say, and Liam would roll his eyes. He seemed to find most aspects of her personality annoying, aside from her potential to make him money.

    Liam liked recording early, before 3 p.m., strange for a cokehead, but it often meant Blue would sleep in the studio, because she had trouble traveling before 5 p.m., especially in this hectic city. Liam had rented out Studio A at Electric Lady for the past two months. Blue hardly left the studio. Liam was running her ragged, as was her lifestyle.

During her first few weeks in New York, Blue went out every night, to speakeasies in the village and dive bars in Dimes Square and underground clubs in the Meatpacking District, really any place that was open or at least unofficially open. But she was getting recognized too much, and people hated her. They called her racist and alt right. Paparazzi took photos of her looking disheveled on the street at 3 a.m. and articles said she was hitting rock bottom. At first she was on so much coke she didn't care, but eventually it became infuriating. People acted like she was some hateful, malicious person. She'd just been trying to make a record that sounded good and would make people happy. She was trying to bring beauty into the world, to make people feel seen and alleviate their pain. That was all she'd ever wanted. She wasn't, as people claimed, making a cartoonish depiction of blackness; rather, she was celebrating and paying homage to music she legitimately loved that happened to be made by Black people. But since the *Pitchfork* review, she'd been afraid to so much as listen to music made by a Black person. And there was some kind of twisted irony here, but Blue was too fucked-up to articulate it, even within her own brain.

When she stopped going out, she started partying with Liam at his place. But Liam soon grew tired of doing coke with Blue, called her a pest. And she quickly realized, given the women she saw entering his building as she left, that she was nearly twenty years too old for him to consider as a sexual partner. She started partying with people from her past, the type of shady musicians she'd hung out with before going to rehab. She was losing weight; all of her clothes hung off her. And on June 20, Blue turned thirty-nine.

Someone threw her a party, but she couldn't remember who. Her apartment in the sky had been filled with bodies she hardly recognized. Her former party friends could no longer keep up with her, so she'd found younger guys, college-age boys with stamina, boys who probably would have had no interest in her if not for her fame and expensive drugs, boys whose names she never remembered. Blue partied with her coke dealer too, who likely tolerated her simply for business purposes. Had he thrown her the party?

Gold balloons had floated up to the ceiling and the floor glittered with confetti. Half-empty glasses covered angular furniture she'd never have chosen—too sleek, too sterile. The room reeked of cigarettes, always reeked of cigarettes. She knew she should open a window but was too tired to figure out if they even opened. The windows were huge and thick and outside them, gold light illuminated the river. For a second, Blue had thought of Malibu, the way the ocean changed colors every day based on the light. She never looked at the Hudson River the way she looked at the Pacific Ocean, with awe and curiosity. She wasn't really looking at anything anymore; everything was filtered through the foggy haze of her addiction. And who was that young, tattooed man who brought her a cake as the apartment glowed amber from the lowering sun?

The strange guests had sung Happy Birthday and Blue felt herself float to the ceiling. When it was time to blow out the candles, she noticed they said *27*. Blue cackled and howled.

"Twenty-seven," she'd said, laughing. She located her best British accent, which was really just Liam's accent. "Brilliant."

"It was your idea," the tattooed man had said.

Blue had been embarrassed she hadn't remembered this so she'd planted her face right into the cake.

The tattooed man had left, telling her she "needed help."

That had been a few weeks ago, or had it been a month?

Since then, or was it before, her coke dealer had said the same thing as the tattooed man. She "needed help." Well, didn't he "need business?" she'd retorted. He said, "Not that badly." He was being dramatic, she thought. All she'd done was light a tiny bit of his hair on fire. And she'd lost her stash. She supposed she'd also lost a friend, but she couldn't even remember his name.

Blue had started stealing from Liam, who had tiny bags of white powder stowed in every pocket, drawer, and nook. But he must have caught on, because Liam was currently out for a smoke and all his usual hiding places were empty. She was furiously rummaging through every secret space she could imagine when the studio door opened and Blue slammed shut the drawer she was looking through just in time.

"I need to go to Duane Reade," she told Liam. Powderless, she wanted to pick up some Hydroxycut—an over-the-counter diet pill whose stimulant effects mimicked those of amphetamines—but she told Liam she wanted a snack. Liam told her to "hurry," and Blue saluted him.

Outside, steam radiated off the sidewalk. Blue had forgotten how humid it could get on the East Coast in the summer. Was it July or August? Storefronts were still boarded up, people still wore masks. Blue had traded the custom diamond mask that fans suspected was not actually preventing the flow of the virus—what did they know? what did anyone know?—for a standard surgical mask so people would leave her alone, and also hopefully not recognize her.

She couldn't find Hydroxycut, so she bought three Monster energy drinks, a can of White Claw, and a pack of blue American Spirits—she had a carton in the studio, but one could never have too many. On the sidewalk, she downed the White Claw while fans sang various lyrics at her through N95 masks.

When Blue returned, Max was in the studio. Blue hadn't seen her since March. She considered running up to give her a hug, but she quickly recognized the look on Max's face. She had a hand on her belly. She was glowing. Blue instantly knew she was pregnant, and that she was here to take Blue to rehab. Blue didn't even protest. She knew she had to go.

She also knew the record would be called whatever Max named her baby.

r/BlueBeards • posted by u/405Tulips • August 2020

Blue's finally getting help :)

Hi all. So, some big news. I have a filthy rich friend from college who's currently at that fancy rehab the Dunes in East Hampton for Adderall addiction. And guess who she just saw checking in? Miss Blue Velour herself. I know we've all been super worried about our girl, but this seems like a positive step in the right direction. I'm just so relieved. It's hard seeing someone you admire lose their way, but I'm so comforted to know she's getting help. Let's send her all the positive vibes. She's not just our icon; she's a human being who needs our support and love right now.

> **Comment by u/CoolRanch**
>
> Finally some good news! I was starting to lose hope. Thanks so much for sharing. Blue, if you see this, we're all rooting for you!
>
> **Comment by u/NeonBruise**
>
> My brother went to the Dunes for a benzo addiction and he's two years sober. They know what they're doing over there. This is a HUGE relief. Addiction is no joke. Blue, we're very proud of you for taking this step!
>
> **Comment by u/GarboMommy**
>
> Thank GOD she's coming to her senses. Maybe now she'll realize what Rose has done to her and get revenge!!!
>
> **Comment by u/PinkCocaine**
>
> U scare me.

Rose

As September approached, Rose became increasingly anxious. Legally, she and Sasha had to vacate the house at the end of the month, and they were almost done with the record. Rose kept asking to rerecord or tweak things to buy time, but Sasha was clearly getting antsy. She kept taking calls from other artists, and Rose had violent thoughts about every single one of them.

And on August 14, Rose's bimonthly check from Blue hadn't come through. Sasha said that Max had taken Blue to rehab. Rose didn't want Blue to die, but she was going to miss those checks. She knew she'd have to get a job soon. She wondered if they'd have her back at the coffee shop. The thought made her sick. Worse, Carly Rae Jepsen had hired Sasha for her next album, which was scheduled to start recording soon.

In bed at night, Rose would stare at photos of Carly Rae and then photos of herself and try to convince herself she was prettier. Every day, Rose's DMs were filled with people calling her beautiful. Some called her ugly too, a "creepy ginger" and a "fire crotch freak," but there were many more complimentary messages. She'd been called a "cherry siren" and "Lindsay Lohan's teenage sister" and "as cute as a baby strawberry." Rose tried to remember all these things when Sasha told her they were done with the record, that she'd be packing up to leave at the end of the week. Rose realized at that point that she would have to ride with Sasha, because Blue had taken the Benz, and Rose had left her Saab at Ella's—well, really it was Ella's Saab. The thought of going back to Ella's made Rose want to die.

The night before Sasha was scheduled to drive them back to LA, Rose considered faking or giving herself a serious illness that would require Sasha to stay and take care of her. She knew she and Sasha couldn't stay here forever. But unlike Sasha, who had a house and work and a life waiting for her back in Los Angeles, Rose had nothing and no one but Ella. She briefly considered jumping off the roof of Velour Chalet. Then she remembered that she and Sasha had made an album. It was currently called *Strawberry Daydream*, and Rose thought it was perfect. Sasha said she was going to set up some meetings with various labels back in LA to get Rose signed, and the thought of that kept Rose going.

But Rose knew life would be wildly different in LA. She and Sasha wouldn't be living together, wouldn't be working together and eating together and falling asleep together every night. She'd see Sasha only occasionally, at meetings. Rose was worried Sasha would forget about their record entirely. That she'd start working with Carly Rae and then someone else even hotter, she'd probably make up with Blue, and Rose and Sasha's perfect time at Velour Chalet would fade into memory, and one day, Rose would start to wonder if it had even happened at all.

Instead of jumping off the roof, Rose woke Sasha up in the middle of the night and told her she loved her. It was 100 percent the truth, Rose had known this since their first night on the couch together, long before Blue left. But Rose also knew that articulating the sentiment was precisely the type of thing to make a perennially single commitment-phobe go running. And yet, she felt desperate, like she had absolutely nothing to lose. After Sasha's reaction, she realized she could lose her dignity, and she probably did. Sasha told Rose she "appreciated her" and then quite literally patted her on the head before falling back to sleep. Even Gigi sat up and barked as if to say, *Rose, you fucking idiot.* In the morning, Rose prayed Sasha didn't remember it, just thought it was a weird dream.

Several times on the way home, Rose thought about jumping out of the car while Sasha was driving over a hundred miles an hour on I-5. But Gigi was in her lap, and also: *Strawberry Daydream*. Their album, their baby. Rose truly felt like they'd made a baby together, and Sasha was about to abandon that baby. As they began winding down the Grapevine—a twisting mountain pass north of Los Angeles—Rose got an impulsive idea. She picked up her phone and gasped.

"Oh my God," she said.

"Everything okay?" Sasha asked.

"My roommate," Rose said. "Or I guess I should say, former roommate. She said she's rented my room to someone else." Rose squeezed her eyes, compelled tears to fall from them. She put her head in her hands. "I have nowhere to go." This was, of course, a lie. Ella had been texting her all day, seeming thrilled for her return. But Rose was frantic. She couldn't go back to her old life.

Sasha seemed unconcerned. "You don't have a friend you can crash with?"

Rose shook her head. "I'd just moved to LA when I started working for Blue," she said, a lie—she'd been in LA for a year. "I didn't have time to make friends other than my roommate, Blue, and Max." She forced some more tears out, turned to Sasha.

"And you."

2021

Didn't anyone tell you? You're supposed to break my heart. I expect you to. So why haven't you?

—BRITNEY SPEARS

Blue

Max's baby was due at the end of May—roughly a month away—and Blue couldn't wait. She didn't feel equipped for motherhood herself, but she loved the idea of having a little baby related to her, one she wasn't fully responsible for but that she could play with and mold ever so slightly in her image. She hoped the baby would be a Gemini like Blue, but either way, she'd love it. Love her.

Max was having a girl. Girls had trouble with their moms but they never complained about their aunts. They loved and admired them, wanted to be them, told amusing anecdotes about them at parties. Blue was going to be that aspirational aunt. Max was going to name the baby Violet, which was what Blue was going to name her next album. Blue's life had, for probably the thirteenth or fourteenth or twenty-fifth time, done a complete 180.

She was back in Malibu, eight months sober. She'd ditched the album she'd been making with Liam. Thinking about him, that album, that time, made her want to throw up in her hand. The skeeze was making her pay him back for studio time, which Blue begrudgingly forked over so he'd leave her alone. She had hemorrhaged money in New York, so badly that she'd been dropping merch to pay her debts.

In February, a magazine Blue had never heard of but that her manager claimed was "very relevant" (*The Draft? The Shift?*) had published a piece about how *Mood Onyx* was unfairly demonized, about how Blue had poetically captured one of the darkest times in the public imagination, that she had done nothing problematic, that there was in fact nothing offensive about enjoying, respecting, and being influenced by music made by Black people. Fans posted it, reposted it; media outlets responded. Soon there was a wave of articles calling Blue Velour the scapegoat for collective racial tension. *Pitchfork* rewrote its review, giving the album an 8.2 and calling it "an important work of quiet desperation."

Prodded by her accountant, Blue capitalized on the album's shift in public opinion by making *Mood Onyx* baby tees, beach towels, booty shorts, and lighters. She even sold a lavender noose. And as of last month, her debts had been paid and she was out of the red and in the black. She still didn't like red things.

For a while, she'd been nervous to hear about an upcoming record from Rose, but she never did, and now she hardly thought about it. When Sasha had come back begging for forgiveness at the end of last year, Blue had turned her away. Rehab had made Blue realize that her relationship with Sasha was completely unhealthy. Made her realize she didn't want to work with a producer she was fucking, or who she wanted to fuck, or who wanted to fuck her. Blue was taking a break from men and sex and romance. She was working with Isaac Altman, a nebbishy man to whom she was not remotely attracted. She felt safe with Isaac in a way she never had with Sasha or Liam. Isaac listened to her, respected her, never objectified her or leered. He lived down the 1 in Pacific Palisades with his wife, Maggie, whom Blue was starting to call a friend. The album they were working on, *Violet*, was the polar opposite of *Mood Onyx*. It was airy and full of hope. Violet wasn't born yet, but she'd saved Blue's life.

Blue was currently on the way back from Shangri-La Studios. Her hair swirled up in the damp ocean air. She'd left her Benz on Broome Street and had been using Max's lime green '70s Bronco—the sisters shared a taste for vintage cars. It didn't have a roof, and Max thought it was too dangerous for a pregnant woman. Her fiancé—yes, Max and Grayson were engaged, and yes, Blue was happy for them and only a little jealous—had bought her a Subaru, one of the safest cars, and Max had moved into his house down the road. Blue had never spent as much alone time in her entire life as she had in the past seven months, but weirdly, she felt less lonely than she ever had. She was meditating, examining the voids she'd been trying to fill with drugs and alcohol and nicotine and sex and older men and Sasha.

At the stoplight before her turnoff, Blue's phone dinged with a message. From Max. It was a video, accompanied by the text: *what the actual fuck???*

Blue pulled over and opened the video.

Rose

When Sasha had texted Rose earlier this week with "an idea," Rose had never been lower in her entire life. She was back at Ella's, working at the coffee shop, using expensive earplugs to block out Ella's late nights, waking up early for shifts where she had to wear a mask that fogged her glasses and made it hard to see or breathe. She hardly saw or even spoke to Sasha anymore. Rose's worst fears had been actualized: her life had returned to exactly how it was before. Except worse. Because she'd tasted heaven and then got dragged back to hell.

Sasha had let Rose "crash" at her place in Silver Lake until Rose "found housing," wording that made Rose feel like a distant cousin at best. She'd nonetheless moved in with Sasha and, in vain, tried to re-create their life in the redwoods. But life at Sasha's home was absolutely nothing like Velour Chalet. The house was hypermodern and sterile, in stark contrast with the cozy rental. Sasha was also different here—hard, cold, in a way that matched the furniture. She'd leave for the studio before Rose woke up and often returned after Rose went to bed. Whenever Rose stayed up until Sasha got home, Sasha was distant and would go straight to bed. Rose had never felt lonelier. And the money in her bank account was dwindling. She knew she needed to get a job. Whenever she asked Sasha about *Strawberry Daydream*, Sasha said she was working on getting meetings, but it was tough because Rose had "nothing to her name." The words *nothing to her name* looped in Rose's head as she tried to sleep that night. Then every night. In the guest room. Alone.

Nothing, nothing, nothing.

When Rose had woken up one night to get water and had run into Zoë Kravitz naked in the kitchen, with Sasha calling her back to bed, she'd packed her things and gone back to Ella's, where she cried herself to sleep. Ella let Rose sleep with Blue the dog for the next few nights. Rose missed Gigi, whom she should have taken with her, but it was too late—she didn't want to go back to Sasha's. Ella was kinder and more grounded than Rose remembered, but maybe it was only in comparison to the sociopaths with whom she'd been spending her time. After a few weeks at Ella's, Rose never wanted to see Blue or Sasha again.

And then Sasha texted her. She'd gotten them three meetings with three record labels. Rose had been excited for the meetings, had gone shopping with Ella, gotten her hair cut and colored by Ella's hairstylist. Ella even did Rose's makeup. But the meetings were all the same. Rose was a nobody, they all said. She needed more followers, more visibility.

"Isn't having an album out the way I get visibility?" Rose had said to Sasha in the car on the way back from the third failed meeting.

"I know," Sasha had said. "But it's just like any other job. You can't get a waitressing job until you've been a waitress, but you can't have been a waitress unless you've had a waitressing job. All industries are hard to crack, and this is probably the hardest."

Rose started to cry the way she had on their drive back to LA, the way she had on her Uber ride to Ella's after seeing naked Zoë Kravitz. Sasha pulled over and squeezed Rose's shoulder. And despite all those weeks of hating Sasha, fantasizing about her dying in a car crash with Zoë Kravitz at the wheel, Rose was instantly propelled back into the emotional landscape of Velour Chalet. One touch from Sasha was all it took, and Rose was right back there. In the land of huge trees and butterflies and dotted yellow light and banana slugs and silver foxes and the scent of damp earth that smelled perfect as long as Rose was on a colossal dose of antihistamines. And once again Rose wanted nothing but to curl up in the nook of Sasha's shoulder and never leave. But as soon as Sasha saw that Rose had calmed down, she removed her hand and started driving again.

"Don't give up, champ," Sasha had said to Rose when she dropped her off. Rose's body shook as she approached her building. Rose had given up. And she hated when Sasha talked to her like some kind of distant uncle. She stopped just before she opened the front door of her building, turned around, went back to Sasha's car and grabbed Gigi. "I'm taking her," she said.

Sasha shrugged, then said, "Great."

Rose had thought Sasha would care, had been preparing to argue her case for keeping the dog. But Sasha clearly only cared about herself. Luckily, Blue the dog seemed to like Gigi, who was so old and still, Blue seemed to think she was a toy. That night, both Gigi and Blue the dog had slept in her bed. Ella had also crept under the covers in the middle of the night like she used to. Ella was growing on Rose. She seemed moderately less self-centered and appeared to be making a concerted effort to cut down on drugs and alcohol. She wasn't entirely successful. Her benders did not disappear entirely, but they reduced in frequency. After several months of sleeping with Ella and both dogs, Rose was finally starting to get over Sasha and their dumb *Strawberry Daydream*.

And then, Sasha texted her.

With this mysterious "idea."

Rose was at work when she got the text. Sasha drove over and picked her up, then took her to her studio in Hollywood, where Blue had recorded her first three records. It wasn't until they got inside the studio that Sasha told her the plan.

"You're going to sing Britney," Sasha said. "Like you did for me at Velour Chalet. Something from *Circus*, probably 'Out from Under,' or maybe 'Unusual You.'" Sasha handed Rose some sheet music. "This is the guitar for both. I can play on the recording, but you will play on the video."

"Video?" Rose asked. She felt dizzy, like she was dreaming.

"Yes," Sasha said. "You need exposure, right? You're a nobody—no offense, but everyone's a nobody at some point. Blue was when I met her. I was too. Anyway, enough about Blue."

Rose smiled. Enough about Blue.

"Britney Spears is a somebody," Sasha said. "Everyone knows her music. Gays go crazy for her. When *Spring Breakers* covered 'Everytime,' people went insane for it all over again. People love her music recontextualized. So you're going to sing one of her songs. We'll record it, here, so it sounds perfect, and then we'll film a video of you playing guitar and looking hot and singing it somewhere outside, somewhere pristine."

The words *looking hot* looped through Rose's brain. Was this really happening? Was this a dream? Was she going to be working with Sasha again? Had Sasha done something to her hair? Was she wearing a new fragrance? Was she somehow hotter than she'd ever been?

"Earth to Rose," Sasha had said.

"I think it's a perfect idea," said Rose.

They started working immediately. Rose picked "Unusual You"—it was more fun, and its theme of heartbreak spoke to her at a moment like this. She learned the guitar pretty quickly—it wasn't complex. Then they started recording. They were in the studio until 2 a.m. And after they'd split a bottle of wine, Sasha leaned in to kiss her.

In the past few months, Rose had pictured this moment—Sasha leaning in to kiss her after a shared bottle of wine—many times, each time with a different outcome. Sometimes she'd reject her, act bored and uninterested, as though she no longer felt a spark. Sometimes she'd kiss her back, elicit in Sasha such extreme pleasure she'd have no choice but to fall madly in love. Sometimes she'd slap Sasha across the face, hard, a physical *fuck you*.

This time, she did all three. First, she dedicated herself to Sasha's pleasure with a meticulous intensity, with the focus of a doctor conducting high-risk brain surgery. She made Sasha scream her name. At Sasha's peak pleasure, Rose slapped her across the face, in a way that seemed to escalate Sasha's delight, precisely as Rose had anticipated. Afterward, Rose acted bored, went on her phone, yawned. When Sasha tried to return the favor, Rose said, "No thanks." Acting uninterested was the most difficult acting job of Rose's life, but one necessary to get what she wanted: Sasha's devotion.

Scrolling on her phone, Rose realized that in the time she'd thought she was getting over Sasha, she had in fact been learning how to draw her in. Because Ella played it at all hours, Rose was listening to Blue's music again. At first it grated on her. But then she fell in love with it all over again, more intensely given the time apart. And in listening to that music, Rose was able to glean exactly what Sasha loved so much in Blue, to understand the way her desire ticked. Sasha adored Blue because she was unpredictable and exciting and completely unavailable. So Rose became that.

They filmed the video the next day in Barnsdall Park in the late afternoon. Rose wore a floral baby doll dress and strummed the cherry red Gibson guitar. Golden hour light filtered through palms and lit up her hair neon red, like it apparently did on her twenty-fifth birthday when Sasha fucked her under the waterfall. Sasha kept making sounds of pleasure while filming on her iPhone, giving enthusiastic affirmation: *you're hot, fuck yes, sexyyy, yes, Rose*. The affirmations fueled Rose, leading her to lean further into the way Sasha saw her: as a strawberry ingenue, waiting for her cherry to be popped.

That night, Rose pretended to be a virgin while Sasha slipped inside of her. The fantasy appeared to electrify Sasha. Rose delighted in deepening Sasha's delight, setting off a positive feedback loop of pleasure. Afterward, Rose told Sasha that *Strawberry Daydream* was too tepid a name for the album. They should call it something more memorable, more evocative.

"How about *Pop My Cherry*?" Rose asked.

"I love it," Sasha said, and then they had sex again, Rose again pretending to be a virgin, again making Sasha go wild.

When Sasha dropped Rose off the next morning, Rose exited the car with a newfound confidence, an airy optimism, a pep in her step. She knew everything was going to be okay. She was twenty-five years old, she was sexy, she was talented, and she had one of the most successful producers in the industry eating from the palm of her hand.

Ella was asleep when Rose got in the apartment. She sat on the couch and calmly uploaded the video. She tagged Sasha.

It had gone viral by the time Ella woke up roughly thirty minutes later.

r/BlueBeards • posted by u/GarboMommy • April 2021

Rose better be sleeping with one eye open

Just when I thought that whole Rose nightmare was over and that mousy little freak had faded back into obscurity where she belongs: THIS. FUCKING. VIDEO. Pathetic Britney Spears impersonation? Criminally cringe!!! And guess what I just saw on Deuxmoi?? I'm so angry I can hardly type. SASHA FILMED IT!!! I swear to God, I'm going to have to go back to anger management for this shit.

How could Rose pull a shady, disgusting stunt like this after everything I did for her? She only got that assistant gig because I went to bat for her, because I wrongly thought she was one of us. And this is how she repays me? Repays us? That SNAKE. Slithering into the spotlight by acting like a garden variety ho! Make no mistake, Rose doesn't care about anyone but herself. She used Blue, she used me, she used all of us. For the integrity of our community, we cannot let her get away with this.

I'm not just mad; I'm out for BLOOD.

Comment by u/NeonBruise

I'm with you, girl. Where does she live? Let's go. I'll bring my Japanese knife collection.

Blue

Max had been in labor for sixteen hours, meaning the baby would be a Gemini—fortunately. But unfortunately, Max was in a lot of pain and Blue wished she could take it away. Every four or five minutes, her sister would start screaming, and Grayson and Blue would rush up to hold her hand. In between contractions, Blue would get Max ice or just pace the halls. Right now, she was roaming the hall for probably the fifteenth time when a male nurse approached her.

"Oh my God, Blue Velour," he said.

Blue was surprised to be recognized at the hospital. She was wearing a mask and a baseball cap. She should have been wearing sunglasses, but also the doctor had said Max's labor could take up to twenty-four hours, and Blue was bored as hell. It was nice to talk to someone.

"Guilty," Blue said.

"I'm obsessed with you," the male nurse said. He was short, shorter than Blue, and had electric green eyes. "I'm so pissed at Sasha," he continued. It was weird to hear Sasha's name. Blue hadn't thought about her much since that disturbing, pedophilic Britney Spears cover that

Max had sent her. The video upset Blue at first, but rehab had recalibrated Blue's relationship to anger. She was starting to experience what she once felt as anger as sadness. When Blue saw the Britney cover, she felt sad that Sasha had once captured her heart, but was really no better than Liam, just another industry sleaze, a user and a perv. And then she let the feeling go.

"Oh, Sasha and I are fine," Blue said. The media and fans were fixated on Sasha and Blue's breakup. Blue was often asked about it by the paparazzi who sometimes camped outside Shangri-La, but she had no interest in fueling a public feud. She'd mourned her relationship with Sasha. She'd moved on. She wished everyone else could too.

"Even after *Pop My Cherry*?" the male nurse said. He put his hands on his chest and inhaled dramatically. "It's like, eleven tracks of 'Lavender Noose,'" he continued. "I can't believe Sasha did you dirty like that."

Blue had no idea what he was talking about, but she knew she needed to leave the conversation. "Thank you for your support," Blue said, then excused herself back to Max's room, where Max was screaming again. Blue went over and squeezed her hand.

After the contraction, Blue sat down and retrieved her phone from her bag. What did that nurse say the album was called? Something pervy and infantile? *Pop My Cherry*? Could it be that dumb? She typed *Pop My Cherry Sasha Harlow* into Google and many results popped up, reviews and articles in publications Blue did not read because they did not nourish her soul. The results revealed a recent album called *Pop My Cherry* by Rose Lush. Very recent. It was dropped just yesterday.

Max started screaming again and Blue took her phone with her to squeeze Max's hand.

"What's stressing you, baby Blue?" Max asked when the contraction stopped. Blue felt a wave of love for her sister, who cared enough about Blue to check in on her feelings while she was reaching her seventeenth hour of labor.

"Nothing," Blue said. But she was looking at her phone, clicking around, gleaning that Sasha had made a record with Rose, that Blue's very own label, Interscope, had signed Rose and released it given the success of the pedophilic Britney cover, that they had recorded the album "in the redwoods." Blue took several deep breaths. No wonder the male nurse was pissed. Had Sasha really recorded a fucking record at Blue's rental that she'd paid for with Blue's assistant, whom she'd also been paying at the time, because she was too fucked-up to cancel her automatic payments? And in addition to the male nurse, several people online were saying the album completely ripped off "Lavender Noose" and *Oleander*.

When Max started screaming again, Blue got up and started screaming with her.

r/BlueBeards • posted by u/AutotuneMe • May 2021

Pop My Cherry??!?!

Seriously, Sasha??? Rose has to be drugging her, that's the only logical explanation. I just can't wrap my head around Sasha purposely making an album like this, that's so misogynistic and male gaze-y and straight up PERVY, from the album cover where Rose looks like a sexy baby to the sleazy-ass lyrics. And can we talk about how the entire album is basically just eleven bad imitations of "Lavender Noose"??? A song, which, by the way, is a sexy little ode to Blue and Sasha's special erotic connection. The GALL. It's quite literally illegal, isn't it? I'm going to ask my cousin in law school and get back to you all.

Why on earth did Interscope sign off on this! Are these idiots forgetting where Rose came from? That Blue literally hired her to help her and Rose just fucking backstabbed her in the grossest possible way? I'm going to be sick. The album is not only tacky but frankly morally corrupt.

> **Comment by u/CoolRanch**
>
> Amen sista. Rose is a sicko.
>
> **Comment by u/GarboMommy**
>
> I was literally just throwing up I'm so angry and disgusted. *Pop My Cherry*? More like Rose is about to get POPPED.
>
> **Comment by u/AutotuneMe**
>
> Seriously, I'm starting to understand the Second Amendment. . . .
>
> **Comment by u/PinkCocaine**
>
> Have you people ever considered that SASHA is the problem here?? SHE's the one who betrayed Blue, not Rose. Rose is literally a naïve twenty-five-year-old just out of college. Sasha

is a forty-four-year-old WOMAN who hit on Blue's assistant and took complete advantage of her and encouraged her to whore herself out for fifteen minutes of fame. She's a CREEP people.

Comment by u/GarboMommy

Sasha would never. Clearly Rose is behind all this.

Comment by u/CoolRanch

Agree. Sasha wouldn't do Blue dirty like that unless she was being heavily manipulated and/or drugged.

Comment by u/PinkCocaine

YOU PSYCHOS DON'T EVEN KNOW THESE PEOPLE!!!!! LITERALLY GET A LIFE.

Rose

Sasha took Rose out to dinner at an upscale French restaurant in Hollywood to celebrate *Pop My Cherry*. But frankly, Rose didn't feel like there was much to celebrate. She'd expected the release to make a major splash, for it to change everything, for her to lose all connection with her former self. For Rose Lutz the mousy loser to evaporate into thin air and for Rose Lush to emerge like a glistening mermaid into the spotlight. But there was no spotlight. Only a couple of lukewarm reviews on websites Rose had never heard of. Interscope had assigned her an A&R rep who didn't even respond to her emails. The album had been out for over twenty-four hours and Rose felt exactly the freaking same.

But she was trying to trick herself into a different reality. For dinner she'd worn a red silk slip dress with Converse sneakers. She'd finally ditched her glasses for contacts—overcoming a lifelong fear of touching her eyeballs with Ella's encouragement—and had therefore experimented with eyeliner tonight.

Sasha had picked Rose up and had come up to meet Ella beforehand. Ella was supportive of Rose's career—Rose had given her an early version of *Pop My Cherry*, and Ella played it constantly, and even encouraged her successful DJ friend Vagablonde to play it too—but she was wary of Sasha. Before Sasha came by, Ella had snorted three lines and opened a bottle of champagne. When Sasha arrived, Ella poured Sasha a glass and asked Sasha about her intentions with Rose, acting the part of an overprotective father. In the car on the ride to the restaurant, Sasha said she liked Rose's "strange roommate" and Rose said, "So do I."

The restaurant had dim lighting and dark wood walls and green velvet booths. Sasha wore a satin black button-down with most of the buttons open and her eyes were lined in smudged black liner. She ordered a dirty martini, so Rose ordered one too. She'd never had a martini before, and it was extremely intense. After just a few sips, she felt drunk.

"I'm so proud of you," Sasha said, gripping Rose's forearm.

Rose pulled away, sipped her drink. "It's an adequate debut."

Sasha smirked. "Adequate? It's fire."

"We can always do better." She didn't want to let Sasha know just how insecure she felt about the lack of press. Sasha didn't seem worried. Rose didn't want to seem worried either. Ella always said everyone in LA was pretending all the time. Maybe Rose should start pretending too.

"You already want to make another record?" Sasha asked.

Rose shrugged. She did. She wanted to make a better record. One people didn't ignore. One that inspired the A&R rep to not only answer her emails but also initiate contact with Rose. To be blowing up her phone all day. Rose wanted to be the one ignoring.

The waitress came over. Rose ordered the steak frites. Sasha, a vegetarian, gave Rose a judgmental glance as she ordered the wild mushroom pasta. Sasha got off on having something to push up against. She lived for tension.

"When do you want to start recording?" Sasha said.

Rose shrugged again. She let a strap of her dress fall down her arm and waited a long moment before putting it back. "Depends on who I work with."

Sasha grinned. As expected, she seemed turned on by Rose's defiance.

"Who are you thinking of working with?" Sasha asked.

"Not sure." Rose sipped her drink. "I've gotten a few offers." This was hardly true. She'd received a DM from Isaac Altman's *cousin*, who was just getting into music production, about potentially wanting to work with her. Rose would never work with him over Sasha, but Sasha didn't need to know that only a newbie nepo baby had expressed interest in her.

"Well, then, do I need to pitch you?" Sasha asked.

Rose bit her lip, taking care not to smudge her lipstick, and nodded.

"Okay," Sasha said. "I like to work with an artist throughout her evolution. I have visions for you, Rose. *Pop My Cherry* is an incredible debut. It's a fresh breeze during a horny afternoon in a cabin." Sasha smiled.

"How original," Rose said.

"I'm not done," Sasha said. "*Pop My Cherry* is sweet. It's pure, innocent, virginal. It's the wide-eyed glance of a young woman new to Hollywood, surrounded by vices and temptations. I want to see Rose Lush evolve into someone who's learning the ropes, someone who's doing the tempting."

Rose nodded.

"Album two will be that, a more mature exploration of the soundscapes and themes dipped into on *Pop My Cherry*—lush guitars, the tempted becoming the tempter." Sasha put her elbows on the table and leaned in. "Then? We're going to corrupt you, pop your cherry, if you will." She grinned. "You have to have your bad-girl moment. Your *Blackout*. Your *Reputation*, in Swiftian terms."

Rose pulled out her phone to appear bored, continued sipping her martini as Sasha kept talking. The waitress came over and Rose ordered a bottle of champagne, the most expensive one on the menu. She knew Sasha would pay.

"I've soured on Swift," Rose said, which was true. That music had made more sense when Rose was falling for Sasha in the soft cocoon of Velour Chalet, when the birds were chirping and life was simple and sweet. Now, whenever she listened, she felt like she was in a Starbucks. These days, Rose preferred the club. Things were finally starting to open and Ella knew all the doormen. Rose wanted pulsing bass lines and vocals auto-tuned into oblivion. She didn't want to be lying around listening to guitar music with some old lady. She took another sip of her martini and stared at the graying hairs around Sasha's temples. She should really get them colored.

When the waitress brought their entrées, Rose carved into her steak with pleasure. She took a big bite, reveling in the juicy flesh. A bead of red fluid rolled down her chin. She wiped it with a red-manicured finger.

"I didn't realize you were such a carnivore," Sasha said.

Rose looked up at Sasha and blinked, then swallowed.

"You didn't?"

r/BlueBeards • u/PinkCocaine is permanently banned from r/BlueBeards

Hello, you have been permanently banned from participating in **r/BlueBeards** because **your post** violates this community's rules. You won't be able to post or comment, but you can still view and subscribe to the sub.

Note from the moderators:
    ignorant takes
    If you have a question regarding your ban, you can contact the moderator team by replying to this message.

Rose

Rose finally had an interview request, from a podcast that both she and Ella had actually listened to. *Pop Empire* was hosted by a sassy gay man who went by DJ Alexander the Great. Ella was a fan; Rose had only listened to the episodes about Blue, back when Blue Velour was her entire life. These days, Rose hardly ever thought about Blue. Well, that wasn't entirely true. She had tried to channel Blue's *fuck it* attitude during her practice interview with the A&R rep's nineteen-year-old assistant. But channeling Blue was semi-impossible, as Rose felt frigid and deferential in the presence of strangers. The nineteen-year-old had given her mostly positive feedback, although she'd said Rose might try "loosening up" a bit. As if that was easy. Rose had relayed this feedback to Ella, who'd given her a pill that she said would make her feel "cool as a cucumber." She'd taken it half an hour ago—Ella had said to take it an hour before the interview—and she was already feeling more relaxed.

Rose made her way into Ella's room, as Ella had offered to drive Rose to the studio. She was still in bed, eyes half-closed. She opened them slowly and sat up on her pillow. "You're wearing that?" Ella eyed Rose up and down.

"It's a podcast," Rose said.

"It's filmed, hon," said Ella. "For YouTube. And DJ Alexander is kind of a bitch."

Fuck. Rose hadn't realized she was going to be on camera. She was wearing a Brandy Melville sweatsuit and no makeup. Ella hopped out of bed and made her way into her closet. She emerged with a vintage red baby doll dress Rose had never seen before. Ella had more clothes than anyone Rose had ever met—Blue included. Rose didn't have time to consider the dress. The interview was in thirty minutes so she just put it on.

Ella had sort of taken up the role of Rose's unofficial stylist slash makeup artist slash right-hand woman, which was nice because literally no one else seemed to care about Rose's career. Rose sometimes felt guilty, as she wasn't paying Ella and was in fact living in her apartment for a majorly discounted price. But then again, Rose had never asked Ella to do any of this, and whenever Rose tried to protest, Ella would just put a finger over her lips.

Ella went back into her closet and emerged with a pair of cowboy boots that smelled horrible, but hopefully DJ Alexander the Great wouldn't be able to smell them. Just in case, Rose took Ella's bottle of Fleur Narcotique and spritzed the fragrance liberally inside both boots.

"Hey, do you know how much that shit costs?" Ella scolded. She brought a brush to Rose's face, and Rose enjoyed the sensation of Ella doing her makeup. She was quite good at it, skillfully accentuating her cheekbones and widening her eyes. Ella always said that she'd be a makeup artist if somehow her money ran out, which seemed unlikely given Rose had never once heard Ella express financial concern. Rose knew Ella didn't actually care about Rose's generous spritzes of her perfume. Also, at this point, Rose could afford to buy her a new bottle.

The pill seemed to have taken full effect and Rose zoned out as Ella massaged various potions into her face. The next thing she knew, they were in Ella's Audi, cruising down Hollywood Boulevard to

DJ Alexander the Great's studio. Ella prepped Rose on the types of questions he typically asked his guests. He was known for being very intelligent and supremely snarky, a combination that frightened Rose. But luckily, she was feeling relaxed from the pill, and being coated in Ella's signature scent gave her a confidence boost. When Ella parked outside the studio, Rose glided into the building like a swan.

A receptionist greeted her with a bottle of water—Voss, ice-cold—and led her into the recording studio. Besides the standard sound equipment, the space was decorated in deep blues, royal purples, and gold accents, with a throne-like chair in which DJ Alexander the Great was sitting. He was really committed to the bit. Rose hardly remembered who Alexander the Great was. Some historical figure in . . . ancient Egypt? Conquered a bunch of innocent people? Low-key evil? High-key evil? She hoped he wouldn't expect her to know anything about history.

DJ Alexander stood up from his throne to greet Rose. He air-kissed her cheek. She could tell from his icy demeanor that he wasn't a fan. They both sat down. She felt small in the tiny chair across from his throne. He told her that their interview would be "a lot of fun" in a vaguely sarcastic tone and said they'd start recording in a minute or so. Rose nodded and sipped her Voss. She was thirsty, maybe a side effect of the pill. She wished she'd taken two. Her heart began to race, defying the meds. DJ Alexander the Great licked his lips like he was about to eat her, his prey.

Rose looked around and didn't see any cameras, just sound equipment. So Ella had been wrong about the show being filmed? Maybe she'd just wanted to dress Rose and do her makeup, like a little doll. Rose felt unsettled. A woman outside the glass held up three fingers, then two, then one. Rose had a sudden urge to ask to go to the bathroom, to bolt from the studio, but it was too late. The red light had gone on and DJ Alexander the Great was introducing her, welcoming her onto the show.

"Thanks for having me," Rose said, her voice slightly slower-paced than normal.

"Well, well, well," Alexander said. "*Pop My Cherry* is quite the debut—what's the release been like?"

Rose smiled at the soft opener. She could do this. "It's been surreal," she said. "I was a barista less than a year ago." She didn't admit the sad truth that it had felt disappointing and normal, that she felt the exact fucking same as she felt before the album came out. Except she was no longer serving coffee given the advance from Interscope.

"Right," he said. He licked his lips again. Why did he keep doing that? He rattled his iced coffee in his hand. "But between being a barista and this album, you were Blue Velour's assistant—yes?"

Rose nodded, then remembered it was a podcast. She had to give verbal responses. "Yes," she said, vaguely irritated. Blue was no longer Rose's favorite topic, no longer even on the top ten list, but she understood why he asked—it was a good story, to him, maybe to his audience, but not to Rose.

"We're huge Blue Velour fans here on *Pop Empire*," DJ Alexander said.

Rose vaguely remembered his effusive praise of *Blue's Beard* when that had come out. She more distinctly remembered him saying that the subreddit was filled with "deranged weirdos" who "should probably be locked up." She also noticed that DJ Alexander had not yet said he was a fan of *hers*, and she was certain that was because he wasn't.

"What was it like working for her?" he asked. "Did it impact your artistry at all?"

Rose exhaled. The nineteen-year-old had asked a similar question in the mock interview, so Rose knew what to say. "Blue was a lovely boss. She was kind and fun to work for." This was mostly true, minus when Blue gave Rose very difficult tasks like finding Chanel nail polish during a global pandemic, or when she lunged at Rose, called her a freak, and fired her for no reason, but it didn't make sense to share any of that. "But I didn't have much access to her creative process," Rose continued. "She made the entirety of *Mood Onyx* in a back house studio that I wasn't allowed inside—she didn't want any outside influence, understandably—so I never heard her make music or anything."

DJ Alexander shook his iced coffee again. Rose briefly pitied the sound engineer who would have to remove all these menacing rattles from the recording.

"But surely you must have picked something up from being around her, right? I mean—forgive me if I'm being forward—but Blue Velour's influence on *Pop My Cherry* is undeniable and frankly glaring."

Rose swallowed. "Well, we worked with the same producer."

"Sasha Harlow, yes, but Sasha's produced for a lot of people who sound nothing like Blue Velour."

Rose shrugged. "I suppose Blue and I share some sensibilities. We aren't as taken by traditional pop hooks." Rose exhaled, feeling satisfied with her answer. She was doing fine.

DJ Alexander sipped his coffee, then smiled at Rose in a way that terrified her. More was coming.

"You were a big fan of hers though, right?"

Rose nodded, then said, "Yes, I love *Oleander* and *Fluorescent Gloom*." She wasn't going to deny being a fan, but she certainly didn't need to get into the extent of it.

DJ Alexander licked his lips again. Rose again felt like she was about to be eaten.

"Come on, Rose," he said. "Let's be real here. This is *Pop Empire*. You can be honest with me."

Telling this man the truth was the absolute last thing Rose wanted. "I am being honest," Rose lied.

"Look, I don't doubt that you love *Oleander* and *Fluorescent Gloom*—those albums are all over *Pop My Cherry*. . . ." He paused and unleashed a high-pitched giggle. "Sorry, I still have trouble saying that album title without laughing. It's so outrageous and . . . pervy!" He stopped laughing and sipped some coffee, resumed the vaguely hostile grin from earlier. "Okay, where was I? Right, I hear those albums you mentioned in your music. But you're obviously downplaying the extent of your Blue Velour fandom."

"Am I?" Rose said. She would play dumb. Her heart started racing again. She should have taken more of these pills.

DJ Alexander unleashed another giggle. "Listen, surely you've been on the internet today."

Rose actually hadn't been on the internet today. She'd slept in, gotten dressed, come here. Instagram stressed her out these days—all the notifications, the rude comments, the people who wanted her dead. What was DJ Alexander talking about? Rose's heart thudded in her rib cage.

"Actually, I haven't," Rose said, telling the truth.

DJ Alexander put a hand over his mouth and giggled again.

Rose felt another urge to run out of the studio.

"Okay, so," he said. "I know Deuxmoi isn't exactly the *New York Times*, but according to a post this morning, which has been picked up by a number of outlets, a tech-savvy Blue Velour fan found out that the BlueBeards' subreddit was created from your parents' IP address in . . . Pittsburgh, was it?"

The floor began to fall beneath her, but instead of falling with it, Rose felt herself float to the ceiling. Was this a nightmare? It seemed real. It was fine, she told herself. She could do this. She could lie. How could someone possibly prove such a thing? She thought of what Blue would do, and she let out a laugh. A loud, mocking laugh.

"That's great," she said.

"So it's true?"

"Honestly?" Rose said. "I wish it was true. That would be amazing."

"So if it isn't true, why did this fan find that the account was created at your parents' house?"

"People can say whatever they want," Rose said. "It's a free country."

"So you think he's lying?"

"I know he's lying," Rose said.

DJ Alexander the great adjusted his headphones. "My producer is reminding me that when Sasha first posted about working with you, Blue commented, 'Our best BlueBeard,' on the post."

Rose had been waiting for someone to bring this up for months, then had forgotten about it, until now. "Blue loves to post cryptic things to get people speculating," Rose said. This was the answer she'd decided upon months ago when this comment resurfacing kept her up at night. "It's her whole thing."

DJ Alexander squinted his eyes at her. Suddenly Rose felt like she was being interrogated at a police station. "So you didn't create the BlueBeards subreddit?"

Rose forced another laugh, then shook her head. "Sadly, no," she said.

"And you were never a member of the subreddit?"

Rage began to radiate through Rose's body. Why on earth had this evil man invited her on his podcast to humiliate her? And why hadn't Ella warned her about this post? She was on her phone 24/7. Surely she'd seen it. But then she remembered Ella had been half-asleep this morning when Rose had gone into her room. Neither of them had seen it, because neither of them had jobs and they both slept until 11 a.m. Fuck. Whatever. DJ Alexander couldn't prove anything. He was clearly one of those obsessive Blue Velour fans who thought Rose was the devil and had brought her on his podcast to watch her crack. But Rose wasn't going to crack.

Rose shook her head again. "I don't even have a Reddit account."

DJ Alexander said nothing, just grinned, seemingly waiting for her to say more. Rose wanted to throw her Voss bottle at his head, then got a better idea.

"Well," she said. She bit her lip, mimicking the host's oral fixation.

DJ Alexander tapped his foot on the bottom of his throne. "Well?"

Rose enjoyed having his attention, waited a bit more before awakening her vocal chords. "I always had this vague suspicion that Blue herself started it," Rose said. "It just seemed like something she would do. She was obsessed with self-created mythology. Is obsessed with it still, I suppose. She seemed to feed off the subreddit, and it seemed to feed her career in return."

"Wow," DJ Alexander said. "That's fascinating. Was there anything you saw when you were working with her that made you think this was true?"

Rose shook her head. "Just a hunch."

DJ Alexander changed the subject, and Rose remained on the ceiling, answering questions semiconsciously, and soon she was being escorted out of the building by the receptionist, and was back in Ella's car, where she let out a very loud scream.

Blue

Blue hadn't left her bed in seven days.

Pop My Cherry was bad enough—tainting what should have been the beautiful experience of watching Max give birth—but making matters worse, *Violet* had been released seven days ago to a disturbingly lukewarm reception.

Spin had said: "*Violet* weaves a pleasing tapestry of hazy lullabies dedicated to Blue Velour's niece—a heartfelt tribute that falls short of breaking new ground in an otherwise familiar soundscape." *The Guardian* said: "*Violet* showcases Blue Velour's mastery at creating atmospheric melodies but ultimately plays it safe, reluctant to delve into the adventurous, boundary-pushing realms that fans have come to expect." *Rolling Stone* said: "*Violet* showcases Blue Velour's technical prowess under Isaac Altman's production, yet it yearns for the mystical synergy she had with former collaborator Sasha Harlow."

Blue refused to read the *Pitchfork* review. Isaac seemed fine with the reviews, said to wait for the Grammy nominations—he expected a few, he always got a few, but would she be involved? Blue was beyond frustrated. Critics had hated her last album for being too out there;

they hated this one because it was too safe. Blue couldn't win. She was so tired of fighting for respect.

Before Sasha had gone and made a bunch of derivative jailbait music with her former assistant, Blue had been doing well. The whole thing reminded her why she was avoiding having sex. She'd had sex with Sasha; it had ended badly. Very badly. Blue had once considered Sasha safe because she thought only men could hurt her. But Sasha had hurt her worse than anyone ever had, man or woman or in between. She'd betrayed her to infinity and beyond. And to think Blue had once thought their relationship was special. Blue would have considered hanging herself with a lavender noose if they hadn't sold them all.

And just when she couldn't feel any more melancholic, Max sent her a link to a podcast. Something called *Pop Empire*. Blue opened the podcast and listened while watching teal paint peel on the ceiling. She needed to pay someone to repaint it, but that type of mundane task was impossible to fathom right now. All the energy and motivation had been drained from Blue's body. Also, maybe she liked the bohemian vibe. She felt like one of those women from *Grey Gardens*. Blue had thought she might end up like that with Max or Sasha—two kooky old ladies singing all day in a dilapidated mansion surrounded by animals. But Max was now married with a family of her own—how had it happened so fast?—and Sasha was persona non grata, canceled, dead to her.

Blue supposed she'd just have to go crazy alone.

Rose was a guest on the podcast, and for a second Blue wondered if Max was trying to kill her. But she kept listening, vaping compulsively to quell the rage boiling up inside her. Of course, the entire interview so far was all about Blue—Rose's working for Blue, Blue's influence on her music—because Blue was literally all there was to Rose.

Blue was starting to like the host, who confessed to being a massive Blue Velour fan and who very obviously detested Rose. Had he invited her on his podcast to humiliate her? Maybe that was why Max had sent it. To hear the bitch get skewered. Blue leaned into the audio. The host seemed to catch Rose off guard by asking about a blind item indicating that Rose had started the BlueBeards subreddit. Blue had heard this rumor a few weeks ago, also via Max, Malibu's resident gossip junkie. Max had been shocked and appalled by the news. Blue less so. They already knew she was *in* the subreddit; it wasn't exactly a stretch that she'd founded it. Rose was obviously a freak. An indoor kid. A loser. Blue wished she could just stop hearing about her. Her voice on the podcast sounded exceptionally juvenile, timid, slow, as though she'd recently suffered a major head injury. Maybe she was just on downers. She was in the music industry now, after all, and maybe it would almost kill her like it had Blue. Or better yet, maybe it would actually kill her.

Rose of course denied that she had anything to do with the subreddit. And at that very moment, Bijou removed her head from the covers and began barking. The pup was so smart. Rose was full of shit, and Bijou had sniffed it day one.

There was a lull in the conversation, and then Rose said something that caused Blue's jaw to quite literally fall to the floor.

"No she fucking didn't," Blue said to Bijou, who was now barking and running in circles on the duvet. Blue shut off the podcast and was about to throw her phone when she realized she needed to text Max.

THAT LITTLE FREAK DID NOT JUST CLAIM I STARTED MY OWN FAN SITE

The next day Max came by with baby Violet. Not even Blue's perfect little niece could cheer her up.

"Auntie Blue made a beautiful record for you," Max said, handing the baby to Blue, who started to cry. A tear fell onto her niece's cheek and the baby flinched. Max went over and opened a window while Blue cried onto Violet's perfect little face.

"It really is a beautiful record, Blue," she said. "Violet loves it. I play it for her every night to put her to sleep."

"You sound like the critics," Blue said. "It's boring. It puts people to sleep. Even babies."

"Well, she fell asleep last night during the *Breaking Bad* finale, so I wouldn't take that personally," Max said.

"I want to kill Sasha," Blue said. Then she kissed the baby's head.

"Sorry," she said. "I don't actually want to kill anyone. Murder is a sin I would never commit. Sins are bad." She tapped Violet's nose. She wanted to be a good influence. "I'm just upset."

Max sat on the foot of the bed. She had that post-pregnancy glow, a luminosity to her skin and her aura. Her hair was thicker and longer than ever. "Have you thought about talking to her?"

"I never want to talk to Sasha again," said Blue.

"I meant Rose," Max said.

"Why on earth would I talk to the girl?" Violet started crying. "See," Blue said. "You've upset Violet with such a preposterous suggestion."

Max took Violet back, rocking her and cooing until she stopped crying. Watching Max soothe the baby warmed Blue's heart, temporarily melting the anger. Blue had a harder time staying angry these days. Maybe it was something about being almost forty. Or she was just tired.

"I just think it might not be the worst idea," Max said once Violet became quiet.

"To talk to my weird former assistant who lied to you?" Blue said.

"It was a white lie," Max said. "No one believed her."

"Of course not," said Blue. "I can hardly use a fucking computer."

"But if you could, it is the kind of thing you would do." A strange grin formed on Max's face.

"Why are you defending this freak?" Blue asked. She turned to the baby. "Sorry, I know it's not nice to say rude things, but this woman did me dirty."

"She did," Max said. She sat back down on the foot of the bed, bouncing Violet on her knee. "And I'm not defending her. I'm just saying—she's obsessed with you."

"She is," Blue said. "I'm all she has! Every single freaking question on that podcast was about me."

"Exactly," Max said. "And I think you could be strategic. You have more power in this situation than you realize."

Blue was listening.

"Let's remember the facts: you fired Sasha and Rose. You let them go, not the other way around. They were hurt because they felt abandoned. And when did Sasha post about making a record with Rose? Right after you announced to the world that you were breaking up with her—professionally, whatever—and working with her nemesis. And let's not forget, Sasha came back begging for you to give her another chance. You turned her away, then started working with her biggest competitor."

"God, kick me while I'm down," said Blue, eyes fixated on the peeling paint, feeling a strong desire to rip off all of it and leave the bare walls to echo her ugly emotional landscape. She felt like an open wound.

"I'm not trying to kick you; I'm trying to inspire you, Blue," Max said. "Don't you see? Everything Sasha does is because of you. And Rose is a superfan. She's literally obsessed with you. She knows every lyric you've ever written, she knows where it was written and when. She started a goddamn *subreddit* dedicated to decoding you."

Blue turned her gaze from the paint and blinked at Max. "I'm not following."

"You're in a perfect position to make the career-invigorating splash you're so desperate for," Max said.

"You think my career needs invigorating?" Blue said.

"I think your career is incredible, Blue. You inspire me every day. And I'm so happy that baby Violet has your tenacity to look up to. You saved us, Blue. You got us out of our shit hometown, and now we're in freaking Malibu, living our literal best lives, and it's all because of you. You could quit making music today and I'd always be proud of you. You could have never made music at all, and I'd still be proud to call you my sister. I've looked up to you since I was born and will never stop."

Blue blinked tears from her eyes. Bijou appeared from under the covers and nuzzled her thigh.

"But making records is what gives you purpose," Max continued. "Being a visionary, contributing to the cultural conversation—these things give you life. And I just think you're in the best position to do what makes you happy."

"I admire your optimism," Blue said. "But I'm having trouble seeing it."

"Well, I see it perfectly," Max said. "Allow me. . . ." She handed Violet back to Blue. Her tiny body felt so perfect in Blue's arms. Bijou licked Violet's miniature fingers.

Max stood up and stood tall, as if she were giving a speech at whatever that place was called where important people gave important speeches.

"Okay, so Sasha would take you back in a heartbeat. Rose worships you. So you go to them. And you tell them you'd like to collaborate."

"Pardon?" Blue said. "Are you well?" She kissed Violet's head again. "Did your momma hit her head on the way in?"

Max frowned, then resumed her speech. "It makes perfect sense. You teaming up with your former assistant who lied about being the superfan who created the subreddit BlueBeards, after which you playfully named your most critically acclaimed album, *Blue's Beard*, which she (badly) copied. Instead of being angry and petty—the old Blue—you make a record together, under the name Blue Rose, it's so fucking shocking and meta and *evolved*—the new Blue. People will lose their shit. That's what you live for, Blue!"

"You're nuts, I'm sorry," Blue said. "I can't make a record with someone I hate."

"If you can't beat 'em," said Max, "join 'em."

"You're saying I can't beat 'em?" said Blue.

"I'm saying you can," Max said. "And this is how you do it."

A cool ocean breeze shot through the window. Bijou licked the side of Violet's face, and the baby started laughing.

Rose

For the seventh morning in a row, Rose woke up with only a faint recollection of what had occurred the night before. She was shocked to be in Ella's bed given she thought she'd fallen asleep at Sasha's. But then a memory came floating back. Of Sasha telling Rose she had to get her shit together, that she was acting precisely as Blue had at twenty-six, that she was on a dangerous path, that she was driving off a cliff, and that Sasha didn't want to be in the car.

Sasha was overreacting. Rose was just celebrating her success, having fun. After she'd been doxed, people had started paying attention to her. She had gotten what she'd wanted—though she wished it hadn't come as a result of being humiliated on a popular podcast. Still, she wasn't exactly complaining. Within days of her being exposed as the creator of the subreddit, *Pop My Cherry* was reviewed in *NME*, and then got reviews in *Paste* and *The Observer* in quick succession. The reviews weren't glowing; they mostly focused on the album's peculiar origin story, Rose's role in creating r/BlueBeards, and its striking similarity to "Lavender Noose." The *A.V. Club* had summed it up with "*Pop My Cherry* is a mostly pleasant yet lackluster debut, its compelling backstory of fandom and controversy far overshadowing the music itself." Nevertheless, the A&R rep had abruptly shifted from disinterested to urgent, organizing a Zoom call filled with phrases like *strike while the iron is hot*.

Rose had immediately been booked for a mix of profiles and video interviews: *Uproxx* did a deep dive; *Complex* filmed a YouTube segment; and *Interview* ran a Q&A. The last one had actually prompted a call from her father, who'd seen one of his students reading the article in class on his laptop. He was scolding the boy when he realized his own daughter was in the photo. She felt like her dad was punishing her when he should have been congratulating her, which was how she often felt when speaking to her parents. So she'd invented an excuse and ended the call.

Rose had also been asked to go "Live" on Instagram with music influencers she'd never heard of, an activity she found extremely uncomfortable and that required a double dose of Ella's calming pills. She'd received a deluge of PR packages, filled with vintage-inspired designer jackets from Acne Studios, sheer bodysuits from Mugler, and enough Balenciaga sneakers to outfit the entire apartment building.

And beyond all that, Sasha suddenly wanted more from her.

Last night Sasha had gotten jealous because Miley Cyrus had been flirting with Rose at Carly Rae Jepson's album release party. And maybe Rose had been flirting back. They had been serving Veuve Clicquot. Rose had lost track of how many glasses she'd had. And when Miley came over and told Rose how much she loved *Pop My Cherry* while rubbing a finger along Rose's forearm, Rose returned Miley's grazes while occasionally making eye contact with Sasha across the room.

Rose had brought Ella, whom Sasha was beginning to dislike, calling her a "bad influence." (Ella said the same thing about Sasha.) Rose and Ella had spent the past month or so—Rose wasn't sure how long it had been—going out nearly every night. The lockdown had loosened and Rose had developed a taste for cocaine, the euphoria, and she was enjoying Ella's company more and more. With the record advance and subsequent royalties, Rose had been able to quit her job at the coffee shop, and Ella had been fired from Interscope for failing to show up, even on Zoom. So between the two of them, they had no real responsibilities. They'd go out until 2 or 3 a.m., then throw after-parties, wake up at around 4 or 5 p.m. She was finally on Blue's schedule.

Occasionally Rose would sleep at Sasha's, but those nights had become increasingly infrequent. Sasha was starting to bore her. Rose was twenty-six years old and had just put out a hit debut record. Sasha was a forty-four-year-old vegan who took herself too seriously. As Sasha herself had said, Rose was young and light and eager and filled with vigor and possibility. Rose suddenly remembered what she'd said to Sasha the previous night before storming out.

"You created this version of me," she'd shouted. "And now you can't stand it!"

In addition to infusing in her an enthusiasm for uppers, Ella had only intensified Rose's dedication to beautifying herself. She had taken Rose to get realistic-looking extensions so that her hair now hung almost down to her belly button. Thanks to keratin treatments, it was redder and silkier than ever. Ella and Rose got laser facials and acrylic manicures monthly, went shopping every day they weren't too hungover. They'd go to vintage stores like the Wasteland and Varsity on Melrose; Vivienne Westwood and Staud in West Hollywood; YSL and Chanel on Rodeo Drive when they were feeling super cocky, often while on cocaine.

Then they'd buy makeup at Neiman Marcus or Saks in Beverly Hills. They'd go home and try on their purchases for a few hours, listen to music, often Blue but more lately Rose. Then they'd go out for dinner at Osteria La Buca in their neighborhood, or Kinkan in Virgil Village, or Musso & Frank in Hollywood. Then they'd do more coke and go out at El Prado in Echo Park or the Frolic Room in Hollywood or the Friend in Silver Lake or Delilah in West Hollywood or Honey's in East Hollywood.

Honey's was their favorite, as it was a lesbian pop-up, and they typically went home with women. Ella was always encouraging Rose to branch out from Sasha, who she said was "washed up" and "dusty." Ella said that Rose was famous now and she should just relax and have fun.

But Rose didn't feel relaxed. She still felt embarrassed about having been doxed, and she was legitimately scared by all the mean messages she got on her social media, many wishing her dead. But Ella convinced Rose that it was very cool and "relevant" to be receiving death threats. And for every death threat there was an effusive and positive message, most from seemingly unwell gay men, saying something along the lines of: *bless you my unhinged princess!!* Rose suddenly remembered screaming something like that last night at Sasha: *there are many people online likening me to ROYALTY so I think I'm doing just fine* right before Sasha had kicked her out. What a narc.

Currently, Ella was snoring and Blue the dog was too, and Rose fell back asleep, confident that she'd done nothing concerning. She and Sasha were supposed to start recording album two next week, but Rose was free to enjoy herself until then. She'd straighten up once it was time to record. And even if she didn't, Blue and Sasha had made some incredible music that had ended up on *Spirit of Sinatra, Oleander*, and *Chateau Velour* before Blue went to rehab. Rose was young and sprightly and she'd be just fine.

When Rose finally fell asleep, she dreamed about Blue. Blue was singing. And smiling, in a kind of scary way. And then her face turned into DJ Alexander the Great's. He said, *I'm a big Blue Velour fan.* Then his face turned back into Blue's. She looked deep into Rose's eyes and said, *Everyone knows you're nobody without me.* She threw a cigarette on the ground and reiterated, *Nobody.*

Rose awoke drenched in sweat. Heart racing, she grabbed her phone and was shocked to see a text from *Blue Velour*, whom she hadn't heard from since she'd been fired over a year ago. Rose blinked to ensure she wasn't still dreaming. She rolled over and woke up Ella, showed her the text.

"Do you see this?" Rose asked.

"Holy shit," Ella said. "Open it."

Blue the dog barked.

2022

In the land of gods and monsters,
I was an angel looking to get fucked hard.

—LANA DEL REY

Sasha

Sasha had created not one, but two monsters.

Maybe in thinking this, she was taking away the women's agency. Maybe they had become monsters all on their own, and Sasha had just enabled it, or maybe even just witnessed it. Either way, she felt like she was on a train to somewhere very dangerous and it was too late to get off.

When Blue and Rose had shown up together at her doorstep several months ago, Sasha had thought she was having a stroke. In retrospect, she wished it had been a serious brain event. Something that would wipe out her memory and confine her to a home where she could just listen to records all day.

But no. It was not a stroke. Blue and Rose—the two women who had most captured Sasha's creative and romantic attention in her entire life, two women who allegedly hated each other—were now asking her to produce an album together under the name Blue Rose.

Blue had been wearing a gauzy blue kimono and Rose a silky red slip dress and they both had thick winged liner and pouty lips and unnaturally tight, poreless faces. Two iterations of the same music industry doll—the blue one and the red one. They both looked so different from when Sasha first met them. Sasha missed those versions of them—Blue in faded Levi's with naturally thin lips; Rose with glasses and freckles she now covered up with dewy foundation. But Sasha worried—for her own sake—that she was more attracted to the women standing before her.

That afternoon, Blue said she wanted to team with Rose because it would make her fans "fucking feral." Rose had giggled, clearly euphoric over the idea of working with Blue, the forever object of her greatest fangirl dreams. Sasha had been shocked but not surprised to learn that Rose had created the obsessive online forum that had inspired Blue and Sasha to troll back with *Blue's Beard*. Rose, as it turned out, had been the original and ultimate troll.

The revelation had somewhat tarnished Sasha's memory of their time together. Did Rose even like Sasha? Did she even mean it when she told Sasha she loved her that night before she left, or was she just an unhinged devotee like everyone on the internet said? But when Sasha was being honest with herself, which was rare, she felt mildly turned on by the idea of Rose as the creator of a subreddit dedicated to fawning over Sasha. Previously, she'd imagined the subreddit's creator as a frizzy-haired femcel, a description Sasha supposed once aptly fit Rose. And honestly there was something inspiring about Rose clawing her way from online admirer to Sasha and Blue's inner circle. The ascent took discipline and frankly the kind of reckless hutzpah that characterized young Blue herself.

Before that afternoon when the women showed up at her doorstep, Sasha was planning to start recording album two with Rose. Sasha had been mildly worried, as Rose had been partying a lot, acting not unlike Blue herself at that age. But when Sasha was honest with herself, and again, she rarely was, she knew that Rose was not an addict and was not throwing her life away, that she was merely a twenty-six-year-old woman with newfound fame who was, as Rose repeated over and over during their brawls, *living her fucking life*. And Sasha also knew in these rare self-aware moments that she herself should not be sleeping with a woman nearly twenty years her junior with whom she was also working, and that Rose was also sleeping with her beautiful and devoted roommate, who was a more appropriate romantic partner in nearly every way. But self-awareness was not where Sasha liked to live. Most of the time, she just saw Rose as a beautiful, young, rosy, tight, talented flower that had previously wanted only Sasha and suddenly wanted more. And that was hard to stomach, seeing Rose want more, realizing that Sasha was no longer enough. Sasha was competitive, a striver, and she wanted Rose's full attention back. And this feeling was familiar. In fact, it reminded Sasha of her relationship with one woman in particular. The truth was, Rose had captured Sasha's attention second only to Blue Velour.

And for that reason, Sasha was, like Rose, also euphoric to be sharing Blue's airspace that afternoon. Before that moment, Sasha had been convinced that Blue would never work with her again. She'd resigned herself to the idea that her transcendent time with Blue was over, and that she could perhaps try to replicate it with Rose, knowing well that it would only be a cheap approximation. That afternoon, Sasha had tried not to smile because she didn't want Blue to see how happy she was. But Sasha couldn't control herself; the left side of her mouth had started to curl upward. When it came to the question of working with Blue, Sasha was always a yes. She was always, forever, a yes.

But Sasha didn't buy Blue's alleged motive—to create chaos. As long as she wasn't drinking, angry, or horny—and Blue didn't seem to be any of these things that afternoon—she was actually quite deliberate. Sasha surmised that Blue's true motives had less to do with chaos and more to do with control. If Rose and Sasha were going to be making music, Blue wanted it to be under her watch.

Accordingly, Blue had asked Sasha and Rose to move in with her in Malibu. She said they could record at the house and at Shangri-La down the road. "Rick says it's cool," Blue had said, as though Rick was some guy she'd once fucked and not Rick Rubin, the founder of Def Jam and among the most celebrated producers of all time.

Sasha was obviously nervous about this idea, but she'd always been excited by that which made her nervous. That was why she'd been initially drawn to both Blue and Rose. When they first met, Blue had the reckless confidence of a downhill skier and the world-weary wisdom of a middle-aged divorcée. She also had the most captivating voice Sasha had ever heard, gliding with ease from delicate high notes to sultry, jazzy lows. But it wasn't just her voice—it was also her energy, the way she moved and breathed, the little sounds she made between words, the way she laughed at her own jokes, the sound of her exhaling smoke on the mic. Blue had one of those auras that drew people to her like a magnetic field, that made people want to be her friend and lover and also made them unable to stop looking at her. Sasha couldn't stop looking at her. She was so utterly desperate to get in the studio with her, to capture not just her singing voice but also the sound of her living, the way she saw the world.

Sasha had taken an immediate liking to Rose as a pleasant antidote to Blue's mercurial, unpredictable nature. Rose had been twenty-four when they met, a couple years younger than Blue had been, but she was nothing like Blue at that age. She was dutiful and steady, with a gentle, controlled voice that she'd honed at a top-ranked music program. When Sasha looked at Rose, she saw herself at that age—hungry, formally trained, sexually repressed. Rose made Sasha nervous because it was like watching a tragic movie knowing exactly how it would end. She was so pure, so off-limits, and so clearly drawn to her. And when Rose kissed her, Sasha was terrified in the precise way that made it impossible to say no.

And now, both of these women were Sasha's roommates in a crumbling '80s manor in one of the most expensive zip codes in the country.

On day one, Blue made a list of rules.

The first: No sex. No sex among the three of them. No sex with anyone outside the three of them. No masturbating. All of the sexual energy would go directly into the music.

The second: No cigarettes. Vaping was okay.

The third: Everyone had to sleep in their own bed, and all conversations about the music had to include all three of them.

The fourth: Generate sublime beauty.

The first rule, to Sasha's knowledge, was broken in week two, when Blue came into Sasha's room at 1 a.m. in a sheer nightgown with a black ribbon around her neck. Saying no to Blue was never an option. Blue was the first woman she'd loved and probably would be the last. She still fantasized about the two of them growing old together. Really, they were cut from the same cloth: impulsive, in love with music, incapable of monogamy, but forever hungry for each other. It was the first time they'd had sex in nearly two years, and for the first time that night, at the ripe age of forty-five, Sasha realized that absence did, indeed, make the heart grow fonder.

They did not break rule three that night, as Blue refused to sleep in her bed. She'd also told Sasha it would never happen again in a way that left Sasha starving for more. And two nights later, Rose appeared in Sasha's doorway, in lacy red lingerie with a literal rose between her teeth. Unlike Blue, Rose did not leave the bed immediately after, did not say it would never happen again.

But Rose was gone in the morning.

And that morning, Sasha saw Blue and Rose breaking rule two. The two of them were smoking on the balcony, giggling like old friends. Sasha didn't buy it, at least not on Blue's end. Rose looked different now—bolder, more red, less trollish—but underneath, she was still the same crazed fangirl frothing at the mouth to share Blue Velour's airspace. But what did Blue want from Rose? Admiration? Submission? Her young blood?

"What are you staring at?" Blue had asked.

"Nothing," Sasha had said as a sudden wave of nausea washed over her.

Roughly a week after rule two was broken, and stayed broken, Sasha witnessed a breaking of yet another rule. It was nearly 2 p.m. and neither Blue nor Rose was downstairs yet. Sasha was antsy to lay down the day's tracks. She went upstairs and knocked on Blue's door. And Blue was asleep in bed, her arms wrapped around Rose. Sasha wondered if they'd also broken rule one. The thought—to Sasha's dismay—turned her on to an epic and uncomfortable degree.

Soon all the rules had been broken: they were all smoking American Spirits, even Sasha occasionally after a few glasses of wine, sleeping with each other, and sleeping in each other's beds. And one night when Rose and Sasha had shared nearly two bottles of wine and Blue was on mushrooms, Blue kissed Sasha in front of Rose, then kissed Rose, then told Rose to kiss Sasha, and soon the three of them were in bed together.

The music was getting better as they continued to break rules, the way it always did. Sasha considered it her job to fall in love with her muses, to get them to reach their artistic peaks, which was often aided by them peaking sexually, together. You could never really know what a woman wanted to say until you'd seen her orgasm. Right? Sasha had learned this somewhere. Oh, right, she'd learned it from Blue. Blue was the very first person to make Sasha feel wanted romantically. Sasha had had sex before Blue, of course, she'd been thirty when they met, but it had all been banal and forgettable. Blue cracked open Sasha's world.

Before Blue, Sasha had, again, been more like Rose when Rose had first showed up at Velour Chalet—timid, cagey, uncomfortable in her own skin. But when Blue first came on to Sasha late one night during their recording sessions, Sasha for the very first time realized she might have something women wanted. Blue helped her figure this out by showing Sasha exactly how to love her, how to love a woman, how to build anticipation until they were both trembling with desire. Under Blue's tutelage, Sasha discovered the power that came from being able to unravel another woman completely.

Beyond sexual instruction, Blue began nudging Sasha's style in certain directions, away from fedoras and Diesel jeans and toward tailored silhouettes and expensive fabrics. Blue encouraged Sasha to ditch the hair straightener and embrace her natural waves, to dye her

American Spirits

mousy brown hair black, to use smudged black pencil to accentuate her almond-shaped eyes. Soon, women other than Blue were looking at Sasha.

Maybe Blue was the one who'd created a monster. Soon, Sasha was a Hollywood music producer who'd established Blue Velour. Everyone wanted to work with her. They were all young, attractive, sexually fluid, and had heard via the rumor mill that Blue's work was so magnificent in part because it was infused with the sexual energy of her collaboration with Sasha. And soon, Sasha was sleeping with every woman she worked with, so frequently that it no longer became special. It started to feel like work. She felt like a sex worker, a prostitute, a shell. That is, until Rose.

Rose was different somehow. Rose seemed to love Sasha, and not just what Sasha could do for her. Of course, Rose wanted to make a record together, but that felt tangential to their primary project of entwining their bodies at the axis of an ancient grove. The music came second; the two of them came first. No one had ever treated Sasha that way before, like she was more important than what she could do for someone. Rose made Sasha feel like she was special, just as she was, just being. But that version of Rose didn't exist anymore, or maybe it never had. Maybe it was all a game. Maybe none of them knew what they wanted. Sasha was a Pisces, a water sign, a watery figure. Blue and Rose were Geminis, also a mutable sign, all mutable figures, always in flux. Impersonating others, impersonating each other. Living in the morally gray waters that defined all the best creative works.

But Sasha started to miss the original versions of these women, the Blue who lived in a studio apartment over a Petco, the Rose whose glasses were always slipping off her tiny face, but most of all, she missed the original Sasha, the corny dyke who never left the house without a fedora and was desperate to be the next Linda Perry. Now Sasha was much more successful than Linda Perry, who'd hit on her several times—and was it she who'd said you needed to see a woman orgasm before you could produce her music?

During the third month of recording, an unshakable sense of dread began to creep over Sasha. She was living this perfect, utopic life in one of the most geographically beautiful regions on the planet, and yet, she had the sense that something was off. Blue said they were living in paradise, but sometimes to Sasha it felt more like a panopticon. It seemed like Blue had invited Rose and Sasha here so she could watch them.

Strange things started happening around the house. Sasha would hear laughter at night and try to follow it, only to find Rose asleep and Blue out somewhere, probably on one of her drives. She'd wake up to find a glass she hadn't remembered putting there on her nightstand, or her toothbrush missing from her bathroom. She figured Blue was fucking with her. When she confronted her, Blue said the house was haunted, that the previous owners had died under "mysterious circumstances." Sasha was pretty sure Blue was lying. But then one night, as she passed the bathroom mirror, Sasha caught a glimpse of her old self—the eager girl in a fedora, the one with tight skin and something to prove. She blinked, and the image was gone, leaving her current, worn expression staring back at her, looking afraid.

Outside, a marine layer filled the sky over the water and stayed for weeks. Sasha's stomach twisted into knots. For the first time, she realized that too much space could compress you, leave you gasping. It was as if the outside was closing in on her, making it hard to breathe.

One afternoon in the studio, Blue told Sasha she wanted to record the sound of her clearing her throat for an interlude. Inside the booth, Sasha was adjusting her headphones when Blue and Rose pressed up against the glass, laughing hysterically.

Sasha had given them a *what the fuck* look back.

Blue cracked open the door. "We were just discussing how much fun it would be to tie you up and leave you here."

Rose cackled.

"Just for a little bit!" Blue said. "We'd come back . . . eventually." She slammed the door.

Blue was obviously joking, but a chill had run down Sasha's spine nonetheless.

That dread intensified when Gigi fell ill during the fourth month of recording. They knew she was on her last legs, but then she stopped eating and literally stopped using her legs. The vet suggested putting her down, but neither Blue nor Rose, who had essentially adopted her at that point, wanted to do that. So for a few weeks, the dog slowly wasted away in a way that was difficult to watch, and incongruous with all the debauchery happening otherwise.

After three weeks, Blue found Gigi lifeless in a flower bed on the balcony. Rose took it harder than Blue. She didn't leave her room for the three days after they scattered Gigi's ashes in the Pacific. They dedicated the album's first single, "American Spirits," to Gigi. The cover art featured a photo of Blue and Rose with both dogs during Rose's first week of work. Bijou also seemed to take Gigi's death hard, assuming a depressive gait and decreased interest in food.

And three days after Blue Rose released the single to widespread shock, acclaim, and awe, that dread inside Sasha calcified into a hard, diamond-like substance that she'd later learn would never, ever go away.

That night, Rose appeared in Sasha's doorway. With her hands behind her back.

"What are you hiding?" Sasha asked with a grin, hoping Rose was wearing handcuffs.

But she wasn't wearing handcuffs.

She revealed her arms from behind her back.

In her left hand, she was holding a gun.

It was gold and glinted in the moonlight that shone in through the window.

Rose pulled the trigger and Sasha flinched. Rose laughed.

"I got it on a kink site," Rose said. "Do you love it?"

Rose

Rose was feeling like Blue for once.

It had taken four years, hundreds of bottles of rosé, and living in Blue's house for three months, but Rose was finally starting to understand what it felt like to be almost pure id. The version of Blue she presented to the world, the one who didn't care what people thought, rather than the actual Blue who Rose now knew rather well, the one who was so desperate for validation, it sometimes seemed it might literally kill her if she didn't get it. Rose didn't mind giving Blue attention; it came naturally to her. But she knew there was a difference between Blue Velour, the woman on the mic and in magazines, and the Blue whom Rose shared a home with—an empty woman plagued by doubt and insecurity, feverishly grasping at anything that might make her feel alive.

Rose wasn't stupid. Unlike Blue, she'd gone to college. She knew that Blue did not have Rose's best interests at heart. She knew that Blue was keeping Rose close because she didn't trust her. And Rose also knew that Blue was planning something that would make Rose look foolish. Rose was already hearing it on the record. Songs that seemed to mock her. The weird part was: Rose didn't entirely care? Whatever sincerity she'd come to Los Angeles with had evaporated into the spooky marine layer that had gathered over the house.

And now, Rose was pointing a kink gun at Sasha's head. And Sasha looked terrified. Rose wasn't planning to let Sasha think it was a real gun for too long, but the fear in Sasha's eyes excited Rose. She was coming out of her grief hole—losing Gigi had been harder than Rose expected—and she missed Ella, with whom things had turned properly romantic just before Rose moved into Blue's house. And it felt good to let all those sad feelings go and direct them at Sasha's terrified face.

Until Rose burst out laughing. She couldn't help it. Sasha was so pathetic. Rose had completely lost touch with the version of herself who wanted Sasha, who craved Sasha's attention and touch. Those things were way too easy to get. Sasha fawned over any woman under twenty-six who could hit a high C. Rose was nothing special.

But Rose's idea was something special, very Blue Velour. Rose knew Blue was only working with her as a stunt. A lot of people were upset. Some at Blue but mostly at Rose. Furious that Rose would interfere with Blue and Sasha's pristine relationship. Furious that Blue would work with someone as pathetic and shady as Rose. Everyone was talking about Blue, which Blue loved, and everyone was mad at Rose. Some people even wished her dead. Rose was the sacrificial lamb. But if there was one thing Rose had learned from ten years of Sunday school, it was that martyrs have power.

And she too was playing a game. During the *Pop My Cherry* press cycle, she'd learned the shameful but undeniable truth that people only cared about Rose Lush insofar as she was linked to Blue Velour. The more attenuated Rose became from Blue, the less likely they would be to listen to her music. So Rose was using Blue for the same reason that Blue was using her—for the rapt attention of a passionate audience.

Rose slunk up to Sasha and dragged the kink gun across Sasha's tired face. Sasha, who now knew the true nature of the gun, pretended to be afraid. She lived for roleplay.

"Please don't shoot me," Sasha said. She took off the silver signet ring she always wore on her left index finger. "Here, take this."

Rose took the ring in her mouth, then spit it out on the bedspread. Sasha reached for Rose's waist, and Rose pulled away.

"I want you to propose," Rose said to Sasha.

Sasha scrambled to find her ring in the bedspread. She found it, then hopped off the bed, got on one knee.

"Not here," Rose said. She pressed the gun into Sasha's temple.

"Okay," Sasha said. She put her ring back on her finger, then leaned into Rose again, held her waist with delicate fingers. "When?"

Rose pulled away again. She put the barrel of the kink gun on Sasha's forehead, right between her eyes.

"The first night of the Blue Rose tour," Rose said. "At the Hollywood Bowl."

Sasha laughed. "Okay." She tried to pull Rose closer, but Rose stayed put.

"What's funny?" Rose said, pushing the kink gun into Sasha's forehead.

"Nothing," Sasha said. "Just, we don't even have a tour scheduled."

"You think we aren't going to tour?" Rose knew they were going to tour. The pandemic was basically over and Blue was addicted to touring. And people loved their single, even if a lot of people also seemed to hate it. Love and hate were two sides of the same coin. While a lot of people wished Rose dead, there were just as many people still calling her mentally ill royalty. They were going to tour. With the album that Blue had designed to mock Rose. Rose was playing dumb, happily giving in to Blue's every sonic request, but Rose was smarter than she let on. Again, she'd gone to college. Rose wanted to prove, if only to herself, that she could have something Blue took for granted: Sasha. And Rose was absolutely high on the idea of Sasha announcing before an audience of Blue Velour fans that Sasha was choosing Rose.

"I'm sure there will be a tour," Sasha said.

"So what's the problem?" Rose said.

"You know people don't exactly like the idea of us together," Sasha said, snatching the gun from Rose's hand and kissing her.

"Yeah," Rose said when she came up for air. "That's the point."

Blue

*D*riving down the empty Highway 1, Blue listened to a track they'd just finished mixing—"Busted Mirror." As with most songs on the record, Blue's vocals were at the forefront. But instead of her typical sultry contralto, Blue mimicked Rose's timid, babyish voice. Blue was an excellent mimic. On the bridge, Rose tried and failed to echo Blue's deep contralto. Blue cackled.

Rose didn't even realize she was the punch line.

Blue remembered the clownish scene she'd overheard last night. Turning in to the canyon, her laugh swelled and filled her belly, nearly causing her to swerve off the road. Blue couldn't believe what she'd fucking heard through the thin Malibu walls: Rose had asked Sasha to propose to her the first night of the tour? Rose wanted Sasha to propose to her before a crowd full of people who hated Rose and only liked Sasha when she was with Blue? It was batshit. And honestly? It sounded like a stunt Blue would have pulled at Rose's age, like when she'd opened for Sia in 2009 and begun her set with a Sia cover that was frankly much better than the original. The crowd had seemed angry, but many had thought it was positively iconic. People still mentioned it to her today.

If Rose wanted to get under Blue's skin, she was going to have to try a lot harder. Blue was all for this proposal, because the crowd would go apeshit. And she knew Sasha would never actually go through with a marriage. Sasha and Blue both saw monogamy as a trap, a source of terrible claustrophobia, a nightmare and a curse.

Blue sped up in the dark, winding toward the Rock Store. She'd been going to her favorite biker bar a few nights a week after Sasha and Rose disappeared to their bedrooms, either alone or together—Blue didn't really care. She wasn't a jealous person. But she was curious. She'd conceived of this whole project to keep an eye on them. If Sasha and Rose were going to be sleeping together and making music together, Blue wanted it to be under her roof. And so far this little experiment had confirmed what Blue already knew: Blue was all these women had. Every decision they made led back to Blue. Hence their idiotic little proposal plan. Blue laughed again.

The parking lot was filled with motorcycles as usual, and as usual, Blue scanned the bikes looking for her next husband for the night. Her eye caught an Indian Scout Bobber, matte black with chrome accents. She knew it belonged to someone who wasn't around here, someone intriguing. As if the universe was reading her mind, a body emerged from the bar and leaned against the bike. He wore a camouflage baseball hat and his skin appeared dark and leathery under the parking lot lights. As Blue approached, he pulled out a pack of Camel Reds. Blue had a full pack of American Spirits in her purse, but approached the man nonetheless.

"Got one to spare?" she asked.

He handed her a cigarette and lit it without saying anything. There was what appeared to be a layer of dust on his weathered hands, as if he'd blown in with the desert wind. Blue felt a pulsing sensation between her legs. The man lit her cigarette, then his own. A gentleman.

"You look familiar," he said after a drag. "You one of those Hollywood movie stars or something?"

Blue shook her head. "I can't act for shit unfortunately," she said. It was true. Her manager had tried to get her a few roles—in the *Charlie's*

Angels reboot and in a Bond film—but Blue could never manage to make her face show the character's feelings instead of her own. She had a very expressive face—not even Botox could freeze it into submission—and many moods. She could only ever be Blue Velour, although there were many Blues, too many to make room for some random Bond girl.

"A singer?" the man asked.

Blue shrugged. She couldn't tell whether to be herself, or which one of her selves to be. An owl hooted in the distance, and Blue shuddered, thinking of Velour Chalet, which had turned her off nature sounds of all kinds. She remembered that Rose was now in her complete control. Her little bitch. And honestly? She kind of liked the little bitch. Not as much as Bijou, but maybe as much as Gigi—RIP.

"I like to sing," she said finally.

He cocked his head at her. She couldn't tell if he knew who she was.

"What about you?" she asked him. "I take it you aren't from around here."

"Name's Jett Donovan," he said. "I live in Nevada—what gave it away?"

"You don't look like a pussy," Blue said.

Jett laughed.

"What brings you to the land of weak men?" she asked.

"Lion tamer," he said. "Traveling circus, currently set up over Ventura."

"Right, okay, and I'm a mermaid," Blue said. She bit her lip. Jett was very sexy, even if he was fucking with her.

"You know, you aren't the first to say something sarcastic when I say what I do for a living." He pulled out a smartphone from his pocket, a mild turnoff, but at least it wasn't an iPhone—Blue didn't even recognize the brand. He clicked the cracked screen—redeeming—with his thumbs and opened a video.

On the screen, Jett stood in a dusty field under a washed-out sky, steady as a statue while a large cat padded toward him. Jett didn't even flinch, his hands loose at his sides. The lion circled him, then leaned into him like they were old pals. Jett raised a hand and the lion sat, its eyes half-lidded as he ran a hand along its back. He flipped through a few more videos, one of him crouched low, coaxing a lion forward with nothing but a whistle. Another of him feeding raw meat to a half dozen big cats under the low light of a circus tent. Finally one of him sprawled on the grass with a cub curled up beside him, fast asleep, his hand resting on its small, rising ribs.

Jett put the phone back in his pocket and smiled at her out of the side of his mouth, the way Sasha did sometimes. But Sasha could never tame a lion.

"Buy me a drink?" Blue asked, nodding toward the door to the bar.

Inside, he looked sexier in the red glow of the bar lights. As Jett ordered her a Red Bull, Blue caught her reflection in the mirror behind the bottles, half-shadowed. She imagined herself as a circus wife, dust on her boots, waiting in some desert town while the lions roared somewhere close by.

AMERICAN SPIRITS   7.3

Blue Rose • 2022

If the internet had its way, this album wouldn't exist. But *American Spirits* materialized anyway, fueled by the messy online discourse surrounding it. On their debut, supergroup Blue Rose spins parasocial lore into something thorny, intimate, and downright mythic.

The album circles a rumored love triangle among the group's members: niche legend Blue Velour, rising ingenue Rose Lush, and alchemic producer Sasha Harlow. It allegedly began in 2020, when the threesome quarantined together deep in the redwoods. Lush was there as Velour's assistant, while Harlow was producing *Mood Onyx* and was reportedly involved romantically with both women during this period. After the harsh reception to *Mood Onyx*, fans claim Velour left the cabin in a rage, firing both Lush and Harlow. Further speculation holds that the terminated pair remained in Velour's rental to create *Pop My Cherry*, widely interpreted as Harlow's ultimate act of betrayal.

Things were already twisted. And then they got weirder. Around the release of Rose Lush's debut, *Pop My Cherry*, online sleuths discovered that Rose was not merely an assistant, but the founder of the infamous BlueBeards subreddit—a 70,000-member forum dedicated to dissecting Velour's suspected romance with Harlow, which Velour referenced on her 2019 masterpiece, *Blue's Beard*. All this time, Rose had secretly been Blue Velour's most obsessive and most unhinged fan. *American Spirits* turns that deceit, tension, and madness into the album's sonic landscape.

The title track unfurls like a religious hymn to nicotine and mortality. Blue's rich contralto, seasoned with experiential wisdom, entwines with Rose's vibrant, youthful timbre, the union embodying the duality of their relationship: mentor and protégé, idol and admirer, rivals turned collaborators.

Aesthetically, the album thrives on contrast. While Rose brims with effervescence, Blue channels a nocturnal, contemplative energy reminiscent of the sound honed on *Mood Onyx*. Released amid 2020's social upheaval, the album was initially criticized as tone-deaf but was later reappraised as a masterful portrayal of a mind undone by self-isolation. On *American Spirits*, Blue adds to this narrative, evoking images of wandering an American wasteland, searching for salvation. (The lore holds that after *Mood Onyx* was panned, Blue embarked on a frenzied, amphetamine-fueled drive across the United States in just thirty-six hours.) Together, Rose's luminous tones and Blue's dusky vocals create a spectral duet through the depths of the collective American unconscious.

The collaboration invites reflection on the cyclical nature of artistic influence and reinvention. On her initial albums, Blue Velour famously channeled the refrain from Nancy Sinatra's "Bang Bang (My Baby Shot Me Down)"—over, and over, and over. It seems almost natural that Rose Lush would echo Blue's "Lavender Noose" on her debut, *Pop My Cherry*. Artists, after all, are merely products of their influences. (Put another way: all artists steal.) In this light, Rose's emulation of Blue's work is less an act of plagiarism and more a rite of passage.

Yet in "Busted Mirror"—titled like a parody of Blue's early work—Blue Velour mimics Rose's bright, conservatory-style vocals, in turn challenging the notion of homage and subtly undermining Lush's contributions. This playful gesture sets the stage for the album's denouement, "Requiem for a Daydream," an apparent reference to *Strawberry Daydream*—an earlier, abandoned version of Rose's debut. This final track bleeds with the melancholy of unrealized dreams.

Ultimately, *American Spirits* confronts the intertwined forces of creation and destruction, of homage and repetition. The album's name nods to the cigarette brand while summoning the spirits of American music legends, proving that "originality" might just be a remix of the familiar ghosts we can't let go. Amid this haunting, Rose Lush emerges as a pivotal figure—initially the earnest newcomer seeking California dreams, only to grasp at fool's gold.

But the question lingers: Is she in on the joke?

r/BlueBeards • posted by u/GarboMommy • September 2022

Ughhhhhhhhhhh

American Spirits is here, i.e., our Black Tuesday, our Pearl Harbor, our JFK assassination, our Challenger explosion, our Hurricane Katrina, our 9/11. Whenever I think Rose can't get any more monstrous, she finds a way to outdo herself. I stuck my neck out for that little ingrate when she was just a nobody with stars in her eyes. And now she hits us with her most unforgivable sin yet!? Parading around making self-indulgent "art" with the two people she fucked over to the nth degree—it's like Rose gets a sick pleasure from twisting the knife. For what? Some misguided attempt to process past trauma through an album of mid Blue Velour B-sides? Shoot me!

I can't believe her sinister spell is working its sorcery on not just Sasha but also Blue?! Blue, baby, I know you're in there somewhere. Snap out of whatever psychosexual trance this devious siren has you under! Sasha, you too! You are the only ones for each other! Get away from this little redheaded devil leeching your creative brilliance!

Rose is a poison, an emotional black hole dressed up as a fire crotch bohemian baby. This album makes an absolute mockery out of something very painful and personal for me and the whole BlueBeards community.

Blue, we bled for you through your darkest days, and now you're dancing on our graves.

Comment by u/Mercury

I dunno, isn't Blue kinda making fun of Rose with the whole thing? The mockery is glaring on "Busted Mirror." Feels like she's not totally letting Rose's disrespect slide. . . .

Comment by u/GarboMommy

Mockery isn't enough.

2023

Bang bang, my baby shot me down.
—**NANCY SINATRA**

Blue

Blue put a French fry in her mouth. It burned her tongue. She was having lunch with a scout from Interscope's rival, Republic. They tried to snatch her up every so often, gave her big pitches about how they'd do something incredible for her career. Blue was loyal. She'd never leave Interscope. Interscope had saved her life. But she couldn't resist an expensive free lunch.

"I don't want to be rude," the Republic exec said. Her name was Dahlia. She was drinking a margarita and wearing a fuchsia blouse. They were eating by the pool at the Sunset Tower Hotel, the Art Deco Hollywood landmark where John Wayne, Frank Sinatra, and Howard Hughes had all lived at various points. Hughes apparently lived in the penthouse and rented some of the lower apartments for his mistresses. John Wayne once reportedly brought a cow up to the penthouse at 3 a.m. and told his guests who were drinking coffee that if they wanted cream they'd have to go right to the source.

Blue loved it here.

"Be rude," Blue said.

"Okay," said Dahlia. She sipped her margarita, made a face, then put it down. "I fucking hate Rose. Hate her ugly red hair and annoying baby voice."

Blue sniffled a smile. This precise attitude had been fueling Blue for several months as the tour approached. Blue Rose was playing at the Hollywood Bowl in three days. She'd spent the last month writing a few songs for the next *Hunger Games*, easy money but a banal pastime compared to the euphoric rush of puppeteering the emotions of a captive audience. Her cells buzzed with that feverish anticipation that always came before a tour.

"Hate everything about her," Dahlia continued. "Hate the naïve posturing, the gimmicky lyrics, *Pop My* fucking *Cherry*? I mean, put Sasha in jail for that." She picked up a fry, then put it down. "And I *hate* that you're working with her."

Blue sighed. "Yeah," she said. "Most people do." Blue had hate mail nearly every day from fans furious at her for teaming up with Rose. But Blue had forgiven Rose and Sasha for the mediocre record they'd made three years ago. At least, she thought she'd forgiven them. A weird thing about being a bipolar drug addict and also an entertainer was that it was hard to know what feeling was authentic and what feeling was simply the byproduct of a chemical imbalance or a desire to ignite the fans who paid her bills and kept her alive.

"You know, I went to law school," said Dahlia. "Passed the California bar at twenty-five."

The pool glimmered silver. Blue pulled her sunglasses closer to her face and tapped her foot on the pavement. "Mazel," she said to Dahlia.

Dahlia laughed. "I'm not looking to be congratulated," she said. "I just want you to know that legally speaking *Pop My Cherry* is your property."

Blue nodded. She suspected this was true, but she didn't care about the law. She wasn't Radiohead. All art is stolen, et cetera. But Dahlia kept talking. Blue struggled to pay attention.

"Okay, so because *Pop My Cherry* was created at a house rented by you during a period when both Rose and Sasha were financially compensated by you, it triggered a work-for-hire situation, which rendered everything they created your legal property." She took another sip of her margarita and Blue's foot started to tap faster. "Moreover, the album's stylistic essence, particularly its resemblance to 'Lavender Noose,' constitutes a direct infringement of your musical style and brand."

Blue hardly knew what Dahlia was saying. "Sorry," she said. "Legalese bores me."

"Listen, I can handle that part. But I have an idea that might interest you. I'll put it in layman's terms."

Blue squinted and tried to pay attention.

"I can draft the complaint," Dahlia continued. "I think you should demand all initial profits and future royalties, but that's not the interesting part."

Dahlia leaned in close to Blue. Blue smelled tequila on her breath.

"I think you should serve the lawsuit onstage at the opening show of the *American Spirits* tour, at the Hollywood Bowl. Light your fucking audience on *fire*."

Dahlia's pupils were huge and Blue wondered if she was on something stronger than tequila.

Part of Blue wanted to make an excuse to leave and forget this conversation. But the less evolved part of her was intrigued. She liked setting things on fire. Her fans were desperate for Blue to enact revenge. Blue didn't believe in revenge, at least not right now, yet she believed in her fans and respected them. This legal maneuver would please them. Sasha would be fine, but Blue knew Rose had nothing to fall back on. This would force her to get some menial job or move back to Pittsburgh. How dreadful. Blue would never go through with the lawsuit. She didn't have much patience for the legal system, nor did she want to ruin Rose's life. But she liked the idea of giving her a scare.

Blue stuck a fry in her mouth. It was cooler now, didn't burn her tongue. All she ever wanted was respect.

"I'm listening," she said when she finished chewing.

Rose

That feeling was happening again. The ground falling out from under her, the breath being snatched from her lungs, the world around her spinning, *spinning*, *spinning*.

Rose was sitting next to Ella at the salon, all chrome and white plastic curves lined with mirrors that multiplied the space into infinity. With silver foils in her hair jutting out at odd angles, Ella looked like some kind of demented angel with a halo of broken metal. Rose gripped the armrests of her chair, trying to anchor herself, but the fluorescent lights were too bright, and the foul-smelling concoction slathered over her hair was making her dizzy. Or diz*zier*. She was always vaguely dizzy these days.

The first show of the *American Spirits* tour was in three days and Rose was having panic attacks every four to seventeen minutes, like a pregnant woman having contractions. She supposed the show would be a birth of sorts. Rose had gone on a petite tour for *Pop My Cherry*, just five cities in venues an eighth the size of the Hollywood Bowl. This tour would be twice as long in venues many times the size. With audiences primed to hate her. Her A&R rep had said this tour would be the birth of Rose Lush, but Rose felt certain it would be her death.

Rose felt like her career had been slowly dying since she'd left Malibu in the fall. Or maybe it had started dying when she left the redwoods, before it even began. She'd left a part of herself in Northern California, the human part that cared what people thought and wanted to be liked and do the right thing. Since she started working with Sasha, life felt like a weird game. For a while, she thought she was winning that game. Going viral with the Britney Spears cover felt like winning. Releasing her debut album to semi-positive acclaim felt like winning. Moving in with Blue and Sasha to make a record felt like winning.

But since leaving Malibu, Rose felt like she was losing. She kept replaying scenes from Malibu, events she'd thought were positive in the moment, but in retrospect felt pathetic and embarrassing, following Blue around like Bijou and doing every little thing she wanted. About a month ago, she'd heard "Busted Mirror" in a coffee shop and a random patron had pointed at her and yelled, "There's the traitor herself!" Rose wanted to be writing music and gathering notes for her next album, but whenever she tried, she felt like an imposter and a loser and a freak. And her notes app remained blank.

Rose received death threats almost every day. Ella now ran Rose's Instagram account so she didn't have to see them. And while Rose had left the subreddit of her own volition years ago, Ella had been ejected from BlueBeards simply for defending her. Ella had heard from a friend that the subreddit had found out and was *furious* that u/PinkCocaine had been living with u/RoseGhost. And now, Ella wasn't just living with Rose. They were sleeping together almost every night. They weren't monogamous, mostly because Rose felt incapable—Sasha and Blue had broken her brain and her heart in so many ways—but Rose's affection for Ella grew every day.

Rose often tried to pinpoint when exactly she'd developed feelings for Ella, the precise moment their relationship had turned romantic. There were many pivotal moments—Ella's first comment on Rose's inaugural r/BlueBeards post, which made Rose feel seen for the very first time; Ella offering Rose a highly discounted room in a glamorous apartment in Blue's city; Ella nursing Rose's heart back to health after Sasha shattered it. Ella had helped Rose realize her dream of becoming a pop star, guided her on how to look glamorous and appear confident. She took photos and posted them on Rose's Instagram, because Rose couldn't look at Instagram without having a panic attack followed by suicidal ideation.

But there was one moment Rose's mind often returned to, the moment she realized that Ella was not as vain or as self-involved as she often pretended to be. Through a friend she'd met at her Interscope internship, Ella had gotten them backstage passes to a Billie Eilish show—Ella's favorite artist second only to Blue. She'd been talking about it for months, obsessing over her outfit and figuring out what she'd say to Billie when she got the chance. Rose liked Billie too, especially since Billie had recently admitted to owing her entire career to Blue Velour's influence. But she was nowhere near as excited as Ella. And then, the day of the concert, Rose came down with food poisoning. (She'd eaten two-day-old sushi for lunch.) She couldn't leave the toilet and told Ella to obviously go without her. But Ella had stayed home, rubbing her back while she vomited all night.

And beyond all the acts of service, Ella was starting to feel like home. Rose had grown accustomed to the feeling of Ella breathing beside her when they slept, the way Ella stroked Rose's back with her fingertips when Rose woke up from a nightmare, which was happening with increasing frequency as the tour approached. Rose and Ella weren't just lovers; they were best friends. Really, Ella was Rose's only friend, the only person who cared about Rose's feelings in a city where no one seemed to care about anyone but themselves.

"You okay, Rosie?" Ella asked. Sharp light bouncing off Ella's foils temporarily blinded Rose, reminding her of stage lights, reminding her of the imminent tour, of that which she dreaded most: sharing a stage with the religiously charismatic Blue Velour.

"I can't breathe," Rose whimpered. She hated this feeling. Rose kept thinking about the tour, about being ridiculed. She had nightmares about being booed offstage every night. And she couldn't stop thinking about that night she'd demanded that Sasha propose to her onstage. They hadn't spoken about it since, and a normal person would think, *It was obviously a joke, there's no way Sasha will propose onstage.* But Sasha liked attention as much as Blue, especially from Blue and Rose. And that would be sure to get their attention.

Sasha had been needier since Ella entered the picture. Rose could tell Sasha was threatened by her. They didn't like each other, and when Rose was feeling vaguely evil in a way that Blue and Sasha had taught her to feel, she liked watching them fight over her. It was perhaps for this reason that Rose hadn't talked to Sasha about the plan, hadn't told her that it was obviously 100 percent off, like a normal person would do. Because part of Rose wanted Sasha to propose. Part of her wanted Sasha to declare to an audience of Blue's fans that she was choosing Rose.

Another wave of panic moved through her.

Ella squeezed Rose's hand. "Let's take a walk," she said.

Rose nodded, her breathing still ragged.

"*Sorry,*" Ella whispered to her colorist. Rose said nothing to hers. Ella took her smock off but Rose left hers on. Ella led Rose outside, where the air was cool but the sun was bright, as it always was.

"Tell me five things you can see," Ella said. She'd suffered from panic attacks her entire life—she said all heiresses did—and she'd learned this method from a therapist she'd gone to when she was eleven.

Rose squinted, her eyes struggling to adjust to the brightness. She looked around. "Red car, palm tree, baby," she said. "Poodle, smashed ice cream cone."

"Great," Ella said. "Now four things you can feel."

"Sun on my skin, hair dye in my hair, cool air, your hand."

Ella squeezed Rose's hand. She was feeling slightly better.

"Three things you can hear."

"Birds, baby crying, your voice."

Ella smiled. She looked adorable with her freckled nose and the silver foils in her hair.

"Two things you can smell."

"Vanilla ice cream, your perfume."

"One thing you can taste."

Before Rose could speak, Ella kissed her.

The kiss felt good, calming, but then Rose felt guilty.

She needed to talk to Sasha, right?

She'd text her as soon as they got back inside.

But Rose never texted her.

r/BlueBeards • posted by u/TrueBlue • January 2023

Who's seeing me at the Bowl tonight?

Hello, BlueBeards, it's me! The real Blue Velour! I swear I'm not a troll! You all probably won't believe me, but you'll just have to find faith in your hearts that I'm the True Blue—Beatrice Vera Clark, born June 20, 1981, in Wilmington, North Carolina. My favorite TV show is *The Bachelor*, my signature scent is Tom Ford's Velvet Orchid, and my favorite album is Nirvana's *Bleach*. I love men over forty-five (sorry) and I have a tattoo on the inside of my index finger that says *Oleander*, which is the name of my second studio album. I had two dogs named Gigi and Bijou, but Gigi passed away last summer and I miss her every day.

These things are all probably easily googleable, but I've never been great with a computer, so who can say? My sister (Maxine Ida Clark) had to teach me how to get on here. I've heard that you all are *so pissed* about *American Spirits*. Thank you so much for your concern about my life. I'm so appreciative that you all are looking out for me and know so much more about my life than I do—even though I'm the one living it! I am so lucky to have you all!

And for those of you upset about me working with Rose, I have a very fun surprise for you all tonight! I won't ruin it, but I just want to let you all know: I've been listening.

Okay, time to return to my favorite pastime: S'ing the D and spending G's! Just kidding. Or am I . . . ?

Bye for now my loves!

Xo,

Blue Velour

Comment by u/CoolRanch

> SHUT UP OMG IS THIS A JOKE? If not: WE LOVE YOU BLUE!

Comment by u/LilacLies

This is obvi a troll. "S'ing the D?" Yeah right. Blue is into Sasha only.

Comment by u/405Tulips

Guys, I think it's really her. I'm almost positive "S'ing the D" is an Easter egg about Sasha? Aren't Sasha's parents Russian and her birthname is Dasha, but she changed it to Sasha to fit in at school? I feel like I heard Blue call Sasha "D" in an interview once. I think she's talking about Sasha! We love you Blue!! Sasha and Blue 4ever!!

Comment by u/DepravedButterfly

Girl, where have you been? Sasha's real name is Alexandra Greta Hardy—check out the deep dive. BUT. Greta = G = "spending G's" . . . just a thought! It always goes back to Sasha <3

Comment by u/GarboMommy

This is obvi a troll. I'm going to ban her now.

Blue

Blue's body pulsated as she stood looking over the empty amphitheater.

Tonight, she was performing for the first time since 2020, that annoying-ass day that had ruined everything. At 8 p.m. this evening, she would play the Hollywood Bowl, her favorite venue, with her personal assistant turned current collaborator, the artist formerly known as Rose Lutz.

Blue knew that after tonight, she would never talk to Rose again. They were scheduled to tour twelve cities, but Blue had recently been diagnosed by a well-renowned energy healer as clairsentient, meaning she could receive psychic messages in her body. And today, her body was sending her a strong message: this would be her last night with Rose.

Tonight would unfold as follows: Rose would open, playing hits from *Pop My Cherry*, if you could call them "hits." Blue laughed to herself as she smoked. Rose was singing said tracks right now at sound check. They were so boring, Blue was worried the audience would fall asleep. After Rose anesthetized the audience, Blue would come out and wake them up with her eight studio albums' worth of actual hits. Then Rose would come back, and they'd perform their bangers from *American Spirits* that were only bangers because Blue and Sasha had made them bangers. Then Blue would execute Dahlia's plan—a disruption that had become bigger as Dahlia consumed more margaritas.

When Dahlia was on margarita number two, Blue had told her about overhearing Rose demand that Sasha propose to her on the first night of the tour. Blue thought the story was charming, recounting the dialogue with a breathy laugh. "She's trying so hard to be me," Blue had said.

"Is she also trying to be dead?" Dahlia had replied, rather morbidly. Dahlia continued that Rose and Sasha were playing checkers, and Blue should play chess.

Blue wasn't good at chess, but now she had a lawyer with anger management issues on her side. Republic was so desperate to woo her away from Interscope, they were literally drafting pro bono lawsuits on her behalf. Blue would never leave Interscope, but she wasn't about to look a gift horse in the mouth, so she'd let them execute a checkmate.

First, Dahlia had met with the lighting guy to switch out the previously agreed-upon visuals, images of red roses and blue velour, of light and dark, sun and shadow. Midway through the first song, the screen would project images Dahlia had dug up of Rose as a young girl in Pittsburgh, smiling acne-faced beside her massive shrine to Blue Velour. Then, Rose would project various comments Rose, under the name RoseGhost, had made in the BlueBeards subreddit. Comments that read as delusional as QAnon, as nerdy as a girl with headgear.

And that was just phase one.

The final image would be the legal complaint. As of tonight, Blue was officially suing Rose and Sasha for copyright infringement, breach of contract, and violation of property rights. The lawsuit demanded all initial profits from the album's sales and future royalties.

Blue would obviously drop the lawsuit—Machiavellian had never been her vibe—but she wanted to please her audience and knew that pulling this stunt in front of her biggest fans in Los Angeles was sure to create a worthwhile explosion.

Maybe Blue wasn't clairsentient. Maybe she just knew the plan would send Rose running. More maybe both things were true.

She lit another cigarette and stared at the Hollywood Hills turning orange in the afternoon sun.

It looked like they were on fire.

r/BlueBeards • u/TrueBlue is permanently banned from r/BlueBeards

Hello, you have been permanently banned from participating in **r/BlueBeards** because **your post** violates this community's rules. You won't be able to post or comment, but you can still view and subscribe to the sub.

Note from the moderators:
   offensive impersonation
   If you have a question regarding your ban, you can contact the moderator team by replying to this message.

Rose

Rose struggled to breathe, let alone sing. The stage lights pierced her eyes, rendering her vision spotty and her brain dizzy. The audience was a vast sea of darkness, invisible except for the sounds—talking, yelling, and not in a positive way. The attendees were bored at best, hostile at worst.

The cabin songs she'd made with Sasha at Velour Chalet did not translate to such a big venue. And even if they did, Rose knew she was performing them terribly. Her own voice relayed back to her in her headphones sounded screechy and amateur, like that of a nervous preteen at a middle-school talent show. She caught an image of herself on the onstage monitor—timid and shaky, with the posture of a crow, like a shy child who'd accidentally wandered onstage.

Rose's heart slammed against her rib cage. She kept fantasizing about running off the stage, out of the venue, to the 101, straight into oncoming traffic. It was what the audience wanted, right? To see her eviscerated in a violent explosion. Rose squinted to see Ella, who was allegedly in the VIP section. But she could see only faceless silhouettes.

Finally, after what felt like an eternity but had actually been twenty-two minutes, she was on the last song of the set. The Britney cover. When Rose started strumming the opening chords of "Unusual You," the audience seemed to perk up somewhat. Although, they were probably cheering for Britney Spears, not her. Also, there were just as many people booing. One person in the front row screamed loud enough for her to hear: *RUDE TO BRITNEY!*

When the set ended, Rose practically sprinted offstage.

She watched all forty-five minutes of Blue's set from the side of the stage while breathing into a brown paper bag. She scanned the space for Sasha but couldn't find her. She'd been there at sound check but had seemed off, distant. Rose kept wanting to talk to her, to say, *Remember that night I told you to propose to me the first night of the tour? Well, that was obviously a completely insane JOKE and STRANGE FLIRT that I never in any way meant!!!* Sasha probably didn't even remember it, and if she did, she wouldn't take it seriously.

Rose put down the brown paper bag and gulped some rosé. Watching Blue, Rose was reminded of all the times she'd seen Blue perform—in Philly, DC, Chicago, New York, and Wheatland—the way it was a religious experience. Blue had a spiritual connection with her audience, an enigmatic and sensual charm that Rose could never learn and would never have, because such things couldn't be taught or learned—they were innate.

Rose considered leaving the venue again, running into a moving vehicle like the audience wanted. But she lacked Blue's courage. She was dutiful, and so she waited where she'd been told to stand and tried very hard not to pass out.

Blue

As the opening notes of "American Spirits" spilled out over the amphitheater, Rose walked onstage with a hollow, tentative gait, like she was on the verge of collapsing. She looked brittle under the lights, her sequined dress hugging her frame, hands twisting around the mic stand. Heavy red extensions tumbled down her slender shoulders. Around her neck, diamonds glittered, oversize and ridiculous. The garish disguise failed to hide the mousy little freak Rose was on the inside, the one Blue was about to project on the screen for nearly twenty thousand fans. And Rose didn't even know what was coming for her.

So why did she look like she was dying?

Even from where she stood, Blue could see Rose's lips quivering, her eyes darting across the crowd like those of a frightened deer. For a moment, Blue almost felt the edges of something resembling pity. But then she remembered the thrill of her plan, the imminent explosion, which morphed her brief flash of sympathy into sheer exhilaration.

As the song reached its second verse, the screens behind them began to flicker. Blue watched the audience, faces tipped up as they strained to catch something out of place. The first image sharpened into view—a cluttered bedroom with posters blanketing the walls, shelves lined with vinyl and merch. Blue's own face was everywhere, looming above a young girl!—a smaller version of Rose, swallowed by a T-shirt several sizes too big, braces gleaming as she smiled at something beyond the camera. Snickers rippled through the crowd, but Rose hadn't yet seemed to notice.

The next image appeared, filling the screens in stark detail: Rose, maybe fourteen or fifteen, standing in front of a wall covered in Blue Velour memorabilia, another Blue Velour shirt hanging off her frame. Her eyes wide behind thick glasses, her smile stretched too tight, acne illuminated by the camera's flash. Blue watched Rose in her periphery, waiting for her to notice. The crowd's laughter swelled a notch louder.

Finally, Rose turned, eyes widening as she caught the corner of the screen. The current image projected young Rose at her laptop, her face lit by its faint blue glow. Then her username, u/RoseGhost, appeared alongside a stream of demented posts: lines dissecting Blue's lyrics, each phrase analyzed into oblivion for hidden messages, coded symbols, references to Sasha. The posts read like pieces of an imaginary puzzle, painting a truly schizophrenic portrait.

Rose's gaze briefly locked on the words as if willing them to disappear, but she kept singing. Blue kept singing. They were professionals.

They had a show to do.

And the fans were fucking loving it.

r/BlueBeards • posted by u/RoseGhost • December 2015

HOLY REVELATION

Hello, my beloveds!!! Surely you've all seen those utterly gorgeous pap shots of Blue and Sasha leaving that little garden house yesterday, right? Perez Hilton confirmed it's Sasha's house (!) in Silver Lake. First time we've actually seen where she lives, right?? I've never even been to LA, but a quick Google search says Silver Lake is like this arty little enclave surrounding a reservoir that feels almost . . . sacred? The pictures are pure magic, and even Perez couldn't help but hint at their undeniable romantic chemistry (using vulgar language I'm too polite to repeat, but the point is crystal clear—the photos scream L-O-V-E).

But of course that is not all!

Today on my way to campus I was listening to *Oleander* (as always) when I noticed this line from "Depraved Butterfly" I'd never really thought about before: "Mossy air, bruised by light, on a blade we meet again." It hit me like a truck. "Mossy air"? That has to be the garden from Sasha's house! The "light" could easily be the reservoir in the background, and "blade"—I don't know, maybe the sense of them hiding in plain sight, just barely out of reach? I swear, it's like Blue is straight-up GRIEVING the fact that she has to keep her love for Sasha a secret, hidden from a world that just doesn't freaking get it. I suddenly *felt* the frustration in her voice, the heartbreak, the utter devastation of not being able to love Sasha openly.

But there's MORE. Remember the peace signs!? How she flashed those *two* fingers *three* times—at *three* locations—at the VMAs in September, the Grammys in January, and at Cannes in May? And we've been like, *What does it mean?!* And then I saw it!! In the new pap shots, if you zoom in, there's a number on Sasha's gate. It's a little blurry but I *swear* it's 222! Sasha's address, people! BLUE HAS BEEN TELLING US THIS WHOLE TIME. It's not just random peace signs—she's been signaling where her heart is. 222!

This is what I love most about Blue—NOTHING is random. Everything is a clue, leading back to her and Sasha. I hope and PRAY the world lets Blue and Sasha walk hand in hand along the reservoir someday, for all to see, forever.

Unsurprisingly, I showed up to class in tears. Legit, like wet eyes, face blotchy. Luckily I have no friends (lol) so no one said anything. And I didn't even care because I was just SO MOVED.

UGH I JUST LOVE THEM SO MUCH. Blue and Sasha FOREVER!!!

Sasha

That demonic feeling that had settled deep in Sasha's gut while they were recording *American Spirits*, which had faded away slightly but not entirely when she left Malibu, had now returned, clawing its way through her with a vengeance.

Sasha wasn't entirely sure what exactly she was afraid of. It was a fear without an object. Or maybe there was an object, many objects: Sasha's career, her livelihood, her dignity. Working with Blue had made Sasha who she was, but she always felt that Blue could take it all away with a snap of her fingers. Of course, it was an irrational fear. Blue couldn't take away Sasha's six Grammys or twenty-one million dollars. No, for some reason, it always felt like Blue could do something much worse.

In between Malibu and the tour, Sasha had made an album with St. Vincent to distract herself, but Annie kept asking what was wrong. Sasha couldn't stop thinking about that night when Rose had aimed the kink gun at Sasha's head and demanded that Sasha propose. It was obviously a joke. It had to be a joke, right? There was no way it wasn't a joke. Sasha had even told Annie, who said it had to be a joke and if it wasn't, Rose was an ideal candidate for inpatient psychiatric treatment. Sasha remembered thinking that a mental health facility sounded nice. A padded cell where she could listen to music and stare at the wall all day.

Sasha hadn't slept in the week leading up to the concert. Now, she felt delirious, half-dead. Her eyes burned. Her throat was dry. Earlier, she'd been downing espresso to stay awake. But since the show started, she'd switched to wine. Rosé, Rose's favorite, but it hadn't made Rose's set any easier to watch. The songs they'd written at Velour Chalet were quiet, intimate, not ideal for a Bowl show. But worse was the audience, who hated Rose in a way that visibly crumbled her.

Now, Rose was performing with Blue, who wasn't much taller than Rose but seemed to tower over her, mostly due to sheer confidence. Sasha was hidden behind a fold in the curtain so they couldn't see her. And now, Blue was smiling at the monitors while the audience roared.

Sasha's eye caught the screens and she choked on her wine. The monitors were suddenly projecting massive images of Rose as a young nerd, as an über-fan and a sycophant. Was Sasha hallucinating or was this a Blue maneuver designed to humiliate Rose? Either way, Sasha thought young Rose looked adorable. And watching current Rose falter under the yellow stage lights, visibly doubting herself, Sasha remembered the girl she'd met in the cabin, the girl who'd captured her attention so fiercely, the version of Rose who, until now, Sasha had forgotten existed.

As Sasha sipped from her third glass of wine, something shifted inside her stomach. Fatigue transformed into levity, then excitement, then euphoria. A revelation moved through her like a rippling current.

Sasha loved Blue because Blue loved music as much as Sasha did. Blue wasn't capable of loving another person as much as the work, and Sasha believed that was true of herself as well. If they could share the work, it became a proxy for loving each other. They couldn't have the true and undying love the very luckiest couples shared, but they could have this acceptable approximation.

But with Rose, it was different. Rose was capable of loving another person, of loving Sasha. Sasha hadn't spoken much to Rose in the interim between recording the album and now, but she'd thought about her often. Sasha had gotten the sense pre-show that Rose was now dating her irritating roommate, Ella, which Sasha didn't entirely understand. Ella was young and pretty, sure, but so was most of Los Angeles. Ella was a nobody. Did she even have a job, or was she just living off Daddy's dime? Sasha had six Grammys and twenty-one million dollars. Sasha didn't like losing out to a nobody. Rose used to look at Sasha like she was a god. And tonight, Sasha had the chance to win that back.

And also, Sasha was realizing, now, for the very first time, that she had the potential to love Rose back. Sasha had thought she was like Blue, incapable of love, but Sasha wasn't Blue. She had simply been mirroring Blue's emotional landscape, the way she did with all her muses. Sasha was her own person. She wasn't entirely sure who that person was, but she could find out. And if there was really nothing there except a mirror, Sasha would rather mirror Rose than Blue. Blue was too bitter, too tempestuous. Seeing Rose tremble onstage, Sasha saw that sweet vulnerability that had first drawn her to Rose. Sasha wanted to be in love with Rose. She wanted to be madly, irrevocably in love with Rose, the type of love expressed in the movies and in the songs she wrote.

Sasha recalled their time at Velour Chalet—days she now knew were the best of her life. Mornings greeted by Rose's bright smile, sharp as the sun cutting through the ancient trees surrounding them. Her soft voice like a lullaby—soothing, a salve for a cruel and heartless world. Nights spent with Rose nestled in her arms, fitting like a missing puzzle piece. In those moments with Rose, Sasha had found unparalleled tranquility.

And it terrified her. So much so that she'd called up Carly Rae Jepsen, an artist she didn't even really like, and offered her production services to get out of Velour Chalet early. The night before Sasha had rushed them back to LA, Rose had woken her up in the middle of the night to confess her love. Sasha's chest had bloomed into warm, hot flames. The response was right there on her tongue, in her heart: *I love you too, I love you more than anything, I was placed in this world to love you, I will love you till the end of time.*

But Sasha was ultimately a coward. So she'd patted Rose on the head and then pretended to fall back asleep. She'd been awake all night, trying to gather the courage to say what she felt: *I fucking love you too.* But she couldn't. She just couldn't.

Sasha should have known that Rose would be corrupted either way. She'd been a twenty-five-year-old redhead with a lovely voice, milky skin, and bouncy tits. She was destined to be devoured by this carnivorous town. And she was. And Sasha should have protected her—from Blue, from Ella, and from the industry. Sasha should have helped Rose grow like the seeds they'd planted. It wasn't too late. Sasha could still save Rose. She could whisk her out of Los Angeles, back to the woods, where they could nurture each other and grow old together. But more importantly, Rose could save Sasha. Rose could prove Sasha was not heartless, that Sasha had the potential to love, to be normal, to be nothing like Blue.

The photos of Rose had been replaced by writing—Rose's early Reddit posts. The words were designed to humiliate Rose, but again, they charmed Sasha. The posts revealed the woman Sasha had fallen in love with at Velour Chalet—eager, enthusiastic, a hopeless romantic. She saw love where others saw nothing. Sasha poured a fourth glass of wine and smiled at the monitors with bemusement.

Until the Reddit posts were suddenly gone. The screen was black for several seconds and the music stopped. Sasha eyed Blue, who was grinning like a maniac. The dread returned, twisting her stomach. Then another image appeared. Black type on a white background. A contract? Sasha blinked at the screen and finally registered the writing. The dread in her stomach hadn't been entirely unfounded. Blue didn't give a shit about either of them. She was fucking suing them; it was right there on the screen. The audience was going wild, and Rose looked like she wanted to hang herself with a lavender noose.

As "Busted Mirror" began, Sasha rushed to get the ring.

SUPERIOR COURT OF THE STATE OF CALIFORNIA
FOR THE COUNTY OF LOS ANGELES

BEATRICE CLARK,
Plaintiff

v.

ROSE LUTZ and
ALEXANDRA HARDY,
Defendants

Case No.: SC1234567

COMPLAINT FOR:

I. COPYRIGHT INFRINGEMENT
II. BREACH OF CONTRACT
III. DECLARATORY RELIEF

PARTIES

1. Plaintiff Beatrice Clark ("Clark"), professionally known as "Blue Velour," resides in Los Angeles County, California, and is the originator of the musical style embodied in the album *Pop My Cherry*.

2. Defendants Rose Lutz ("Lutz") and Alexandra Hardy ("Hardy") reside in Los Angeles County, California, and were compensated by Clark for work related to *Pop My Cherry*.

GENERAL ALLEGATIONS

1. *Pop My Cherry* was a musical album created at a residence rented by Clark, during which time both Lutz and Hardy were financially supported by Clark.

2. Under the work-for-hire doctrine, *Pop My Cherry*, created while Lutz and Hardy were compensated by Clark, is Clark's property.

3. Defendants' unauthorized release of *Pop My Cherry* infringes Clark's copyright and appropriates her unique musical style as established in the song "Lavender Noose."

4. Plaintiff seeks an injunction, a declaration of her ownership rights, and all profits and royalties derived from the album.

PRAYER FOR RELIEF

WHEREFORE, Plaintiff prays for judgment against Defendants as follows:

1. Declaratory judgment that *Pop My Cherry* is the property of Clark under work-for-hire;
2. All profits derived from *Pop My Cherry*, including future royalties;
3. An injunction preventing Defendants from further use, sale, or distribution of *Pop My Cherry*;
4. Attorneys' fees, costs of suit, and such other relief as the Court deems just.

DATED: January 23, 2023

Dahlia Montalvo,

Attorney for Plaintiff Beatrice Clark

Rose

Rose worried she might pass out. She hoped she would. Anything to end this agony, this humiliation ritual. Blue was singing "Busted Mirror" with absolute glee—mocking Rose's vocals as the text of the lawsuit was projected on-screen. The crowd was screaming. Rose was trying to stay upright. She glanced backstage for Sasha. Where the hell was she?

As lights washed over the audience, Rose finally spotted Ella, who was singing along enthusiastically, a bright spot in a hostile crowd. Ella smiled at Rose as if to say, *You got this*. But Rose did not have this. And she couldn't believe she'd even showed up tonight. She was such a fucking idiot, masochist, a sacrificial lamb.

On the final bridge of the song, Rose finally spotted Sasha in the wings, drinking straight from a bottle of wine. What the fuck was she celebrating? Their demise? Sasha suddenly put the bottle on the ground. And then—to Rose's absolute horror—she began to charge onto the stage.

The crowd erupted into chaos.

Sasha approached Rose, who tried to focus on her lyrics.

But it was nearly impossible.
Because Sasha was getting down on one knee.
And oh God, no.
No, no, no.
Sasha was pulling out a glinting ruby ring.
The air split with screams.
A voice in Rose's headphones told her to stop singing.
Blue stopped and ran off the stage.
Sasha followed, a blur of black hair and silk.
Rose was about to run when she looked into the audience.
And she looked directly into the barrel of a gun.
This didn't look like a kink gun.
No, this gun was very, very real.

2024

*I died a hundred times. You go back to her.
And I go back to . . . I go back to us.*

—AMY WINEHOUSE

Blue

Blue turned onto the 1 as twilight bruised the edges of the horizon. The ocean blurred past in soft shadows. She was driving home from Violet's second birthday party, thinking back to last year, this same stretch of highway—only that time, she'd been hyped about the upcoming *American Spirits* tour. Her enthusiasm was embarrassing to admit in retrospect, even to herself. Blue couldn't imagine being excited to perform ever again. Which was sad, because she used to live for it.

Since the incident, Blue had been going to therapy. Her first time talking to a professional since rehab. Her therapist was a redhead, which at first gave Blue pause, until she confirmed the color was natural, which Blue did before saying anything about herself. Therapy had been Max's idea given that Blue had, according to Max, "been a victim of a mass shooting." Blue had thought that was dramatic. Only one shot had been fired. And she'd been offstage by the time the bullet left the gun. Rose had been the victim, not her. But Max had convinced her somehow. And now she had a naturally redheaded therapist, and together they were working through Blue's PTSD, from the show and many things before that.

Blue not only had what they called "survivor's guilt" but she also felt convinced that the entire shooting was her fault. She'd teamed up with Rose for the precise purpose of riling up her audience, a goal that had ended with an enraged fan firing a loaded gun right at the stage. Max had reminded Blue that under that logic, the shooting was Max's fault as Blue Rose was initially her idea. Blue's redheaded therapist—her name was Rachel—assured Blue that it was neither of their faults, that they were in no way responsible for the actions of a "deeply disturbed individual."

The craziest part was that Max had allegedly gone to camp with said disturbed individual. Her name was Grace Sable. She'd been the one to recommend Rose for the assistant position! It was all so uncanny. Making it all even more wack, Grace had met Rose in the creepo subreddit Rose herself had founded, the one dedicated to dissecting evidence that didn't exist.

Blue had told Rachel that she felt like people were tearing apart her shadows, picking through everything she kept hidden for a fucking reason. Or seeing things that were never there at all. She said she felt trapped in someone else's narrative, like Ophelia—obsessed over, romanticized, but never able to tell her own story. Blue didn't want to end up like that, reduced to some tragic figure people couldn't look away from, yet never really saw. She didn't need anyone's flowers, especially not roses. If she could choose, she'd take something like blue orchids—something that felt hers.

But Grace had latched on to this projection of Blue's life, was committed to Blue's romantic entanglement with someone who was legitimately horrible for her: Sasha. Blue had recently skimmed an article Max had sent her about the shooting, written by the same woman who'd profiled her in 2019: Zoe Alexander. That interview felt like an eternity ago. Anyway, according to the skimmed article, Grace had recommended Rose for the assistant position given her "esteemed role" in the subreddit. Vom.

Rose got hired but didn't end up giving Grace the insider access she craved (Blue internally thanked Rose for that). And when Rose got fired and started making music with Sasha, Grace felt deceived, even though she didn't actually know any of these people. Grace was also pissed because Rose had lied about how she knew her, telling Max they'd met on a cruise. Frankly, Blue understood why Rose lied; she would have lied too—what normal person would admit to meeting someone on REDDIT?

Blue could still remember the voice in her ear telling her to run. And the way Rose had looked, frozen, even after the shot was fired. The blood trickling down her ear. Grace had confessed to everything and even claimed she'd do it again if given the chance. Sicko. Given her lack of remorse, the judge had landed on the maximum sentence of thirty years. Blue slept better knowing the bitch was locked up.

Rose had apparently escaped to some mountain town with Ella, somewhere far from LA, somewhere safe, and Blue didn't blame her. According to the article, Rose and Ella had recently gotten engaged. Ella was quoted as saying, "I knew Rose was the one from the first time I saw her." It was so romantic. Rose had told the reporter something about Ella being there for her when literally no one else was.

Blue drummed her nails on the steering wheel. She hadn't been there for Rose, hadn't done a damn thing for her beyond sending an overpriced bouquet to the hospital. But at least she hadn't bolted across the country like Sasha—right after freaking proposing, literally causing Grace Sable to pull the trigger. Blue hadn't spoken to Sasha since that night either, but she remembered another quote from the article she'd skimmed. When asked if the proposal had been real, Sasha had said something along the lines of "it was real at the time" but "the whole thing's too tainted now." Classic Sasha. Such a fucking coward.

Blue's headlights brushed the edge of the coast. Sasha hadn't even reached out. But Blue hadn't reached out to her either. Maybe they really were the same. Cowards, destined to be alone.

As she turned onto Broad Beach Road, Blue's phone buzzed on the seat next to her. She glanced over and smiled—a text from Jett. The guy she'd met at the Rock Store two years ago. He'd been a great lay, but she'd never thought she'd see him again, until she did, a few weeks ago. She recognized his bike first, the Indian Scout Bobber. He'd been leaning against it, smoking a Camel Red in a patch of sun, his skin bronzed and leathery. She'd taken him to her house that night, which she rarely did. But she trusted Jett for some reason. And he was decent enough not to act overly impressed by her house, not that it was really that impressive—it was becoming more dilapidated by the day—but more importantly, he'd been as good in bed as she'd remembered.

In the morning, she'd asked him to show her more videos of him and the cats. He asked if she wanted to see them in person. On his bike, he took her down to a dusty lot on the outskirts of Ventura, where the circus was camped. Behind a row of weathered tents, lions paced in their cages like shadows, their eyes lit up gold. Jett had let her hold a cub in her arms. It was such a happy day. She couldn't stop thinking about it, about him.

Now, Jett was back in Nevada, the Cowboy Corridor, of all places. He lived in Elko, where Blue had bought the Dexedrine that had powered her thirty-six-hour drive to New York. Blue had liked it there, that little cowboy town, imagined she'd like it sober as well. She let herself picture it for a second—living in the high desert, with a guy who could tame lions.

She let out a laugh.

God knew she could use a little taming.

Rose

It was Ella's idea to invite Sasha and Blue to the wedding. Neither of them responded to the RSVP, which was fine by Rose. Her life no longer revolved around Blue and Sasha, had stopped revolving around them as soon as the shot was fired. In that sense, Rose was thankful for the bullet that had grazed her ear.

The wedding was held at a vineyard in Dahlonega, Georgia, the small mountain city where Rose and Ella now lived. Ella had grown up here and her family was essentially Dahlonega royalty. Nestled in the foothills of the North Georgia mountains, the small city was known as the site of the first major US gold rush, a lineage from which Ella directly descended. Unlike Los Angeles, downtown Dahlonega was filled with well-preserved nineteenth-century buildings. The streets were filled with antique shops, art galleries, and ice cream parlors. It sometimes reminded Rose of Stars Hollow from *Gilmore Girls*—wholesome charm from another era. Today, Dahlonega was mostly known for its hiking trails, scenic views, waterfalls, and vineyards, like the one in which they were marrying.

Ella and Rose lived in a small but comfortable house tucked into the trees about ten minutes from downtown, a home that reminded Rose somewhat of Velour Chalet. Well, it was like all the good things about Velour Chalet—the canopy, the forest scents, the crickets, the damp soil and fresh air, the cozy intimacy—and none of the bad: the mood swings, the mind games, the impending lawsuits. Also, Rose was somehow less allergic here, only needing medicine occasionally in the spring.

Their house had weathered wood siding and a wraparound porch overlooking the Appalachian foothills. Its small garden was bursting with flowers that Rose had planted, applying the knowledge Sasha had imparted to her at Velour Chalet. Rose was proudest of her blossoming rosebushes. Inside, they had a stone fireplace and plush rugs and large windows that framed the outdoors. At night, they'd light candles and listen to records. They still listened to Blue, and Rose had finally gotten Ella into *Fluorescent Gloom*. In fact, it was one night during a spin of the record that Ella got on one knee and proposed to Rose with a delicate red diamond.

Saying yes was the easiest thing Rose had ever done.

The vineyard where they were marrying was set atop a rolling hill with views of distant mountain peaks. Ella had been worried about the weather, but today, there was hardly a cloud in the sky. The fifty guests, most of them Ella's family, were seated on wooden chairs on a lush lawn. The aisle was lined with roses leading to an altar. Blue the dog would walk the ring down the aisle. The light could best be described as heavenly.

Violins started to play. Rose was standing on the opposite side of the venue from Ella, whom she couldn't see. But she knew Ella was with her dad, who would walk her down the aisle. Waiting on the side of the altar were Ella's sisters, her bridesmaids. Rose didn't have any bridesmaids. She'd asked her sister, who said she had a "work thing." Rose's parents were her only family members in attendance, but they hadn't paid for any aspect of the wedding and acted as if the whole thing was a big inconvenience. Rose hadn't asked her dad to walk her down the aisle because she knew he didn't want to. So Rose was standing here alone.

Finally, the opening notes of "Rose Ghost" started playing. Rose saw Ella and her dad begin to approach the top of the aisle. Ella looked luminous in a custom Chanel sheath dress. Her creamy hair glowed in the light. Rose's stomach buzzed. She was excited but also felt very alone. As if God was listening, suddenly, there was a hand on her back. Rose figured it was the wedding planner. She stood up straight, ready to go.

But something about the familiarity of the touch told Rose it wasn't the wedding planner.

Sasha

Sasha had flown down to Buttfuck, Georgia, for one reason and one reason only: to see Blue.

She hadn't spoken to Blue since that disastrous night at the Hollywood Bowl. Blue Rose had dispersed with the sound of the gun, the three of them scattering like magnets with the same polarity. Sasha wasn't actually sure if Blue was mad at her or avoiding her—Sasha hadn't exactly tried to reach out. She was weak in that way, in many ways. She hadn't reached out to Rose either. She hadn't even visited her at the hospital. Instead, she'd gotten on a plane to New York, looking forward to avoid looking back. Sasha figured Rose hated her. She was shocked to receive an invite to the wedding, but also relieved. She'd never wanted to hurt Rose, had experienced guilt about proposing, then abandoning her. Sasha hardly got close to that guilt, instead throwing herself into other things—buying and renovating a farmhouse in upstate New York, building a new studio, making new music. She still loved Rose in the way that she'd forever love everyone she'd made a record with. But Sasha realized she hadn't just been mirroring Blue when she decided she couldn't be in a monogamous, committed relationship. That was all Sasha, and she and Blue were the same in this way.

The music always came first.

Since being in New York, Sasha had tried dating. Well, she'd slept with people she'd been making music with. No one excited her creatively the way Blue did, the way every recording session was a surprise, the way they put themselves into the music, the way they became it, the way it became their entire world and nothing else existed.

For these other women, the music felt more like the means to an end. A vehicle for more Instagram followers, or to sell merch, or to tour. None of them wanted to stay up all night the way Blue did, to sleep in the studio, to crack themselves open and bleed all over the mic. And when they were done with the music, they all stuck around wanting more from Sasha. They wanted her to commit, to worship them. Blue was never done making music. When she was done with one record, she was thinking about the next. Her career was a never-ending thrill, just as it was for Sasha. And today, provided that Blue would show—Sasha had a feeling she would—Sasha was going to try to get back on the ride.

Sasha had been late to the wedding, hoping maybe to secretly miss the ceremony because they tended to be boring and go on forever and the booze didn't come until later. But unfortunately she arrived right as Ella was starting to walk down the aisle with her father. At least Sasha thought it was her father—they had the same slim nose. Ella was lucky her parents weren't homophobes like Sasha's, whose dad would sooner shoot himself in the foot than walk her down the aisle to marry a woman.

Ella looked pretty, her hair shiny and golden in the last of the afternoon light. Sasha thought back to that first night she'd met her, when Sasha had gone to pick up Rose for their date and Ella had grilled her with the intensity of a homicide detective. Sasha should have known then that Ella was in love with Rose. But she'd started suspecting it not long after, the way Ella was always short with Sasha, always pulling

Rose away from her. Ella had shown up a few times when they were recording *American Spirits*, only at Shangri-La because Blue wouldn't let anyone who wasn't family or involved in the album come to her house. Blue could be so rigid. But whenever Ella came to the studio, she looked at Rose like she was a slice of heaven. Sasha wondered if anyone had ever looked at her that way. She imagined it was how she looked at Blue when she was singing. Sasha realized at this moment that the string quartet was playing an instrumental version of "Rose Ghost." She laughed. She'd never seen a bride, let alone *brides*, walk down the aisle to music she'd composed.

Sasha craned her neck to look for Blue. But she didn't see her. Instead, Sasha spotted Rose at the top of the aisle. Sasha remembered talking about their families late at night in the redwoods. Rose wasn't quite as estranged from her family as Sasha was from hers, but Rose described her family as cold and disinterested. Sasha's heart sank seeing Rose all alone. She walked over to her, trying not to think about all the traumatic shit involving Rose that Sasha was overpaying a therapist to help her not think about. Well, the therapist said Sasha needed to "process" it. Sasha was a lesbian; she'd had enough processing. She wanted to forget about it, to bury her head in the sand. The therapist said that the point of therapy was to see, not be blind, so Sasha had stopped showing up to appointments, ghosting the therapist the way she ghosted most women who wanted anything approaching intimacy with her.

Whenever Sasha thought about that night, her mind went limp. The person she was that night seemed like a stranger—confused, lost, terrified. Sasha was still afraid, but in a different way. She was plagued by nightmares about the show, varying only in their gruesome conclusions. Sasha never wanted to go to a concert again. In fact, this wedding marked her first trip out of New York in nearly a year, a journey she'd only managed with the liquid courage of three Bloody Marys in an airport bar. Now, Sasha found herself constantly on edge, terrified of violence lurking at every corner.

But then, that night at the Bowl, she'd been terrified of not being wanted. She felt like her stock was up. She was officially in her mid-forties, middle-aged, Blue was over her. And Rose had looked at her with the most eager eyes that made her feel so special. Sasha had proposed to Rose because she wanted to be looked at that way forever.

But instead, she'd put Rose in danger, almost gotten her killed.

And now, Sasha was happy to set Rose free.

She reached out, gently touching the back of Rose's arm.

Blue

Blue arrived just in time to watch Sasha walk Rose down the aisle to an orchestral version of "Rose Ghost." As soon as she recognized it, Blue couldn't help but smile.

The aisle was made of grass and surrounded by soft, rolling hills. Blue was impressed with this town Rose and Ella had settled down in. It was charming and historic and nothing like Los Angeles. She was staying in a bed-and-breakfast in a building that had been built in 1846, with original pinewood floors. Her bedroom had its own fireplace and a crystal chandelier hanging over the bed. Blue was thinking of extending her stay, exploring the town and writing a new song. Maybe afterward, she'd go home to see her parents. Her hometown wasn't too far away, and Blue's anger at her parents was dissipating with age. They wouldn't be around too much longer, and she wanted to make peace with them before it was too late.

Watching Sasha smile with a teary, angelic Rose on her arm, Blue couldn't help but feel emotional. She loved love, and the three of them had been through so much. It was heartwarming to see Sasha step up in this way. Although it didn't exactly cancel out her bolting after putting

Rose in the gravest danger. But Sasha was here now, and that impressed Blue. It wasn't everything, but it was something.

The kind of love celebrated at weddings remained elusive to Blue. She hadn't even told Jett she loved him, despite living with him in Nevada for the past few months. She'd invited him to the wedding, but he had a circus in Chicago. She wasn't exactly upset by their time apart. They had great sex, and she felt protected. She loved the lions and living in cowboy country, the sprawling desert. But something was missing.

Something was always missing.

Sasha deposited Rose at the altar, then moved to the side. Rose looked stunning in a silky blush dress. Her hair fell in soft tendrils beside her face, covering up, Blue imagined, the missing tip of her ear.

Under the last gasps of light, Rose's hair appeared more natural than it had when they were working together, less neon red and more its original auburn—nowhere near as red as Rachel the therapist's—and she was no longer covering up her freckles with foundation. Blue couldn't help but see that girl who'd appeared in her kitchen that afternoon five years ago. Rose had been so nervous, so green. Now, she walked with the confidence of a woman who had seen things. Blue felt partially responsible for that, but she'd never meant to hurt Rose. Well, maybe just a little. All Blue ever wanted was respect. And Rose inviting her to this wedding was an act of respect. And Blue was therefore thrilled to watch Rose get her happily ever after.

Blue didn't know Ella well, but she was very beautiful—a patrician, delicate-featured blonde—and, given the looks of her frigid family members and the slight upturn of her nose, appeared to be very rich. Blue could also tell from the way she looked at Rose that she was madly in love. Blue couldn't imagine being looked at the way Ella was looking at Rose right now. Fans looked at Blue like she was a goddess and a treasure, but Ella's look was something else. She was looking at Rose like nothing else mattered.

When Ella kissed the bride, Blue cheered along with everyone else. During the reception, Blue approached the brides.

"You're radiant," Blue said to Ella.

"I'm so glad you came," Ella said, taking Blue's hand in hers. Her hands were warm and soft. She really was a nice girl. Blue remembered liking her from the few times she'd stopped by recording sessions at Shangri-La. Sasha had always seemed less taken, but Blue could now identify that reaction as jealousy. Sasha could be very childish.

Rose appeared from behind Ella. She smiled sheepishly, and Blue immediately recalled Rose sitting in her kitchen drinking a Diet Coke the day of her interview. That version of Rose had felt so distant while they were recording *American Spirits*, but suddenly it seemed resuscitated somehow.

"I love seeing your freckles," Blue said.

Rose laughed and instinctively, it seemed, put a hand over her face. Her ring sparkled in the light coming in through the side of the tent.

"Thank you for coming," Rose said. "You don't know how much it means to me."

"Well, you did walk down the aisle to my song," Blue said. "So I have an idea."

Rose laughed again. Her cheeks reddened. Without thinking, Blue wrapped Rose in a big hug. She wasn't typically a hugger and couldn't remember if they'd ever hugged before, but Blue felt a sudden motherly instinct. Rose hugged her back, her fingers cold on Blue's skin.

"I'll let you get back to your fans," Blue said when they pulled apart. "But I really am very happy for you, and thank you for inviting me." Lately, Blue had been trying out sincerity. She used to think life was only interesting from a place of ironic posture. Now, that felt lame. Blue wanted to be closer to something real.

Rose kissed Blue's cheek and went to greet another guest.

Blue turned around to find herself facing Sasha.

"Hi, stranger," Sasha said.

"You sound like such a perv," Blue said.

Sasha shrugged. They laughed.

"Can we talk?" Sasha said.

"I think we are," Blue said.

Sasha took Blue's hand and dragged her outside the reception tent. The sun was turning purple over soft green hills. Sasha dropped Blue's hand, and Blue couldn't help but momentarily miss it. Her hand fit so perfectly inside Sasha's.

Blue noticed an eyelash on Sasha's cheek. Sasha had the world's longest, thickest lashes, the type of lashes Blue paid people big money to fabricate on her face. Blue swiped the eyelash with her finger, held it up to Sasha, and said, "Make a wish."

Sasha closed her eyes and blew on Blue's finger. Her breath was warm and firm.

The eyelash floated into the air, toward the setting sun.

2025

*Rock on, ancient queen.
Follow those who pale in your
shadow. Rulers make bad lovers.*

—FLEETWOOD MAC

QUEEN OF MY HEART   9.3
Blue Velour • 2025

In 2014, Blue Velour famously told a journalist she wished she was dead. And for what seemed like years after, scarcely an article was written about her that didn't mention it. The singer was miserable at the sour critical reception of *Fluorescent Gloom*. She was, perhaps, peddling its underlying fatalism, pushing back on allegations that her dark persona was fabricated. Almost certainly, she was harboring the sort of creative ambition that craved association with tragic geniuses like her hero Kurt Cobain. But Velour's latest album represents a rather dramatic pivot from the macabre, showcasing an artist who has flirted with the abyss but has emerged with an unflinching desire to—unlike her heroes—remain alive.

Queen of My Heart crowns both music itself and longtime collaborator Sasha Harlow the leader of Velour's heart, her life force. Her bond with Harlow has been the subject of endless speculation, notably by the infamous BlueBeards subreddit. This now-defunct online community once fervently dissected every interaction between Velour and Harlow for hints of romantic entanglement. In an ironic twist that feels plucked from daytime television, the group's founder, Rose Lush, ended up in a perverse love triangle—and an eventual supergroup—with Sasha and Blue. The soap opera took an especially dark turn on the opening night of their tour when an angry member of BlueBeards opened fire.

While fans and Redditors demonized Rose Lush as the wedge that split their queen and queen, Blue Velour's latest album paints a different story. On the shimmery track "Rose-Tinted Glasses," Velour unveils a surprising truth: Rose Lush was not a barrier between Blue and Sasha, but rather the unexpected force that strengthened their bond and brought them closer than ever.

And really, Rose Lush is merely a blip on the epic timeline that is Blue Velour and Sasha Harlow. The two met in 2007, when Blue was just twenty-six years old. Neither of them had yet released an album. They could help each other break out, and they did. Over the next eighteen years, they made eight studio albums together, culminating in the euphoric *Queen of My Heart*. Fittingly, the album's title comes from a lyric from Nirvana's "Love Buzz"—the first song Harlow ever heard Blue Velour sing.

Over eleven tracks, Velour revisits and reinterprets the range of sonic landscapes she has explored with Harlow. From the initially dismissed baroque pop sensibilities of *Spirit of Sinatra* to the cinematic orchestral sounds of *Chateau Velour* and the brooding trap influences of *Mood Onyx*, each element is woven into *Queen of My Heart* with a newfound maturity. It's a retrospective and a reimagining, showcasing a sonic richness and sui generis magic missing from 2021's *Violet*, the only album Velour has made without Harlow.

The evolution of Velour's perspective is most powerful in "Back to Us," which takes its lyrics from "Back to Black" off Amy Winehouse's acclaimed album of the same name. Reflecting on Winehouse's powerful relationship with music, touring pianist Sam Beste said in the 2015 documentary *Amy*: "It was like she needed music, as if it was a person, and she would die for it."

While Winehouse's fate led her to the Twenty-Seven Club alongside other legends, Velour forges a different path. "Back to Us" departs from the solitary anguish of Winehouse's single and instead unfolds as an unconventional love letter to Sasha Harlow. The song paints a relationship that transcends romance; a deep and enduring connection through music—not as a destructive force, but as shared lifeblood. Winehouse died for music, but Blue Velour vows to live for it.

The album's artwork features a silhouette backlit by bright sunlight. Initially, the figure might be mistaken for Blue or a stranger. However, upon closer inspection, it becomes apparent that the figure is none other than Ms. Harlow. This visual metaphor speaks volumes: Sasha is not only the queen of Blue's heart but also a symbol of the profound bond they share. Music emerges as the sovereign ruler of both their hearts—a shared realm they've forged together, a divine gift that will outlive both of them and us all.

r/GayVelour • posted by u/DeathBaby • 3 hours ago

Death Baby's first fanfic

My sweet GayVelours! Thank you from the bottom of my heart for reading and supporting my very first fanfic novel. I know it is unhinged. But hopefully sexy too, right? For those who have questions or left angry comments, I'm leaving some "author's notes" below. This is what authors do, right? I wouldn't know, I've never met one! Well, I did go on two dates with a very obnoxious author (let's just call her "Asterix") who acted like I should know who she is?? And I was like, babe, I wouldn't recognize Stephen King if I saw him in the street, I certainly don't know who the fuck you are. Anyway!

    Rose is entirely a work of fiction. And even though a lot of people have commented that they hate Rose, she is loosely based on me. Part of the reason I'm so drawn to Blue is because she's completely unlike me in a way that is exotic and captivating. I've always wanted to be daring and sensual and effortless. I'd kill to have a *fuck it* attitude. To ride on the back of a lion tamer's motorcycle or drive across the country on an impromptu amphetamine bender. But unfortunately I'm a control freak who cares . . . just so much. So, so much. Hence why I went to law school, a tragic scene Blue Velour wouldn't be caught dead in. Sorry to bring up Taylor Swift on this subreddit, but as she says in her song "Mirrorball" from *Folklore*—watered-down Blue album, I know—"I've never been a natural, all I do is try, try, try." Taylor Swift embarrasses me because when it comes to my own music, my own work, my personality, my life, whatever, all of it, I'm more Taylor than Blue. Blue is a natural, a genius, a savant, and Taylor is a mediocre try-hard who's stuck around through sheer persistence. Rose is a try-hard. I'm a try-hard with significantly less talent than Rose. (I can't sing for shit!)

    A lot of people also seem pissed that I concocted a plot in which Sasha falls for someone other than Blue, even briefly. I mean, come on people! Isn't the primary reason we're all in this group, beyond finding Blue Velour to be among the greatest songwriters of all time, because we're attracted to Sasha, or Blue, or both? Like Rose, I want to be Blue and fuck Sasha. Ban me, I don't care. I'm just being honest. Y'all should try it sometime. So duh, I wrote my fantasy. Is there any reason to create anything other than to make yourself laugh or turn yourself on? Seriously, is there?? I feel like Blue would agree.

    Also, in case you have poor reading comprehension like I do, Sasha and Blue end up together in my book!!! It is not ambiguous!!! As I wrote, Blue and Sasha both love the music more than they can love any person. But they share the music, which is the closest they can come to loving another person. In real life, they've both said similar things in the media. In 2019, Blue told the *New York Times* that Sasha was her soulmate. When the interviewer asked if Blue meant in a romantic or creative sense, Blue said, "What's the difference?" I think about this quote a lot and put it directly into my novel. (Is that illegal? I went to law school but I remember nothing!) Anyway, at the 2020 Grammys, Sasha told an interviewer on the red carpet, "Music is the one relationship that consistently sweeps me off my feet and keeps me coming back for more." Blue and Sasha make music together, which means they keep coming back to each other. This is what their latest album, *Queen of My Heart*, is about! I mean . . . talk about romantic!!!

    Since I began writing this book years ago, Sasha and Blue have both entered serious relationships whose validity has been called into doubt in this subreddit. Sasha with Zoë Kravitz, who makes several appearances in my novel, and Blue with Jett Donovan, a lion tamer who is also featured in my book. I do believe both of these relationships are legitimate—and in Blue's case, deeply Jungian—but I still think what Sasha and Blue has surpasses any connection they could possibly share with anyone else. (And frankly, I think the only reason Blue is living in Nevada right now is because her house burned down in the Malibu fires—broken heart emoji.)

    For those upset that I cast our subreddit in an unflattering light, ever going so far as to suggest one of our members would commit an act of violence with a deadly weapon, I cannot stress enough: this is a work of FICTION!!! And I changed the name of the subreddit for a reason (although I did paraphrase some brilliant album analyses with the authors' permission). I doubt anyone will publish this book, I mostly wrote it for myself, but if they do, please rest assured that I will protect the innocent. And I will make clear that this is a novel and not meant to depict reality in any way whatsoever. That no characters are based on any members of this subreddit. Except Rose, who is loosely based on me. Except that I can't sing. And I'm not a redhead. And I'm closer to Blue's age than to Rose's. And a lot of other differences I don't have time to get into. But Rose's emotional experience is similar to my own, and we share an encyclopedic knowledge of Blue's discography.

Anyone pissed about the nonexistent producer Liam Sterling—let me clarify! This *fictional* character is loosely based on Nigel Godrich, a British producer who worked with Radiohead, Pulp, Warpaint, and Arcade Fire, among other similar bands. About the Radiohead inclusion—yes, some of you are pissed because Radiohead sued Blue Velour for alleged similarities between Blue Velour's "Polaroid Is the Void" and Radiohead's "Paranoid Android," but the lawsuit was quickly dropped. Blue Velour owns 100% of the song's royalties, so calm down. Also I'm not exactly exalting the band in this book in case you didn't notice lol.

Oh, and if you're mad that I wrote Blue as horny for men, including the fictional Liam Sterling and the real Jett Donovan, I do believe that Blue is horny for men, which is all over her music. I do not believe this diminishes her profound connection with Sasha.

There is of course an irony here. One of my primary gripes with this subreddit is the mental gymnastics y'all go through to find evidence of homosexuality that simply isn't there, a practice I satirize in my novel. But then in writing this fanfiction novel, in which Blue and Sasha are actually sleeping together, and in which they arguably end up together, I am perpetuating the same cringe crime—imposing a gay narrative onto apparently heterosexual material. But whatever! Isn't everyone a hypocrite? To quote Blue, who is quoting Walt Whitman, which is quoted in my novel: "Do I contradict myself? I contain multitudes!!!!!"

FINALLY, a few of you commented about the parallels between

the bullet that grazed Rose's ear at the Hollywood Bowl and the one that grazed Donald Trump's ear at a 2024 campaign rally. BUT I wrote that scene before Trump was shot! (Writing a book takes forever lol!)

Okay, I'm tired of defending myself. Blue has never defended her art and neither should I. But I'm a try-hard and a pick-me, so I can't help but be myself. After this, I will make a graceful exit from this group. You all have helped me through some strange and difficult times, and I love being united with people who worship Blue as intensely as I do. But all great things must come to an end. My posts will disappear. If you'd like to keep in touch or read my book, I've left my contact info below. As usual, I'm dropping a link to my SoundCloud. I'm no Blue Velour, but maybe one day Sasha will notice me and I'll have my Rose Lush moment. Don't shoot me!

Xx,
Prue
prue.vanteesen@gmail.com
http://soundcloud.com/VAGABLONDE

P.S. YES I make two brief cameos in the novel, and again it's obvi fiction because I am described as "a successful DJ" lol

P.P.S. I'm going to drop my favorite Blue lyric below because I'm sentimental and corny and it also feels applicable to this post and this group and to my novel:

When you feel those baby blue moods
Just hum this tune, it's just for you
It'll echo on, long after we're through

Acknowledgments

Thank you to my perfect agent and friend Sarah Phair. I'm so proud of us for turning all of our cultural obsessions into book deals. Thank you to my amazing editor and friend Olivia Taylor Smith. I am pinching myself that this is our fifth book together. Thank you, Martha Langford, Danielle Prielipp, Brittany Adames, and the entire Simon & Schuster team. And thank you, Math Monahan, for the absolutely gorgeous cover.

Thank you to KK Wootton, Catie Disabato, Maggie Murray, Jon Doyle, and Andrew Extein for reading an early version of this and giving the most brilliant notes. Thank you to my perfume consultant, Léonie Chainé.

Thank you to my family, for not disowning me (yet).

Thank you to Vanessa, the queen of my heart.

And finally, thank you to the ultimate woman, Lana Del Rey.

About the Author

Anna Dorn is the author of the novels *Perfume & Pain*, *Exalted*, and *Vagablonde*. She was a Lambda Literary Fellow and *Exalted* was a finalist for the Los Angeles Times Book Prize. She lives in Los Angeles.